About the Author

In 2006, Edinburgh-born D.D. Johnston quit working at a Manchester coach station to chase the dream of becoming a writer. One scrap of the dream existed – the start of a story inspired by derelict council housing in Hulme. Two novels pushed it to one side. The first, *Peace, Love & Petrol Bombs*, a 2011 book of the year in the *Sunday Herald*, has been recorded as an audio book and translated into Spanish. The second, *The Deconstruction of Professor Thrub*, was a 2013 book of the year in the *Morning Star*, where it was described as 'determinedly extraordinary.' With the publication of this third novel, D.D. Johnston finally tells the story that started it all – the story of *The Secret Baby Room*.

THE SECRET BABY ROOM

DD JOHNSTON

BARBICAN PRESS

First published in Great Britain by Barbican Press in 2015
Copyright © D.D. Johnston 2015

The right of D.D. Johnston to be identified as
the author of this book has been asserted by him
in accordance with sections 77 and 78 of the
Copyright, Designs and Patents Act, 1988

Barbican Press, Hull and London
Registered office: 1 Ashenden Road, London E5 0DP
www.barbicanpress.com
@barbicanpress1

A CIP catalogue for this book is available
from the British Library

ISBN: 978-1-909954-18-2

Typeset by Tetragon, London
Cover by Jason Anscomb of Rawshock Design

Printed by Totem, Poland

For mothers. For all our mothers.

One

CLAIRE WILSON was in the spare room of her new home, unpacking a box marked 'miscellaneous,' when she glanced up and saw the strangest thing. High up in the abandoned tower block that overshadowed their estate, a woman was bottle-feeding a baby.

She watched for a few seconds, straining to make out more detail. Then she returned her attention to the unpacking. The box at her feet was one of those they had filled at the last minute, and it was full of all the stuff that had no proper place: a collection of batteries, her husband's football shin pads, an empty picture frame, the plunger from a cafetière that so far remained lost in transit. She thought for a moment and then carried the plunger downstairs, setting it on the kitchen windowsill. When she looked back at the tower block, the woman and the baby had disappeared.

Already the image was fading in her mind. She thought the woman might have had blonde hair, but it could have been grey. She thought the baby might have been wrapped in a purple blanket, but it was difficult to be sure. And yet, for some reason, it occurred to her that the figure she'd seen in the distance was not dissimilar to the girl who lived next door. She had blonde hair. She sunbathed topless in her garden and drank cocktails through a straw and played dance music in the early afternoon. Claire had yet to speak to her neighbour, but she knew every beat of her music collection. In fact, the present silence was unusual and she wondered whether perhaps—

But then why would the blonde neighbour, or anyone else, take a baby up *there*? *How* would she take a baby up there? The tower and its grounds were fenced off with construction barriers, and yellow-black warning signs were spread around the perimeter. Beyond that, the weeds had grown unchecked, a forest of thistles and nettles and rosebay willowherb. The building's entrances were blocked with plywood and clearly marked: DANGER. DEMOLITION IN PROGRESS. DO NOT ENTER. Above that the lower floors were wrapped in dark tarpaulin that flapped at night like the rigging of a ghost ship. And yet, higher still, beyond the fire-charred glassless windows, at a window on the eighth or ninth floor, there had been – she was certain of it – a woman cradling a baby.

If the demolition had gone according to plan then Sighthill Tower, like the other high rise flats in this part of Manchester, would have been demolished before the Wilsons moved in. While the other blocks had disappeared, built over by privately-owned semi-detached suburban homes, Sighthill Tower had made a defiant stand. Claire had followed the news online from their old home in Birmingham: a resident in new-build suburbia, Morgana someone or other, had challenged the council on a point of health and safety – something to do with asbestos. The complaint was upheld and the controlled implosion was postponed. The rescheduled demolition would now go ahead – touch wood – in four weeks' time.

Feminism was a wonderful thing, Claire thought, but in her opinion women had been conned when it came to work. Once upon a time, or so it seemed from old sitcoms, men did a day's wage labour and women did a day's domestic labour; now, most of her married friends seemed to do a day's wage labour, and then come home to do a day's domestic labour. They should have made the men do half the domestic labour and offered to do half the paid work in exchange. Everyone would have worked part-time, and everyone would have enjoyed a healthy balance between employment and home life. She'd come to this conclusion over the last week when, for the first time ever, she'd done the whole housewife thing. When Dan was offered the manager's job at Manchester coach station, she'd seized the chance to escape unhappy memories. But fleeing the past had meant doing something she'd always said she wouldn't: she'd quit her job and moved with her husband's work.

'I applied for a job today,' she told Dan when he came in.

'Oh yeah? Doing what?'

'Same thing – medical secretary. It's a pay band lower, it's only twenty-eight hours a week, and it's fixed term, but it's something to tide me over, right?'

'Where's it at?'

'That's the best bit – it's in Wythenshawe. I could walk there if I wanted to.'

Dan opened the fridge and pulled out a Carlsberg. 'Is it ophthalmology again?' he asked without looking round.

'No – urology.'

'Isn't that penises and stuff?'

'It's genitourinary, yeah. Kidneys, bladders, urethras, testes, prostates, penises . . .'

'So you're going from looking at eyes to looking at bollocks. Is that progress?'

'I don't look at anything. I keep the records, type the notes, find the files.'

'Files filled with pictures of diseased penises,' said Dan, easing into the sofa. 'What a day I've had, Babe – you wouldn't believe it.' He clicked on the TV. 'A pile up closed the M6 in both directions near Knutsford, so the London coach were two hours late, meanwhile the shuttles were delayed cause of some road rage incident on the M62. Bloke with a machete, they said on the news.'

Claire had learned to stop listening during Dan's traffic reports. The state of Britain's highways was of great importance to Dan and his colleagues, but it bored the hell out of her. Last Christmas she'd accompanied Dan to the Birmingham region's annual staff party, where she'd spent the night listening to Dan and his colleagues debate the M42 road works.

She sat next to him and took a sip of his beer. 'I saw something really weird today.'

'Oh yeah?' said Dan, flicking through channels.

'I looked out at that tower block and quite high up, the seventh or eighth floor or something, there was a woman with a baby.'

Dan paused. There was a beat before he spoke. 'Really?'

'I swear they were there.'

'Weird. A homeless woman sheltering from the mid-day sun? A mother wanting to visit her childhood home before it disappears forever?'

'I guess. There was just something really freaky about it — something haunting.'

Dan started to laugh. 'One of the 350 drivers, Tommy, is dead into all that ghost business. According to him, that church up the road—'

'St. Michael's?'

'Yeah. It's the most haunted place in Manchester, he reckons. All the ghost hunters go there and camp overnight.'

'I think the solution may be more mundane.' Claire lowered her voice to a whisper. 'It was hard to tell from here, but the woman looked a bit like her from next door.'

'The hippy woman?'

'No, her on the other side.'

'Oh. I spoke to her this morning.'

'Why?'

'In a neighbourly way. Her name's Lianne, she seems sound, and she certainly didn't have a baby with her.'

'Well, whoever it was put that baby in needless danger. Do you think we should phone someone?'

'Claire,' said Dan, rubbing her shoulder, 'don't go mithering social services. Let it drop.'

Later, when the bell rang, Claire expected it to be the pizza guy. Instead, she opened the door to her new neighbour – not Lianne, but the hippy woman who lived on the other side. Snakes of hair stuck out from her green headscarf, and despite the heat she was wearing a woollen poncho. From her neck there hung a wooden triple-moon symbol, which seemed to Claire like a new-age version of the Coco Chanel logo. The woman was flanked by two young children. 'I do hope we're not disturbing you,' she said. 'Adrian, my husband, said we should let you two settle in before pestering you with the business of the neighbourhood, but I did so badly want to stop by and say hi. I'm Morgana Cox, and these are my children, Mooncloud and Unity.'

'That's very kind of you.' Claire wanted to shake Morgana's hand but saw that she held a clutch of photocopied leaflets. 'Dan,' she called into the house, 'come and meet Morgana Cox from next door.' After a shuffle of awkward greetings, during which the children smiled rigidly as if hypnotised, Claire asked whether Morgana was the same woman who had intervened to delay the demolition of Sighthill Tower.

'Oh, that was nothing,' said Morgana, as if to deter an impending chorus of praise. 'It was just my duty as a concerned member of the community. I mean, for all we know there isn't any asbestos up there, but it's the principle of the thing, isn't it? It's just such a masculine attitude: if there's a problem, blow it up. There's a lot of energy in the tower – both good and bad – and it needs to be handled carefully, don't you think? It's the same with the redevelopment of the old church house, isn't it, children?' The children maintained their glazed smiles. 'I swear half the people working on that site are illegal immigrants. But we mustn't talk about that here,' whispered Morgana; 'that lot are owned by her father, Neville Shaw.' Morgana nodded her head towards Lianne's house.

At that moment, a woman in a trouser suit pushed open Lianne's gate. She wasn't how Claire imagined one of Lianne's friends would look, and she was too well-dressed to be a Jehovah's Witness. An insurance saleswoman, Claire decided. Whatever her purpose, she rang twice and received no answer. Lianne was still out. Involuntarily, Claire glanced at the tower, the peak of which was just visible over Lianne's garage.

Her attention returned to the conversation when Morgana said 'Yes, there are some disturbing things going on around these parts. Still, you probably don't want to hear about all that just now.'

'We do have a fair bit to do, right enough,' said Dan.

'Wait,' said Claire, 'what do you mean?'

Unity had for some time been tugging Morgana's poncho. 'Mummy, Mooncloud and I want to do the leaflets now.'

'Oh, of course, my treasures. You take these ones. And can you manage these ones? One through every door, okay? Remember, don't cross the main road, and don't do the house on Riverside Grange with the doggie. That doggie isn't very friendly, is he?' Morgana watched her children run off with a doting attention that struck Claire as somewhat false.

'What did you mean,' Claire asked again, 'that disturbing things have been going on around here?'

'It's not something I'd want to worry you with,' said Morgana, 'what with you just having moved in.'

'You're right,' said Dan, who hadn't paused his gangster film. 'We've got enough on our plate.'

'I'm sure we wouldn't be worried,' said Claire.

'Let me ask you this, then,' said Morgana: 'are you expecting?'

'Pregnant?' said Claire, sucking in her tummy.

'Na,' said Dan.

'A lot of people move here to start a family,' said Morgana.

'That is our plan,' said Claire.

'But not any time soon,' said Dan.

'Quite soon,' said Claire.

'Then I shouldn't tell you.' Morgana looked up the street where Mooncloud and Unity were racing to complete their respective deliveries.

'I think now we'll worry more if you don't tell us,' said Claire.

'Yes,' said Morgana, with an affected sigh of resignation, 'you're probably right. Well, did you meet the previous owners of your property?'

'No, just the estate agent.'

'And did it occur to you why they were moving so soon? These houses were only built eighteen months ago.'

'It were summat to do with his work, no?' said Dan.

'Not exactly,' said Morgana. 'They were a lovely couple – Asian. We got on very well. But the wife was pregnant when they moved here. Oh, I really don't think I should be telling you this.'

'Go on,' said Claire.

'Their baby was born horribly deformed. I didn't see the poor thing, but it sounded terrible. They had to move to be near a special hospital.'

'I see,' said Claire.

'And that's not the only thing. You know the real reason I don't want the kids to leaflet at the doggie house? That poor couple suffered a miscarriage, and I'd hate to stir painful memories.'

'That's enough,' said Dan, holding his hand up to stop Morgana from speaking.

'There's more. The woman—'

'Why are you telling us this?' asked Claire.

'We think it's something to do with the mobile phone mast. Have you seen it? It's across the river, beside the nursing home. It's like this big phallic presence – this sword in the earth. You can probably see the top of it from your bedroom window. That's what the leaflets are about.' Morgana handed Claire a Xeroxed sheet of A5: 10pt font and a line drawing of an ankh. 'Are you free tomorrow?'

'Tomorrow?' said Claire. She looked at Dan for help.

'Tomorrow I've got to— We've got to . . .'

'Well,' said Morgana, 'if you've nothing planned, we're having a meeting at our house. It will be the perfect way to welcome you to the neighbourhood.'

Two

WHEN CLAIRE left Birmingham (itself no Costa del Sol), the nurses on the ophthalmology ward clubbed together to buy her a pink Banana Republic raincoat as a leaving present. During the move, she had taken it with her in the car, partly because it symbolised her life past and future, and partly for the more practical reason that she expected to arrive in a downpour. Everything she had seen and heard of Manchester had made her anticipate rain. Instead, she and Dan had arrived during a heat wave that broke new records every day. The people of Manchester rediscovered, in sheds and garages, the optimistic purchases of the previous spring – garden furniture, hosepipes, boules sets – and for a month they devoted themselves each day to this miracle of sunshine, and gamely tackled the problem of what to *do*.

Yes, the sun made people spend time together – in parks and beer gardens, around trampolines and paddling pools – and for the first time, Claire recognised the extent of her isolation: besides Dan, the only person she knew in the whole of Manchester was Ozzy, Dan's childhood friend who'd been the best man at their wedding. Somehow, against all laws of natural selection, Ozzy had recently managed to reproduce – his girlfriend had given birth to a . . . Claire couldn't remember if it was a boy or a girl. In his whole life Ozzy hadn't managed to move more than five minutes from the Burnage suburb in which he and Dan had grown up, and it depressed Claire that Dan had now returned to a neighbourhood only twenty minutes away. Ozzy brayed at his own stories and told interminable anecdotes about altercations he'd had with retail workers. He leaned too close to you when he spoke. He sprayed spittle. He delivered long monologues about the best way to take out the bikers at the airfield when you're playing as Trevor in Grand Theft Auto 5 on the Xbox 360. Ozzy was the entirety of Claire's social connections in Manchester. And maybe that's why, mid-afternoon, she decided to introduce herself to her next-door neighbour Lianne.

When Claire left her new house, the force of the sun was unexpected. Heat waves bent the air, turning the horizon to rubber. Beside Lianne's gate, a dead frog stretched out on the pavement, baked dry and transparent. The sight made Claire stop, look around. The houses, and their waist-high red-brick garden walls, were architecturally identical, but the gardens were very different. At number thirteen, Morgana and Adrian had erected bird feeders and hung dream catchers from the roof of the porch. They grew parsley and chives in window boxes and their small lawn was sprinkled with daisies. In Lianne's garden, dandelion clocks poked out through the knee-high grass, and wasps buzzed around an overgrown cotoneaster bush. An empty pizza box lay in the corner, its corporate branding bleached pale by the sun.

Lianne's windows were open, and a song Claire didn't recognise played out into the street, but there was no answer when Claire rang the doorbell. She watched the wasps crawl on the cotoneaster and listened to the hum of a lawnmower a block or two away. She waited an abnormally long time, and then, resisting the urge to return home, she rang the bell again. This time, she heard steps in the hallway. The music stopped. She wondered whether Lianne was watching her through the peep-hole. Eventually, the door opened to the extent allowed by the security chain. Lianne peered out into the afternoon brightness. She wore a long T-shirt over her underwear and her face was smeared with yesterday's makeup.

'I'm Claire Wilson. My husband and I have just moved in next door.' Claire started to extend her hand, and then pulled back, for some reason fearing that Lianne might slam her wrist in the door. 'I just thought I'd stop by, introduce myself, say hi.'

'Ah,' said Lianne, as if this were the explanation she'd been waiting for. She closed the door, and for a moment Claire thought it wouldn't reopen; then she heard the scratch of the chain, and Lianne reappeared still holding the door as if in readiness. 'I'm Lianne,' she said.

'It's nice to meet you. We've just been, you know, getting unpacked and stuff, but I thought it'd be nice to introduce myself.'

'Cool. I think I met your husband. Brown eyes, right?'

Claire couldn't think what colour Dan's eyes were. 'That was probably him,' she said.

'Yeah, it were him. He's nice.'

'Not if you have to live with him.'

'Most men are nice if you don't have to live with them.'

For some reason, Claire laughed at this, longer and harder than the comment was funny. It was forced laughter, but it seemed to relax Lianne, and after a few seconds she joined in. As Lianne laughed, Claire saw that she had overlapping front teeth that seemed out of place with her peroxide hair and acrylic nails.

'So how are you, like, finding the area then?'

'We love it,' said Claire. 'How long have you been here?'

'Forever,' said Lianne, folding her arms across her chest.

Claire knew the question she wanted to ask but was unsure how to broach the subject, so she stood there, smiling, as a rare gust of breeze sent dandelion seeds drifting across the street. 'I hear they're knocking down that tower,' she said at last.

'September eighth,' said Lianne.

'Right. This might sound a weird question . . . Do you ever, I don't know, ever go up there?'

'Sighthill Tower?'

'Yeah, I thought I saw you up there the other day.'

Lianne shook her head.

'It must have been someone else. I thought I saw you with a baby.'

'You what?'

'I saw someone with a baby and I thought—'

'A baby?' Lianne's face had gone white. 'Nasty bitch.'

'What? I—'

'Piss off ya manky cow!' said Lianne, already wiping her tears.

Claire opened her mouth to apologise, but before she could speak, Lianne slammed the door with an animalistic howl. The force of Lianne's rage was so great that as the door slammed Claire stumbled backwards. Then the day seemed eerily quiet and the only noise was a distant siren passing at speed on St. Michael's Street.

Back at home, Claire locked the door and lay on the sofa, waiting for Dan. When he arrived, she'd want to tell him what had happened, but to do so would open herself to the inevitable 'I told you so.' She'd be unable to blame him for such a response because she – or anyone else – would do the same. 'I told you so' seemed to Claire an inescapable human reflex. You go to see the captain of the Titanic: 'shouldn't you slow down, Sir?' 'It'll be fine,' he says. Next time you see him you're clinging to debris, hypothermic, hallucinating lights in the sky. Exhausted, you bob your head out of the water just long enough to say, 'told you so.'

So when Dan came home, Claire kept quiet about the incident with Lianne. Instead, because she needed to say something, rather than because she thought Dan might actually consider it, Claire asked her husband whether he was going to Morgana's phone mast meeting.

'I'd sooner stick my head up a dead bear's bum.'

'So the mobile phone mast doesn't worry you?'

'D'you know what that hippy's got in her garage?'

'How d'you know what's in their garage?'

'If you press the fob before you're on the driveway, it opens the garages on both sides. It's the same roller code or summat. You have to go round and shut them all once you've parked.'

'So what?'

'So nothing. It doesn't matter so long as our next door neighbours aren't burglars.'

'No – so what's in their garage?'

'Oh. They've got this weird sort of altar thing. It looks like something from Harry Potter. It's carved with pentagrams and strange lettering.'

'No way!'

'I'm telling you – it's well freaky. Anyway, Babe, I don't think that meeting would be good for you.'

'One of us has to go.'

'Why?'

'She'll know we're home.'

'We'll pull the curtains shut, pretend we're out.'

'It would be too rude. What will we say the next time we see her?'

'Say we got food poisoning.'

'In any case, it will be nice to meet the neighbours. I don't know anybody in Manchester.'

'True,' said Dan, scrunching his empty can. 'But I don't think Morgana's going to be your new bessie.'

'It won't be just her there.'

'Na, but it might be just the two of you.'

It nearly was. The official minutes will testify that seven local residents were present, but one of those was a cat. Unity had insisted that the family pet, Smudge, be allowed to air his opinions, and she and Mooncloud spent much of the meeting bewitching the disorientated feline with a mini chakra wand. Morgana's husband, Adrian Cox, sat on the Ottoman, smiling benignly at the children. He had tousled ginger hair, and he was wearing a worryingly tight pair of denim shorts. The only delegates from outside the Cox household were Claire and an elderly woman, Mrs Hilary Brompton.

Despite the small attendance, Morgana (the meeting's self-appointed chair) felt it was necessary to discuss ground rules for establishing a safe and mutually supportive environment in which everyone felt empowered to express herself. As far as Claire could see, assuming Adrian didn't open his legs any wider, the only attendee in any danger was Smudge, whose tail was being pulled about like an anchor rope.

If the opening exchanges seemed dull and pointless, there was plenty to interest Claire in the Cox's living room. For a start, they had the most candles she had ever seen outside a catholic church. None were lit, but there were candles of every size and colour. There were oil burners and incense sticks and crystals. The walls and seats were festooned with hand-woven rugs and tapestries, and the whole room smelled of camel. There were ornamental coffee pots and wood-carved masks ('we're great fans of the ethnic,' as Morgana explained), and in the alcove there was a crude statue of a figure with a disproportionately large vulva. For many reasons, it struck Claire as an unsuitable house for two young children.

When Morgana deemed everyone felt safe and empowered, the meeting finally commenced. It was immediately apparent that Mrs Brompton wasn't quite on message. 'I don't wish to seem like an old busybody,' she said, 'but I do worry about those ne'er-do-wells in the tower. An awful rough lot they seem to be. And where are the police?'

'Yes,' said Morgana, 'I think that's a concern we all share. Perhaps it's something we can return to once we've discussed the mobile phone mast?'

'They lit a fire the other week,' said Adrian.

'Glue sniffers, I bet,' said Mrs Brompton.

'Quite,' said Morgana, 'but I think the urgent matter here is the phone mast and the effect it's having on pregnant women.'

'The effect it *may* be having,' said Adrian, before he registered Morgana's stare. 'Sorry but I just think we need to clarify our language for the minutes. We mustn't cause unnecessary panic.'

'Tell that to the grieving mothers,' said Morgana.

'Wiccanzabar!' said Mooncloud, swinging the wand at the cat.

'That's a little unfair,' said Adrian.

'Is it?' asked Morgana. 'Do you know what it's like to carry a child? To nurture a life in your womb?'

'And all the graffiti,' said Mrs Brompton. 'Why, it's even appeared on my street. A baby with a crucifix staked through its heart? It's most unpleasant.'

'Wiccanzabar!'

'I do share your concern,' said Claire, because she felt Mrs Brompton was being ignored, or because she wanted to change the subject. 'About the people in the tower, I mean.'

'Thank you, dear; it's an awful worry to have at my age.'

'It might be worth co-authoring a letter to the chief constable?' said Adrian.

'Right, that's it,' said Morgana. 'As chairperson I'm empowered to enforce the agenda. We are talking about the mobile phone mast. Is that clear?'

'Wiccanzabar!'

The meeting finally concluded in a spirit of compromise: it was agreed that they would campaign against the mobile phone mast *and* the ne'er-do-wells inhabiting the derelict tower. Afterwards, Claire stayed behind to talk with Morgana – she needed to tell someone what had happened with Lianne. She explained how she'd seen a blonde woman holding a baby high up in the tower block, how she'd tentatively accused Lianne, and how the door had been slammed in her face. 'Oh dear,' said Morgana, when Claire had finished, 'you weren't to know.' She leant back and massaged her temples. 'It's not your fault. You mustn't feel ashamed. Please, sit down. Let me get us some tea.'

Claire had hoped for a cup of Tetley's, but Morgana returned with a pot of fennel and dandelion. As they sipped their tea, Claire could hear Adrian reading a bedtime story upstairs. 'I should have told you before,' said Morgana.

'Should have told me what?'

Morgana kicked off her sandals and massaged her temples once more. 'Lianne is another one. She was pregnant. At the start of the year, her baby was stillborn.'

The previous year, when flying to Corfu, Claire's plane had dropped 5000 feet without warning; she now experienced the same sensation. 'Oh God,' she said, covering her mouth in appalled shock.

'You weren't to know.'

'I'm an idiot!'

'No, you're not; you were trying to do the right thing.'

'Dan told me not to stick my nose where it wasn't wanted.'

'Now, come on,' said Morgana; 'if everyone had that attitude there would be no community. What's important is that you counteract any bad karma. If you let this thing fester . . . well, the consequences could be tragic. Tell me, do you believe in magic?'

'Magic? Not really.'

'Then you've nothing to lose. Wait there.'

She returned from the kitchen with a green cooking apple, a knife, half-a-dozen cocktail sticks, a pencil, and a small scrap of paper. 'Is it your moon time?' she asked.

'My what?'

'Your moon time, Claire. Your cycle.'

'What? No!'

'Now, now, it's not something to be ashamed about. I only ask because you're especially receptive during your moon time. Not to worry. This is an old Romany spell. They use it for mending love affairs, but it works just as well for friendships.'

Morgana wrote 'Claire Wilson' and 'Lianne Shaw' on the scrap of paper, and then she sliced the apple in half. 'It works best if the seeds stay whole . . . Yes, that looks fine.' She placed the paper between the halves of the apple and pressed them together. 'Now, visualise you and Lianne surrounded by a pink aura. Got it?'

'I think so.'

'Good. Get the cocktail sticks, and skewer them through the apple, pinning the two halves together.'

In doing this, Claire touched Morgana's hands, and she recoiled at their coldness.

'There,' said Morgana, releasing the apple once its two halves were pinned, 'how do you feel?'

'Better,' said Claire.

Morgana laughed. 'It takes some time.'

'I did see a baby,' said Claire. 'I admit it was too far to make out the detail, but I know what I saw.'

'Of course you did – I don't doubt it. Mrs Brompton's right, you know: there are druggies camped out in that building. One of the poor wretches probably has a child. Isn't it awful?'

'Tell me something,' said Claire; 'do you really think what happened to Lianne – and those other women – happened because of the phone mast?'

'Wait.' Morgana looked at Claire as if she'd had a sudden realisation. Her eyes narrowed and then closed, and she held her hands up as if about to catch a basketball. She sat like this, breathing deeply through her nose. 'I sense negative energy, Claire. Something's troubling you.'

Claire shook her head.

'Do you want to talk?'

'That's very kind of you,' said Claire, 'but my husband—'

'Hold my hand.'

Claire laughed awkwardly, stood up. 'Thank you for the tea. This has been really nice, but I should . . . you know.'

Morgana sighed and lowered her extended hand. 'Don't bottle it up,' she called as Claire reached the door.

Outside, Claire stood for a moment, reluctant to go home. At this time, in the settling dusk, she could hear the faraway whoosh of motorway traffic on the M60 flyover, and then from the direction of the tower block came a howl; she imagined a feral dog stalking between the tower's stilts. The sky was dark purple, the stars not yet visible, but the evening was clear and the low moon was a few days off full.

She knew that if she didn't do it now, she would never apologise to Lianne. She argued with herself that it was too late to call on a neighbour, but Lianne's windows were open, R&B still playing into the street. So Claire walked past her own house, watching TV-light dance behind the curtain, and for the second time that day she pushed open Lianne's gate. She reached her finger towards the door bell and then paused, pointing. Then, finally, she pressed the bell, stepped back, and waited half-way up the path.

This time there was no delay. Lianne opened the door fast, as if she'd been expecting Claire's visit. 'What?'

'I came to apologise.'

'Go on then.'

'I'm very sorry for what I said. I didn't know about your loss.'

'Anything else?'

Claire didn't know what to say. 'I know what it's like.'

'Good,' said Lianne, starting to close the door.

'Wait – Lianne, can I talk to you?'

Lianne paused, holding the door ajar, and then her countenance softened, and she pushed the door open. Claire followed her inside to the living room. Lianne's house had the same newly-built smell as did her own: paint, recently cut wood, fibreglass insulation – a smell almost like sweat. 'I'm going out in a minute,' said Lianne, dimming the music, 'so I can't talk for long.' She was now wearing a strappy top and white hot pants, with thick mascara lashes and sparkles of glitter around her eyes. Her push-up bra was the sort of bra that Claire hadn't worn since she and some school friends had celebrated finishing their A-levels in Worcester town centre.

A half-empty bottle of Chardonnay stood on the coffee table next to an overflowing ashtray. 'I'll get you a glass,' said Lianne. As she watched her host leave the room, Claire noticed that Lianne's legs did not suit shorts that small. Cellulite rippled down from her bum, and her fake tan was smeared at the back of her knees.

Lianne came back with a mug instead of a wine glass. She poured Claire a drink and then squeaked back onto the sofa and lit a cigarette.

'Big night planned?' asked Claire.

'Meeting some of the girls, you know? Just, like, have a few drinks, hit a club, whatever.'

'Sounds good.'

'D'you go out?'

'I was going to ask you where's good to go – we're new to Manchester. Well, I am. Dan grew up here.'

Lianne flicked her ash. 'Depends what you're into. From here you can go into, like, Fallowfield and Withington and all that. But it's the student bit so it's kind of stuck up. You're not a student, are you?'

'I'm twenty-eight now. I haven't been a student for a long time.'

'Yeah, well, that scene's probably a bit young for you.' Lianne swigged her wine. 'Go into town then. What music you into?'

'I like a bit of everything,' said Claire.

'Give over,' said Lianne. 'Why do people say that? Like, you really saying you like, I don't know, death metal, experimental jazz, big band marching music?'

'Then I guess, probably, indie.'

'I hate that crap. Skinny jeans, corduroy, converse trainers.'

'What are *you* into?'

'Oh, this and that,' said Lianne, looking very pleased with herself. She stubbed her cigarette out and exited the room with an ungainly attempt at the strut of a femme fatale.

Left alone, Claire tried the wine – it was sweet as apple juice – and then, because doing nothing made her uncomfortable, she stood up and looked around. Lianne's home was weirdly bare, especially after the clutter she'd seen at Morgana's; it hardly seemed lived in. One of the few features that personalised the living room was a postcard-sized framed photograph of a young man in military uniform. It had the faded look of a moment captured before Claire was born. The man was pictured as if riding side saddle. After a moment, Claire heard the toilet flush, and then Lianne returned, now followed by a swarm of perfume.

'Is this your . . . ' Claire paused, nervous of saying the wrong thing.

'Yeah, that's me dad – well, he's me stepdad. Me biological dad pissed off before I were born.'

'Has he . . . ' She didn't know how to phrase it. ' . . . Passed away?'

'Na!' said Lianne, laughing. 'Haven't you heard about Neville Shaw yet?'

As Claire retook her seat, she remembered that Morgana had said something about Lianne's dad. He owned a building company or something. Claire decided it was best to shake her head.

'Quick version or long version?'

'You're the one who's going out.'

'Okay, quick version. He did two tours of Northern Ireland, and when he got out he were all, like, messed up and stuff. Back then they didn't have all your counselling and that, did they? So he's moved down here – he were from Scotland – for me mam, I suppose, and he started driving taxis. Like I say, he weren't right. He started drinking, like real bad, and he were at it with the gambling as well. He lost his license, ended up owing money to the worst sort of people. One morning, he left home and didn't come back. Two months later, he shows up: sober, clean, rebuilding his life. Turns out he's, like, discovered Jesus or whatever, joined the church and everything. So he finds a job on a building site and for two years he doesn't drink a drop or gamble a penny. Then one day he's out doing some shopping, right, and he hears this voice, you know? Like, in his head. And it's the voice of God, he reckons, and God's telling him to put on a bet. God's saying, like, lay on this accumulator or whatever. Me dad's not bet nothing in two years, remember, but he hears this voice and goes down to the bookies and puts on the bet just as God suggested. Guess what? All his results come in, just as God said they would. He won £820,000.'

'That's incredible.'

'It happened,' said Lianne, 'swear down. He didn't waste it neither. He bought the company he worked for, doubled his money inside ten year. Then they got the contract to build all these houses.'

'They did a good job. They're beautiful.'

'He lets me live in this one.'

'Thanks be to God,' said Claire. 'Are he and your mum still together?'

'Yeah, I suppose they are. She's in care now.'

'I'm sorry.'

'She's a bit, you know,' said Lianne, making a screw-loose gesture, 'but we see her often.'

'Any brothers or sisters?'

'I did have older sisters, yeah. Half-sisters. But they're not around anymore. Me mam were pretty old when she had me. She wanted a boy. She never wanted me.'

Claire nodded, sipped her wine, unsure what to say.

For a moment, the only noise was Lianne tapping her rings against the rim of her mug. Eventually she said, 'So you lost a baby too?'

'I'm sorry?' said Claire.

'You said, "I know how it feels."'

'Oh. Yeah, I had a miscarriage. Six months ago. I was only fifteen weeks.'

'It's hardly the same thing.'

'Perhaps not. We'd always spoken of our baby as a boy, but we'll never know, will we?'

'What did you do?'

'What did I *do*? I don't know. I . . . It was an unexpected pregnancy. We were just getting used to the idea.'

'Well, it's better it happens early.'

'I cried. I blamed myself, blamed Dan. I mean, with the grief there was also this guilt. And this *anger*, as if what had happened had happened because we – because he . . . because I – didn't want our baby badly enough.'

Lianne nodded as she poured more wine.

'Because,' continued Claire, 'we were too slow to love him.' Claire's breath grew heavy and Lianne nodded in silence. 'He would have been born this month. I would have loved him. I would have loved him so much. I just didn't know how little time I had.' Neither of them knew what to say. And then, unexpectedly, in the company of a stranger, Claire did what she hadn't done with Dan in months – she put her hands to her face and wept.

Three

WHEN CLAIRE arrived home, Dan was already asleep. She sat on one of the final unpacked boxes and listened to his snoring. Tomorrow, she would finish the unpacking in an hour or two; what would she do after that? The only people she knew were her neighbours: a crazy white witch and a tragic alcoholic. At Claire's age, how do you meet people? All her life she had made friends accidentally – at school or uni or work. What now? Take up a hobby? Pottery lessons? A Spanish evening class? Interior design? It occurred to her that when she finally emptied it of boxes, she could decorate the spare room. It was painted magnolia like the rest of the house, but when she and Dan had viewed the property, they had discussed it as a baby room, and she imagined it brightly coloured with dangling aerials and cartoons as big as the walls.

That night she lay awake, breathing with the rhythm of Dan's snores. They slept with a window open, naked, covered only by a sheet, but the night was still uncomfortably hot. At the top of the mobile phone mast there was a red light to warn off low-flying aeroplanes; for an hour, she watched its pulse-like blink redden her bedroom wall. Then, at what time exactly she couldn't say, just as she was dozing off, there came a crack from the back garden. It sounded like a piece of wood snapping. She sat up and shook Dan by the shoulder. 'Dan, wake up.'

'380 to Bangor? Door A, stand two, 16:45,' mumbled Dan.

'Dan!'

'Okay, yeah.'

She shook him harder. 'Dan!'

He rolled over, wrapping himself in the sheet's entirety.

Claire sat still, listening to the silence outside, and then, because her pulse was still thumping, she got up and put on her dressing robe. Edging down the stairs, she decided she'd feel safer with a weapon. She turned the living room light on, decisively, as if in doing so she would vanquish a vampire. No intruders. Nothing she could use as a weapon, either. She checked the downstairs toilet, where she briefly considered arming herself with the toilet brush.

Then, in the kitchen, she grabbed the peppermill from the counter. It felt good to hold something heavy. Keeping the light off so she could see the garden, she crept up to the sliding patio doors and clicked on the garden light.

When she saw the man, she screamed and dropped the peppermill. He was staring right at her – a man in a black beanie hat. Later, when she thought back on the moment, what most alarmed her was that he had not seemed the least bit startled. The man didn't run or panic or even look guilty. He noted her presence, and then, disinterested, he continued what he was doing at languorous pace. He strolled to the fence that separated Claire's garden from Lianne's, vaulted it, and continued towards the derelict tower block.

'Babe?' Dan was thudding down the stairs, too late as usual. 'Babe, what's happened? You okay?' He turned on the kitchen light and stood naked, breathing heavily. His eyes were screwed half shut and he seemed unaware that he'd woken in a state of semi-arousal. 'Babe, you look like you've seen a ghost.'

'Not a ghost, Dan, just a crack-head intruder from the crack-head tower in our crack-head new neighbourhood. I hate this place!'

'Calm down, okay? Come here. Tell me what happened.'

It felt good to be held by him, but when he told her to calm down a second time, Claire thought, Screw you, Dan. You were asleep when I needed you. She pushed past him and ran upstairs to phone the police.

Nobody teaches you when you should and shouldn't phone 999. The operator listened to Claire's story with professional courtesy, but all the time Claire sensed she was keeping this woman from some more urgent part of her job. It didn't help that she remembered no details: she could only describe the intruder as a white man in a black beanie hat, and she couldn't even recall her new postcode.

She and Dan sat up for a bit and watched TV, but every channel seemed to be showing a slasher flick or a documentary about a serial killer, and so, when it became apparent that no police officer was coming, they returned upstairs and locked the bedroom door. In some belated attempt to be her masculine protector, Dan armed himself with a hammer, a cook's knife, and a cricket ball in a sock, but he was snoring again in minutes.

Claire was still awake at three or four when she heard a taxi idling on the street outside. A door slammed and then the engine revved, fading into the distance. She heard Lianne's key scratching at her lock. Laughter. A man's voice – 'come on. I'm bursting!' Then she listened as they climbed the stairs, played music, flushed the toilet. At one point a glass smashed. And then, inevitably, from a few centimetres on the other side of the wall, Claire heard the squeak of her neighbour's mattress. She listened to their accelerating rhythm, straining to hear the details of something she should have wanted to ignore. They paused, whispered. She heard a noise like someone being smacked. Then the rhythm was slower and louder, each thrust crashing against the wall. Claire looked at her snoring husband and realised that, apart from the night they moved in, when Dan had insisted they 'christened' the bedroom, it hadn't occurred to either of them to make love. Lianne was shouting now, demanding obscene acts, screaming desires that in four years of marriage Claire hadn't even contemplated. And then, with no audible climax, it was over.

Claire lay still, listening to the silence. After a minute or two, she padded to the bathroom as if she'd been party to the act. She sat on the bath, enjoying the sensation of cool ceramic against her bum. A toilet flushed through the wall and she wondered at this strange synchronicity. And then, conscious of her nakedness, aware that the door was open and that Dan, if he woke, could step in and see her, she opened her legs and stroked her thighs. She hadn't waxed in weeks – pubic hair had spread over her groin – and after a moment she stood on the edge of the bathtub so she could inspect herself in the mirror. Her boobs were okay, she thought, though her nipples were asymmetrical. Her shoulders were too broad. She'd got a good

BMI, statistically, but fat slumped to her waist and sat dolloped on each hip bone. She sat on the rim of the bath and thought about the morning. Maybe she should do Zumba, an exercise DVD, take up running, something like that?

When she returned to bed, she could hear Lianne crying through the wall. She thought of the man in the beanie hat – she couldn't get his image from her head. Then Lianne was shouting that the man had to leave and the man was shouting back. She heard something crash against the wall. More crying. She heard the man call Lianne a psycho, and then Lianne was screaming at him to get out. A minute or two later, Lianne's front door slammed, and after that the only noise was delivery traffic on the M60, and birds singing their survival to the lightening sky.

The next morning, after Dan had gone to work, the bell rang. In her dressing gown, Claire opened the door to two twenty-something policemen, who introduced themselves as constables Young and White. 'We understand that you disturbed an intruder?'

Claire nodded and invited them in, even though the way he'd phrased it suggested she'd behaved a bit inconsiderately.

The policemen sat down on the couch with a great effort of shuffling and rearranging themselves. They were so bulked up with stab vests, so burdened with handcuffs and radios and truncheons, that the manoeuvre took them several attempts. Can you tell us when last night this happened? No. Can you describe the man? No. Can you show us where he forced entry? Well, no. 'He wasn't in the house,' explained Claire; 'he was in the garden.'

'I see,' said one of the policemen, standing up to inspect this so-called garden. He peered through the open kitchen door and nodded. 'You should keep those doors locked at night.'

'The thought has occurred to me.'

'Do you live here alone?' asked the other policeman.

'With my husband, Dan.'

The policemen looked at each other. 'We'll leave you our card. If you see anything else suspicious, don't hesitate to be in touch.'

That was it? thought Claire. They weren't going to search the garden for footprints? They weren't going to check if a fragment of the intruder's clothing had snagged on the fence? They weren't going to interview the neighbours? If Claire ever joined the police force, she decided, she would always at least *pretend* to perform the sort of investigation expected by citizens reared on cop movies.

'There are people living in that derelict tower block,' she said as the policemen reached the door.

'Yes,' said the taller of the two, 'we've already had complaints about them.'

'Can't you do something?'

Young and White looked at each other and smiled ruefully. Both waited for the other to respond. Eventually the shorter of the two said, 'We might move them on in the next few days, but they'll only go somewhere else. They're junkies – they don't think about anything except drugs. They were squatting in the old church house up there, till Neville Shaw's men moved in.'

'Yeah,' said the other cop, laughing, 'I think Neville Shaw's men are pretty persuasive, if you know what I mean.'

'We can't even draw our truncheons without completing a mountain of paperwork.'

'We can't handcuff someone without being taken to the European Court of Human Rights.'

'Political correctness, isn't it?'

'The criminals have got more rights than the law officers.'

'Then there's the paperwork.'

'Don't even mention the paperwork.'

'If we go in there, move them on, we'll be filling in forms for the rest of the week.'

'I think they've got a baby in there,' said Claire, when the policemen finally paused for breath.

'A baby?'

'I saw a woman, high up in the tower block, holding a baby.'

'Did you report this?' asked the taller officer.

'No,' said Claire, feeling guilty. 'Well, I suppose I'm reporting it now.'

'You can't report it to us.'

'No, not to us.'

'That's a matter for social care, isn't it?'

'If we were to get involved with something like that . . . ' Both policemen laughed. 'We'd be wrapped up in the Children Act, hit over the head with the ACPO guidelines.'

'I understand,' said Claire, opening the door to the morning heat.

She did go for a run that afternoon. She'd planned to burn off some weight, but when she stepped into the sunshine, dressed in joggers and trainers, the heat overpowered her, and before she'd left their road, her pace had slowed to a stroll.

She crossed St. Michael's Street, with no particular route in mind, vaguely heading for the church. Dan had said it was the most haunted building in Manchester, and it did look spooky – it was hundreds of years older than any other building in the neighbourhood. The stones in its walls had become so used to each other that the lines between them were faint, and its steeple, adorned by no spire, resembled the watchtower of a medieval fort. At some time, a transept had been added to the building, cutting through the nave, its stones lighter-coloured but still ancient. The slated roof was shaded green with moss and lichen.

But was it haunted? Claire walked up the gravel pathway, towards the half-open oak doors, and peeking inside she saw an elderly woman leaning against a pew, polishing something. Eager not to be seen, Claire circled the building, stepping through the shin-high churchyard grass. If there was anything creepy about this place, then it was the churchyard. A fern-lined staircase led to a tiny door, a side entrance to the church's undercroft, the wood of which looked so old it might crumble in your hand.

Tombstones leant at angles, tangled in ivy and lined with moss. She walked among them, noticing that time had dissolved the inscriptions. She strained to read the softened carvings: 'In hopes of a blessed immortality are here deposited the remains of Samuel

Brewster, beloved son of Charles and Agnes. Born 1902, died 1907.' 'Frances Mary, the beloved child of Kingsley and Edith Brompton, died Oct 7th 1874 aged 9 months.' Almost every gravestone seemed to commemorate at least one child, including the gravestone that bore Claire's married name: 'Here lieth the remains of Sarah, the daughter of Edward and Mary Wilson, who died June 12th 1809, aged 26 years, & also Richard and John, sons of the aforesaid, who died in their infancy.'

She walked out, crossed the road, planning to pick up her pace again. They had built a roundabout in preparation for traffic flowing to houses not yet built, and Claire paused there a moment, looking around the quiet crossroads. Far down the empty road, heat waves trembled the tarmac. She jogged on, concentrating on her stride. Ahead of her loomed a giant billboard, on which a computer-generated image advertised the architect's vision of the new development. 'Live like this,' it said. But, as she neared it, she saw that over the writing someone had spray-painted graffiti: a picture, two-metres tall. It was the image that Mrs Brompton had complained about during their meeting at Morgana's. The picture was of a baby, in foetal position, sucking its thumb. She stopped to catch her breath and stretch her triceps. From the proportions of the drawing, and the smoothness of the curves, it was obvious that the vandal had some artistic ability, but at places he or she had let the paint drip and run, and this gave the image a frightening raw anger. What was horrific about it, of course, was that, as Mrs Brompton had described, though the baby looked serene and peaceful, it had a crucifix staked through its heart. There was a crow perched atop the billboard, and when Claire finally jogged on, it cawed and flew into the sun.

The area on which they planned to build was now a barren scrubland. The last time she'd been here, when she and Dan had been house hunting, the old council housing had been half-demolished. It was a Saturday, and the workers had left one house barely standing; its front wall was missing and its concrete second floor drooped on construction wire, like dog-eared cardboard. Since then they had cleared the site, built a mountain of rubble, and tarmacked a road that ran nowhere, but the project would not continue until Sighthill Tower was destroyed.

At present, the new road ran as far as the construction fence and stopped. This was as close as she'd ever been to the tower. Seen from this angle, it looked enormous. It wasn't rectangular, she now saw, but was built to a cruciform design – it was almost like four towers joined in the middle. She counted twelve storeys. How high up had the baby been? It was hard to say. About two thirds up, she thought. Everything was quiet, and the tower was less frightening in the sunlight, so she decided to jog to their side of the building, to see up close the view she had from her kitchen window. When she tried, however, she discovered that the barriers went right to Lianne's fence, allowing no way through. She looked across her own fence, worried how easy it would be for someone to climb over, and then she retraced her steps, not yet ready for home, planning to go round the tower on the far side.

The only construction work currently taking place was at the old building on the far side of the tower, and even there the work had slowed in the heat. Two men sat topless, hard hats at their sides, reading tabloids. This must be the church house, Claire thought, remembering what she'd been told about Neville Shaw's redevelopment. On either side of the construction barriers, apples had already fallen to ground, where they lay crawling with wasps.

Claire hesitated, nervous of walking past the men. Would they shout at her? Wolf-whistle? There are women, she thought, who can probably predict how men will react to them: some women are obviously attractive; others know they're unlikely to be the object of indiscriminate lust. Claire belonged to the awkward middle ground. All her life she'd felt appraised, her looks assessed and debated. When she used to date, she had always felt that whether she was classed as fanciable would be decided by some minor detail. The balance could be tipped by good mascara, or badly chosen accessories, or concealer that rubbed off to reveal a spot. Worse, she had never established in her own mind whether she was attractive. As an adolescent, she'd heard herself described as 'well doable' one week and 'a minger' the next. She remembered in shopping malls and changing cubicles, catching glances of her reflection from unusual angles, and changing her opinion of her prettiness with each new look. For a long time, she had talked to boys with her head fixed in one position, convinced this was the only angle from which she looked attractive. She was twenty-eight and still worried about how she appeared to builders. When she finally passed them, they looked up from their papers, saw nothing of great interest, and returned to their reading. She realised she'd subconsciously sucked in her stomach.

Soon after passing the church house, Claire came to the River Mersey. It was just two-metres wide, flowing slowly, and it was hard to believe that this was the beginning of a waterway that, sixty miles from here, near Ellesmere Port, became an estuary five-kilometres across. The past week of sunshine had dried the river, and its water trickled between banks of earth-grey rocks. She couldn't go upstream because around the tower block the track had been blocked by the demolition company. She still hadn't seen how the junkies got in and out – like a fortress, the tower was surrounded by barriers on three sides and protected by water to its rear. The barriers went right into the river, so that you would have to wade to get round them. She looked through the bars and saw that reeds grew through a shopping trolley and around the skeleton of a bike. A girder slumped into the water, as though a kid had tried, and failed, to build a bridge.

So she jogged west, following the course of the river, until she found a bridge and crossed to the other side. On this side, the track bordered a golf course, and so she slowed to a walk, listening to the melodic ping, and the sporting patter of applause, as balls were struck down the fairway. As she strolled, she saw a figure in a kayak, gliding with the flow of the stream. The man paddling the boat was wearing a protective helmet and life vest, and it was only as he passed her that Claire saw the protruding tufts of ginger hair and recognised the man as Morgana's husband, Adrian. She called out but he was past her too quickly, lost in thought.

At the end of the golf course, she had the option to re-cross the river and arrive just metres from her house, but she felt she should burn a few more calories and do a general cool down. An old man, spine C-shaped by time, leant over the bridge rail, muttering into the water. Behind a line of lime trees, she could see St. Michael's Residential Care Home – a building that, for all its luxurious embellishments, couldn't shake off the oppressive quality inherent to all Victorian-built institutions. She wondered whether the old man lived there.

As she started to walk on, the old man called out to her. 'Are you adopted?'

'I'm sorry?' said Claire.

'Are you adopted?'

'I'm not sure I know what you mean.'

The old man turned, shaking, with one talon hand clinging to the railing, the other pressed down on a walking stick. His voice trembled, as if someone were patting his back as he spoke. 'I'm asking if, when you was little, you was adopted by someone other than your parents?'

'No,' said Claire, bemused by the question.

Without any explanation, or any conclusion to the conversation, the old man resumed muttering into the water.

She kept to the far side of the river and walked on until she stood beneath the phone mast. So this was what all the fuss was about. It looked innocuous: like a miniature Eiffel Tower with satellite dishes at the top. Spike-topped palisade fencing surrounded the mast, and on either side the grass grew tall and yellow. There were no radiation-wilted weeds. No dead birds. No two-headed squirrels.

Soon she walked under the flyover, where skater kids clattered their boards on the concrete slope protection. A young man with a big zirconia ear stud was rolling a joint in a long Rizla. The roar of traffic, far overhead, sounded to Claire like one enormous gust of wind. As she hurried through, grateful for the shade, she noticed that on both abutments of the bridge, the staked-baby graffiti had been painted, even bigger than it was on the billboard.

On the far side, she climbed up to the pedestrian walkway, sweating heavily in the heat. Even when on the other side of crash barriers, it was frightening to walk beside such a weight of traffic.

Tied with string to the fence were three posies of wilted flowers. A crash or a suicide jumper? From up here, the dried-out river looked like a thread.

Claire was relieved when she descended to St. Michael's Street and passed back under the motorway. She'd walk on to the church and then turn left for home – a perfect circle. She felt good for the exertion: sunshine and exercise, endorphins and serotonin. The world seemed a better place, and this new neighbourhood, she had to concede, was a perfect area in which to raise a family. In a few weeks, the tower would be gone, the junkies would be gone with it, and her home would be— But even as she was thinking this, even as she was reneging on her worries and suspicions, she passed their only local shops. There was an empty unit, a small general store, and a Chinese takeaway. The takeaway was shut at this hour, and its corrugated shutter was padlocked in place. And there it was again. Sprayed across the shutter: the staked baby.

Four

'I'VE SEEN the graffiti you were talking about,' Claire said to Mrs Brompton, the following week, when the anti-phone mast assembly met for a second time at Morgana's.

'You've seen the what, dear?'

'The graffiti. The baby with a crucifix staked through its heart.'

'Isn't it vile?' said Mrs Brompton. The women sat in silence, listening to splashing and singing from upstairs. A few minutes earlier, Mooncloud & Unity had arrived at the front door, covered in leaves and soil. They had been playing 'mud pigs' and Adrian and Morgana had disappeared upstairs to bathe them.

'Of course, it never used to be like this,' said Mrs Brompton. 'Everything went wrong when they built the council housing. Don't get me wrong, dear; I'd never look down on anyone for being poor. My father, rest his soul, was a philanthropic Christian, who taught me, from before I could walk, to understand that all men are equal before the Lord.' Mrs Brompton closed her eyes and stroked the butterfly brooch she wore near her left shoulder.

Claire was unsure whether Mrs Brompton would continue. 'Absolutely . . . ' Claire said in encouragement.

'Well, then everything changed. There were some fine people moved in at first – even into those awful towers. The deserving poor, we used to call them. But then . . . My father was the last vicar to live in St. Michael's church house.'

'You lived in the church house?'

'Yes, dear. I was born there. Spent my whole childhood there. I wish you could have seen what it was like. My sister and I used to swim in the river. Can you imagine? We had a rowing boat and a hammock in the garden. You can't imagine what summer used to smell like.'

Claire tried. She imagined orchards, spring blossom like dollops of ice cream.

'There were farms and the church and the hospital, and that was our world. And . . . It's hard to explain, dear; it was a different time. When I was a child, ten or eleven, I thought I'd fallen in love with a soldier. You know the building across the river—'

'The nursing home?'

'Yes, where the oldies like me say farewell to our failing bodies. It was built as an orphanage—'

'You look fitter than I do, Mrs Brompton.'

'Oh, you dear thing. Well, sooner or later we will all say goodbye, and I will take my leave in that old building, looking out on the river I played in as a child. Everything here has changed, but when I close my eyes and listen to the river, it could be 1945 again. Back then, the nursing home was a military convalescent hospital. Can you imagine, dear, the impact that had on a child? There were men wandering the fields, talking to themselves, not knowing who they were or what they'd done. Men with no limbs. A man whose face had been burned beyond recognition, whom I saw wheeled out for fresh air, his head wrapped in muslin. And I fell in love, or so I believed, with a young man from Llandudno, who had lost both his arms. We used to walk in the fields, lie down amidst the corn, or sit on haystacks, and I would play at nursing him. I was only twelve, and if it happened today, the poor boy would probably be arrested, but these were different times. He was younger than I was in many ways.'

'Mrs Brompton,' said Claire, 'what do you think of the church house being redeveloped?'

'Well, after the war, eventually, life went back to normal. And it was in the 1950s they started building the new houses. How could one object? Did those poor men who had been wounded for King and country not deserve a good modern house? But then things started to deteriorate. Many people blamed the blacks – the coloureds, I should say. But there were never very many back then – coloureds, I mean – and the locals were just as bad. We left in the early 1960s. By then the neighbourhood was overrun with toughs. The new vicar decided to live in Didsbury, and so the church sold the house.'

'What did you do?'

'We moved to Oxfordshire. My father was appointed rural dean. But my heart stayed here, and two years ago, when I learned that the neighbourhood was to be redeveloped, I decided it was time to come home.'

Morgana clumped down the stairs and entered the living room holding a bottle of Ecover dishwashing liquid. 'It's important for children to interact spiritually with the earth.' Morgana said this determinedly, as though in response to some imagined criticism of her parenting. 'I'll make some tea and then we'll start.' So while Morgana brewed her latest herbal infusion (rose hip and hibiscus), Claire and Mrs Brompton sat in clouds of smoky jasmine incense. Now and again, Mrs Brompton's eyes flicked to the bulging fertility statue, and each time Claire saw her look away in discomfort. 'What were you asking me before, dear?'

Claire couldn't remember.

'Oh, the church house. Well, nobody wants her childhood home altered,' said Mrs Brompton. 'As long as the past remains in mortar, then we can revisit our youth. But it was awful to see the building in ruin, its roof crumpled, its garden overgrown. And so, given the choice, I'd prefer it become an apartment block for some nice young newlyweds, than that it be left to rot.'

'Tell me something,' said Claire. 'My husband says that some people think the church is haunted. Do you know how that story started?'

'Oh, what a load of fiddlesticks. My father once caned Doris and me for discussing such nonsense. He made us write, a thousand times, "The Holy Spirit is the only spirit in the Holy House of God." Still, I suppose the story is harmless now. Sometime in the eighteenth century, before the hospital was even an orphanage, a peasant woman killed her babies. She had triplets, you see, and by the grace of God they were all born healthy. But the family were poor, and the woman was hungry and overworked, and so, before the father had seen them, she drowned two of the babies in the river. She thought, God have mercy on her, that she and her cousin, the woman who'd helped her give birth, would be the only ones who ever knew. But the guilt weighed upon the cousin, and she broke her silence, and the babies were found, and the woman was sentenced to death. Well, when they hung her, her neck didn't break, and nor did she strangle. She hung by the neck for two whole hours, or so the story goes, and even then she kicked and screamed and wouldn't die. According to legend, her cousin took pity on her and cut her throat so that she would suffer no more. Of course, the superstitious peasantry claimed her crime had been so awful that Satan had shut the gates of hell. She was trapped, forever to wander the village. Even when I was a child, the more ignorant people whispered about the "White Lady." I don't know where the white bit came from.'

'Did she have blonde hair?' asked Claire.

'The woman or the ghost?' Mrs Brompton laughed. 'The ghost never existed, and, who knows, the woman maybe never existed either.'

'What ghost?' said Morgana, entering with the tea and some organic shortbread.

'I was telling Claire about the White Lady.'

'That ridiculous story,' said Morgana. 'As if spirits are evil presences skulking around graveyards.'

'So you never saw her?'

'Of course not,' said Mrs Brompton. 'Mind you, Doris, my sister, used to try to scare me. She'd come running from the attic or the basement, swearing she'd seen the White Lady cradling her dead babies.'

'I think I saw her,' said Claire. The two women stopped smiling and Claire was aware how crazy she sounded.

'Saw what?' said Adrian, who entered with the children, once again wearing dangerously small shorts.

'The White lady,' said Morgana.

'I saw her too,' said Unity, who was now clean and wearing rainbow pyjamas.

Adrian ruffled her bowl cut. 'Of course you did.'

'I don't mean I saw a ghost,' said Claire, feeling embarrassed, 'but don't you think it's strange that I mentioned seeing a woman holding a baby, up in that derelict tower block, before I'd even heard this White Lady story?'

'I did see a ghost,' said Unity. 'Didn't I, Mooncloud?'

Mooncloud looked puzzled and shook his head.

'Yes I did, stupid. After we'd been to the Secret Baby Room.'

'What's the Secret Baby Room?' asked Claire.

'Unity's telling a fib,' said Mooncloud.

'That's not a nice thing to say about your sister,' said Adrian. 'Maybe she genuinely believes she saw a ghost, even if no ghost existed.'

'Yeah!' said Unity. 'It was walking on the river, and its feet were on fire, and its chains were all rusted, and it had spiders in its hair.'

'Don't try to frighten your little brother,' said Adrian.

Claire tried again. 'What's the Secret Baby Room?'

'She's lying!' said Mooncloud, starting to cry.

'Nothing,' said Morgana. 'It's just a game they play.'

Mrs Brompton tapped a teaspoon against her saucer, in an attempt to bring some order. 'Children,' she said, and it seemed she was addressing them all. 'There are many mysteries we will never solve, so let us not invent new ones where none exist. My late husband, rest his soul, used to refer to Occam's Razor. Many centuries ago, a Franciscan Friar, William of Ockham, said that the best explanation is usually the simplest. So, if we wonder what Claire saw, then we could invent a whole world of ghosts and spirits. Or, given we know the building is filled with ne'er-do-wells, we could say that one of these glue-sniffing rough types has a baby. Which explanation requires the fewest assumptions?'

The meeting did finally begin, and it finally ended, too. The time for talking was over, declared Morgana; the time for strongly worded letters was nigh. And so they sat in companionable silence and composed complaints to their elected representatives and the local press. Claire was appointed to contact the *Manchester Evening Chronicle*, and she sat, pen in hand, unsure what to write. She worried that her objection wasn't entirely sincere – that, if pushed, she would be unable to back her arguments with science and figures and salient facts. After all, it would never have occurred to her that the phone mast was problematic, had the idea not been placed in her head. She had a peak at Morgana's notepad and saw that every paragraph Morgana wrote began with 'Speaking as a mother of two' or 'As a mother' or 'It is my duty as a mother.' Why did motherhood give her opinion such authority? Claire was not a mother. She wrote, 'Speaking as a former badminton enthusiast,' and then she scored it out. She wrote, 'As a keen reader of historical fiction,' and then she scored that out too.

When Claire left Morgana's, the sun was brushed orange across the horizon, and she looked west, where the tower stood silhouetted against the bright strokes of the sky. She thought of some giant pagan standing stone. Then she saw something new: high up on the tower, near where she'd seen the baby, was the biggest version of the staked-baby graffiti she had ever seen. Whoever painted it must have— How was it even possible? It was painted black and white, a storey tall, hundreds of feet in the sky. He must have been on a harness or something. Why would anyone go to such effort? Why would anyone want to paint *that*?

'Have you seen the graffiti?' she asked Dan, who was watching highlights of the cricket. 'Dan?'

'What graffiti?'

'A baby with a stake—'

'Oh, the sort of foetus shape with a crucifix thing stabbed in its chest? That's all over the motorway.'

'It's everywhere round here.'

'Never seen why those guys bother.'

'But don't you think it's weird?'

'Very weird. Imagine creeping around in the middle of the night, just so people recognise your tag.'

'No, I mean the baby graffiti.'

'Suppose it's a kind of celebrity. A way to make a mark on the world.'

'I mean, don't you think it's weird that the graffiti's of a baby, and I saw a baby, and the previous owners of our house had some problem with their baby, and the area's supposed to be haunted by a White Lady who killed her babies, and—'

'Woah,' said Dan, 'where's all this coming from?'

Claire sat next to Dan and rested her head on his shoulder.

'Tell me which bit is weird,' said Dan.

'Okay, isn't it a strange coincidence that I saw a woman holding a baby in an abandoned tower block, and then, later, I heard a story about a ghost who's supposed to walk around here holding the babies she killed?'

'Na,' said Dan, after a moment's thought. 'Babe, what it is, right . . . cause we're new here, you've just learned a thousand things about the neighbourhood, right? As per the law of averages, a few of those things have summat to do with babies. But cause of what happened, you emphasise those stories and ignore everything else. It's not healthy, Claire.'

Claire took a moment to think. 'You're saying this is all in my head, right?'

Dan's face was tight with concentration, and Claire could see the effort he was making to phrase his next sentence tactfully. 'I think it's absolutely normal, given what happened, that you're psychologically fragile just now.'

'*Psychologically fragile*? You make me sound like some fainting Victorian debutante.'

'I mean that it's normal for you to be . . . I mean that obviously you want to have a baby and—'

'Now it's just me who wants to have a baby?'

'And you just need to be sure it's for the right reasons.'

'Okay, fine. Are you saying you don't want a baby?'

'Don't start mithering me, Babe.'

'Well, do you or don't you?'

'You know I do.'

'Great, Dan. That's great. Do you know how babies are made? You know there's a thing you have to do?'

'I just think that, after what happened—'

'Stop saying that!' She stood in front of him, blocking the TV.

'We shouldn't rush into anything, you know? We're still young.'

'You're thirty-four, you great baby. You're going grey. Stop acting like a student.'

'*You're* young.'

'I'll soon be twenty-nine. Even if I get pregnant tonight – and barring an immaculate conception, that won't be happening – I'll be nearly thirty when I give birth.'

'Exactly. That's young. It's not 1834.'

'And what am I supposed to do while you're playing football and crushing on the female cast of Hollyoaks? Just sit around, wait for you to grow up?'

'You've just applied for a job.'

'Does that bother you?'

'Of course not, Babe. Why are you trying so hard to fight? I'm glad you've applied for that job. It's not healthy for you to be sitting at home dwelling on what . . . dwelling on the . . . '

'Dwelling on the fact that we lost our baby? Dwelling on the fact that I had a miscarriage while you were still lamenting your youth?'

'That's not fair, Claire. It were a shock for both of us.'

'I know. I'm sorry.' She sat beside him. 'I'm just upset. I'm upset – I don't know why I've not heard about the job yet.'

'Give them time, Babe.'

'And I don't know why you've reneged—'

'Reneged?'

'Backtracked about starting a family.'

Dan laughed. 'I didn't realise I were contractually obliged to knock you up within a fortnight of moving in. I should've read the small print.' He looked at her, his eyes appealing for her to laugh with him, but it was the wrong time for jokes.

'Oh yeah, Dan, cause I'm so desperate for your sperm. Women are queuing up for the chance to reproduce your genes. Get over yourself, Dan.'

'Right, then what are we arguing about?'

'We're arguing,' said Claire, 'because I screwed up my life by marrying you.' Even as she said this, she knew she didn't mean it. She was mad because he was right; something inside her – something that defied reason – did want to have his baby, and that was the infuriating paradox. 'That reminds me,' she said, because it seemed the only way to hit back. 'I've invited the neighbours round.'

'You've done what?'

'They're coming . . . next week.' Claire hadn't invited them, but she soon would – especially now she'd seen how much it would irritate Dan.

'You can't just invite people round without discussing it. This is my house.'

'*Your* house?'

'Our house.'

'Exactly. And I'm having my guests round. If you don't like it, stay in your bedroom and play computer games.'

Five

THERE WAS one problem with Claire's retaliation; she was almost as reluctant to host the neighbours as Dan was. She had decided, to minimise stress, that she would invite only the immediate neighbours: Morgana and Adrian, and Lianne plus one. For food, she had tried to keep things as relaxed as possible. A sit down dinner was too formal, so she had prepared a buffet of finger foods – in Claire's experience, that made it easier for guests to tactfully avoid food they found revolting. Not that anybody would find Claire's fayre unpalatable; she had worked on it all day. She'd marinated chicken cubes in ginger, garlic, orange zest, and honey, and she had skewered them between cherry tomatoes, and chunks of red onion and pepper. She had cooked chicken drumsticks coated in lemon juice, crushed pistachios, and cayenne pepper. Against her better judgement, she had spent all morning wrapping Parma ham around dates she'd stuffed with basil leaves and goat cheese. They tasted fine, even though they looked nothing like those pictured in the recipe book: some were fat and some were skinny, and the cheese oozed out onto the plate.

And then, an hour before her guests were due to arrive, it occurred to Claire that Morgana and Adrian might be vegetarians. In fact, she'd be amazed if they *weren't* vegetarians. Claire had nothing against vegetarians – she was a lapsed vegetarian herself – but Morgana and Adrian, she imagined, would be the sort of vegetarians to talk to you about abattoirs. The sort of vegetarians who would lecture you about the conditions of battery hens. Evangelical vegetarians.

Dan had still not returned with the car (and no way was his lateness unintentional), so Claire hurried out to the local shop, hoping they'd at least have some hummus. On the way, she saw that the Jaguar with the N3V registration plate was parked outside Lianne's again. When Claire and Dan had been house hunting, they'd seen that car and assumed they were looking at property in a particularly exclusive neighbourhood. Now she knew that the car belonged to Lianne's dad. She turned onto St Michael's Street, sweating though she'd only walked 100 metres, and up ahead she saw the old man who'd spoken to her on the bridge. He looked so frail that Claire was surprised he'd been able to walk this far. When she smiled at him, he showed no recognition, but held his cane up in a gesture of address. 'Are you adopted?' he asked.

'You asked me that last week,' said Claire. 'On the bridge, remember?'

He tilted his liver-spotted head and looked overburdened by his memories. 'And are you?' he asked.

'No,' said Claire. 'Do you live in the care home?' she asked, but he was already shuffling past her. He moved in inches, and each step seemed to Claire a small act of heroism.

The local shop did not let her down. She bought hummus, which, once plated with slices of lemon, drizzled in olive oil, and sprinkled with coriander, looked almost homemade. And she bought bags of cashew and pistachio nuts, more wine (Lianne did seem to drink a lot), carrot juice (Morgana and Adrian probably didn't drink at all), and a vegetarian pizza. Finally, getting slightly desperate, she bought a tin of pineapple chunks, which she served, in children's-birthday-party style, on cocktail sticks next to chunks of cheddar.

Of course, as it turned out, Morgana and Adrian ate meat. They arrived first, before Dan had bothered to come home. 'I was looking forward to meeting your husband,' said Adrian, who, mercifully, was wearing full-length cords.

Claire had this weird feeling, as if Dan was a boyfriend she'd made up. 'I think he's been detained at work,' she said, and then in an attempt at levity she added, 'or he's having an affair.'

'Oh,' said Morgana. They stood in awkward silence.

'I don't think he is,' said Claire. 'I mean, who else would have him, right?'

'We've brought you a hand-woven Bedouin cushion,' said Morgana, who was wearing enormous pentagram earrings.

'As a house warming present,' explained Adrian.

'That's lovely,' said Claire, receiving the cushion (it smelled strongly of goat droppings).

'We bought it when we holidayed in Jordan,' said Morgana.

'Really? That's very kind of you.' Claire lowered the cushion to the hardwood floor, patting it reverentially and admiring it for long enough to show suitable appreciation. 'Shall we go into the garden?' She had opened the patio doors and set glasses and plates under the parasol. For now, the food stayed in the kitchen, covered in cellophane. 'Let me get you drinks. Wine, beer, cider, carrot juice?'

'Do you have any ales?' asked Adrian.

Right then, the door opened and Dan called hello. Rarely had Claire been so glad to hear his homecoming. 'Here comes the philanderer,' she said, determined to dig out Morgana's sense of humour.

'Look who I met at the gate,' said Dan. He had entered with Lianne and an older man. The man wore a suit and moustache. He had dark clouds sagging under his eyes, but the rest of his face was taught and angular, as if he'd been carved in granite. He stood in the hallway and rapped his knuckles against the wall.

'This is me dad, Neville,' said Lianne.

'Ah,' said Claire, who'd worried this old guy was Lianne's latest squeeze. Lianne's cocktail dress was so short that Claire could see the creases below her buttocks; it was not what Claire would have worn to go out with her dad.

'It's nice tae see what folk have done with the houses,' said Neville, kicking the skirting boards and assessing the light fixtures.

'Can I get you a drink, Lianne?' said Dan.

'What sort of kitchen did they fit in this one?' said Neville, striding past Claire. He paused for a moment, surveyed Morgana and Adrian as if he'd found two unicorns, and then, with a bemused shake of his head, he turned his attention back to the kitchen. 'Oh aye,' he said, recognising the pine cabinets. He started opening and closing the cupboard doors.

'Neville, meet Morgana and Adrian.'

'How do you do,' said Adrian.

'Number thirteen yous are in, aye?'

'Why don't we go outside,' said Claire.

'Yeah, I could do with a fag,' said Lianne. Neville, however, strode back into the hallway, and Claire heard him climbing the stairs.

'Are you looking for the bathroom, Neville?' asked Claire, running after him.

'No, no, just having a wee nosey. Is this your bedroom, aye?'

Claire ran upstairs; she hadn't thought to tidy the bedroom and her dirty underwear was strewn across the floor.

'Aye, you get decent light in here, don't you?'

'Come downstairs, Neville. Let me get you a drink.'

'Are the pipes up here noisy? No too bad, aye? The lads were told tae put a wee bit of insulation around them all, which should help, ken?'

'Yes,' said Claire.

'And the windows? How are they working out for you? They're cheaper than the ones we were supposed tae use, but there's no much difference in terms of performance.'

'Right,' said Claire.

Neville backed out of the bedroom and opened the door to the spare room, which was still filled with unplaceable clutter. 'What yous doing with this room?' he asked.

'We hope it will be the nursery,' said Claire.

'Are you pregnant?'

'No, not yet.'

'We did always see these as being family homes.'

'We do plan to start a family.'

'Good. It's a family sort of place, ken? I was devastated when Lianne lost the bairn. Devastated.'

'What would you like to drink, Neville?' said Claire, escorting him downstairs with an arm on his shoulder.

'I don't drink.'

'Of course. Sorry.' Claire now remembered what Lianne had said about her dad's alcoholism.

'What ye sorry for?'

'I've got carrot juice?'

'*Carrot* juice? Why would anybody drink carrot juice? Do carrots even contain juice? Just gie me a tap water.'

At least Dan had managed to pour wine and settle the others around the parasol.

But when Neville walked outside, the conversation stopped. 'So,' said Neville, looking Adrian up and down, 'what do you do, son?'

'I'm currently a freelance nature writer.'

'You're what, sorry? You're unemployed, are you?'

'No,' said Adrian, 'I'm—'

'Here, I'm only messing with you. That's all writing about flowers and that, aye?'

'Actually,' said Claire, trying to help out, 'I saw you out on the river the other day, Adrian.'

'In the old kayak, was I?'

'What's this,' said Neville, grabbing one of Morgana's pentagram earrings. 'I didnae ken it was fancy dress.'

'Ignore him,' said Lianne, laughing.

'Your glass is empty,' said Dan. 'Let me go get you a top up.'

Lianne had finished her wine in two big gulps. 'Thanks, honey,' she said, smiling at Dan as she lit a cigarette.

Claire followed her husband inside. They stood in the kitchen and she whisper-shouted at him: 'This is going awful! Where were you? God, I can't believe that Neville Shaw. Does the food look okay? I had to run out to get something vegetarian and – You stop flirting with Lianne, okay? I didn't buy ale and – If I'd known Lianne was bringing her bloody dad . . . He's an alcoholic.'

'An alcoholic?'

'*Shhhh!* Oh God, I didn't have a chance to do my makeup. This is a disaster, isn't it?'

'Babe, you were the one who organised this. Just chill and deal with it. It's going to be fine.'

★ ★ ★

What actually happened was that Lianne drank glass after glass, smoked fag after fag, and eventually threw up in the hydrangeas. Neville talked about the pros and cons of EPDM roofing and recounted his rags to riches tale. ('And the Lord spoke tae me, as clear as I'm speaking tae you now, and he said, "get yersel doon tae the bookies and put on an accumulator. Oh, and Dunfermline will get an away win."') Morgana collected flower petals and made a potion, which she said Claire should rub on her belly to enhance her fertility. And Adrian, poor Adrian, sat quietly and identified the evening calls of migrant bird species.

And yet, believe it or not, the evening was almost a success. Though the vegetarian dishes were largely ignored, Morgana said she *adored* goat cheese and Parma ham, Lianne ate – and then puked up – three or four chicken drumsticks, Neville ate five of the spicy chicken kebabs (he said the stuffed dates looked like 'something gynaecological'), and Adrian politely sampled a bit of everything. Dan kept everyone's glasses full – particularly Lianne's (which wasn't easy) – and by quarter past eight they had, against all odds, found a mutual topic of conversation: the neighbourhood.

For example, everyone had encountered the old man and everyone had been asked the same question: are you adopted. Nobody knew what it meant, and everyone agreed the man was mad, but Neville knew the man's name and biography. 'Aye, I ken Old Man Jack. Lost his marbles, ken? But what can ye expect at his age? He used tae be a pro-golfer, believe it or not. He was runner up in the News of the World Matchplay. Lost by three strokes tae Dai Rees. Course, there wasnae the money in the game that there is now, but he did alright for himself. He'd worked here, farming, one summer before the war. Something like that. Anyway so once he was ready tae retire, he remembered the fields across the river, and he thought tae himself, with folks getting cars and all that, that's no far for a Mancunian tae drive for a round of golf, is it? So he bought the land and built a golf course. Before you ken it, the city's expanded out tae his course. Aye, he wasnae so daft in those days.'

And they talked about the tower, of course, for its shadow traced time across Claire's garden. Claire was counting the days (nineteen) until it would be demolished, but once again Neville had a different perspective. 'It might just be an eyesore tae you, but it was home tae us. Wasn't it, Lianne? Aye, it's time for the tower tae come doon, but dinnae yous forget that I raised my daughter there. That tower was our home.'

'Yeah,' said Lianne. 'Folk think it were pure scally central but they know nothing about it.'

'Dead right,' said Dan. 'I remember visiting those towers as a lad. I grew up in Burnage, see.'

'Yeah, so Claire told me,' said Lianne.

'There were a lad at our school – African fellow. Abukar, his name were, and his family were refugees from Somalia, I think. He were ace at football, which qualified him as me mate in those days. And a couple of times I went to play at his flat, up in one of them towers.'

'You never told me this,' said Claire.

'His dad had been a doctor back in Somalia, if I remember right.'

'How come you've never mentioned this?' Claire was alarmed to discover there were still things she didn't know about her husband.

Dan shrugged. 'Their tower's been knocked down now, of course. I wonder if they stayed here or went back to Africa.'

'Stayed here, I'll bet,' said Neville.

'We used to play in this fort he'd made in a little space behind the water tank. The two of us would squeeze in there and piss about.' Dan laughed. 'Then one day he showed me his willy—'

Claire noticed Lianne gazing at Dan with an expression she couldn't quite read.

'Dirty bastard,' said Neville. 'Shows what they're like, doesn't it?'

'I don't think that's fair,' said Adrian.

'Yeah,' said Dan. 'I probably showed him mine back. We were only nine or so.'

'Still, if I'd have caught some darkie waving his tadger at Lianne, I'd have beaten the bastard blacker than God made him.'

Claire coughed and caught Adrian's eye.

Adrian shuffled in his seat. After a pause, he said, 'These stuffed dates really are delicious.'

Despite all this, there was a moment, just as dusk settled, when Claire drifted off from the conversation and gazed contentedly as daisies closed themselves and her lawn grew dark green in the fading light. She smelled sun-hit skin, cigarettes, wood smoke, the charcoal scent of barbecues. In a nearby garden, children kicked a football, commentating on their achievements as they played. And then Claire heard the sirens.

It seemed ironic that after Claire had spent two weeks hoping the police would clear the addicts from Sighthill Tower, they finally did it on the night of her garden party. By the time the commotion started, it was dark enough that the police torches cut beams through the night. They heard the sirens first, and then van doors opening and dogs barking. It was impossible to talk any more. Claire and her guests ran to the fence, peering at Sighthill Tower over the angle of Lianne's garden. They saw the police shaking the construction barriers, heard them crash to the ground. Then there were more sirens, and the dogs were barking as if they'd been starved. They heard the thud of feet, policemen shouting commands: 'Get down! Get down on your knees!' There was screaming and swearing and breaking glass.

'That'll teach them,' said Neville Shaw, laughing as loud as the dogs. But his good mood didn't last, for it was at that moment, while they were all distracted, that Lianne lurched to the bottom of the garden and puked in the hydrangeas. By the time anyone noticed she was missing, she had curled on the grass in a foetal position.

Predictably, it was Dan who ran to her first. He stood over her, stroking her hair, and talking to her in the voice one would use to address a small child. It would not have escaped his attention, Claire thought, that as Lianne sat up her legs opened, or that she made no attempt to hide her lace thong. Her makeup had run from her eyes in streaks of black, and her mouth was open in a coat-hanger wail. 'I'm disgusting,' she howled.

'It's okay,' said Claire. 'Would you like a glass of water? Dan, get Lianne a glass of water.'

'What have I done? Oh God, what have I done?' Lianne crawled on all fours, exposing her big white buttocks, but she retched only a spit of bile.

'I'll come with you,' said Adrian, following Dan inside. It was strange how men feared women's bodies even more than they desired them.

'Pull yourself together,' said Neville. 'Look at yourself! Filthy wee tramp.'

'There's a lot of angry energy here,' said Morgana. 'I think we should all try to find a more compassionate discourse.'

'Get up!' Neville grabbed Lianne by the wrist, but only spun her round until she fell face first onto the grass.

'I'm disgusting,' wailed Lianne.

'No, you're not,' said Claire. 'You've just had a bit too much wine.'

'You're an embarrassment,' said Neville. 'Pull your dress down for God's sake. You sicken me. And look at me when I talk to you.'

'I'm sorry! I'm sorry!'

'Now,' said Neville, in an awful whisper, 'get up.'

Lianne stood up, supported by Morgana. She had green stains on her knees and her stilettos were anchored in the lawn.

'Apologise to our host.'

'I'm sorry.' Lianne was crying and drooling and it was impossible to tell which water on her face came from where.

'Don't be silly,' said Claire, relieved to see Dan and Adrian returning with the water.

'Gie me that,' said Neville. He took the tumbler and launched its contents against Lianne's face. 'Pull yersel together, right?'

'Now that's not on,' said Adrian, as Lianne cried harder.

'Yeah,' said Dan, uncertainly. 'Let's all calm down a bit.'

Neville looked as if he might hit one of them. His fists were clenched and his chest was rising and falling with each breath. Though he was the shortest of the three men, he had more presence than Adrian and Dan combined. When he finally spoke, his voice was slow and quiet. 'Don't ever tell me how to look after my daughter.'

The other men nodded in apology and stood aside as Neville dragged Lianne by the wrist. She had taken her shoes off and was clutching them in her other hand. As they reached the patio, she tripped and fell, and Neville dragged her, scraping her side, until she scrambled to her feet. Claire hurried after them, concerned for Lianne – sure – but also filled with the absurd notion that manners demanded she ought to see them out.

'That went well,' said Dan, half-an-hour later, when they'd bid farewell to Morgana and Adrian.

'Don't, Dan. Just for once, save the "I told you so" speech.'

'Do you think she's going to be alright?'

'I don't know, Dan. Why don't you go and tuck her in?'

'I mean it, Babe; that Neville seems a bit of a psycho—' Dan stopped, startled by the doorbell.

Who would ring their bell at this time? Claire didn't unlock the Yale until she'd seen through the peephole that it was Morgana and Adrian. They must have forgotten something, she thought.

But when she opened the door, Morgana and Adrian seemed almost apologetic, reluctant to speak. 'We're, uh, sorry to be the bearers of bad news.'

'Yes, I'm afraid to say—'

'As we were leaving we saw—'

'It appears you've been targeted by vandals.'

Claire followed them down the path, conscious that she'd left the door open, and worried that someone might sneak inside while her attention was diverted.

'Look,' said Morgana. The paint was so fresh that it smelled toxic like a car exhaust. She remembered, for no particular reason, that the estate agent had boasted that the garden walls were made of mill brick. Now, the street-facing side of her front wall had been painted with the staked baby. A black silhouette, sucking its thumb, staked through the heart with a crucifix. She could see her neighbours' walls, up and down the street, illuminated by street lamps, and she saw that they alone had been targeted. 'Why us?' She started to cry. 'What does it mean?' she said, as the streetlights blurred to yellow asterisks.

'It's okay, Babe.' Dan held her and kissed her head. 'I'll hire one of them graffiti blasters. I'll do it tomorrow.'

'No,' she said, remembering that she still had PC White's card. 'It's evidence. I'm going to phone the police and put a stop to this.'

Six

THE NEXT DAY, mid-morning, the phone rang while Dan was still asleep (Dan worked alternate Saturdays, and on his Saturdays off he rose at noon in time to eat breakfast in front of Football Focus).

'We've got good news for you, Mrs Wilson.'

'We cleared that bunch last night.'

'I heard,' said Claire. 'What's happened to them?'

PC White looked at PC Young and both smiled. 'I don't think they'll be bothering you again anytime soon.'

'Do you think they were responsible for the graffiti?'

PC White removed his cap. His hair was cropped a millimetre from his scalp and sweat trickled across his temples. 'Maybe. Maybe not.'

'They were crack-heads,' said PC Young, who since Claire last saw him had cultivated a light down on his upper lip. 'They probably didn't have the energy to do anything except get high.'

'Why do you think the graffiti was sprayed on *our* wall?'

'You tell us,' said Young. 'Is there any reason you can think of?'

'Do you have any enemies in the neighbourhood?' asked White.

It occurred to Claire that the paint was still wet when she went outside, and the street was empty except for Morgana and Adrian. She dismissed the thought as paranoid. 'Tell me one thing,' she said; 'when you cleared those people from the tower block, did one of them have a baby?'

'A baby, ha! If that lot came by a baby, they'd eat it.'

White laughed. 'They'd try to smoke it!'

'So you searched the building—'

'We cleared it out, Mrs Wilson.'

'And there definitely wasn't a baby? Because I saw a baby—'

'So you keep saying, Mrs Wilson.'

'Did you search upstairs?'

'Can't go up there,' said Young.

'Health and safety,' said White.

'Red tape,' said Young.

'Political correctness, isn't it?'

'I think you need to search upstairs. I think there might be a baby upstairs.'

'Very well, Mrs Wilson; we'll mention your theory to our commanding officer.' White nodded a bow, replaced his cap. 'You have our card.'

'Wait, may I mention something else?'

'Is it about the baby?'

Claire looked down, embarrassed. Young's boots were enormous black things, with shiny leather uppers that curved like the shells of beetles. 'I'm a bit worried about – I don't know how to say this.' She lowered her voice to a whisper. 'We had our neighbour round last night and her father was quite violent with her.'

'Do you want to report an assault, Mrs Wilson?'

'Kind of, I guess.'

White sighed in exasperation, but he took out a notepad and began to write. 'Describe what you saw then.'

'He kind of dragged her across the patio, she was crying—'

'Do you have children, Mrs Wilson?'

'No, I—'

'Maybe when you've kids of your own, you'll have to discipline your child.'

'But Lianne's in her twenties.'

Both policemen burst out laughing. 'Sorry,' said Young, 'we just thought—'

'We thought you were reporting child abuse.'

'I think she's probably learned to handle her old man by now, don't you?'

'Families have arguments. This doesn't sound like a police matter.'

'Of course,' said Claire, still whispering. 'But just for my own peace of mind, I'd like you to note my concern.'

'Very well,' said White. 'What's the gentleman's name?'

'Neville Shaw.'

White folded his notepad and looked at Young and then back at Claire. 'That's quite an allegation, Mrs Wilson.'

'I'm not alleging anything. I just—'

'Don't worry, Mrs Wilson. We'll be sure to mention your concern the next time we see Mr Shaw. Now, if you'll excuse us, Manchester's criminals are capable of more than a patch of graffiti and a row between father and daughter.'

Claire finished clearing up the mess from last night's party, glad she had something to distract her. Working as a medical secretary, she had spent so long on computers, that hitting control and z had become an automatic response to a mistake. The reaction was so ingrained in her that sometimes she thought to hit ctrl and z to undo some error she'd made in life. She wished she could undo the conversation with the police: hit ctrl z and start over again.

When she heard Dan clumping out of bed, she wanted to avoid him, and so, before he came downstairs, she laced her trainers and stepped outside. There was low cloud for once, and further up the street, a man hoed his front borders, looking up in hope of rain. Claire had started timing herself as she completed her circuit, but despite the cloud, the air was still warm and humid, and she was unsure how far she could run.

She stopped to look at the graffiti, shuddering to think they'd been targeted for some reason, and she noticed that Neville's Jaguar was still parked outside Lianne's house. But when she began to jog, her muscles loosened, and she found a rhythm that shook the fear from her. She ran onto St Michael's Street, past the church, and turned left across the scrubland. She was breathing heavily, watching the ground, counting the steps in her head. One, two, three, four, past the mountain of rubble. One, two, three, four, over caterpillar tracks baked in the earth. She passed a JCB, which was rooted, its wheels overgrown by nettles.

When she reached the fence that surrounded the tower, she stopped, wheezing for breath. It was a start, something to build on. She would run a little further every day. She lifted her T-shirt to check the flatness of her stomach, as though her three-minute jog might have had an instant impact, and then, disappointed, she looked up at the derelict flats: the plywood boards had been knocked off the lower windows and the black tarpaulin flapped loose at one side. She was surprised that the council hadn't barricaded the entrance. There were beer cans and polystyrene bags suspended in the weeds, and she saw that a bonfire, extinguished but still smouldering, wisped an ascending spiral of smoke.

She walked on, towards the old church house. Work was adjourned, this being a Saturday, and the only noise was the orange 'Shaw Construction' banner lapping against the scaffolding. Recovering her breath, she turned left towards the river, and that was when she saw it.

She stopped, crouched down, at first unsure what she was seeing. As she waited, she felt her pulse in her ears. Thirty metres away, pushing through loose fencing at the rear corner of the tower, was a pram.

A man in a bomber jacket pushed the pram out onto the rough ground, looked left, looked right, and walked towards the river. Tentatively, Claire followed him, treading softly from clod to clod. As the man turned onto the riverside path, Claire accelerated, scared she would lose him. But there he was, up ahead, pushing the pram along the side of the river. Claire started to jog, panting, still out of breath from her earlier run. 'Excuse me!' she called to the man. He looked over his shoulder, but then continued his journey, as if he thought Claire was hailing someone else. Claire jogged on, gaining ground. 'Excuse me!' she called again.

And then, suddenly, the man ran. He charged, pushing the pram, bouncing its wheels on the rough path. Claire ran faster, almost sprinting. Her lungs hurt and lactic acid burned her thighs. Just before the bridge Claire normally crossed, the man charged the pram down a cycle path, a route Claire had never before explored. 'Hey!' she yelled, stopping, hands on knees. 'Wait! I just want to talk!' The man disappeared round the corner and Claire ran on as hard as she could. Her pulse was roaring in her ears and every time her trainers crunched the clay-grit, pain racked her knees.

Soon the path opened onto a quiet street, flanked by pine trees. The man had maintained – maybe even extended – his lead and was still running, pushing the pram so recklessly that Claire worried he might tip out the baby. As she chased him, she wondered for the first time what she would say if she ever caught up. Then the man veered across the road, bumped over the opposite curb, and continued, shoving the pram through the pine needles that carpeted the pavement. This slowed him down, and Claire, though staggering, began to gain ground. She heard the traffic on the main road, the revs of buses – she had never walked these streets before. There was a pub on the corner, and two girls, sipping rosé at the benches outside, watched open-mouthed as a man charged a pram away from a pursuing woman.

When they reached the main road, Claire was only a dozen metres off pace – she could hear the rattle of the pram's wheels – but the man, glancing over his shoulder, accelerated once more, and Claire didn't have the energy to go with him. Her legs were cramping and she stopped, doubled over; her body ached so badly that she thought she might be sick.

When the man saw she'd given up, he slowed to a stroll, and seconds later he flagged a bus. It was a kneeling bus, and seeing the pram the driver lowered the front axle to kerb height. As Claire listened to the bus's hydraulic sigh, she determined to make one last effort. She started to run, face screwed in pain, holding her arm out for the driver's attention. But the bus rose to its normal height, the doors swished shut, and with a great puff of exhaust, the vehicle lurched forward.

Why is it so embarrassing to run for a bus and miss it? Imagine missing a bus when you've run so hard that you're dizzy and trembling, gasping for breath, your back soaked with sweat and your fringe matted flat on your forehead. She wanted to explain to the dog-walkers and baby-strollers that she had been chasing the man and pram, not the bus. Then she remembered her digital watch and made a big show of stopping the time. 'New record,' she said, smiling, to a man with a Dalmatian. She wanted to collapse, but she stood for a moment, stretching her quad muscles in the style of an Olympic athlete.

When she had recovered, she retraced her steps to the river and continued her circuit at a stroll. She walked along the far bank, where a heron flew along the course of the river, its great wings casting a light shadow on the water. She looked between the poplar trees and saw men in Pringle sweaters and flannels, pulling golf carts, squinting in search of misfired balls. She remembered from last night that, according to Neville, this golf course was designed by Old Man Jack. As she approached the nursing home, she wondered whether she would see Jack today. If she did, would he ask his usual question?

She passed the phone mast, walked under the bridge, and soon she was climbing the steps to the flyover, hauling her tired legs up with aid of the handrail. She paused at the top, looked out at the view, flinched each time a lorry displaced the air behind her. She listened to the Doppler effect, hearing how the roar of an engine dipped in pitch each time a vehicle passed her. Then she descended to St Michael's Street, and stopped again at the general store, where she bought a copy of the local paper. She bought the paper only to see whether her protest letter had been printed, and she hurried home eager to check.

When she got home, Dan was up. Kind of. He was on the couch, dressed in an old T-shirt and a pair of boxer shorts. 'Hey, Babe,' he said, without looking up from the TV. The room smelled of male sweat and morning breath.

'Guess what I saw?'

'I don't know, Babe. Lord Lucan galloping about on Shergar?'

'I was out jogging, and I passed the tower block, and I saw a guy come out with a pram.'

No matter how deeply he was already reclined, Dan had this ability to throw himself still further into the couch. He did this now, and Claire was struck by how genuinely frustrated he seemed. 'Babe,' he said, 'so what?'

'So the baby's still there.'

'You saw a guy with a pram. Maybe he just went in to take a leak.'

'He ran from me. I called out to him and he ran.'

'Wouldn't you run if you were chased by some crazy woman?'

'Oh, now I'm "some crazy woman"? Thanks, Dan.'

'Babe, I didn't mean – Wait, where you going?'

'I'm going to take a shower. You should try it.'

Claire turned the shower on, and while the water warmed up, she balanced on the edge of the bath tub and examined herself in the mirror. The running had so far done nothing to reduce her paunch. She sucked her stomach in, until it looked flat like a model's, and then she pushed it out, arching her back so that she looked pregnant. Apart from her forearms, which had freckled in the sun, her skin looked cadaverously white, and she remembered that during her unpacking she had discovered a half-used tube of St Tropez gradual tan body moisturiser. It was a purchase from a year ago, something she'd used before she and Dan had holidayed in Corfu – that seemed ages ago now. The prickly hairs on her legs looked black against her white skin, so she found her razor and laid it by the bath. What was the point, she wondered. Would Dan notice if she never shaved again? Her face looked lined and tired, and as she studied herself she found a grey hair in her fringe; it was only the third grey hair she'd ever found, but how many lurked beyond her view? She plucked the hair, pulling five others out with it, and draped it across a black bottle of conditioner. Irrefutable evidence. She remembered from a school exchange trip that Italians call grey hairs 'white hairs.' Their version, she saw, was more accurate. The shower was hot now, steaming up the mirror, and she stood for a long time as the glass clouded and her image disappeared. Then, without planning to, she reached forward and traced the staked-baby shape into the steam.

When she'd finished in the bathroom, she remembered about the newspaper and turned eagerly to the letters page. There was a letter from a local councillor, responding to an allegation of expenses fraud; there was another from a pensioner, bemoaning the demise of the hat industry in Stockport; there was even one from a concerned parent, opposing local school closures; but Claire's letter had not been printed. She searched the rest of the paper, thinking that they might have decided to run an article. She would be credited, she imagined, as 'local campaigner, Claire Wilson, 28.' She found no such article, but on page eleven she encountered a face she recognised: it was Neville Shaw.

He was pictured outside the church house – she recognised the apple trees and the orange 'Shaw Construction' banner. He was smiling, grimacing against the sunshine. The headline read, 'MYSTERY AT ST MICHAEL'S.'

> The skeleton of an infant or foetus was found by builders redeveloping a Manchester property, police said yesterday.
>
> The skeleton, believed to be the decades-old remains of a baby, was discovered by workmen on Friday. Formerly a church house, the derelict building in St Michael's is being redeveloped into luxury flats. The work was interrupted by the macabre find after builders knocked through a false wall in the basement. 'It was the last thing the lads expected,' said the owner of the construction company, Neville Shaw, 58. 'They knocked through a wall and found a suitcase. The skeleton was inside.'
>
> The remains were wrapped in a *Manchester Guardian* newspaper dated 1936, police said. 'This is obviously a tragic discovery,' police Inspector Page told the *MEC*.

'It may be too late to prosecute anybody, but we will await the coroner's report and conduct an investigation in due course.'

Page told the *MEC* that police would research the history of the residence and use cutting-edge forensic techniques to identify the victim and bring closure to any family members.

Work at the property is due to recommence on Monday.

Claire's first thought was to wonder why Neville hadn't mentioned this at the party; it was, after all, much more interesting than his rants about roofing materials. But then she remembered that even Neville Shaw wouldn't bring up such a topic in front of his daughter who had recently suffered a stillbirth.

Her second thought was to run and show the article to Dan, but on reflection she imagined that he would only scoff. Somehow, the existence of this article would be attributable to her 'obsession.' So Claire decided to keep this information to herself. She snipped the article from the paper and resolved to visit the church house on Monday.

Seven

IT WAS MANCHESTER, and the weather had held for three weeks straight. Shoppers and bus drivers and local radio hosts were muttering about climate change, discussing global warming, testing the phrases uncertainly. Though they complained about the heat, it was hard for Mancunians to accept this global warming business was a bad thing. Beneath the jokes, however, there remained an edge of anxiety, a sense that this weather was disturbingly irregular, and now and again Claire envisaged mosquitoes and malaria and crumbling coastlines, or the Gulf Stream shunting south, leaving in its wake a new ice age.

The fruit had fallen early in the garden of the church house, and already the apples were rotting to pulp, crawling with flies and wasps. The insect hum reminded Claire of Greece or Spain. Brambles grew around the old wrought-iron fence, and in the sycamore tree, blue tits sped from branch to branch, evading the acrobatic ascent of a grey squirrel. Then metal crashed inside the house, and the birds flew towards the river, shrinking from view until they appeared no bigger than punctuation marks.

Claire would have loathed anyone to know it, but she'd worn a strappy top and balcony bra in the hope of garnering the workmen's assistance. She'd straightened her hair and applied mascara and lip gloss, but now she felt silly, tarted up, waiting at the gate of a construction site. 'Hello?' she called in a weak voice.

A radio played a jingle-backed traffic report: queuing traffic on Princess Parkway and two lanes closed at junction 18 on the M6. She imagined Dan surrounded by angry customers. 'Hello?' she called again, but the only response was the crash of a sledgehammer.

She stepped past the warning sign – DANGER: CONSTRUCTION AREA, HARD HATS MUST BE WORN ON SITE – and pushed open the gate. The metal was warm to the touch, the paint flaked and patched with rust. She walked under the scaffolding, between a dormant cement mixer and great bags of sand, and then she stepped over yellow lengths of timber, inhaling the fresh smell of sawdust. 'Hello?'

On entering the open doorway, the shade hit her, and she remembered visiting renaissance churches to escape the blazing Venice sun. She walked into the grand entrance hall, where the thick plaster dust made her cough and her steps left footprints on the floor. She removed her sunglasses, straining to see in the dim light. 'Hello?' She could hear the workmen upstairs, boots thudding, the radio, louder now, playing REM. As she began to climb the stairs, she leant on the bannister and the whole thing lurched to the right.

The radio was on the first landing. Its aerial had been snapped off, and comet tails of paint crossed its speakers, but the volume was cranked up to ten, and the tune pounded out, crackly in the dusty air. Then, as she reached the first floor, she saw legs dangling from a ceiling trapdoor. She waited, silently, as the boots thumped down the rungs of the ladder, and then the man turned, saw her, and yelled in fear.

'I'm sorry!' said Claire, hands raised in apology.

The man had his hand on his heart. He emitted a big breath of relief and then smiled. 'You have frightened me,' he said. He spoke with an Eastern European accent, and he was the most gorgeous man Claire had ever seen. He was stripped to the waist, tanned from outdoor work, his biceps like the muscles on an action man. 'You should not be here,' he said, removing his hard hat to wipe his brow. 'It is not allowed, yes?'

Claire felt herself blushing, unable to speak. His obliques formed a suggestive triangle. On the radio, the DJ gave a shout out to Debs and the barbecue crew. Claire still didn't speak.

'Hello?' said the builder, speaking slowly as if she were the foreigner. 'Can I help you?'

'I'm Claire,' she said, extending her hand.

He looked confused, but he passed his hard hat to his left hand so that he could reciprocate her greeting. 'I am Lukasz.'

'Lukasz,' she repeated stupidly.

The silence held for a moment. Lukasz was waiting for her to speak, bemused by her presence, but averse to being rude. He had a slight snooker player's chin, dark tousled hair, stubble dusted white with plaster.

'I read in the paper,' said Claire, remembering why she was here, 'about the skeleton of—'

'Yes!' said Lukasz, nodding emphatically. 'I have found this. You are a reporter?'

'No,' said Claire, 'not exactly.' Not at all, in fact. She paused, trying to think what she *was*, and what she was doing here. 'I'm . . . investigating . . . suspicious circumstances.'

'You are a detective?' His smile was full of childish excitement.

'Not exactly,' she said, 'but I'd be grateful if you could show me where you found . . . it.'

From through the trapdoor there came a harsh shout in Polish, and Lukasz called back in a big voice that emphasised the gentleness with which he'd been speaking to Claire. The other man shouted a question and Lukasz's answer provoked both men to laugh. Were they making fun of her?

'Come,' said Lukasz. 'I will show you.' As they descended the stairs, he lowered the volume of the radio, and then they walked on, shoulder to shoulder in silence.

'How long have you been in the UK?' she asked to make conversation.

'Three years,' said Lukasz, leading her through a door that was propped open with a power drill. 'I will go home soon. In one year or two. Definitely before I am twenty-five.'

'Oh,' said Claire, shocked he was so young.

Lukasz laughed. 'You are disappointed? You will miss me?'

Claire walked with her hands clasped behind her back, twiddling her wedding ring.

'In here,' he said. The door was locked and he opened it with a rusted iron key.

They entered a small cupboard – a coal bunker, perhaps. The walls were unplastered, the exposed stonework meshed with spider webs. Half a dozen bare stone steps led to a brick wall, through which a hole had been knocked. Lukasz pulled a torch from his belt and pointed it at the ground. 'When we entered here,' said Lukasz, 'there was a door, flat, here, covered in dust – like it was the floor, you understand? Then we sweep the dust away and see we are standing on a door. So we have lift it up and found these stairs. And this wall,' he said, gesticulating with the torch, 'is not original. And it is obviously not structural, so we have knocked through the wall so that we can see where the steps are leading. Come.' Lukasz jumped down the stairs and dropped onto his hands and knees to crawl through the crumbled wall. Claire hesitated. From where she stood, the hole, dissected by the torch beam, reminded her of a slashed zero, or a letter from a foreign alphabet: Ø. 'Come on,' called Lukasz, 'there are no ghosts.'

She had to crawl through on all fours, and the space was so confined that as she entered her face brushed against Lukasz's pecs. It was so dusty she wished she had a mask, but she could also smell his fresh scent of male exertion. Embarrassed by their physical proximity, she shuffled round so that they were side to side, hips and shoulders touching, both on all fours.

'This wall, here,' he said, pointing the torch to his left, 'is also a false wall; on the other side, it is just the foundations. You can walk around in there, but you have to stoop. It is too small to develop. Maybe if we—'

'The skeleton was here?' asked Claire.

'It was there,' said Lukasz, pointing the torch into the half-metre ahead of them. 'In a suitcase. We opened the suitcase with a crowbar. It was wrapped in old newspaper. We didn't know what it was.' For the first time, Claire realised that, though he was trying to hide it, Lukasz was traumatised by what he had discovered. 'It had been bricked closed for so many years,' he said, lowering the torch beam.

'The Secret Baby Room,' said Claire, remembering Mooncloud and Unity's game.

★ ★ ★

When Lukasz led Claire outside, she squinted in the noon brightness and reached for her sunglasses. She looked better wearing her
sunglasses, she thought, and she felt more confident shielded behind
them. Her clothes were grey with dust. 'Well, goodbye,' she said.
'Thanks for your help.'

Lukasz laughed, reached out, brushed a cobweb from her hair.
She flinched when he stretched towards her, but stood still as he
stroked her cheek. The action seemed to take a very long time. 'It
was my pleasure. If you want me to show you anything else, Claire,
you let me know, yes?'

She turned, walked away from the church house, forcing herself
not to look back.

At home, she stripped in the bathroom and turned on the shower.
Why was the sun such an aphrodisiac? Was it something to do
with vitamin D? Serotonin? Increased blood flow to secondary
erogenous zones? Perhaps the answer was simpler. Maybe we're
just excited by the sight of half-naked bodies? Or, perhaps, the
libidinous thrill comes from exposing your own body. Standing in
the bathroom, it seemed to Claire that the really sexy thing about
sunshine was that it made being naked so easy. In winter, you
had to blast the heating and then unbutton and unzip layer after
layer; in the summer, one lifted skirt, one unbuckled belt . . . She
thought of Lukasz's body, remembered the feel of his hip against
hers; how easy it would have been for— And why was it, Claire
wondered, that women's sex drives increased as men's sex drives
declined? What evolutionary sense did it make for the sexes to pass
each other like ships in the night? Her first serious boyfriend, she
remembered, had ground against her thigh – morning, night, and
afternoon – seemingly in a state of permanent arousal. For her,
on the other hand, the best thing about their coitus had been its
predictable brevity.

She would have gone on with these thoughts had she not turned
to see her reflection and screamed so loudly that she must have disturbed the neighbours. She screamed before she remembered what

she was looking at: the mirror had steamed up, and the steam had resurrected her drawing of the staked baby.

When she had washed and dressed, Claire set out to see Mrs Brompton, worrying that it was bad form to call at her house unannounced. On the contrary, however, Mrs Brompton was delighted to see Claire, and invited her into a living room that seemed ordered in expectation of guests. Her furniture, presumably transported from a previous residence, looked out of place in this new-built home. They sat on Queen Anne armchairs and the room's centrepiece was an Anglo-Indian coffee table with a brass tray. 'Let me make some tea,' said Mrs Brompton. She seemed to be recreating a previous life, Claire thought. The houses were all fitted with wall-mounted flat-panel electric fires, whose faux flames were just illuminated ribbons, but Mrs Brompton had screened her heater with a mesh and brass spark fender.

Mrs Brompton's approach to tea was as old-fashioned as her furnishings. She returned with a serving tray. The tea was in a porcelain pot from which emerged the chain of a strainer, and the milk was in a matching jug. 'How many lumps do you take, dear?'

'No sugar for me, thank you; I'm watching my weight.'

'You silly thing,' said Mrs Brompton, placing a lump in her own cup with miniature serving tongs. 'I'll forgive you so long as you have a scone.' Two scones were arranged on a side plate, next to a china butter dish.

'That's very kind of you, Mrs Brompton.'

'Not at all, dear; it's lovely to have you visit.'

'There is a particular reason why I called today.'

'Oh, do tell,' said Mrs Brompton, shuffling forward in anticipation.

'I'm afraid it's a bit of an unpleasant topic.'

'Is it that wretched phone mast?'

'No, it's—'

'The tower?'

'Not the tower.'

'Then it's the graffiti, isn't it?'

'Actually, Mrs Brompton, I wanted to talk to you about your old house.'

'Oh,' said Mrs Brompton, settling back into her chair.

'I don't suppose you happened to see the *Manchester Evening Chronicle* on Saturday?'

'No, dear. I only read *The Telegraph*.'

Claire paused, worried it would be inappropriate to share the article. 'I'm afraid you might find this a bit distressing,' she said. She reached into her handbag and unfolded the news cutting.

Mrs Brompton's hands shook as she received the paper. Her hands were like maps: her veins, waterways; the wrinkles around her knuckles, contour lines. 'I see,' she said, when she had finished reading. And then the full horror of it seemed to strike her and she put her hand to her mouth. 'All those years!' she said. 'Do you know exactly where it was found?'

So Claire recounted her trip to the church house, described meeting Lukasz ('a gorgeous builder,' was all she said), and explained about the secret room.

Mrs Brompton removed her reading glasses, which hung from a chain round her neck. She pinched her nose, her memory rewinding through decades. At last she said, 'I remember. It was on the corridor that led to the kitchen: a small box room. My parents used it to store empty trunks, fishing rods, our old wooden sledge. Doris and I used to play hide and seek in there. How awful,' she said, shaking her head. 'How awful.'

'Do you have any idea who might have . . . put the baby there?'

'Let me see,' said Mrs Brompton, restoring her reading glasses. She read the article again. '1936 . . . it must have been just before we moved in.'

'Do you know who lived in the church house before you?'

Again, Mrs Brompton squeezed her nose in the manner of one about to plunge underwater – perhaps, at a certain age, that's how delving into the past must feel. 'Yes,' said Mrs Brompton, uncertainly. 'I think they were the Robertsons. I know this only because we received mail for them even years after the war. It was something of a family joke.'

'And do you know anything else? Why they left? Where they went?'

'Maybe it wasn't Robertson. Radcliffe? Richardson? No, I think it *was* Robertson.'

'And do you know where they moved to?'

'Yes, dear. That I certainly do know. They went overseas to do missionary work.'

'That was in 1936?'

'It was about then, dear.'

'And where did they go?'

She squeezed her nose again, straining very hard. 'No. I want to say Africa but I think that's just in my head as a place a missionary ought to go. Australia? No, I only think that because my brother-in-law moved there. Greenland is in my head for some reason? I'm sorry, dear; I really don't know.'

'That's okay, Mrs Brompton; you've been a wonderful help. There's a lot for me to think about.'

'Good,' said Mrs Brompton, sipping her tea. 'I hope it keeps your mind off that gorgeous builder.'

Eight

ON FRIDAY, after a week of waiting, Claire finally heard about her job application. She answered the phone expecting it to be Dan and had to adjust her manner when it turned out to be someone from HR at University Hospital of South Manchester. Claire's surprise must have confused the caller because she asked whether she had applied for a position as medical secretary to the urology ward.

'Yes,' said Claire. 'Yes I did.'

'We're wondering if you're available to interview for the position next Thursday?

'Yes,' said Claire. 'Yes I am.'

As soon as she got off the phone she ran upstairs pumping her fist. In the spare room, she looked out the job description and person specification and hurried to the garden to re-read them. She lay a towel on the grass and stretched out in the sunshine. The more times she read the person spec, the more her confidence grew: she already knew about the PAS system and the Caldicott guidelines. She knew medical terminology and had processed endowment payments. She was familiar with the JN391 form. She was going to walk the interview.

She was still in the garden, still feeling good, when Lianne hailed her from across the fence. A week had passed since Claire's disastrous party, and during that time the neighbours hadn't spoken. But if Lianne felt any embarrassment about how she'd behaved, she didn't show it. 'There's something I need to tell you,' she said.

'Okay,' said Claire, bemused.

'Wait there – I'll come round.'

'Okay,' Claire said again, for she'd been lying in the sunshine all morning, and now she could hardly claim to be busy.

Seconds later, Lianne arrived at the front door, wearing shorts too small for her bum and fake tan that made her look like an Oompa Loompa. She carried a plastic bag that clinked with bottles. 'We should get a gate put in between our gardens,' she said.

Claire laughed nervously. 'Shall we sit out the back?'

'Cool,' said Lianne. 'Let me put these in the fridge.' She did put the bottles in the fridge, but first she poured them both large glasses of wine. Her T-shirt said, 'Don't bother: I'm not drunk yet.' Claire wondered how long it would be before she needed to change.

Outside, they sat under the parasol, and Lianne lit one of her Lambert & Butler's. 'So, listen,' she said, leaning in for a close whisper. Claire could smell her perfume: Britney Spears Fantasy, or Cosmic Radiance, or something like that. 'So what you said before about how there's, like, a baby in the tower, yeah? Well, I think there may be summat in that.'

'Why?' said Claire, leaning away from Lianne's bubble-gum-and-tobacco breath.

'It's . . . ' Lianne silently mouthed three syllables. The only noise was the meeting of her lips.

'What?'

'Morgana,' said Lianne, leaning back, attempting to exhale a smoke ring. 'Listen, right. Guess who I saw playing in the tower this afternoon? Unity and Whatsit.'

'Unity and Mooncloud?'

'Whatever. I looked out my window, yeah, and I seen them running around under the tower. Then they went inside.'

'That's not safe!'

'Yeah, like, you've no idea. Guess what I saw yesterday?'

'Hold on. Where are the kids now?'

'Shhh!' said Lianne, nodding towards Morgana's house. 'I think they're still in there.'

'Then . . . we need to tell Morgana.'

'No!' said Lianne, grabbing Claire's wrist. 'This is what I'm trying to tell you, yeah? Yesterday I saw Morgana in the tower. Not in the tower, right, but in the, like, grounds or whatever, yeah? And she were – It's hard to explain.'

'Go on.'

'She were doing like a ritual or spell or summat, yeah?'

'You need to tell me exactly what you saw.'

'She had a staff, you know? Like a druid or summat. And she made this circle in the ground. And then she's poured summat into the circle – petrol probably – and set it alight. She were dancing in this ring of fire, like . . . leaping about like the devil, you know?' Lianne stubbed her cigarette out while maintaining eye contact.

'Was Adrian with her?'

'I don't think so.'

'The kids?'

'Na, she were alone, I think.'

Claire took a second to think. She looked at Lianne's cigarettes and for the first time in years she felt an urge to smoke. 'There's probably some reasonable explanation,' she said. 'Morgana believes in magic.'

'Yeah, black magic.'

'I don't think so. She did this spell on me after you and I fought. She wrote our names on a piece of paper and put them between the two halves of an apple.'

'What did that do?' asked Lianne.

Claire shrugged. 'Made us friends?'

'We *are* friends, right?' said Lianne. 'I don't have that many friends.'

'Sure we are.'

At this point, Lianne clumsily pulled Claire's head to her chest in an embrace. Claire tried her best to reciprocate, reaching her arm to pat Lianne's back, but she felt Lianne's body begin to tremble and soon heard her sniff back tears. 'I'm sorry,' wailed Lianne. 'I just get over-emotional.'

'There, there,' said Claire, patting Lianne's back, wondering how long this embrace needed to last. Her right forearm was pasted to Lianne's clammy thighs and she could smell the turmeric scent of fake tan. Lianne squeezed tighter until the backs of Claire's ear studs stabbed into her neck. There does come a point when it's necessary to use a degree of force to escape an embrace, Claire thought, and after a few seconds more, she gently pushed Lianne away. This increased the volume of Lianne's sobbing. 'It's okay,' said Claire. 'Wait here while I get you some tissue.'

'Thank you,' said Lianne through her tears. 'Will you bring the wine too, yeah?'

Claire didn't respond. She walked inside, wondering what she should do: it was two o'clock on a weekday, and it seemed irresponsible to serve Lianne more wine; on the other hand, if she refused then Lianne might be even more upset. As she found a box of tissues, she rationalised that it was Lianne's wine anyway, and it was really up to her when she drank it.

When Claire returned outside, Lianne was fanning her eyes with her hand, breathing as if she'd just surfaced from a long dive. Wiped in criss-crossed streaks, the mascara on her cheeks reminded Claire of Japanese lettering.

'There you go,' said Claire, handing her the tissue.

'Ta, honey.'

'Listen, Lianne, I think maybe we should go check on Mooncloud and Unity.'

'Now? Really? I'm kind of enjoying chilling out.' Lianne tossed the crumpled tissues onto the garden table; they were as black as boot cloths. 'Okay, tell you what: let me smoke a cigarette, drink this, and then we'll go, yeah?'

Claire nodded. It's weird, she thought, how you never really stop being a smoker; it's like how an alcoholic can relapse even after a decade of sobriety. 'May I pinch one of your fags?' she asked.

'For sure!' said Lianne, pushing the box towards her.

One wouldn't hurt; it wasn't like she was pregnant.

Once they reached the top of the road, their progress slowed because Lianne was wearing platform heels and stumbling on the rough approach to the skyscraper. She took her heels off, but the rubbly ground, ridden with stones and glass, was too rough on her feet. As Lianne replaced her shoes, Claire said, 'There's something I haven't mentioned yet.' She wondered whether she should tell

Lianne about the skeleton discovered in the church house, but at the last moment she decided not to mention it. Instead she said, 'The other day, I saw a guy pushing a pram out from the skyscraper.'

Lianne held Claire's arm for support and the two of them wobbled forward. 'A guy with a pram?' she said. 'I haven't seen nothing like that.'

'He goes in and out on the far side of the building.'

'We're not going in,' said Lianne.

'We might have to.'

'We'll call to them.'

'God,' said Claire, 'why would they go in there?'

They stopped by the fence, where a red admiral opened and closed its wings with a balletic flourish. Dragonflies chased each other above the rosebay willowherb, and two were mating mid-air: a weirdly impractical-looking head-to-toe coupling. It was a grotesque sight in many ways, but Claire noticed that the shape of their joined bodies formed a love heart. When Lianne spotted the dragonflies, she pointed and laughed. Claire laughed, too, but her eyes flicked to the church house. There was no sign of Lukasz.

'So?' said Lianne.

'Shall I show you where the pram guy goes in?'

'If you want,' said Lianne.

They walked on, Lianne still holding Claire's forearm. Lianne was wearing bug-eye Versace sunglasses, and Claire felt like she was leading a blind woman. They stepped over a rusted iron pipe and walked on, past a small trench filled with beer cans and goose grass. Claire listened to the noise from the church house: Daft Punk, crackly on the radio, just audible above the low throb of an electric saw or drill.

When they reached the point from which the pram man had emerged, Claire demonstrated how the fence opened. Each barrier had been planted into a concrete base, but the wire connections between two fences had been cut, so that when one was lifted from its base, it swung open like a hinged gate. Behind her big sunglasses, Lianne's expression was inscrutable. 'We're not going in,' she said. 'It's not safe.'

'Okay,' said Claire, 'but we need to get the kids out.'

'I think Morgana runs a cult or summat. They do blood sacrifices. You shouldn't be friends with her, you know. Like, you could be in danger.'

'I think that's getting a bit . . . Where did she do the ritual?'

'Up near the tower,' said Lianne, pointing.

'Well, let's not jump to conclusions.'

'What if Morgana's in there now?' Both women stood by the open fence, neither crossing an imaginary line that separated the demolition site from the rest of the neighbourhood. 'Call them then,' said Lianne.

'Mooncloud? Unity?' Claire sounded ridiculous to herself. Her voice was probably too quiet to be heard in the tower, but it still seemed to reverberate around the neighbourhood. They waited, straining to hear some noise other than birdsong. 'Children?' called Claire again.

They seemed to wait a very long time. Claire imagined she could see the tower's shadow inching across the earth. 'We'll need to go in,' she said.

'No,' said Lianne, grabbing Claire's arm. 'MOOUNCLOUD! UNITY! GET DOWN HERE, NOW!'

Lianne screamed so loud that Claire had to cover her ears. When she'd finished, the echo of her voice seemed to rebound off the tower's walls. But it worked. They soon heard the slap of the kids' sandals, and then they emerged, squinting against the sunlight.

'Over here,' Claire called, waving her arms.

The kids ran through the long grass and weeds, breathless with alarm.

'Are you okay?' asked Claire.

The kids nodded.

'What the hell were you doing in there?' shouted Lianne.

Mooncloud started to cry. 'We were playing,' he sobbed.

'It's okay,' said Claire. 'We were just worried about you.'

'Look at this sign,' said Lianne, dragging Unity by the wrist. 'Can you read, yeah?'

Now Unity started to cry, too.

'"Danger: do not enter." You do speak English, right?'

'Lianne,' said Claire, 'I don't think we should—'

'Did your mum take you in there?' asked Lianne.

Both children were now crying too much to talk. 'Let me handle this, please?' said Claire.

Lianne stepped away to light a cigarette, unsteadily kicking the earth in frustration.

Claire crouched down to meet the children's eyes. 'Listen, guys,' she said. 'You've not done anything wrong, and we're not angry with you. We're just worried because this isn't a very safe place for you to play.'

The children nodded, tears subsiding.

'There are lots of safe places for you to play: in the garden, on our road, even down by the river – if your mummy allows it. You can play in my garden too, if you like. But this is a very dangerous building,' said Claire. 'We're grownups and even we wouldn't go in there, would we, Lianne?'

A few feet away, Lianne shook her head with a sarcastic look and blew smoke vertically. They had somehow become good cop and bad cop.

'Shall we go and see your mummy now?' asked Claire.

The kids shook their heads.

'Don't worry, guys; she won't be mad at you. I'll bet she knows some brilliant places where you can play. Come on,' said Claire, extending her hands to the children.

Unity put her hand in Claire's and started to skip towards her home, but Mooncloud folded his arms. 'But the Secret Baby Room is in *there*,' he said.

As soon as he said this, Unity ran back and stomped his exposed toes.

'What you talking about?' said Lianne.

Mooncloud looked at his elder sister, eyes big with fear and shock.

'We can keep a secret,' said Claire. 'What's the Secret Baby Room?'

Lianne lifted her sunglasses onto her hairline and crouched in front of the children. 'Come on, you brats! What the hell are you talking about?'

'Did your mummy take you to the Secret Baby Room?' asked Claire.

Children have this attuned sensibility to adult attention. We think that we can fool them, row or praise them out of duty and pass it off as the real thing. But both Unity and Mooncloud sensed that Claire and Lianne's interest was frighteningly real. The basis of this interest was, to the children, a mystery, and so they responded the only sensible way – they resolved to say as little as possible. Claire could tell that they sensed they might be in trouble, didn't know exactly *why* they would be in trouble, and worried that anything they said would land them in *more* trouble. And, like most siblings, no matter how much they fought, when confronted by adult discipline their solidarity was resolute.

'You better get talking,' said Lianne, 'or I'll slap you both myself.'

Crying again, the children looked at each other, communicating wordlessly.

'Can we play in the Secret Baby Room, too?' asked Claire.

'We're not going in there,' said Lianne.

'Is there a baby in there?' asked Claire. Okay, she thought, when they were met with more silence; she wasn't proud of herself, but she could think of only one way to make the kids talk. 'Nobody's angry with you, kids, but we need to know that everybody's safe. If you won't tell us about the Secret Baby Room then we'll have to call the police.'

'You won't like it in prison,' said Lianne.

'Lianne, please! Let me handle this.'

She saw that it was possible for the children to have a whole conversation without speaking a word. Their communication was almost telepathic – a series of tics and gestures, many of them too subtle for adults to detect. 'Come on, Unity,' she said, smiling very hard; 'whisper in my ear.'

And after a final consultation, Unity did shuffle forward and put her lips to Claire's ear. Claire felt the air change as she entered the child's world: Unity smelled of talc and tangerines and a stickiness that was nothing like adult sweat. After a hesitant pause, Unity said, 'The Secret Baby Room is where you get sent when you're acting like a baby.'

'Good girl,' said Claire. 'Does your mummy send you there?'

Unity shook her head. 'I did it bad,' she whispered. 'I sent Mooncloud there because his knee hurt and he was crying like a baby. Please don't tell on me, Mrs Wilson. Please don't tell?'

Nine

CLAIRE DIDN'T TELL, but she did start to watch Morgana's parenting with concern. 'Do you think we should call someone?' she stupidly asked Dan that night.

'Like who?'

'I don't know: the NSPCC?'

'Fucksake, Claire. It's the first rule of neighbourly behaviour,' said Dan; 'you don't go mithering folk about their childrearing. You just don't do it. Like, unless they're abusing the poor buggers, you just keep your beak out. What's got into you, Babe? I mean, do you think you need to talk to someone?'

'Yeah,' said Claire, 'I need to talk to you.'

'Okay,' said Dan, 'talk.'

'We're going out. To the pub.'

'There isn't a pub,' said Dan, gesturing a sweep of the neighbourhood.

'There's one further down the river. I saw it when I was chasing the pram guy.'

Dan emitted a huge sigh – a gust of breath like an old man blowing out candles. That's some stage of laziness, Claire thought, when even going to the pub becomes an unconscionable effort. 'I've been at work all day,' he said.

'We're going to the pub, Dan, not running the London Marathon.'

'We can chat here, can't we?'

'Please, sweetie; I want to celebrate getting an interview.'

Dan sighed in acquiescence.

Claire kissed his cheek. 'Just give me ten minutes to get ready.'

Claire walked upstairs, leaving Dan to tap his foot irritably in the living room. She turned her straighteners on and looked for her eyeliner. She was going to 'make an effort.' What a sad phrase that was, she thought. An effort: an exertion of body or mind; a piece of work produced by way of attempt. What a joyless, dutiful phrase.

She stripped, rubbed herself in sun shimmer, and then, standing naked, she chose a short summer dress with a string-tied halter neck. Dan had especially liked it, she remembered, when she'd worn it on their last night in Corfu. But when she tried it on with a strapless bra, she was shocked by the armpit fat that overlapped her bust. She looked in her cupboard for something else to wear; perhaps jeans and T-shirt would be more appropriate for the local pub?

'If we're going, let's go,' called Dan from downstairs.

'Hang on!' she said. She looked in the mirror again – it *was* a nice dress. What the hell, she thought.

She found eyelash curlers in her makeup drawer – she'd forgotten she even owned any. Then she overdid the bronzer, realised she looked like Noddy, and wiped it off with the T-shirt she'd worn that afternoon. Her eyeliner and mascara seemed heavy, too – almost gothic. Her silver kitten heels could have done with a polish and her matching clutch bag was shedding sequins. When she returned downstairs, Dan said 'You look nice' in a surprised tone that undercut any compliment.

They walked into the warm evening and Claire linked her arm in Dan's. As they strolled arm in arm by the riverside, joggers passed them, their breaths and footfalls a rhythmic backing to the Wilsons' evening stroll.

'This is nice,' said Dan.

'It feels like being on holiday, doesn't it?'

On the far side of the river, a bat flew from the fourth floor of Sighthill Tower. 'Look!' said Claire. Its small silhouette flicked left, then right, and then it passed through the poplar trees and disappeared from view. 'Did you see it?' she asked.

Dan shook his head, looking belatedly at the sky.

'It was a bat, I think.'

'Oh yeah?' said Dan. 'Adrian said there were lots of them around here, nesting or whatever. Do bats nest?'

'They roost, I think. They must be roosting in the tower. Do they bite, is what I'm wondering.'

'Vampire bats do. I saw a documentary about how they can, like, swoop on cattle and stuff. They can carry a whole sheep away.'

'Really?' said Claire. Dan was no David Attenborough.

'But that's in South America. Most bat bites are pretty harmless. Unless they give you rabies.'

'It's just not a safe place for kids to play, is it?'

'It's just not your business.'

Claire didn't answer; she probably couldn't avoid an argument, but there was no harm in postponing one.

They crossed back over the river, watching a mother mallard lead a wobbling line of ducklings. The ducklings punted in jostling formation, spreading a V in the still water behind them. Claire paused to watch the ducks, admiring the mother's patient maternal pace, and then she led Dan down the cycle track and onto the pine-needle softened side street.

The pub was nicer than Claire had realised when she'd been running. It was housed in a grand red-brick building, whose chimneys were tall as spires, and whose walls were partially covered with ivy. Inside, where the ceiling was webbed with fairy lights, a scatter of drinkers sat on buttoned leather armchairs, but Dan and Claire took their drinks to the busy beer garden, where laughter resonated amidst the parasols and trestles.

'Okay,' said Dan, watching a young woman carry a Chihuahua towards the main road. 'What d'you want to chat about?'

On the walk to the pub, Claire had considered how to make her case, and she'd decided to hit him with the most objective evidence she had. She unfolded the newspaper article and slid it across the table. Dan read the article, typing a rhythm on the desk. 'Why are you showing me this?' he asked when he'd finished.

'I've been to see where the skeleton was found.'

'The church house?'

'I went inside, spoke with one of the builders.'

'Jesus, Claire. I don't think I can cope with this.'

'He showed me where this baby's skeleton was hidden all these years. Whoever put it there built a secret baby room below a box-room.'

'You went to a building site, alone, with a bunch of builders?'

'I only spoke to one builder and he was really sweet.'

'What you saying that for?'

Claire folded her arms across her chest, feeling her armpit fat stick to her triceps. 'We were having a nice evening. Just for once, let's try not to argue, okay?'

'I'm not the one who's argue—'

'Dan, stop it. Listen, I asked Mrs Brompton about who lived at the church house in 1936, and she thinks it was a family who emigrated to do missionary work.'

'Did you really fancy the builder?'

'You fancy Gabby Logan, don't you? But you love me, right?'

'That's different; she's a sports presenter.'

Claire wasn't convinced by this logic, but she stood up quickly before Dan could add anything more to this silly argument. It seemed that the adult responsibilities of being a manager and a homeowner had caused him to regress in every other area of life. She walked fast, feeling at the centre of some unseen stare. She didn't really need the toilet, but she wanted to inspect how she looked. As she hurried inside, her heels sounded like a horse at the trot.

The ladies was perfumed, a chemical blossom, and the fittings were set in slabs of cool marble-effect plastic. Claire studied herself in the wall-length mirror: yes, you could see fat under her arms, but you'd have to be staring. At least her complexion looked good. Maybe it was the bronzer and sun shimmer, but had she seen another woman looking so well, she would have described her as 'glowing.' As she calculated how long it had been since her last period, she guessed she might be ovulating. She enjoyed the quiet of the empty bathroom: just the noise of her heels and the whisper of the pipes.

When she returned downstairs, she stopped at the bar and ordered two more drinks. She ordered herself a large wine this time; what the hell, she thought.

'Wow, thanks Babe,' said Dan, when she returned with his pint.

Before he found something else to sulk about, Claire decided to broach what had happened that afternoon. 'So I saw this secret baby room at the church house, yeah?'

'Babe, I know it's nine months since you lost the baby. Since *we* lost the baby. I feel it too—'

'Just listen to what I've got to say.'

'And I understand what you're going through. Or I'm trying to, you know?'

'Will you just listen to me, Dan?'

He nodded and shrugged all at once.

'Morgana and Unity play this game called the Secret Baby Room in the tower block.'

'Don't worry about the tower block, Babe – they're knocking it down in a week.'

'Nine days,' said Claire.

'Seven days or nine days – who cares? It's gonna go *kaboom*.'

'Exactly. We've only got nine days in which to make sure that the building's empty. Now, let's look at the evidence. First, I see a woman with a baby high up in the tower block. Second, I see a guy coming out of the tower block pushing a pram.'

'You think there's a family living there?'

'Third, Unity and Mooncloud are playing a game in the tower that they call "the Secret Baby Room."'

'What's this got to do with the skeleton from the 1930s?'

'That's what I'm trying to figure out. Maybe nothing, I don't know.'

'And the graffiti of the staked baby?'

'Exactly,' said Claire, 'that's the fifth thing.'

'I don't think we've had the fourth thing.'

'The skeleton was the fourth thing.' Claire was drinking faster than usual, and she was unsure of her own counting. 'The skeleton, the graffiti . . . the baby that I saw . . . What else did I say?'

'The guy with the pram.'

'Right. The sixth thing is what Li—'

Dan was laughing now. 'Babe, you've only said four things.'

'The guy with the pram, the baby, the skeleton . . . '

'The graffiti.'

'Yeah, and the children's game. Look, there are too many pieces of evidence to count. You've got the ghost that's supposed to have murdered her babies. You've got the birth problems that Morgana tries to blame on the phone—'

'And our miscarriage.'

'No, Dan. That didn't happen here. That isn't anything to do with this. Is it?'

Dan stood up without answering. 'I need the toilet.'

Claire watched him walk under a trestle, on which grew a rose that had bloomed a single apricot-coloured flower. People were smoking at every other table. It's strange, she thought, how pleasant tobacco smoke smells outdoors. When Dan was out of view, she leaned back to check the cut of her dress when seated. She didn't remember it bulging her underarm fat in Corfu. Maybe she was thinner then. Drinking alfresco, slightly tipsy, she could almost imagine they were back on holiday, in a bar dug into the chalky hillside. That last evening, they had climbed to the top of the cliffs as the sun set, and there they had sat on a terrace, nibbling mezes and sipping beer. The after-trails of motorboats, far away, just tiny white scratches on a perfect turquoise sea.

When Dan returned he brought more drinks: he'd put her back on the small wine, which she might have complained about had she been able to focus. She remembered going clubbing as a student and drinking eight vodka tonics, followed by who knows how many tequila slammers, and still being able to arrhythmically thrust her hips in what, to a white girl from Worcester, was a reasonable attempt at booty shaking. Now, after two glasses of wine, the lines of the world had softened, as if it were being gently trembled.

'What I'm building up to,' said Claire, 'is about Morgana. Today Lianne told me she'd seen Morgana in the tower, performing some sort of fire ritual.'

Dan laughed. 'I don't know which of you three is craziest.'

'Think about it: Morgana is the link to everything. Who tries to blame the still births and deformities on the phone mast? Morgana. Who stopped the tower from being demolished? Morgana. Who happened to be outside when fresh graffiti appeared on our wall? Morgana. Whose kids talk about the Secret Baby Room? Morgana's.'

'But Morgana weren't alive in the 1930s. Or is she immortal?'

'I don't know, Dan. I'm trying to make sense of it all, too. Maybe there's some sort of . . . cult that's been going on here for decades – centuries, perhaps.'

Dan laughed.

'I'm not joking. I'm . . . theorising.'

'But you must have some idea how crazy you sound, right? I mean, fire rituals? A cult that's existed for centuries? Secret baby rooms? You're losing the plot.'

It did sound absolutely bonkers.

'And what's Morgana's motive?'

'I don't know. She's doing experiments. She poisons pregnant women, collects all the deformed babies, stores them in the tower.'

Dan leant forward and banged his head on the table, sloshing his cider overboard.

'That last bit was kind of a joke,' said Claire. For the first time in a while, she started laughing. Dan looked up, relieved, and when he laughed too, Claire's laughter became uncontrollable. It felt good. 'Okay,' she said, breathless from the hilarity, 'laugh all you want. At least I'm brainstorming. What's your theory?'

'If you ask me,' said Dan, 'it's more likely summat to do with vampires. The bat we saw today were probably Morgana in her night form.'

'She feeds on children. She's been doing it since the 1930s.'

'Longer than that, Claire. She's—'

'Wait, how do I know you're not in on it, Dan? You were the one who decided we should move here. Then it turns out you've been in the towers as a kid with that . . . whatshisname?'

'Abukar.'

You try to dissuade me from investigating—'

'You've got me, Babe – Morgana is just one of my servants.' They were laughing together for the first time in ages – giggling like children – and it felt *so* good.

'Your real name is Euronyme the Awful, Dark Prince of the Night.'

'This appearance is an illusion.'

'Couldn't you have chosen a nicer one?'

'My true form has flaming eyes set in a maggot-ridden skull. I can kill with a stare.'

'And yet you still can't un-ball your socks.'

It felt *so good*! Claire remembered seeing a TV feature on laughter yoga: a ring of Indian guys standing in a public park. They started clapping and shaking and gurning. And then, in unison, they *forced* themselves to laugh. After a while, the laughter was contagious, and they were belly howling, stomping the floor, fighting for breath. At the time Claire had thought them ridiculous, but now she could see the cathartic benefits. She and Dan could have gone on like this, too busy laughing to fight, and they might have walked home hand in hand – who knows, perhaps they would have made love. Perhaps—

But even as they were laughing, even as she was thinking how good it felt, she focused on a man who was pushing a pram past the pub. She had read somewhere that according to neuroscientists human actions commence before we're conscious of them: we think our conscious minds choose the things we do, but in fact by the time we're thinking about those things, we've already started doing them. So it was with Claire's recognition of the pram guy. She had been watching him for a second or two before she realised what it was that fascinated her. Her laughter slowed to a stammering stop. 'It's him,' she said.

And then she was up, trotting as fast as she could to the entrance, and Dan, confused, stood up, still laughing. But as he saw where she was going – as he guessed what she was about to do – he ran after her, vaulted the low wall. 'Excuse me,' called Claire, reaching for the man's shoulder. The man glanced right, recognised her, and pushed the pram forward like a tobogganist starting a race. The pram crashed into Dan and overturned.

There was a long, horrible moment as Dan and Claire looked to the ground expecting to see a baby tip out. Dan, poised like a goalkeeper, crouched to make a sprawling save. From the beer garden, Claire heard a choric intake of breath. Then the pram was on its side, wheels spinning in the silence.

Was the baby strapped in? Claire crouched to peer inside and saw, to her relief then shock then embarrassment, that the pram was empty. The man, who was wearing the same bomber jacket as before, righted the pram as Dan babbled apologies and consolations. Claire could hear the drinkers murmur admonishments, unease spreading from table to table, but the only dialogue she would later remember was spoken from the man with the pram. He didn't respond to Dan, but he looked right at Claire and said, 'Leave us alone.' He spoke with a speech defect, and he smelled of unwashed clothes. He was unshaven, his tongue hanging out, as if it were too big for his mouth. His knuckles were tattooed with 'MCFC,' the ink faded algae-green.

He pushed the pram on, glancing back once or twice. Dan stared at Claire but didn't speak. They returned to their seats as the other drinkers stole glances, curious and appalled, but wary of provoking a reaction.

'Finish that,' said Dan. 'We're leaving.'

'I'm not leaving,' said Claire.

'You're drunk. You've humiliated us both and frightened some poor guy with learning difficulties.'

Claire started to cry. It was like some great black cloud had passed over their evening.

'Don't make a scene, Claire. I'm taking you home. I know this isn't your fault, but tomorrow we're getting you some help.'

'I'm not going,' she said, gulping the last of her wine.

'Well, *I'm* going. Are you going to stay here on your own?'

Claire didn't answer. If he was going to treat her like a child then she was going to behave like one.

'Fine,' he said, 'do what you want.' He walked five steps, but then he turned back to her. 'Babe, please come home with me?'

The other drinkers were watching the scene with embarrassment.

'Come on,' said Dan.

She felt sorry for him, but she couldn't back down now. She shook her head, stood up, lurched towards the bar. The whispers behind her were inaudible and yet amplified. Inside, where nobody had seen the incident, she felt safer. She climbed to the bathroom, looked at herself. The last gulp of wine had gone to her head and the image was hazy, undefined. Her makeup had blurred: dripping raccoon eyes. As she tried to clean her face with tissue, a toilet flushed and a lock clicked. It was a girl in a black dress that Dan had been ogling before. 'Are you okay?' she asked.

When Claire finally descended the stairs, she ordered another large wine, and sat alone at a corner table. She stared straight ahead, fancying herself as a mysterious heroine (dangerous, desirable, empowered), but fearing she looked like a desperate, emotionally-disturbed divorcee. Soon she staggered to the cigarette machine. What the hell, she thought, the mantra sounding weak in her head. She bought Marlboros, took them outside, and asked a group of men for a light. One of them slid her a lighter, disinterestedly, as their conversation continued unbroken. She sat as far from them as possible, sipped her wine, and watched the smoke dissipate in the night air.

By the time she left, the lights were impressionistic streaks. She started home, conscious she was walking in diagonals. Had she been sober, then no way would she have walked alone up that cycle path. It's strange, isn't it, how we're at our most fearless when we're at our most vulnerable. She imagined she was warping through the galaxy: the streetlights on the cycle path were spaced wide enough that each emitted its own puddle of light; each time Claire passed a lamppost she held her breath, stepped into the dark, and counted the seconds until she entered the next solar system.

A dog barked in a nearby garden, but the only other noise was the sound of her feet. She imagined how this scene would be shot in a movie. It was quiet, she thought. Too quiet. She said this to herself in a melodramatic voice that made her laugh – the voice used to narrate film trailers. Then, as she neared the river, she heard someone shaking an aerosol can. The rattle of the ball bearing sounded like a percussion instrument. She knew it was a can of spray paint.

Claire stopped, afraid to go on. She was suddenly conscious of how silly she'd been. The cycle path bent to meet the river, and, though hidden from view by the curve of the wall, the vandal was only yards ahead of her. She listened to the rattle of the can, and then heard a faint hiss, like air being released from a tyre. She recognised the toxic exhaust smell of freshly-sprayed paint. Then the cap clicked onto the can, and the vandal walked towards her. She realised her only option was to walk towards him, to pass him nonchalantly as if unaware what he'd been doing.

When you're conscious of the need to conceal your nerves, you start to think about how you're walking, and it becomes impossible to act normally. While passing the man, Claire looked up at the streetlights and hummed the theme tune from *The Muppet Show*. But she did sneak a glance, and she did recognise him. On her runs, she'd often seen him hanging around the neighbourhood – on the bridge or under the flyover. He was twenty-ish, she guessed, wearing baggy combats and a retro Adidas hoody. His clothes changed from day to day, but he always wore the same big zirconia ear stud.

The paint smell intensified as she rounded the corner. The man had sprayed the staked-baby graffiti on the red brick wall that flanked the cycle path. She clenched her fist: she had caught him in the act.

Ten

IN THE MORNING, Claire woke with a headache and a vague sense of self-disgust. It was eleven o'clock. Next to her, Dan was reading a football magazine. This at first disorientated her, for she thought it was Dan's Saturday to work, but then she recalled that he had swapped shifts with his assistant manager, who had needed Sunday off for— What did it matter? 'Good morning,' she said, but Dan, who was a sulker's sulker, ignored her.

She stood up, determined to conceal the extent of her hangover. She was so thirsty! Her throat felt full of dust, and her stomach was cramping. She stumbled to the bathroom, half-expecting she would be sick. She was reminded of morning sickness – the nausea that at first she'd been unable to explain. Every room in the house was so hot! Who would have thought she'd move to Manchester and daily pray for rain?

She threw the toothbrushes from their pot, rinsed the pot, and ran the taps until the water flowed as cool as it would. She drank two cups without a breath, and then she turned the shower on, setting the temperature just cooler than lukewarm. She had fallen asleep in yesterday's underwear, and her skin had been bitten red by the elastic of her knickers. All her clothes were so tight on her, and she worried that her life would be marked by a trail of once-loved garments, each of which had become unwearable on a different birthday.

Standing in the shower, goose-bumped by the cold, she thought through her hazy memories of the preceding night. There was no one incident ruinous in itself, and yet the evening as a whole produced in her feelings of self-loathing that she couldn't articulate. It was the very vagueness of her unease that made it so powerful and so impossible to rationalise.

She had worked hard at improving her fitness, controlling her weight, and then she had undone all her efforts with a needless night of bingeing. She imagined herself, alone in that pub, her makeup streaked by tears, drinking and smoking as if she had nothing else in the whole world. What a desperate, pitiable creature.

When she'd finished in the bathroom, she resolved to jog her circuit as penance. She would sweat out the hangover, compensate for last night's excess. At the back of her mind, however, she was also aware that she now knew exactly who was responsible for the staked-baby graffiti. At this time of day, there was a good chance he would be lounging under the flyover, or she would pass him at some other point on her route. If she didn't see him today then she would see him tomorrow or the next day. But what would she do? Would she have the courage to confront him?

Outside, Morgana was stocking her bird feeders. 'Hello, Claire,' she called. She looked up at the sky with a big, radiant gesture. 'We are blessed by Sol once again.'

'Yeah, nice day,' said Claire, walking on.

'Claire,' called Morgana.

Claire turned, looked at Morgana properly. She was wearing an old Greenpeace T-shirt over a long orange dress.

'Are you coming to the meeting tomorrow?'

'Tomorrow . . . ' Claire's life was currently so empty that it was hard to think of an excuse. 'I'm not sure. Perhaps. I think Dan maybe wanted to do something.'

'I see,' said Morgana.

Don't provoke her, thought Claire. 'If not tomorrow then I'm sure I'll see you soon.'

'No doubt,' said Morgana.

Claire waved and tried again to walk away.

'Claire,' called Morgana.

'Yes?'

'She's hurting, you know.'

'Sorry,' said Claire, 'who is?'

'Mother earth, Claire. She tells me she's hurting. She wants us to help.'

Claire didn't know what to say. After a second of silence, she raised a clenched fist in what she thought would pass as an eco-warrior's salute, and then she jogged away before Morgana could call her back once more.

She felt sick as soon as she started to jog, but she kept going, refusing to admit the extent of her hangover. She made it as far as the river, and then she bent over and vomited red bile onto the weeds. She was in view of a mother and toddler, but she couldn't stop herself. It was years since she'd last been sick, and she'd forgotten how much she loathed the feeling: the pain in your throat, the lumps in your sinuses, and that awful abdominal emptiness. The young mother called her toddler closer and hesitantly asked whether Claire was okay. While the child was stomping his tiny buckle shoes in hopeless pursuit of birds, the mother was resting her Mulberry handbag on the seat of the pushchair. Claire straightened herself, sniffed back more vomit, and spat into the long track-side grass. 'Yes, thank you,' she said in her poshest voice. Then she put her hand to her belly and said, 'They tell me it gets better in the second trimester.'

'So they say,' said the mother, smiling in sympathy. 'Here, I'm sure I have some tissues. Ben! Keep away from the water!' She passed Claire a packet of Kleenex. 'When are you due?' she asked, stooping in a gesture of concern.

Claire's head was too clogged to do the maths. If she was in the first trimester then it would be another seven months, which would take them up to— she started to count in her head.

'Poor thing,' said the mother. 'Are you sure you're going to be okay?'

'Yes, yes, thank you so much.' She held out the unused Kleenexes.

'Please, you keep them. It *does* get better,' said the mother.

It's safe to say that this was not the time that Claire would have chosen to once again encounter the graffiti artist. He overtook her just after she'd crossed to the far side of the river, and at first she didn't recognise him. Then, as she realised it was definitely him, she thought she might just ignore him. After all, she saw him hanging around almost every other day; if she ignored him this time, then she would not have to wait long for their next encounter. Besides, if he ran from her the way the pram-man had run from her— God, she thought, remembering the horror of what she'd done last night. The pram had been empty and— Why would anyone push an empty pram? She dithered so long that the moment to confront the graffiti artist had passed. Nevertheless, her curiosity was even stronger than her hangover, and so she decided to follow him.

She waited until the graffiti artist was twenty metres ahead of her, and then she accelerated to match his pace. On a hot, clear Saturday, the golf course was busy, and every few seconds a flock of birds would squawk, flapping into the sky, as a player struck a ball, launching it into optimistic flight. Sometimes Claire heard the balls landing: a noise that diminished with each bounce, like the leaps of a stone skimmed across a lake. The graffiti artist was oblivious to this, but Claire noticed that as they passed the tower, he glanced back to inspect his work. It was still there, she saw: the staked-baby graffiti, high in the sky, flanked on either side by a flash of reflected sunlight.

Claire had expected the graffiti artist to continue straight, past the mobile phone mast, to the flyover, under which she had most often seen him. Instead, he turned right and entered the grounds of the retirement home. Was he going to paint that old building? she wondered. Did he paint during the day or only at night?

She followed him along a woodchip pathway, passing through the shade of sycamore trees. Soon, the path joined the retirement home's driveway, which was bordered with whitewashed boulders. To the left, the lawn had been mown in careful stripes; to the right, rhododendrons bloomed in big cushions of colour. The building itself was redbrick and sandstone, neo-gothic architecturally. With its spired bell tower and its lancet windows, it seemed to have been designed to terrify the orphans it was built to house.

When the graffiti artist was near the main entrance – a pointed arc carved with cherubic gargoyles – an old man shuffled outside and the two stopped to talk. Claire stopped, pretended to tie her shoelaces. She imagined she was being watched from behind the tall, pointed windows. As she watched the old man, however, she began to think he was familiar. We're more aware of the differences between people our own age than we are of the differences between those who are much older or younger than us, and so Claire wasn't at first sure whether this was the same old man – Jack, Neville Shaw had called him – who habitually asked local people whether they were adopted. Certainly, his conversation with the graffiti artist was going on longer than his usual interrogations.

Claire could no longer pretend to be tying her shoelaces, so she strolled into the car park and crouched behind a Volkswagen. When the old man began to stagger onwards, she heard the graffiti artist laughing. 'Stay out of trouble, Jack,' he called. Then he entered the building, taking the steps at a jog.

Claire took her keys from her pocket, dangling them as if she'd just locked her car, and then she stepped out onto the driveway and walked towards the old man. As she had expected, he stopped in front of her, blocking her path, and he asked her, 'Are you adopted?'

'No, Jack,' said Claire, 'I'm not.'

Jack didn't seem surprised that she knew his name, and he had no wish to extend the conversation. He seemed to be shrinking – the old suit he wore looked even bigger on him than it had last week – and his wheezing breath sounded three times with every step he took.

The entrance porch smelled of fresh paint and newly-printed brochures. Claire picked up a brochure, flicked through pictures of grey-haired people (all of them far too young and healthy to be in a care home) laughing and grinning and looking as if their physical and mental decline was everything they'd ever dreamed of.

On the far side of the glass door, behind a reception desk, a girl in a white uniform was on the telephone. Maybe Claire could sneak past while the receptionist was distracted? Or maybe she should ask for a tour – say she was exploring care options on behalf of her elderly father?

She pushed open the door, breathed bleach and disinfectant, potpourri and lavender air freshener. The reception desk was cluttered with vases of flowers, but the receptionist saw her and gestured that she should wait in one of the chrome seats affixed to the near wall. 'Yes,' she said into the phone, 'and that'll be at ten o'clock on Tuesday?' Claire crossed to the seats, listening to the little screams her trainers made on the linoleum floor. The receptionist clacked the computer keys and asked, 'That'll be with Doctor Fielding?' Only when Claire sat down did she hear the ambient music that was playing through overhead speakers; it was barely audible above the hum of the climate control system. Claire waited, still unsure of her next move. It was uncomfortably hot, the air stuffy and recycled tasting, like the air on an aeroplane.

'Sorry about that,' said the receptionist, hanging up the phone and lifting a manila file from under a clutter of papers. 'How can I help you?'

Claire stood up and approached the desk. She saw that the receptionist had the name 'Amy' pinned to her chest. She couldn't have been much older than eighteen, but she was carefully made up, with conditioned blonde hair pulled back in a ponytail. She didn't look at Claire but continued to search for something amid the clutter on her desk. 'Are you here to visit a relative?'

'No,' said Claire, suddenly inspired. 'I wanted to speak to a guy I saw come in here. I think he dropped his keys by the river.' She held out her own keys, but the receptionist wasn't looking. 'I called out to him but—'

'Okay,' said the receptionist, swivelling her back to Claire. 'Do you want to leave them on the desk? I can log them in the lost property book when I get a minute?'

Claire watched the receptionist struggle with the filing system. 'I think I'd best speak to the owner, make sure I've got the right building.'

'Okay,' said the receptionist. The phone rang again and she didn't answer it. 'Shit,' she said under her breath, removing the file from the pigeon hole she'd just placed it in.

Claire waited while the phone rang out, wondering whether this was the standard of applicant she'd be interviewing against on Thursday. Not wanting to embarrass the girl, she stood back and pretended to examine a framed photograph – the Duke of Wessex visiting the home in 2005, according to the caption.

'Okay,' said the receptionist, finally turning to deal with Claire. 'So could you describe the gentleman who dropped the keys? Was he in a wheelchair?'

'No, he was a young guy, baggy jeans and a big earring.'

The receptionist laughed. 'Ah, that'll be Seth. I'll just give him a shout.' She picked up a walkie-talkie and pressed it crackling into life. 'Front desk to Seth?' They waited in silence, both staring at the radio in the receptionist's hand.

'What's up, Amy?'

'Hey, Seth, I've got a lady here who says she's found your keys.'

Silence. The receptionist examined her manicure.

'Not my keys.' Silence. 'I've got mine right here.'

'No worries, Seth.' Seth's reply was just a blast of static. The receptionist set down the radio and looked up at Claire with a shrug.

'Seth works here?'

The receptionist nodded in a manner designed to emphasise the stupidity of Claire's question.

'What does he do here?'

'He's a Care Assistant. He's a Care Assistant who hasn't lost his keys.'

'Do you think I could speak to him anyway?'

The receptionist looked Claire from head to foot, her expression one of incredulity. 'Don't you think you're a bit old for him?'

Now Claire saw why the receptionist was so carefully made up, and she realised how Seth must have appeared to a girl of Amy's age. He was handsome in the pretty way of a boy band member, and to Amy he probably seemed unfathomably cool, but he was also a little bit wild, something dangerous, a project to which Amy could devote herself.

Claire forced a laugh. 'Don't be silly,' she said. 'I think he might have information about a crime.'

'What sort of crime?' asked the receptionist, folding her arms.

'I'd sooner speak to Seth about that.'

'I don't think so,' said the receptionist.

'Perhaps you could just let him know that I'm here.'

The receptionist grabbed the radio, this time staring at Claire as she spoke into it. 'Seth, it's front desk again. The key woman's still here. Says she wants to speak to you. About a crime or something.'

This time the silence lasted twenty seconds. Claire rested her elbows on the desk and leaned into Amy's space, for that was a client habit that had driven her mad back at the ophthalmology ward.

'I'm kind of busy with Mr Caruthers, Amy.' Static. 'Take the woman's number and I'll call her back.'

The receptionist's smile was purposefully antagonistic. Claire didn't want the graffiti artist to have her number, but in any case she knew there was no way that the receptionist would pass it on. 'Forget about it,' Claire said. She felt humiliated. Instead of leaving, she leant even further over the desk and pointed at the mess of papers. 'Patient-identifiable information should be filed and locked away. I recommend a clear desk policy.' She turned, not waiting for a reply. At the door she hesitated. 'Maybe someone can retrain you on Caldicott.' She swung the door open and walked out, weirdly elated by her parting shot. When she looked back from the porch, she saw that Amy had ignored her warning about confidentiality and was already running from the reception desk, presumably to warn and protect the object of her affection.

When Claire got home, Dan had gone out. On their garden wall, the staked-baby graffiti, which Dan had promised to remove, was as bright and as intimidating as ever, and Claire decided she would remove it herself. From the pavement, she hit the garage fob, forgetting what Dan had told her about the neighbours' doors. Lianne's garage door stayed shut, but Morgana's started to roll upwards. Claire hurried to press it shut, fearful that Morgana would emerge from the house.

Claire's own garage had a masculine smell that didn't seem to suit her husband. It smelled of oil and wood shavings and newly-mixed cement. Dan's tools, unused in years, were in a trunk behind the car. Though the garage was lit by only one dim bulb, she soon found a paint brush. It smelled of white spirit and its bristles had hardened into a point. It would do, she thought. The only paint in the truck was a tub of magnolia, which she vaguely remembered Dan using to patch up the living room wall of an old rental flat. It didn't matter to Claire that the garden wall was redbrick and the paint magnolia; she just wanted to cover that haunting picture.

On the street, she struggled to open the paint. It was caked shut and the handle of the paintbrush wouldn't open it. She went back to the tool trunk and found a chisel, which she then hammered under the lid with a small rock. Inside, the paint had separated into water and goo. She stirred it together, reviving the smell, and then she started to paint.

As Claire was working, Morgana passed with a wicker shopping basket. 'Covering it up, are you?' asked Morgana.

'Yes,' said Claire. The problem, of course, was that the paint wasn't designed for such a porous surface, and it was so light-coloured that the graffiti showed through as clear as ever.

'Perhaps I could have a look in the garage and see whether Adrian has any cement-based paint?'

'No thank you,' said Claire. She continued to work, trying to ignore her neighbour.

'Actually, I meant to ask when I saw you before: have you had any luck with your letter to the *Evening Chronicle*?' asked Morgana.

'No, not yet,' said Claire. Don't offend her, Claire thought; be neutral, detach yourself, but don't incur her wrath.

'Oh dear. Well, we'll meet to discuss a new strategy, won't we? Next week, if you really can't make it tomorrow.'

'I'll need to see,' said Claire, continuing to paint.

'Is everything okay?' asked Morgana.

Claire rested the brush in her pot and turned to look at Morgana. Morgana had pulled a black hoodie over her Greenpeace T-shirt; the print on the hoodie said 'I'm pagan and I vote.' She wore a snake goddess headband and she was barefoot. Don't offend her, thought Claire. 'I'm sorry,' she said, 'I'm just . . . You know, just—'

'That's okay,' said Morgana. 'You're feeling kind of over-whelmed, aren't you?'

' . . . Right,' said Claire.

'You just need some time to ground yourself, don't you?'

Claire nodded politely, smiled, and returned to her painting. She could feel that Morgana hadn't moved.

'Have you ever been tested for clairsentience?'

Claire thought Morgana was asking her about some infectious disease. 'At school, probably, I think,' she said.

'If you'd like to explore how you're feeling then—'

'Thank you,' said Claire.

'Or if there's anything else I can do to help, please just—'

'Thank you,' said Claire. 'I think just now I'd be best trying to finish this.'

'As you wish,' said Morgana. She waited a moment longer and then barefooted to number thirteen.

Twenty minutes later, all Claire had achieved was to paint a drip-ping white splodge that emphasised rather than concealed the staked baby. The wall looked far worse than it had before.

The sun was high overhead, the heat maddening. Suddenly, Claire's pent up rage demanded physical expression. It was the sort of petulant gesture of temper that she normally resisted, but she kicked the paint can into the street and watched as it dribbled a mess of dots and strings across the tarmac.

She left it there, walked inside, slammed the door, punched the sofa. She was just so angry at Dan and Morgana and that bloody vandal and his little – In fact, she realised, she was going to confront this Seth, and it didn't matter whether he knew anything about dead babies and secret rooms. Maybe he was just an everyday sad case vandal, and it would still be worth confronting him, even if only to make him clean her bloody wall. She punched the sofa again and again. She realised she was acting like her father – taking her temper out on inanimate objects. As a child, she'd hated his impotent expressions of fury, and the realisation that she was copying him made her stop. After one last punch, Claire gathered the cushions, re-plumped them, and smoothed the sofa cover.

It took two minutes to walk to the retirement home, but more than ten minutes to drive there. She had to turn down St Michael's Street, loop back onto the motorway, come off at the first exit, and drive down past the golf course. Still, it felt good to be driving. Dan drove to work every day and this was the first time Claire had been behind the wheel since they'd moved. She rolled her window down and turned up the radio. When she joined the motorway, she pressed her foot to the floor. The wind cleared her head. It occurred to her that she was heading south, that she could drive out of town, be back at her parents' house in time for dinner; but the thought frightened her, for she knew that if she left now, she might never return.

She parked in the shade of a sycamore tree, in a spot that afforded a clear view of the retirement home entrance. She had no idea how long she'd have to wait. If Seth's shift started at twelve then it could go on until – God, Claire thought, if that receptionist saw her camped out here, she'd think Seth had attracted a crazy stalker.

Looking west, beyond the retirement home, Claire saw that the horizon had darkened – a great streak of black had spread across South Manchester. Seagulls circled, their bodies bright white against the dark background.

Claire kicked her shoes off and reclined her seat. She closed her eyes then opened them quickly, worried she'd doze off and miss Seth leaving. The car smelled of Dan's cricket equipment, which at some stage he'd slung in the boot. She was probably the only woman in the world who associated that smell with romance. She and Dan had held their wedding reception at Dan's boss's cricket club – an idea she had vigorously resisted for months. In fact, when she finally conceded, she and Dan drove to Sherrardsbrook, and she saw it was the most perfect setting imaginable. The pavilion, which on the day was flanked by two marquees, was bright white, with a tiny clock tower (replete with a weather vane), and a planked veranda that resounded tunefully with every footstep. The spire of the village church, in which they married, was visible between two willow trees, and beyond that the Malvern Hills stood black against the setting sun.

On the day of the wedding, as they sipped champagne and strolled across the confetti-dotted lawn, the only thing that reminded her it was, in fact, Dan's boss's cricket club, was the cricket-kit smell that a dozen flower bouquets could not eclipse. And so, three years later, the smell – of leather and sweat and Deep Heat and linseed oil – still evoked in her feelings of love and happiness.

Soon, despite her mission, she dozed off. She slept for an hour, dreaming in the evening heat, and only woke when the storm broke. At first it was just the distant cannon rumble of thunder, and then, on the horizon, she saw forks of lightning, crawling across the earth like great silver insect legs. Then the rain broke, and she wheeled up her window as the first drops freckled the dry ground. Soon it was thumping the car roof, machine gunning into the dusty soil under the trees. Sycamore seeds whirled to ground, landing in puddles that swelled from nowhere. The day had gone dark as night.

The storm was ten-minutes old when Seth emerged from the home. He stood in the porch, watching the downpour, but when the receptionist ran out to offer him an umbrella, he jokingly shoved it back and ran into the storm, pulling his tracksuit top over his head.

Claire hit the ignition, stalling the car in her haste. The radio came on, startling her with its volume. She turned it off then flicked her lights on, their beams hitting the rain. The windscreen wipers were lashing back and forth, but she could hardly see where she was going. She skidded onto the driveway, hooting her horn, shooshing surface water into the grass.

She rolled down her window and the rain spattered the upholstery. 'Hey, Seth!' she called. He sped up but didn't run, so she drove at his pace, calling through the window. 'I just want to talk to you. I'm not the police.'

When he reached the woodchip path, he left the driveway and jogged away from the car. She threw her door open, ran after him barefoot. She was wearing a light summer dress and in seconds it was soaked transparent. 'Seth!' she called. 'I know you do the graffiti – I saw you.' Wet ropes of hair fell over her face. Her dress stuck to her skin. 'I don't want to make trouble for you. I just want to talk!' She was standing ankle-deep in a puddle.

'What d'you want, yeah?' He turned, arms spread, chest puffed out. 'What's your problem?'

'You spray-painted my wall and I—'

'And what? What you gonna do about it?'

'Please?' she said. 'Come into the car. I need your help.'

Seth made a visor with his hand, squinting past the headlights to see if a burly husband or a policeman lurked in the car. 'Why d'you need my help?' he asked, his tone less hostile.

A clap of thunder startled them both and two seconds later the lightning flashed and the scene appeared, momentarily bright – a snapshot of an argument. 'Please,' she said. 'Just a minute of your time?'

Seth walked back, squelching off the path so he could keep his distance from Claire, and then he circled the car, peering suspiciously inside. 'Okay,' he said, and flung open the passenger door.

Claire ran back to the car, water splashing her calves, and slammed the door closed behind her. They sat, staring at the rain-blasted windscreen. The flicks of the wipers sent water spraying to either side of the bonnet. When Claire cut the engine, the only noise was the thudding of raindrops.

After a moment, Seth reached across her and pulled the keys from the ignition. 'So what's the deal?' he asked. 'You gone to the police?'

'No. And I don't plan to. I told you – I want your help.'

'Let me guess,' said Seth; 'you liked the tag on your wall so much that you want me to do you a mural?'

They both laughed and the laughter broke the tension. The car now smelled of their damp clothes and the windows were steaming up.

'I want to know why you paint what you paint – what it means. And I want to know what you know about the Secret Baby Room.'

'What's the Secret Baby Room?'

'That's what I hoped you could tell me.' They sat, side by side, never looking at each other, and Claire told Seth about the baby she'd seen in the tower, the man with the empty pram, Morgana's spell, and Mooncloud and Unity's game. 'I know you went in there to paint and—'

'Yeah,' said Seth. 'That one took hours. I had to climb out the window and everything. Next day, I find out they're knocking the fucker down in a week.'

'But you've never heard of the Secret Baby Room?'

'Never.'

'And you didn't see anything strange when you were in there?'

Seth rubbed his chin, demonstrating deep thought. He was determined to appear helpful, Claire thought. 'There have been people living there, I'd say. Like, there's beer cans and tinfoil – you know, like junkie stuff, yeah? And the first way I tried to go in, which turned out to be a dead end – just like a storage room or whatever, yeah? – it were all filled with, like . . . It were padlocked shut, but I had me bolt-cutters, yeah? And it were all filled with stuff.'

'What sort of stuff?'

'I don't know. Clothes and stuff, innit?'

'Children's clothes?'

Seth shrugged. 'Maybe. I only had a small light.'

The windows had steamed opaque. They were parked in the middle of the driveway, but it seemed unlikely anyone would try to drive through while the storm was still so intense. 'So why do you do it?' Claire asked.

'People always ask me that. Look at the world, yeah, and ask yourself what impact you have. Okay? See, if you go up town, there's a McDonald's here, a big billboard there, a posh chain pub next to that, yeah? The whole city's been designed by rich guys. If you sit on a bench, crack open a beer, they spy you on their CCTV, okay, and they send their cops to harass you, cause they don't want nobody in their city that isn't paying the businesses they work for. You get me?'

'I guess,' said Claire.

'See, public space isn't public space no more, yeah? It's corporate space. A whole city controlled by rich guys. Why don't they let you do flyposting?'

'To keep the city looking tidy?'

'You think billboards look tidy? Listen, don't be naïve, yeah? They don't let you flypost cause only the rich are allowed to make a mark on the city, cause the city belongs to the rich. You get it? A guy like me, a mixed-race, poor kid from Hulme, I'm not allowed any say in how the world is, yeah? I'm not allowed to make any kind of mark. But when I spray me message on the walls, they can't stop me. You get it?'

'You can vote.'

Seth scoffed, shaking his head. 'Look at this,' he said. With his finger, he sketched ten Xs into the steam on the passenger window. 'That's your lifetime input to how the country's run. You call that democracy? Those guys are all the same anyhow. You telling me you can really tell one lot from the next?'

Claire remembered that she wasn't there to argue politics with a teenager. 'That's very interesting, about why you do graffiti, but it wasn't really what I wanted to ask. I want to know why you spray what you spray.'

'What the tag means?'

'Yeah, why a baby with a crucifix through its heart?'

'It means from the cradle to the grave, yeah? My art's a protest against suffering, innit? Like, there's a woman in the home, yeah, who wakes up screaming every night. Like, she's suffering every night, in her subconscious. You get me? She's screaming, "Why didn't I stop him?" "Why did I do it?" over and over. Sometimes the noise is so awful it breaks me heart, innit? But in the morning she can't remember nothing, and she can't think why she might be upset. You start life screaming, you end life screaming. From the cradle to the grave, yeah?' They sat for a moment, listening to the thudding rain. 'You know what my job is?'

'You're a Care Assistant.'

'Right. You know what that is?'

'Not really,' said Claire.

'When people get too old to work, when their bodies start to fail them, when society's got no more use for them, when they need to be spoon fed, when they can't wipe their arses no more, I'm the guy that they pay to do that. You get it now? You know how much it costs to live in there for a year? Over forty grand. You know how much they pay me an hour?'

Claire shook her head.

'£6.53. The boss of a bank, a bank that's gone bust and been bailed out by the taxpayer, is worth millions just for his bonus, yeah? I'm worth £6.20 an hour. So I'll never have savings, and I'll work until I'm seventy-five – if I live that long – and then they'll pay some kid on the minimum wage to wipe me clean. That's what I mean, yeah? From the cradle to the grave.'

When the storm subsided, Claire drove Seth home to Hulme. They passed some punks who were sitting around the remains of a bonfire, drinking Special Brew. Further on, kids on BMXs cut across the road, forcing her to brake. A group of men, heavy with jewellery, stood guard outside a pub, and a Mercedes, its roof open now the storm had passed, blasted music so loud it shook Claire's car. When they paused at traffic lights, she saw the staked baby painted across a boarded shop front. She watched a woman struggling with a pram, and when the lights changed, Seth directed her to turn right by a peach-coloured high-rise. Then, at no place in particular, he asked her to stop. 'I live over there,' he said, gesturing vaguely. She watched him enter the park, cross a playground that was strewn with broken glass. And then, as he disappeared from view, she turned her car for home.

When she arrived back, she saw the graffiti and realised it no longer scared her. The truth is rarely as bad as we imagine, she thought. She looked up at the tower block, saw Seth's work framed by the receding storm. The building would be knocked down in eight days. One way or another, the mystery of the Secret Baby Room would soon be over.

Eleven

THREE DAYS LATER, Claire found Old Man Jack collapsed near St. Michael's Church. Her first reaction was to look around for help, for it seemed she was the worst possible person to deal with a medical emergency, and then, when she saw that the road was empty, she crouched beside him and asked, rather stupidly, 'Are you okay, Jack?'

There was no reply and it occurred to her that he might be dead. His face was yellow and puffy and there was no sign of breathing. She saw that he'd been sick; the vomit had dried on his chin. She recalled, all at once, fragments of information from a hundred medical dramas and a first aid course she'd taken at school. Her head was too full and busy and she couldn't focus on any one idea. Should she put him in the recovery position? Be careful not to move him? CPR? Mouth to mouth? The— what was it called? The Heinrich manoeuvre? She checked his wrist for a pulse; at first she thought he had no pulse, then she thought he did, and then she thought the pulse she felt might have been her own.

She had her mobile with her, so she dialled 999, thinking how grateful she was for mobile phone masts. 'Ambulance,' she said, her voice faltering.

'What's the problem?'

'I've found a guy, collapsed. I don't think he's— We need an ambulance.'

'Can you tell me your location?'

'We're outside a church.'

'I need an address.'

'St. Michael's Church, St. Michael's Street, in— I don't think he's breathing.'

'I need you to calm down for me, okay? What's your name?'

'Claire Wilson.'

'Okay, Claire. Can you repeat the address for me?'

'It's St. Michael's Church on St Michael's Street. It's in South Manchester. I don't know the postcode. I'm really sorry. He needs an ambulance, I think. You need to hurry up.'

'St. Michael's Street, Manchester?'

'You need to hurry up,' said Claire.

'Don't worry, Claire. The ambulance is on its way. All the time you're talking to me the ambulance is on its way. Okay?'

'Okay.'

'Are you with the man now?'

'Yeah, I'm with him. He's right beside me. I think he's gone.' At that moment Jack emitted an enormous groan. It was a noise that started far down in his belly and burst from his mouth with a splutter. 'No, he's alive!'

'Is he conscious?'

'I don't think so. I don't know. He just groaned.'

'Yes or no, Claire – is he conscious?'

'No.'

'Is he breathing?'

'Maybe. I can't tell.'

'Can you check for me, Claire?'

She leant closer, put her ear to his mouth. Later, what she felt worst about was how revolted she'd been by the smell of vomit, and how, as Jack balanced between life and death, she'd prayed the operator wouldn't ask her to perform mouth to mouth. 'I think he's breathing. He's trying to breathe, I think.'

'Okay, that's good. You're doing well. Did you see him collapse?'

'I didn't. I just found him. I was out jogging and—'

'How old is he?'

'He's old, really old.'

'Can you see any visible wound?'

'No. He's been sick. He's been sick and I think he's wet himself.'

'Okay, do you know what I mean by the recovery position?'

'Where's the ambulance?'

'I need you to put him on his side in the recovery position. Can you do that for me?'

'Hang on. I need to put the phone down.' Claire heaved him onto his side. Jack's body felt empty and saggy, like the underbelly of a cat. She wasn't sure whether she'd done the recovery position right. A car passed, slowed, stopped. A man watched her for a few seconds and then got out. Claire fantasised that he'd turn out to be a doctor.

'Have you done that for me?' said the operator from the mobile at Claire's feet.

'Yes, there's someone else here now.'

'Is he okay?' asked the man. He kept his distance. He wasn't a doctor.

'Now I need you to look in his mouth, okay? Can you see any food or vomit in his mouth?' Jack's jaws were surprisingly difficult to prise apart. He let out another groan and tried to speak.

'He's trying to speak,' said the man.

Claire imagined that Jack's first words upon recovery – because surely now he was going to recover – would be to ask her and the man and the operator whether any of them were adopted.

'There are some bits in his mouth.'

'Okay, Claire, you're doing great. I need you to reach in with your finger and, very carefully, pull those bits out.'

'Where's the ambulance? Come on! They need to hurry up!'

'The ambulance is just around the corner. It'll be with you any minute.'

Claire reached into Jack's mouth, poked between his toothless gums, lifted his leathery tongue, and scooped out green and red phlegm and bile and part-digested food. And then, in the distance, she heard the sirens, and she saw the lights, and the paramedics parked kerbside, and they exited the vehicle at a stubbornly-steady pace, which simultaneously frustrated Claire and brought to the scene a welcome sense of calm.

She rode with Jack in the ambulance, conscious that her fingers were still wet with his drool and vomit. She would have been more repulsed had she not been in shock; as the adrenaline left her system, she began to shake, teeth chattering, as if *she* had collapsed. Later, she couldn't remember much about the ambulance ride, except that given the noise of the sirens, and the pace they must have been driving at, the journey was surprisingly smooth. When they arrived at the hospital, the paramedics threw the ambulance doors open, and on a count of three they lifted Jack's stretcher onto a hospital trolley. He was underneath a grey blanket, unconscious, wearing an oxygen mask. Never rushing, they pushed him through the automatic doors, and Claire followed, ignored now. For a minute, Jack was parked in the A&E waiting room. The paramedics spoke to the receptionist, argued with a nurse (Claire couldn't hear what they were saying, but the body language of all three suggested mutual antagonism), and then they shoved the trolley towards the emergency room, through swinging double doors, and out of Claire's view.

Claire took a seat in the waiting room, unsure whether she was allowed to follow the trolley. To her left, a short-haired girl held a blood-soaked dishtowel over her right hand. Behind her, an older woman elevated a sore ankle. Near the door, an adolescent boy in cricket whites cradled his left hand, and at the far side of the room, a man wearing dirty jeans punched and shook the vending machine.

After a minute or two, the paramedics walked past Claire, sharing a joke as they returned to their ambulance. 'Excuse me,' said Claire. 'Is he going to be okay?'

'He's in good hands. He's comfortable now, and they'll do all they can for him.'

'Be good if you could stick around,' said the other paramedic; 'the nurse will want to talk with you.'

Claire thanked them for their help and retook her seat. It didn't sound good, she thought. On the ophthalmology ward the doctors and nurses said 'he's comfortable' and 'we'll do all we can' when a patient was admitted with irreversible ocular trauma, or advanced diabetic retinopathy, or some other condition where the prognosis was fairly hopeless.

She looked through the magazines, flicked through pictures of bikini bodies and fashion disasters. She read a comparison of how

Kate Moss and Kate Middleton were performing as wives. She read about a Chinese woman who was forced to have an abortion. She looked at celebs on yachts. She looked at magnified celebrity cellulite. She learned the things '*we*' like, and she wondered whether she was part of that 'we'. (Did it refer to the magazine's editors? The magazine's readers? All women? A certain kind of woman? Those women who have achieved a certain standard of womanhood?) She learned that she applied her eyeliner incorrectly. She learned that she should wear more yellow. She learned that she should diet. She learned that if she wanted to conceive she needed to increase her uptake of folic acid.

She read this stuff for fifteen minutes, until a nurse exited the emergency ward and scanned the waiting room uncertainly. Claire could see the nurse excluding the injured and their relatives. She approached Claire hesitantly. 'Is it Claire?' she asked. She spoke with an Irish accent. 'You're a relative of the older fellow that just got brought in?'

Claire explained that she wasn't a relative, but that she had found Jack unconscious and had ridden with him in the ambulance.

'Would you happen to know his full name?' asked the nurse. 'He's not been able to tell us.'

'I just know him as Jack. People call him Old Man Jack. He lives at St. Michael's Residential Care Home, in South Manchester.'

'That's a big help,' said the nurse. 'We'll give them a call.'

'How's he doing?'

The nurse, a smiley woman by nature, affected a grave expression. Claire could imagine that during her training she had practised that expression in front of a mirror. 'We'll need to do some tests, I'm afraid. He's very sick, but he's comfortable, and he's in good hands.'

An hour later, Seth arrived. Claire looked up from an article in an old edition of *Look* – 'The Rise of the "Drip Feed" Generation' – and saw he was waiting at the reception desk. Given she'd been afraid of Seth until a few days ago, she was surprised that now her immediate reaction was to run to his side. 'Seth!' she said.

At first he looked shocked – appalled – to see her again, but he relaxed when she explained what she was doing there. They sat together, both resting their chins in their hands, their elbows on their knees. Claire was still wearing her running gear – Lycra leggings, a zip-up sports top, and a bum bag that held her purse and phone. It was not a flattering look, and she worried that she smelled of BO. 'Are you here to take him home?' she asked.

'Depends,' said Seth. 'The doctor's gonna come see me in a bit.'

'What time do you finish at?'

'Work? I were on the early today: six till two.'

Claire looked at the clock, saw it was after three. 'Will you get overtime?'

Seth laughed. 'I'm not working just now. I just— Jack hasn't got any relatives, you get me? Like, when he comes round or whatever, I want him to see somebody he knows. Nowadays, he knows me as well as he knows anybody.'

'That's really sweet of you,' said Claire.

Seth looked embarrassed, pulled out a packet of tobacco. 'Yeah, I'm a real boy scout, innit?' He started to roll a cigarette.

Maybe it was a reaction to the trauma of discovering Jack unconscious, or maybe she just wanted a moment of companionship, but Claire felt a great urge to join Seth for a smoke. 'Do you think maybe I could have one of those?' she asked.

'Sure,' said Seth, passing her the tobacco and Rizla.

Claire held them in her lap, embarrassed she didn't know what to do.

'You can't roll?' asked Seth. 'Here, swap.' He passed her the cigarette he'd made and started to roll himself a new one.

Outside, they walked far from the hospital doors, and then they smoked in silence, watching the carousel of ambulances. 'You know Jack,' said Claire. 'Every time I saw him, he asked me if I was adopted.'

'He asked everyone that,' said Seth. 'He didn't ask me, mind you. He knew it couldn't be me.'

'What couldn't be you?'

'He were looking for his child. He knew I couldn't be his child because—' Seth stopped. Perhaps he'd realised, as Claire had realised, that they were talking about Jack in the past tense. 'Jack's lived an amazing life, you know?' Seth continued. 'Did you know he were a pro-golfer?'

'Yeah, my neighbour's dad said something about that.'

'He made enough money to build a golf course – you can see it from his room at the home. But before all that, he came here to work the fields. This were years and years ago, before the war, you get me? Back when Jack were a teenager, which is hard to imagine, right, but one summer he falls in love with this girl from the village – St. Michael's was just a village back then, yeah? He's in love with this girl called Ellie, right, and so they're, I don't know, rolling about in haystacks and whatever. And you can imagine what happens, right? He gets her knocked up, innit? So – and this is his story anyway – he's in love, right, and when they can't hide her bump no more, he goes to ask her father if he can marry her, yeah? Now, when the father finds out what's been going on, he's proper crazy, yeah? Like, for a start, Jack's an uneducated farmhand. A casual labourer, you get me? What's more, his daughter's been doing it unmarried, right? This guy – the dad – is, like, totally Christian – he's a priest or summat, yeah?'

'Oh shit,' said Claire. 'Let me guess – the family emigrated. They went abroad to do missionary work.'

'Yeah, exactly,' said Seth, surprised. 'The dad couldn't live with the shame, yeah?'

'Oh shit,' said Claire, throwing her cigarette away and holding her head in her hands.

'The father keeps Ellie in the house, cause he don't want her to see Jack, yeah, and cause he don't want people to know about her sin or whatever. And then, like you say, he announces in a sermon that they're leaving England to do the Lord's work overseas.'

'So Jack never saw her again.'

'Well, on the day they were leaving, Jack hid in the bushes, right, and he watched them packing, you get me? He'd hoped he'd get a chance to speak to Ellie alone. Like, if the father went indoors and left her outside, he'd call her over, yeah? Well, Ellie's dad weren't taking any chances, right, and so Jack never got to speak to her. But he did see her. How's it Jack puts it? She weren't "with child" no more. You get me? She didn't have a baby and she weren't pregnant no more.'

'Oh shit,' said Claire, almost not wanting to listen.

'So Jack figured they must have put the baby up for adoption, yeah? He went off in the world, played all this golf, fought in the war, but sooner or later he knew he were going to come back for his child. This Ellie, right, were like his one true love, you get me? So he came back, opened his golf course, and investigated people who'd adopted babies in 1936. He never found his child, and in the end he went crazy. Now he just walks the area of the old village, asking strangers of all different ages if they're adopted. Proper sad, innit?'

'I know what happened to his child,' said Claire. 'I think you better see this.' In her purse, she still carried the newspaper article about the baby's skeleton that was found in the church house. It was crumpled and smudged and torn at the corners, but she unfolded it and passed it to Seth. When he realised what he was reading, when he saw how the dates coincided, he slumped against the wall.

'I spoke to a neighbour of mine, Mrs Brompton, who lived in the church house as a little girl. The family that lived there before her – the family that lived there in 1936 – were called the Robertsons, or something like that. The father was a priest. They moved abroad to do missionary work.'

Eventually, Seth handed back the article. 'From the cradle to the grave,' he said.

Twelve

WHEN THEY LEARNED that Jack would be staying in hospital overnight, Claire gave Seth her mobile number and he promised to call her when he heard anything. This he did the following night. It was not good news. Jack had stomach cancer. The cancer was advanced, inoperable. The doctors gave him only days to live.

'It's spread to his liver and pancreas. They said chemo might buy him time, but not at his age, you get me?'

'Can I go to see him?' asked Claire.

'Sure,' said Seth, 'but he's back here now. The hospital couldn't do anything except smack him up against the pain, yeah? The nurses here can do that just as well. I figured if he's gonna die, he'd sooner it were here, in view of where he met Ellie, in view of his golf course. You know?'

'Yeah, I do. When should I come?'

'Soon. I hate to say it, but Jack's got no use for a year planner.'

'Tonight?'

'That'd be good, Claire. I gotta go home soon – I'm on the early tomorrow – and it'd be nice if there were someone to sit with him tonight. Just for a bit, yeah?'

When Claire hung up, Dan shouted from the living room. 'Who was that?'

'Seth,' said Claire.

'Seth? Who the fuck's Seth?'

Claire didn't answer. She wasn't silent because she was guilty, or because she had anything to hide; she was silent because she had no idea how to explain who Seth was. What would she say? He's the guy who spray-painted our fence? He's a Care Assistant at a nursing home I nearly got thrown out of? He rolled me a cigarette when I was at the hospital, waiting on news about an old man called Jack? She realised how much of her life Dan knew nothing about. They had stopped communicating.

'Well,' said Dan, as Claire walked past him, 'who is he?'

'He works at the nursing home. I've been visiting a terminally ill patient.'

'You've been visiting a terminally ill— since when?'

'Since yesterday.'

'What, yesterday, all of a sudden, you've decide you're Florence Nightingale or summat?'

'I found him collapsed and I rode with him in the ambulance and at the hospital I met this Seth guy who I already knew because— Look, it doesn't really matter. I have to go out.' She squeezed her shoes on, examined herself in the mirror.

'You're going out, now? It's after eight.'

'I know. He's got stomach cancer. I—'

'Why haven't you told me about any of this?'

She closed the door decisively – not quite a slam – and she strode past Neville Shaw's shiny Jaguar. She saw Shaw letting himself into Lianne's house, and she called a cheery greeting. Shaw turned, lifting his hand in vague recognition as Claire crossed onto the riverside pathway. The water was streaked red by the setting sun, and Claire wondered whether, after two days of drizzle, the warm weather was set to return. She paused on the bridge, watched long fingers of waterweed reaching downstream with the current. She was hesitating, she knew, because she didn't know what to say to Jack. Would she tell him the truth and break his heart before he died? Or would she let him die without ever finding out what happened to his baby? Both options seemed awful.

She crossed the woodchip path, heard an owl hoot from the sycamore trees. If she already felt foreboding, the nursing home did not put her at ease. They had painted the window frames sky-blue, perhaps to brighten its façade, but the turrets and pointed doorways suggested the building, like the church house, might hold some macabre secret. When something flapped from the clock tower, she looked up expecting to see a bat, but it was a collared dove that flew to the trees, landing heavily, sagging the branch upon which it sat.

Inside, she saw to her dismay that the desk was manned by Amy, the same receptionist whom she had encountered before.

'Yes?' said Amy.

'I'm here to see Jack.'

'Lost his keys, has he?'

'Seth's expecting me.'

This obviously hurt Amy, and she glanced down – a look of defeat. Then she grabbed the radio and said, 'Seth, visitor for Jack. Says you're expecting her.'

A few seconds later, her radio crackled with Seth's reply. 'Okay, I'll come down and show her through.'

Amy didn't respond. She filed her nails, ignoring Claire who took a seat as far from the desk as possible. When Seth arrived, Claire stood up to follow him, remembering to thank Amy for her help. Amy smiled sarcastically and returned to filing her nails – at least there was one thing she knew how to file.

Claire followed Seth, past side tables busy with flowers, down a corridor that was wallpapered peach with a lilac border. Through an open door she saw a woman pulling at her grey hair. As they started up a spiral staircase, the lift door opened and a middle-aged nurse wheeled out a mobile stand holding a blood pressure monitor, a pulse oximeter, and other equipment Claire didn't recognise. 'You still here, Seth?' she called.

'You know I can't stay away from you, Mags.' They climbed up two floors and then Seth stopped beside a fire door. 'He's just down here. You going to tell him?'

'I don't know,' said Claire.

'Please don't, Claire? He doesn't need to know.'

Claire didn't say anything, but Seth took her silence as assent. He pushed open the fire door and led her past a common room, in which two old men played cards. 'Gambling again?' called Seth. 'These guys are sharks, Claire – they took me car last week, innit?' The men laughed. One of them had tubes entering either nostril. A third man slept in an armchair, wired to a drip.

'In here,' said Seth. Jack's room was like a hotel room from long ago. The bedside lamps were pink and there were fresh flowers on the writing desk. The curtains were pulled closed and the smell was awful – the same scent of lavender and urine and disinfectant, but also a gastric odour like nothing Claire had smelt before.

'There's someone to see you, Jack. This is Claire – she helped you after you fell.'

Jack didn't reply and it was unclear whether he'd heard. He was on his back, his gurgled breaths loosely in sync with the beep of an EKG.

'Hi Jack,' said Claire. She felt silly – she was speaking in the voice people use to address small children and pets.

'Am I okay to leave you two?'

Claire nodded, not really wanting Seth to go.

'The nurses will be in regularly, but if you need anything, press that button there, okay?'

When Seth had said goodbye to Jack, Claire sat on the suede armchair. She shuffled it as close to Jack as she dared. He was wearing a hospital gown, with red stains on its chest, and his yellow eyes were open but unfocused – Claire didn't know whether he could see her. 'How are you feeling, Jack?' She was very conscious of her own voice. It was like talking to yourself when you could be overheard. His right hand was white and hanging off the bed. She wondered whether she should lift it up, but it had an intravenous drip taped to the wrist, and she was worried she'd dislodge it. She sat in silence for a minute, listening to the beeps, the clatter of something metal spilled on the floor below, the click of a heater that smelled of singed hair.

What should she say? When visiting the terminally ill – she had no idea where she'd heard this – you're supposed to say something interesting about the outside world. She wished she'd learned something about golf – she could have told him who won the Open or something like that. His colostomy bag – an awful amber colour – was lashed to the side of the bed. She averted her eyes and watched a bubble swim to the surface of the saline solution that hung above them on a tall stand.

'Listen, Jack,' she said. 'There's a particular reason why I wanted to talk to you. It's about your child.'

It wasn't a big change in his posture, but Jack's facial muscles twitched, and he nodded slightly, and he tried to say something.

'I know what happened to your . . . daughter,' said Claire. She had no idea whether what she was doing was right, but it was now too late to stop.

Jack hawked phlegm and writhed in pain. He might have been trying to repeat 'daughter,' but Claire couldn't be sure.

'She was named Ellie, after her mother. Ellie . . . Robertson. She lives in . . . Australia. In Melbourne. I found out about her on the internet. You know those modern computers, Jack? You know, you can find all sorts of things on those computers. She has a website, all about how she had to leave England and about her life in Australia. She's old herself now, Jack, but for years she was a . . . ' Claire couldn't think what job to give her. 'She ran an equestrian school. She worked with horses and taught little girls to ride. And her husband's an accountant, so he handles all the business side of it. They have two kids, a boy and a girl – your grandchildren, Jack. The girl, Jane, is a real beauty – she was Miss Australia when she was younger – and the boy's . . . The boy's called Jack, after you, I guess. And he must take after you because he's a really good golfer.'

Claire talked like this for hours. Sometimes a nurse would come in to check on Jack, change his drip, or inject him with more pain relief, and Claire would pause to exchange pleasantries with the nurse. But as soon as she and Jack were alone again, she would resume her stories. She told him about Ellie's house, and the problems they had with ducks in the swimming pool. She told him about the equestrian school and how it had begun when Ellie adopted two lame mules that were otherwise set for the knacker's yard, and how today they had eighty well-bred horses, and a canteen, and even a gift shop. She told him about Jane's wedding reception, which was held, she said, at a revolving seaside restaurant, from which guests could see the Great Barrier Reef. Sometimes she cried, but she kept talking for hours.

She woke in the armchair in the early a.m. Two nurses and a doctor had gathered around Jack's bed, and somehow Claire knew immediately that he was dead.

Thirteen

IT WAS STRANGE to witness the early-morning rush in the nursing home. All over St. Michael's, people were still asleep, but in the nursing home, breakfast trays were being wheeled on rattling trolleys, and sleepy-eyed nurses, their breath smelling of coffee, hurried from room to room dispensing medicines. It was something Claire had never understood: why do old people get up so early? You would think that in retirement, freed from the pressures of work, pensioners would exert their well-earned right to doze until noon. She suspected there was some biological explanation, but she preferred to think that life, in one's twilight years, becomes something valuable that ought not to be wasted in bed.

A nurse led Claire to a reception room, a ground-floor version of the common room in which she'd seen the men playing cards. It had basket chairs and coffee tables, and its walls were adorned with oil paintings of cherubic children at play. The nurse offered consolations, thinking Claire was a granddaughter or some other relation. Claire kept apologising for having fallen asleep, but she realised that the nurse, despite her kindness, was exhausted and not really listening. 'You have a seat here,' she said. 'Rosie, will you fix this woman a cuppa, please?'

At ten to six, Seth arrived for work, and before starting his duties, he called in to see Claire. 'You okay?' he asked. He was still adjusting his blue polyester uniform.

'Yeah,' she said. 'You?'

'Always,' said Seth. 'You wanna go out for a smoke before I start?'

They walked out to the front of the home and stood quietly as Seth rolled two cigarettes. Claire watched the day awakening. The sky was shades of purple and blue, the edges of morning light golden on the leaves of the sycamore trees. The birds were louder than she'd ever heard them – a chorus of defiant tweets and chirps and coos – and the lawn was dark green, beaded with dew, its scent rising and fresh.

'I lied to Jack,' she said, as they started to smoke. 'I told him that his daughter lived in Australia. I made up a whole life for her, with kids and a husband and an equestrian school. I couldn't tell him the truth.'

Seth thought about this, blew smoke into the damp morning air. 'You did a good thing. He'll have died happy. I've seen a lot of people die – trust me, most of them don't die happy.' An ambulance rolled up the driveway, its headlights still on. No need for sirens now.

'What'll you do now, Seth?'

'I'll collect the breakfast trays, load the dishwasher, and then I'll assist the oldies bathing. What about you?'

Claire shrugged. 'Go home, try to sleep, argue with my husband.'

The ambulance driver backed up to the nursing home and opened the ambulance's rear doors, ready to receive Jack. Seth and Claire were still outside when they wheeled him down the ramp. Claire heard the trolley clatter into the ambulance, the slam of the doors. She didn't look.

As the engine started, a woman in a nightdress ran out to see the ambulance depart. She was younger than most of the residents, and she looked unusually healthy. 'They're taking Jack, aren't they?' she said to Seth. 'He's gone and died, hasn't he? I knew it!' She grabbed her hair and started to pull, hard, as if wishing to rip it out.

'Don't do that, Mrs Shaw,' said Seth.

'I knew it!' she said, gouging her cheeks with her nails.

'Come on now,' said Seth, grabbing Mrs Shaw's wrists. 'It's okay.'

'He promised!'

'Were you very close?' asked Claire.

'Close?' said Mrs Shaw. '"Are you adopted?" "Are you adopted?" "Are you adopted?" Day after bloody day. No! I'm bloody not. He stank – that's the truth. And he was a Pisces. You know what that means, don't you?'

'I think you had a secret crush, Mrs Shaw,' said Seth.

'I'm a happily married woman, I'll have you know. And I've always hated fish. Even when I was a little girl, I didn't like fish. But that old git promised!'

'What did he promise you, Mrs Shaw?' asked Seth.

'My husband's coming this week. And my daughter.'

'What's your daughter's name, Mrs Shaw. Can you remember?'

'Yes, of course I can remember.' Mrs Shaw lifted the hem of her nightdress and stamped back up the ramp.

'What did Jack promise her?' asked Claire, when Mrs Shaw was back indoors.

'He said she could watch the demolition from his window. Jack's room had a good view of the tower block, you get me? She used to live in the flats, yeah, so she wants to see them come down,' said Seth. 'That's the woman I told you about. Sometimes she wakes in the night screaming and shouting and pulling her hair. But if you talk to her about it during the day, she'll only talk about how much she loves her husband and daughter. It's sweet, you get me? She can't hardly remember their names, but she knows how much she loves them.'

'Am I right in thinking she's Neville Shaw's wife? Has a daughter called Lianne?'

'That sounds familiar, but they don't come that often, you know? The husband's a Scottish guy. Moustache.'

'Yeah, that's Neville,' said Claire.

'Listen, I better clock in. You sure you'll be okay?'

'Of course.' Claire patted Seth on the shoulder. 'Stay out of trouble, okay?'

'Sure. I'm a boy scout, right?' He started to walk up the ramp, but when he reached the front door, Claire called him back.

'Hey, Seth,' she said. 'You know the young girl who sometimes works on reception?'

'Amy?'

'That's the one. You do know she's madly in love with you, right?'

Seth laughed. 'Amy? No way. She wouldn't go for someone like me.'

'She's crazy about you.'

'Really? I can't see that. She's never said anything.'

'Well,' said Claire, laughing, 'welcome to suburbia: everyone has a secret.' She turned for home but she looked back a second later and saw Seth entering the nursing home with a bounce in his step that defied the early hour.

She didn't go straight home. Instead, she walked the second-half of her circuit, head bowed in thought. At this time of the morning, she saw a totally different set of people. She saw old men with droopy-eared dogs. She saw wiry runners in fluorescent tops, pounding the grit path. She climbed up to the flyover and watched the one-way rush of commuter traffic. She saw delivery drivers, their shifts nearly finished, shaking themselves alert as they sped towards their depots.

She looked back at the mobile phone mast and thought about Morgana and her campaign. There was no grand conspiracy, she realised. The entombment of Jack's baby was a tragedy, but it wasn't connected to the miscarriages and deformities. What mattered, she decided, was to ensure that another tragedy didn't occur. She looked back at the tower block: how many days until demolition? Three, she thought. What day was it? Thursday . . . Thursday! She'd totally forgotten about her interview.

She ran home to find Dan in his pyjamas, eating cereal in front of breakfast TV. 'Hi, Sweetie,' she said. 'How are you?'

Dan threw his spoon into his bowl, splashing milk onto the carpet. He stood up and crashed through to the kitchen.

'Dan?' said Claire, following him.

He dumped his bowl in the sink and turned the tap on, full blast, so that its spray fanned out, splashing the floor and worktop. 'How am I?' he said, turning to face her. 'I've been up half the night worrying about you! You come in at 7:30 – fuck knows where you've been – and the first thing you say is "how are you, Sweetie?" How d'you think I am?'

She reached out to hold him, but he pushed her away.

'Where you been, Claire?'

She reached for him again but he pushed her away so hard that her back crashed against the worktop.

'Ugh,' he said – he seemed genuinely revolted by her.

'The guy I was visiting died – I fell asleep in his room. I would have phoned but by the time I woke—'

'What have I done to deserve this? It's not enough that you stay out all night, but you come home and insult me with this—'

'It's true,' said Claire. 'His name was Jack.' She wondered whether she would believe Dan if he stayed out and in the morning told her he'd fallen asleep in the room of a terminally ill cancer victim. Probably not.

'Why d'you wait till now? Why wait till we've bought the house and everything. Jesus, Claire – if you weren't happy, why didn't you say so before?'

'I was happy, Dan. I was, I really was.'

'And now you're not?'

'Dan, I've got my interview at nine. Can we do this later?'

Dan ran upstairs and slammed the bedroom door. Claire chased after him and tried to push the door open, but he'd locked it. 'Let me in, Dan, please?'

'I'm changing. Do you mind?'

'Come on, Dan – don't leave things like this. Not today.' She took the key from the spare room and tried it in their bedroom lock – it didn't fit.

She could hear him crashing drawers, throwing clothes against the wall. After a minute, he shouted through the door, 'I won't be home tonight. Don't call me.'

'Where you going?'

'It's none of your business, Claire. You've lost your right to ask.'

When Dan left the house, Claire listened as he screeched the car out the driveway and sped towards St. Michael's Street. She entered the bedroom, viewed the damage. All her dresses had been dragged from the wardrobe, thrown across the floor. Her shoes were scattered across the bed. She tipped them off, too rushed and tired to right the mess, and then she stripped, throwing her dirty clothes on top of her clean ones.

Naked, she searched for something suitable to wear. She found a blouse and a smart black skirt. The blouse was creased and the shirt smelled musty from having been too long in storage. She searched for the iron and couldn't find it – Dan wore blue polyester work shirts that he never ironed, and Claire realised she hadn't seen the iron since they moved. Perhaps it was in the loft? There was no time to look, so she hung the skirt and blouse in the bathroom and turned the shower up until the room filled with steam.

When she'd washed, dried, and straightened her hair, she checked the clock on the bedside table: 8:05. She had no idea how long it would take to get to the hospital and she knew no Manchester taxi numbers, so she typed 'taxi Manchester' into her phone and waited while GPRS cranked into life. While she waited, she began to search for underwear. She needed a white bra to go under her blouse, but where were they all? In desperation, she started looking through the dirty laundry basket, but soon realised that anything that had been in proximity to Dan's dirty football kit could not now be rescued. Black bra? Red bra? *No* bra?

She arrived at Wythenshawe Hospital, two minutes before her interview was due to start. The Iranian taxi driver had spent much of the journey describing the almond-filled *Qottab* pastries that were a delicacy in his home town of Yazd, but Claire was too stressed to understand why he thought this relevant.

Inside, she waited her turn at the main reception desk as an older man stooped over the receptionist, telling a story that seemed to concern his throat. 'So the doctor says to me that I had to get them cut out – me, what d'you call them?'

'Tonsils?' asked the receptionist.

'Course this were in the fifties, you know? So it were all different then. Didn't look like this at all. But it were me ma, walked up here with me, and I had me jim-jams folded under me arm, you know? And it were Christmas, I remember, cause after I'd woke up I were sat under a tree, you know? A Christmas tree. And in those days—'

'I'm sorry,' said Claire, 'I'm really sorry to butt in, but I'm here to interview for the position of medical secretary to the urology ward and—'

'What's that, love?' asked the receptionist. 'The urology ward? You go down there past the toilets, yeah, and you follow the yellow route, right, until you get to the outpatients' wing, and then you turn left onto the green route, till you can go up the stairs, okay, and then you're going sort of that way,' she said, pointing, 'onto the first floor green route, and you keep going until you get to the F block, and then—'

'Great, thank you,' said Claire, running in the direction of the first instruction (the only instruction she remembered), as the old man resumed his tale.

Ten minutes later she arrived at the urology ward, which she soon discovered wasn't where the interviews were taking place. Having left her confirmation letter at home, Claire had no choice but to admit that she was hopelessly lost, and, five minutes later, after the receptionist had phoned a dozen people on her behalf, the only consolation Claire could think of was that the receptionist seemed like a very nice person to work alongside. 'Okay,' said the receptionist, finally hanging up the phone in relief. 'You should be down in the Education and Research Unit. Go back out the way you came in, turn left then right, then follow the green route until you get to the stairs. You want to go down the stairs, turn right past the café, and switch on to the orange route. You follow that round the corner, turn right, and you should see the South Entrance. When you get to the South Entrance—'

'Brilliant, got it – thank you,' said Claire, and once again she started to run.

By the time she was admitted to the holding room, Claire was twenty-five minutes late. A man in glasses showed her to a seat and handed her a clipboard that contained a personal questionnaire and a filing test. The other applicants seemed to have finished their tests and were making small talk about hospital experiences: a freckly woman was sharing a story about a man who'd presented to doctors with an Elvis Presley statue stuck in his rectum.

Claire tried to block this out and concentrate on the filing test: 19119 came before 19919, which came before 91191, which came before 99119, which came before 99191. But which came first out of Marshall and McGregor? She couldn't think. She was halfway through the test when the door opened and a woman in a trouser suit called her name.

The interview panel was comprised of this woman (who smelled of potpourri), a fat bald man whose head was striped with rivulets of sweat, and an older man whose eyebrows reminded Claire of snowy mountains. 'May I take your test and questionnaire?' asked the woman.

'I haven't finished the test,' said Claire.

'Oh.'

'I was late, I'm afraid. Hospitals are really confusing!' she said with a laugh.

The sweaty man looked at the older man, who raised his mountainous eyebrows and murmured something about that being why they employed secretaries.

'Sit down, sit down,' said the woman.

Claire sat, folding her arms to hide her black bra. It wasn't ideal body language. 'I don't find them confusing when I work in them,' said Claire. 'Hospitals, I mean. I worked very successfully at Birmingham Midland Eye Hospital.'

'And that's in your questionnaire response, I presume?'

'No, I didn't get round to the questionnaire because – The thing is . . . I know this doesn't look very good, but it's been a difficult couple of days. I was with a . . . with a patient all last night.'

'A patient?'

'Not my patient – I'm out of work just now.' '

'Somebody else's patient?'

'Yes.'

'I see.'

'And he died. I was talking to him, I fell asleep, and when I woke up . . . he was dead.'

The woman looked at the bald man who looked at the guy with the big eyebrows and all three looked totally at a loss.

'So you can imagine,' said Claire, 'that it's been a bit of a rush to get from there to here. I didn't even have time to find a white bra!' She laughed nervously as she unfolded her arms to reveal her bust.

For a long while, nobody spoke. Eventually the woman shrugged and referred to the questions in front of her. 'Okay,' she said, her tone procedural. 'What do you consider to be your biggest strength?'

'Timekeeping,' said Claire. Nobody laughed. 'Honestly, I haven't been late for work in forever. Today was most out of character. It's just been . . . one of those mornings. The taxi driver wouldn't stop talking about some Iranian—'

'And where do you see yourself in five years' time?'

Claire took a moment to think. It was hard to imagine; after all, that morning her husband had told her he wouldn't be coming home. 'I've always imagined starting a family,' she said, thinking aloud. And then she added, quickly, 'and I'd very much like to be part of a successful team on the urology ward at this hospital.'

From the panellists' expressions it was apparent they knew only one certainty about Claire's future. They could not say whether in five years' time she would be rearing a family or living as a man in the Albanian Alps. But they could say, with absolute certainty, that whatever else her future held, she would never work at Wythenshawe Hospital.

Fourteen

CLAIRE WALKED HOME, her eyes red from crying, her only thought to drink herself numb. There are explanations for many causes of unhappiness and envy: why do your friends have more friends than you have? Because you're more likely, statistically speaking, to be friends with people who have lots of friends. And if you go on a date, the chances are your date will be more experienced at dating than you are, because you're more likely, statistically speaking, to date someone who goes on a lot of dates. And if you go to the gym, chances are the girl on the next treadmill is fitter than you are, because – you guessed it – you're more likely, statistically speaking, to be in the gym alongside people who regularly go to the gym. That's all harsh but true. But nobody has yet come up with an adequate explanation for the triptych structure of misfortune – for why bad things come in threes.

Jack had died, the interview had been a disaster, and when Claire got home her house seemed to be undergoing some sort of quarantine. Men in high-visibility vests and hardhats were shouting and pointing, screeching duct tape from giant rolls, holding tarpaulin flapping in the wind. They seemed to be sealing up her windows, and her first thought was that Dan had somehow had her evicted. But as she got closer, she saw that they were doing the same to other houses: Lianne was on her doorstep, wearing a babydoll nightshirt and holding cups of tea; Morgana was blocking her gate, arguing furiously on the telephone.

'Hey!' said Claire, grabbing a man by the shoulder. 'What's going on?'

The man turned, startled but friendly-looking, and removed his hard hat. 'Don't worry, love, we'll be out your way in no time. She saw that he, and the other men, had 'Skacel & Black Demolition' printed on their luminous vests. 'It's just for the dust and any stray debris,' the man explained. Now, belatedly, Claire remembered something about this. 'It should all be contained in the demolition zone,' the man continued. 'We use water cannon to limit the spread of the dust, but you can never get it all.' He nodded towards the tower; 'That's a whole lot of building we're going to blow up.'

Amid the workmen's shouts, the hiss of the flatbed's airbrakes, the clatter of extendable ladders, and the sound of screeching tape, Claire could barely hear what Morgana was shouting, but she understood that Morgana was trying to halt the demolition. 'You don't know what you're doing,' she said. 'I am making a protest. That building cannot be demolished until you've taken our views into account.'

Morgana was too busy shouting into her telephone to acknowledge Claire or Lianne, though both were watching her. As Claire unlocked her door, she caught Lianne's eye, and they shared a conspiratorial look of bemusement.

Inside, Claire sat on the stairs wondering what to do. She was exhausted and upset and she wished only to go to bed, or to drink a bottle of wine, or, ideally, to drink a bottle of wine in bed. But she had no wine and it would be impossible to sleep while workmen were clambering outside her windows. She could hear the men all around her, closing her in, sealing her from the outside world, and she started to worry about the disarray her house was in. She had still not tidied up after Dan's tantrum, so her clothes were scattered across the bedroom floor. Dan's breakfast dishes still cluttered the living room. Worst of all, she had discarded her dirty underwear – where, she couldn't remember – and it had probably already become a workman's joke. Then she put her head in her hands and laughed. It felt like liberation. 'Who cares,' she said aloud. 'Who really fucking cares?'

By the time the workmen left, her windows offered the same visibility as salt-coated ferry portholes: through them she could see light and shapes, but all detail was blurred. She made herself a coffee and sat in the kitchen – where the patio doors had been covered over, rendering the garden inaccessible – and she considered what she ought to do about Dan. The first thing was to convince him that she wasn't having an affair, but then why should she? She *wasn't* having an affair, and the more she stressed that fact, the guiltier she would sound. Why did Claire feel that *she* had to make the peace?

In the early afternoon, the bell rang again, and Claire opened the door to Lianne. Lianne was wearing white jeans and a yellow boob tube. She'd painted her lips hot pink, and circled them with a redder lip liner. Through Lianne's sandals, Claire saw that the pink on her toenails had chipped to reveal a blackcurrant undercoat. Predictably, she was holding a bottle of white wine.

Claire found two glasses, unscrewed the wine. They sat at the kitchen table and Lianne leant forward as though afraid what she was about to say might be overheard. Her breath smelled of coffee and cigarettes. 'Did you see her this morning?' she asked.

'Morgana?'

'Like, what is wrong with her?'

'Who knows,' said Claire, glugging two fingers of wine.

'Do you think we should do something?'

Claire shrugged. 'Like what?'

'I dunno. Like, phone social services – like, both of us, you know? She's a devil worshipper and that's . . . I mean, knock yourself out, love. But she's got kids, innit? Like, she lets them play in that dirty old tower block, yeah? It's just not right. I mean, why would she want it to stay there?'

Claire poured more wine. It was the first time she'd ever drunk quicker than Lianne.

'You okay, honey?'

'Yeah, I'm fine. I just . . . I interviewed for this job this morning and—'

'How'd it go?' said Lianne, her voice trailing off as she realised the redundancy of the question. 'Not so well, huh?' She shuffled closer and seemed to be attempting some gesture of comfort – some expression of intimate female friendship and solidarity – but she seemed unsure what to do. A hug might have been welcome – albeit a bit over-familiar – and a squeeze of the hand would have been fine, but Lianne leant close to Claire, stroked Claire's fringe, and blinked her clumped lashes, as if making some clumsy advance. 'Don't worry about it. Work's shit anyway. Last job I had was on a sex line – swear down. I had to sit in this big open plan office in Deansgate, yeah, with all these fat old black women, and I had to get guys off, you know? I were too good at it, me. It were like you had to keep them on the line as long as possible, yeah, but my ones always spunked after two mins.'

Claire was crying a bit but laughing too.

Encouraged, Lianne continued. 'They were dead filthy, the callers. This one bloke, right, he phones up and asks me to torture him, yeah. So I were like, okay, get a glass and break it. So he does – I can hear him, yeah? And I says, put that broken glass in another glass of water, right, and then get your cock and balls and dunk them right in. He were loving it!'

Claire laughed again. It was both reassuring and frightening to be reminded that things could definitely be worse.

'See? Work's not worth worrying about, honey.' Lianne settled back in her chair and they lapsed into silence while they sipped their wine and stared in the direction of the garden.

After a while, Claire asked, 'What was it like to live there?'

'Where?'

'The tower.'

Lianne blew her fringe from her eyes, shrugged, swigged some wine. 'Yeah, it were okay. Like . . . One day, I'll never forget this, when I were little, I got into the lift and there were a man, like, lying unconscious holding his dick, yeah? Like, his trousers were round his ankles and— He'd wet himself, yeah? Like, he were a junkie and he'd, like . . . He were going to inject himself into his dick, yeah?' Lianne laughed. 'Me mam grabbed me, pulled me out the lift, cause I were just staring, and— But that were only one time. He were just some bum who'd come in for a place to shoot up. I mean, there were really good people who lived there. Like, across the landing from us, yeah, the Hoggs – they were really good people. They used to let me stay with them, after school, just, like, do some colouring in, watch some TV. Like, you think we were all just chavs and scallies, yeah, but it weren't like that. There were good people. A lot of good people. A lot of bad people too, you know? Last time I seen me mam, yeah, they'd given her some drugs or summat, and she were all weird and slurring, and she would only talk about how she wanted to see the tower explode. Like, she called it "a place of evil" and that surprised me cause she'd never said nothing like that before. But I know what she meant, I think. Like, I won't be sorry when it's gone. That Morgana, mind you – like, what's she doing in—'

'I met your mum this morning,' said Claire.

This seemed to make Lianne uncomfortable. She shrugged – a petulant adolescent gesture of 'so what' – and then she picked up her cigarettes. 'Can I smoke here?' she asked.

Claire shook her head. 'I'm sorry, Dan would—'

'Yeah, I heard you two this morning,' said Lianne. 'You okay?'

'Of course. I— He thinks I'm having an affair.'

'Yeah, well, if he were, like, a little bit better in the sack then maybe you wouldn't be looking elsewhere, right?'

'What do you— How do you know what he's . . . '

Lianne flicked open a compact and checked her makeup. Incredibly, she seemed satisfied with what she saw. 'Oh, come on,' she said after a moment. 'Like, your bedroom's through the wall from mine, yeah? See the couple that lived here before you, yeah? Like, I don't know what he were doing to her, but I'd have liked a shot, you know? I mean, they were . . . you know, like, Asian or whatever. But she were screaming every other night. He must have been working his way through the Karma Sutra or summat. They're meant to have really small dicks, aren't they? I wouldn't have minded a go on his, mind— Hey, hon, I haven't offended you, have I? Hey, at least you've *got* a husband, right?'

Claire tried to smile. This exposure of her sex life – or lack thereof – felt to her like a violation.

'Come on,' said Lianne, rubbing Claire's shoulder. 'Let's go out for a fag.'

'I don't think we can,' said Claire, nodding at the tarpaulin that covered the patio doors.

'Just cut a door in it,' said Lianne. 'That's what I did. She stood up, shook open Claire's kitchen drawers, and then spotted the knife block near the cooker. Holding a cook's knife, Lianne looked more like a serial killer than a chef.

'Is that allowed?' asked Claire, but Lianne had already opened one side of the door and was lunging and stabbing at the tarpaulin window. She stuck the knife through the plastic and then hacked a slash across at shoulder height. Then she sawed downwards, pulling the flap of tarpaulin. Soon she had cut an opening big enough that she could pass through it at a stoop. 'Come on,' she called, throwing the knife point-first into the lawn.

Outside, under the parasol, Claire accepted a cigarette and sat with her knees pulled to her chin.

'So, who's the guy?' asked Lianne.

'What guy?'

'The one you were out with last night.'

'Last night I was with a ninety-year-old man who was dying of stomach cancer.'

'Takes all sorts, I suppose.'

'Lianne!'

'Come on, I'm not gonna tell.'

'I'm serious – I was with that guy Jack. You know the one who asked everyone if they were adopted? Well, he died last night.' Claire described how she'd met Seth, how she'd found Jack collapsed, and how she'd sat at his bedside and lied about his child.

'You poor pet,' said Lianne, leaning forward, her big breasts resting on the table.

Claire leant back, realised her cigarette had burned to the butt, stubbed it out. 'And then, in the morning, I met your mother.'

Lianne lit another cigarette, sat back in her chair. 'Yeah, well, you can't listen to nothing she says. Like, she's lost the plot, hasn't she?'

'She said you were visiting her this week?'

Lianne shrugged – the same adolescent gesture of 'so what'. 'Maybe,' she said, looking towards Morgana's house.

'What do you think your mum meant when she described the tower as "a place of evil"?'

'She said that to you?'

'No, you told me she said that a minute ago.'

'Yeah, well, like I say – you can't listen to what she says too much.' They sat quietly, the only noise Lianne splashing more wine into their glasses. 'Listen,' said Lianne, leaning in with her conspiratorial air, 'wait till you hear this. The other day, yeah, I saw something that was, like, weird, but that at the time I didn't think much of.'

'Okay,' said Claire.

'I was going to the get the bus, to go into town, yeah, and I was walking along by the river, right, and I— You know Adrian, Morgana's husband?'

Claire nodded.

'Well, he's got this little, like, boat, you know?'

'I've seen it,' said Claire. 'Like a canoe or a kayak or something?'

'That's it. I don't know if you know this, right, but he often paddles this thing along at the back of the tower block.'

'I've seen him going that way, yeah.'

'This day I'm talking about, right, he'd, like, pulled up at the riverside – a few metres from the tower – and he were talking to a guy with a pram.'

'What did the pram guy look like?'

Lianne tried to think. 'He wore, like, a black bomber jacket.'

'That's the guy I saw!'

'Tattoos on his knuckles?'

'Yeah, that's him.'

'Well, Adrian had summat with him in the boat. It was, like, sort of a bundle. Like, the size of a small child, but all wrapped up. Anyway, he took this thing out and gave it to the pram guy.'

'What did he do with it?'

'He's, like, put it in the pram, yeah, and then he's given summat to Adrian out of his jacket.'

'What was it?'

'I couldn't see. Summat small enough it fit in his hand. It could have been money. I don't know.'

Claire squeezed her cheekbones, deep in thought. Lianne watched Claire think in silence.

'And then?' Claire asked.

'I didn't see nothing more. Like I say, I didn't think much of it until today. What d'you think they were doing?'

'I don't know,' said Claire, lighting another cigarette. 'We need to search the tower.'

'No way,' said Lianne.

'We have to.'

'It's too dangerous. Look, it's falling down and— There could be explosives and stuff.'

'We can't let them blow it up until we've figured out what's going on inside.'

'I'm not going in there,' said Lianne. 'Like, I'll do anything to help you, Claire, but I'm not doing that, yeah? That place creeps me out too much.'

'Aren't you curious?'

'Sure I am. But we don't know what we're messing with. Black magic and sacrifices and who the hell knows what? Trust me, Claire, it's like— Listen,' Lianne said, whispering, 'you've got to leave this to the proper channels, yeah? Like, we phone Childline or whatever, okay? We get, like, social services involved and then— Look, they'll get Mooncloud and Unity out of harm's way and then— They'll get to the bottom of it, won't they?'

'Meanwhile the tower's demolished and whatever's inside is lost forever?'

'Don't you think they check these things? Like, they make sure a building's empty before they blow it up, you know.'

'I don't know,' said Claire. 'I'd feel happier if we looked ourselves.'

Lianne shook her head vigorously. 'It isn't safe. And you're getting too stressed, yeah? Listen, Claire, when's the last time you had any real fun?'

Claire smiled, but she didn't answer.

'This is Madchester, yeah? You should be mad for it, right?'

'I'm a married woman,' said Claire, laughing. 'I'm nearly thirty.'

'Yeah, and, like, you look amazing. I mean, I'd love to have your thighs. Have you even been up town yet?'

Claire shook her head. 'I made it to the local pub once.'

'Hon, maybe Dan doesn't see how sexy you are, but you're— Listen, tonight, we're going out—'

'I'd love to, Lianne. I really would. But I can't – I really have to speak to Dan.'

'Claire, when you guys are shouting, I can't help but hear. Dan won't be coming home tonight, will he?'

Once again, Claire didn't answer.

'So . . . while the cat's away . . . Come on, what d'you say? Girls night out, yeah? You come round mine about six. We get made up, have a few drinks, hit the town.'

'It's really kind of you, Lianne – I do appreciate it – but I think I'm a bit past it.'

'You're only as young as you feel,' said Lianne, squeezing Claire's thigh, 'and you feel pretty young to me.'

Claire laughed nervously. She felt trapped and coerced, but she was also desperate to say yes. She was reminded of how it felt to be hit on when she was younger. Even when she was talking to a guy she really fancied, as soon as he showed any interest, one part of her had always felt as if something obscene was being forced on her. Of course, another (secret) part of her had thrilled at the attention, had longed to feel the guy pressed against her. And when, inevitably, the guy had turned his attention to another girl – when Claire's shyness, her inability to flirt, her apparent coldness and disinterest, had driven him to one of Claire's more appealing rivals – she had always felt a pang of hurt and loneliness.

'Okay,' said Claire; 'we'll go out. Just for a bit. Not—'

'Yes!' said Lianne, pumping her fist. 'You'll come round mine at six?'

'Okay,' said Claire.

Lianne pulled Claire's head against her chest. 'This is gonna be, like, mega.'

'Okay,' said Claire, trying to escape Lianne's embrace.

'And you promise me you'll stay out the tower block? Cause, like, I only just made a friend, yeah, and I'm not ready to lose you.'

'Okay,' said Claire, laughing and breaking free. But this last agreement was a lie. Claire knew that as soon as Lianne went home, she would check Morgana was in her house, and then she would run to the tower. Maybe it was to do with Jack dying, or to do with her failure at interview. Maybe the wine had made her bolder. Maybe she was panicked by the impending demolition. Maybe the first signs of autumn – the yellowing leaves, the seeds that drifted cloud-like on the breeze – made Claire think of endings. But one way or another, Claire was through waiting: that afternoon, she was going to explore the tower.

Fifteen

SHE LEFT a note on the kitchen table: 'Dear Dan,' it said, 'if I'm not back when you get home, please come to search for me. I have gone to explore the tower and something bad must have happened. Love you, Claire xxx.' If she was caught, imprisoned in the tower, then maybe Dan would arrive to save her, but even if he got the note too late, at least Claire's last words to him would be an affirmation of her love. It's strange, she thought, how love seems connected to death. You only have to remember your mortality and the urge to express your love becomes stronger than any argument.

Outside, the afternoon was shaking off a September shower. Worms coiled on pavements and a rainbow stuttered across the sky. That woman, the smartly dressed one that Claire had imagined to be a saleswoman, was ringing Lianne's bell again. How many times had Claire seen her now? Three or four at least – a persistent seller. Once again, Lianne wasn't answering the bell, though Claire knew she was at home. Good for Lianne, Claire thought.

When Claire reached the scrubland, she looked up at the tower with something like inverse vertigo. It seemed impossibly tall and unsteady, creaking from side to side. Clouds passed high overhead, little white scars in the post-rain blue sky. In fact, Claire was so busy looking upwards that she tripped on rubble and stumbled a few steps, crashing though clumps of dock weed and St John's wort. After that, she walked head down, concentrated on where she placed her feet, and tried not to look at the tower. But she *felt* when she entered its shadow. The air went cold and she shuddered and her heart rate accelerated. She glanced over at the church house, startled by the crash of a sledgehammer – a noise that seemed to echo off the tower walls.

She walked over a shattered concrete block, out of which metal wires protruded like grotesque hairs. She balanced, like a child, heel to toe along a giant rusted girder. She jumped over a rain puddle. Soon she reached the gap in the fence – the spot from which she and Lianne had shouted to Mooncloud and Unity. She lifted the untied side of the fence out of its concrete base. It didn't swing open as easily as it had before – it stuck in the dirt, and Claire had to lift it from the soil and heave it open with her shoulder. She opened it a yard, stepped through, stopped.

The wind lifted as she started to walk along the path of flattened grass. It whistled through the tower's open passageways, flapped loose tarpaulin slapping against the derelict walls, threw seeds from the clumps of rosebay willowherb. A crow hopped, beat its wings, rose up to perch on a higher ledge. Claire saw, resting in a shallow ditch, a vodka bottle, whose label had been bleached by sun and time, and next to it a discarded nappy, tied up and crawling with flies.

Then she was out of the grass and weeds, standing at the edge of a two metre-wide circle of ash. In the centre, partially burned, she could see Formica-coated chipwood planks, a pair of trousers, the melted stumps of a plastic chair. Claire imagined Morgana, staff in hand, bellowing to the moon as Unity and Mooncloud danced naked around the flames. She tiptoed across the ash, kicked through the white-grey powder near the centre.

Walking across the remains of the fire felt like a dangerous transgression, and she was glad to step onto tarmac. The tarmac was patched with moss and cracked by weeds, and its colour – lightening as the rain dried – was uneven, blotched with dark continents where the ground was still damp. Her feet crunched on broken glass. She saw the wheel of a bike. She watched a beetle climb a strand of grass.

Then she stopped, just short of the tower's entrance, reluctant to walk between its graffiti-covered concrete legs. The writing on the tower spanned generations. She saw a punk-style circled A. She saw, brush-painted in faded white capitals, 'NO POLL TAX.' She saw a faded swastika: NF, BNP. She saw spray-painted scrawls for Manchester United, Manchester City, the Longsight Crew. She saw the inked messages of younger kids – random obscenities, initials, declarations of enduring love, school feuds played out on the tower block's walls (Shirley Wick was a slag; Johnny Mac was gay). She saw the bubble letters of older graffiti artists, the centres of letters squished like screwed up faces. She saw newer tags, multi-coloured metallic paint rolled, brushed, and sprayed in 3D blockbuster lettering. And then, painted most recently, she saw Seth's work: a mini-stencil of the giant graffiti he had painted upstairs.

She stood for a long time, watched a drip slide from a moss-choked pipe. She read the warning signs: DANGER. DEMOLITION IN PROGRESS. DO NOT ENTER. And then, knowing she couldn't rest until she'd seen for herself, she walked under the tower and looked for the entrance. She saw a padlocked door – perhaps the one Seth had broken into (had someone repaired the lock?) – and then she saw the main entrance.

She stepped towards it, feet crunching broken glass. To the left and right of the door, by the entry buzzers, some family names were still legible. The names were engraved on oxidised metal plaques, printed on stickers, or scribbled onto sticky tape. There was something nostalgic about the names – a reminder that once, before its ruin, the tower was a place that children explored and mapped and loved; it was a place where young couples moved, filled with excitement at the prospect of starting a family. She looked for a name she recognised – Shaw or Hogg – and when she found none, she stepped into the building's entrance foyer.

The first thing that surprised her was the dark. The tower was built on stilts, and besides those, the ground floor comprised only the utility rooms and this brick entrance hall. The lowest flats were on the first floor, and the entrance foyer gave access to nothing except the lifts and the two stairways. In the absence of electricity, it was lit only by the beam from the doorway, and the light that filtered down from the first floor. Still, as her eyes accustomed to the gloom, she saw that this was where the homeless had established their base. She saw two stained mattresses, some blankets flung against the wall. She saw beer cans, crisp packets, scraps of tinfoil. In the middle of the room there was a cigarette-burned armchair, from which a spring protruded like a claw. The room smelled of urine and damp. Then she sensed movement, screamed, covered her face. It was a frog. Just a frog. The scream was so loud in the silence that it seemed not yet to have ended. She felt her pulse race, tried to catch her breath. The frog traversed the linoleum floor, hopping irregularly. Shlap. Shlap. Shlap.

Before she climbed the stairs, Claire crept across the room and peeked into the lift. Somebody had slept in there, too. Cardboard boxes had been flattened into a bed and a smiley face was drawn in lipstick across the elevator wall. But other than that, the lift was weirdly unchanged; its buttons and lights and ceiling tiles were all still in place. She half-expected to hear the doors close, the turn of wheels, the creaking of wire; she would feel that momentary give, and then the slow sensation of rising. Across the entrance foyer, the doors to the other lift were firmly closed, and she imagined it hung suspended, frozen during its unfinished last journey. For the first time it occurred to Claire how much there was to search. Twelve floors, according to the lift buttons. The entrance buzzers had covered panels on either side of the door. How many flats? Fifty?

She backed away from the lift, scared to look behind her, and then she took the stairs two at a time. As the light improved she saw footsteps on the dusty floor. There were at least a dozen different prints. The landing was rectangular, with stairs up and down on each long side, and a window at each end. She saw discarded aerosol cans, cider bottles, more graffiti – a wailing skull with red eyes and wings extending from its temples. The windows had no glass, but the black tarpaulin that enwrapped the lower floors had been ripped around the openings, and the daylight was welcome after the gloom of the entrance foyer. She saw that there were doors to four flats. She did the maths: four times twelve floors meant there were forty-eight flats. How many rooms in each flat? Her task felt impossible. Where the light was best, she crouched to look at the footprints. There were dozens of different treads. Most of the footprints were the heavy treads of workmen's boots, but she also spotted trainer prints and the fossil-like ribbed pattern of a child's sandal. The doors to the flats were all smashed open, and Claire followed a path of footprints across the landing. 'Hello?' she called as she pushed open the broken door. 'Hello?' she called again.

She was in a small, unlit hallway. The walls were fire damaged, blackened with soot. She kicked open a half-burned door – its sealant falling off in curls. This room was even worse. Everything was black – the smell of smoke still strong months after the blaze. Nothing had survived except the springs of a bed frame and a saucepan with no handle – things reduced to their essence. Claire backed out of the flat, struggling to breathe.

She tried the next door, unsure what she was searching for. In the hallway, she could just make out that junk mail still lay on the hall floor: an advert for Sky TV, a free newspaper, a takeaway menu for a now-closed restaurant. It was as if some ghostly postman had continued his deliveries after the building had been abandoned. She pushed open a door. It creaked, crashed against something.

When she heard no noise, Claire stepped through, entered a small kitchen. It was brighter than the hallway, half-lit by a tarpaulin-covered window. The spiral-ring-hob cooker had been ripped from the wall, turned on its side. Above where it used to stand, the walls were textured yellow with grease. The other appliances had been removed, leaving dirty black rectangles. She opened a cupboard door, saw circles of mould, grains of rice, one or two red lentils.

She spun round, as if being watched, stepped across the hallway, breathless with fear. She entered a big room, half-lit like the kitchen had been. The room was empty. The plaster had been smashed with claw hammers or axes. There were big scars where piping or wiring had been ripped out. She stepped back into the hallway, entered the bathroom. The floor was covered with shattered ceramic. The sink and the toilet had left their shapes on the walls. A mouldy Fireman Sam lampshade hung from the ceiling. There was a cupboard, a small storage area above a water tank. Someone had kicked a dent in the door. Peering under the water tank, Claire saw the flattened bristles of a dirt-covered Thomas the Tank Engine toothbrush.

When Claire entered the bedroom, a cat screamed, ran past her, so fast Claire didn't move. Only after it had gone – out the door like a bullet – was Claire hit by the full force of her fear. When her heart beat again, it seemed to restart heavily, uncertainly, like some machine that badly needed to be oiled. She kept her hand on her heart, reassuring herself it was still beating. She counted each deep breath, wiped her eyes with her sleeve.

Back on the landing, where the light was brighter, she held her hand outstretched, willing it to hold steady. She felt dizzy, unsure what to do next. The building was too big, too frightening. She couldn't search every room in every flat on every floor. She ran up the stairs, two steps at a time, as if she could outrun her fear.

And then, on the second floor landing, Claire saw the most horrific sight she'd ever seen.

Sixteen

ON THE LANDING FLOOR, there was a crudely painted pentagram. The lines were wobbly and the star's points were unequal in length. Still, Claire recognised the symbol. At each point of the star there was a candle – a tea light like the ones she and Dan had at home – but the real horror was in the middle. At the centre of the pentagram, streaked with blood, there sat a decapitated pig's head.

Claire stared in breathless terror, too startled even to run. The pig smelled putrid and flies crawled in and out of its snout. Its eyes were closed, its ears perky, and it appeared to be smiling. It seemed, grotesquely, to be quietly amused. Later, the thing Claire most remembered was that the pig had eyelashes – fine blonde lashes – but at the time she just stared, appalled, struggling to believe what she was seeing.

And then, of course, when she'd fully registered what she was looking at, she turned and ran back the way she'd come. One thing that surprised her, when she looked back on her panic, was that at no point did she remember screaming. She had screamed when she saw the frog, and she had screamed when she was startled by the cat, but the pig's head in the pentagram instilled in her a terror that seemed beyond noise.

She ran to the first floor landing, but then she heard the noise of a padlock. She stopped, listened. A door hinged, crashed against a wall. Then she heard heavy footsteps, the turning of a wheel, perhaps. The noises were coming from the bottom of the building. For a moment, she stood on the landing, immobilised, and then she turned and ran back towards the pig's head.

She couldn't stay near it. She would take her chance with whatever lurked above. But as she ran upstairs, she began to imagine still greater horrors – corpses with no eyes, axe men in blood-stained aprons, skeletons shackled to walls. It was, as Mrs Shaw had said, a place of evil.

Then, when she found the third-floor landing empty, she stood with her hands on her knees, trying to compose herself. Okay, she thought, don't panic. So, she thought. That was a pig's head. In a pentagram. Okay. Don't panic. So Morgana was doing a ritual. Maybe she was a Satanist. So? It was hocus-pocus, the sort of black magic games that Goth kids play before they grow up. It didn't mean—

The door slammed downstairs and she started to run again. She didn't know where she was running to. She climbed higher and higher, breathless, face covered with snot and tears. God, she wanted out of there. Why hadn't she listened to Lianne?

She was vaguely heading to the top of the building, out onto the roof, perhaps. At least there she wouldn't be enclosed; she'd be— She had her mobile with her and perhaps she could phone for help? But what would she report? A pig's head? A pentagram? This wasn't Elizabethan England – she couldn't report someone for witchcraft.

By the time she saw the Secret Baby Room, she'd lost count of how many floors she'd ascended, but she saw on the wall, where once a numeral had been affixed, a light-shaded figure of eight. Had she not been tiring, her motivation to reach the top diminished, then she might have charged onto the next flight of stairs without realising she'd found what she was looking for. She had always imagined that the Secret Baby Room would be a room in one of the flats – maybe even a secret chamber like the one built beneath the church house – but in fact it was laid out in the middle of the eighth-floor landing.

What did it consist of? The first thing she noticed was an old-style doll. The doll's right leg was melted to a stump, its big wax face cracked open where its papier-mâché insides had expanded and burst out. It sat, leaning against the stairwell, its arm pointing into the middle of the landing. In the middle of the landing, there lay a grey woollen blanket, a paint-coated dust sheet, a ripped Hannah Montana quilt cover, a brown curtain, and a soggy-looking yellow pillow. These items had been arranged into something like a bed, but they were surrounded by junk, as if children had attempted to build walls. They had used lengths of pipe, chunks of plaster, a frying pan, a cupboard door, a broken strip light, the rusted frame of a bicycle, even one of the security signs from downstairs. All these things were piled around the bedding to make an enclosed space. The walls were knee-high in some places, as high as Claire's waist in others, and the only entrance was a gap through which the half-melted doll was pointing.

But what was most eerie about the Secret Baby Room was that the insides of these walls were lined with children's toys. There was a blood-stained wooden giraffe on wheels. Next to that was propped a naked Barbie doll, whose feet and hands had been chewed until they had no digits. The Barbie doll's tummy was open, revealing a contorted plastic baby. Claire saw a stuffed gollywog, the first one she'd seen since childhood. Beside that sat a giggly doll, whose head, unpowered by batteries, was frozen in an open-mouthed toothy cackle. She saw a plastic baby with a smashed face, an action man whose head had been deformed by fire, a faceless teddy bear whose pink and white stuffing protruded from its severed leg.

Claire ran to the window. Outside, the sun was shining. She could see the church house, the river, the golf course. She ran to the other window, calculating whether this could have been where she'd seen the baby. She could see Lianne's house and then hers. She could see the window she'd looked through – the window of her own baby room. But *this* window – the window of the landing – seemed the wrong shape. She thought the woman had held the baby at a bigger window. Maybe a window in one of the flats?

She crouched down, examined the footprints in the dust. Here, there were fewer prints than downstairs. There were still some large boot prints, but also the medium-sized prints of an adolescent or a woman wearing flats. The most common prints, however, were those that Claire believed had been made by Morgana's children's sandals.

Then, before Claire could check which flat had been most vis-ited, she heard a thud – a noise like something being dropped. She spun round, alert again. Someone – or something – was nearby, but she couldn't be certain where the noise had come from. One of the flats? The floor above? She started to edge towards the stairs, flight or fight responses kicking in. She stepped backwards. Listened. Stepped backwards again. Silence. She slid her toe behind her, listening all the time, shifting her weight gradually so she wouldn't make a sound. Whoever – whatever – had made the sound was now silent, too, listening to Claire's movements. As she inched backwards, Claire's eyes were flicking from door to door to door. Now and again she glanced towards the floor above, but she never looked behind her.

She trod on the pointing wax doll. It made an awful crunching noise then rattled down the stairs. Claire stumbled after it. The noise, after the silence, was percussive. She ran downstairs, leaping steps four at a time, the pain in her ankles not registering, the world burned white by her fear. It's strange how, when life really matters, we shut down those parts of ourselves that we normally deem most important. Claire did a thousand things in those seconds. She ran and balanced and jumped and breathed; and though the world appeared simplified, reduced to the negative of a photograph, in some animal way she saw where she had to run, chose her route, and never fell or stumbled. But in those seconds, or however long it took her to escape the tower, she didn't have a single conscious thought.

She didn't start thinking again until she was outside, running to the fence. The sun was bright, birds were singing, 'Insomnia' by Faithless was playing quietly from the church house. She closed the fence behind her, slammed its feet into the concrete block, and then she risked looking back at the tower. She saw a kestrel glide from a high window. It flew without a beat of its wings, curved over Claire's head, and hovered still, leaning into the breeze. It waited like that, occasionally stroking the air with its wings, and then it swooped, plunged vertically, changed its mind, and curved out in a rising arc.

She rested for a moment, until she had her breath back, and then she started to walk home. She tried to make sense of what she'd seen. This was beyond anything she could cope with. She needed to phone someone, but whom? Social services? The NSPCC? Then she remembered that she still had Constable Young's card; she'd phone him and report a child-protection issue. After all, if the truth was half as macabre as appearances suggested, this was a matter for the police.

'Ah, Mrs Wilson,' said PC Young. 'We haven't had a call from you in a while. I was beginning to wonder if you were okay.'

'I want to report a child-protection issue.'

'Aha. Would this have anything to do with the baby that lives in Sighthill Tower?' From his tone, Claire imagined that there was someone else in the room – probably PC White – for whose amusement Young was performing.

'I have concerns about my neighbours' children. Their names,' Claire whispered, 'are Mooncloud and Unity Cox.'

Young laughed. 'I think that's evidence enough. Mooncloud and Unity Cox,' he said, away from the mouthpiece. Claire heard more laughter.

'Their parents,' Claire whispered, 'are called Morgana and Adrian.'

'Okay,' said Young. There was no pause to suggest he was recording this information.

'The children—'

'Mooncloud and Zebedee?'

'Unity. Mooncloud and Unity have been playing in the tower block – a game called the Secret Baby Room.'

'I see. Do you think this a case for the Serious Organised Crime Agency or the Territorial Support Group?'

'Please,' said Claire, 'would you at least listen to what I have to say?'

Silence.

'I went into the tower today, and I saw . . .'

'Yes?'

'I saw a severed pig's head in the middle of a pentagram.'

This time the laughter was prolonged. 'What's that?' she heard someone say, and then she heard Young repeating what she'd said, and then she heard more laughter.

'I'm serious,' she said. 'Go and see for yourself. It's on the landing. On the second floor.'

'We'll be sure to investigate, Mrs Wilson, but first we're going to identify some suspects. Top of the list: Snape and Voldemort.'

She hung up, threw the phone against the sofa. How had it happened that the only person she could talk to was Lianne?

At four o'clock, Claire decided to visit Lianne early: she had to tell her what she'd seen, and maybe she could excuse herself from their planned night out. However, when she walked outside, she saw that Neville Shaw's Jaguar was once again parked outside Lianne's house. Through Lianne's open windows, Claire heard Neville shouting: 'Useless wee tramp . . . Take that off . . . You'll do what I tell you . . . Don't make me . . . You're not too old for me to . . . ' Claire listened for a minute, and then she returned to her house.

She waited by the living room curtains, peering out on the street, hoping to see Shaw's Jaguar depart. She must have been there fifteen minutes when she saw Unity exit Morgana's. She heard Morgana call 'Be a good child, don't go on the main road, and be back by five!' Claire watched Unity skip past her window. The child was wearing a sky-blue sunhat and dungarees. She carried an A4 plastic polypocket – the sort of thing in which one would file papers in a ring binder. Claire listened for the sound of Morgana's door closing, and then she stepped onto the street.

She followed Unity at a distance. The child skipped and sang to herself, oblivious to her tail. Unity, Claire had to admit, did not seem like a kid trapped in a satanic cult. She walked along the riverside and Claire followed, watching as Unity threw a stick into the water. Unity was hopping now, left leg for ten jumps, right leg for ten more. She paused when the stick was caught by reeds, and restarted when the current pushed it free.

Soon she walked under the footbridge, on the other side of which the path was blocked by the demolition company's fencing. Claire slowed her pace – it was dark under the bridge and Claire couldn't see what Unity was doing. Then, as she got near, she saw that Unity had found a child-sized gap between two fences: sideways first, breath sucked in, the child squeezed through the fence, still humming contentedly.

Claire climbed onto the bridge and stood at the spot where she had first met Old Man Jack. She could see Lianne's garden and the back of her house – Lianne's curtains were closed against the sunshine. Unity hadn't run directly to the tower, as Claire had expected, but was meandering through the tall weeds. Often, only her head was visible. She was picking flowers, Claire realised. She was collecting the heads of weeds and storing them in her plastic pocket. Claire tried to remember the names of weeds and wildflowers, thinking of words she hadn't used since childhood. She thought of Nipplewort – Nipplewort sounded like something Morgana would use in a spell.

She watched Unity for ten minutes, during which time the child flattened a twisting maze of pathways. Claire waited to see whether the girl would enter the tower, but when the plastic pocket was full of seeds and blossom, Unity returned to the river path via the same gap in the fence. 'Hey, Unity,' Claire called, waving from the bridge. 'What you doing?'

Unity turned, momentarily startled. She saw Claire, smiled shyly, waved back. 'Collecting flowers,' she said in a quiet voice.

'Wow,' said Claire, 'I love flowers! Can I see?'

Unity shuffled forward and stopped at the start of the bridge.

'Come on,' said Claire.

'I'm not allowed to cross the bridge.'

'Why not?' she asked the child.

'Mummy says.'

'Does your mummy cross the water, Unity?'

Unity appeared confused by the question but shook her head.

So Claire walked to meet the child at the foot of the bridge, gazing in pretend awe at her flowers. 'Wow, they're beautiful!'

'These ones are pink and these ones are purple.'

'They're very pretty, aren't they?'

Unity nodded. 'These are seeds.'

'Ooh,' Claire said, as if the concept was new to her. 'What are seeds for?'

'Make baby plants,' said Unity.

'And what are you going to do with all these beautiful flowers?'

Unity shrugged.

'Are you going to give them to your mummy?'

The child stuck her fingers in her nose, thought for a moment, and then nodded.

'What will mummy do with them?'

Unity shrugged.

'Will she use them in a spell?'

'Aaaaah—' She spun a circle on the ball of her foot. '*My* spell.'

'You can do spells?' said Claire, talking with the animated excitement of a children's TV presenter. 'Wow, I've never met someone who can do real spells before!'

Unity giggled, spun on her foot once more.

'Would you do a spell for me? Unity? Would you?'

Still giggling, Unity reached into the plastic pocket and scrunched a fistful of flowers and seeds. She threw these into Claire's hair and shouted 'Wiccanzabar!' with both her arms outstretched in magical command.

As was the case when Morgana had performed the friendship spell, Claire had no idea how she was supposed to react. 'Thank you,' she said. 'What does that spell do?' She was afraid of the answer.

Unity was watching a millipede crawl between the stones at the side of the bridge.

'Unity?'

'That spell is . . . a sweet dream spell. You will dream of princesses and roses and unicorns.'

'Thank you,' said Claire, unsure whether she should pick the weed petals from her hair. 'Unity, maybe you can explain another spell to me? I don't know anything about magic, you see. Do you think you could help me?'

No longer interested in the millipede, Unity nodded enthusiastically.

'Earlier today I saw a magic symbol, but I don't know what it means. Look, I'll draw it.' Claire bent down and found a small sharp stone. On the big rock at the side of the bridge she scratched her best attempt at a pentagram. 'Do you recognise that symbol?' she asked, throwing the stone into the river. It landed with a small splash and Claire counted the rings in the water while Unity thought.

'Yes,' said the child, eventually.

'Can you tell me what it means?'

'It means . . . magic.'

'Good magic or bad magic?'

Unity pulled her lip down with a dirty hand and sunk her eyeballs under her lids.

'Do you know where I went today?' asked Claire. 'I went into the tower.'

Unity looked at her feet – the millipede had gone.

'Have you been there today?'

'Not allowed,' said Unity.

'Who says?' asked Claire. 'Unity, who says you can't go in the tower? Did your mummy say that?'

Unity nodded.

'I saw the Secret Baby Room today. You and Mooncloud built it, didn't you?' Claire saw that Unity was on the precipice of tears – her mouth was twitching, her eyes were moist, and she was sniffing and swallowing. Claire knew she had to slow down, take this easy. 'It's amazing,' she said. 'It must have taken ages to build. I would never have found so many things to put in it. Did it take a very long time?'

Unity nodded, hanging in there for now.

'Did you have to carry all those toys, all those blankets, up all those stairs? You must have worked *soooo* hard! One thing I wondered, Unity, was why you built it so high up? I mean, wouldn't it have been easier to have built it lower down?'

'The river's lower down,' said Unity, skipping to the water edge.

'Why did you build it on the eighth floor, Unity?'

'Fishies.'

'Leave the fish just now, darling.'

Unity turned to face Claire. Her face was pink and trembling.

'Is there something special about that room?'

'That room is . . . '

'Unity?'

She shook her head.

'That's okay, darling. You've been a very good girl. But Mooncloud probably knows these things better than you do, doesn't he?'

'No! Mooncloud's a baby!'

'I'll bet he knows why the Secret Baby Room had to be so high up.'

'It didn't. It's just that – Sometimes . . . '

'Yes?'

'Sometimes, up there . . . ' Unity looked around three-sixty degrees. There was nobody to tell her what to say. 'Up there,' she whispered, 'sometimes you can hear a baby cry.'

Seventeen

WHEN HAD CLAIRE last done this? She was standing in Lianne's bedroom, wearing only her underwear. The room smelled of smoke and perfume and nail varnish, and Lianne's clothes – dresses and skirts, shorts and playsuits and T-shirts – were draped over chairs, hung from cupboard doors, crumpled on the floor, or sprawled across the bed. Claire had tried on *at least* a dozen outfits, none of which she'd even momentarily considered wearing, while Lianne lay on the bed, her newly-painted toenails webbed out by pink separators. They were drinking wine too fast and playing a Ministry of Sound compilation so loud they had to shout. Claire remembered from her youth that often this was the best bit of a night out: the anticipation, the optimism. For an hour, nothing seemed to matter – not her disastrous interview, the pig's head, the ghost baby, or the tower. For an hour, she even forget that Dan was AWOL, that she'd given up her job, that she'd moved to Manchester for a marriage that was failing.

'Try this,' said Lianne, throwing Claire a sparkly-golden halter-neck top, 'with these.' She threw a pair of glittering, sequin-covered, red hot-pants. If Claire were to wear those two items together, she would look like a Christmas cracker. 'Take your bra off,' shouted Lianne, as Claire quizzically dangled the halter-neck.

'What about this?' asked Claire, picking up a black dress. A black dress – she could do a black dress, right? She held it against herself then realised it had slashes on the back and across the hips. 'Or maybe this?' she said, finding another black dress.

'You do realise it's not a funeral we're going to?'

'Don't you think this is nice?' said Claire.

'*That*? I'd forgotten I had that.' It was a scoop-necked T-shirt dress. It would cover her up a bit at least. She pulled it over her head. It fitted well, Claire thought (it must have been obscenely tight on

Lianne, whose breasts were two or three sizes bigger than Claire's). It showed more cleavage than Claire would have wanted, and she worried about the fat under her arms, but at least it covered her back and shoulders. When Claire tugged the dress over her hips, however, she realised it was shorter than anything she'd worn in years. 'I won't be able to sit down!'

'What?'

'The dress,' she shouted, as the music reached a crescendo. 'I'll be tugging it down all night.'

'I told you! You've got amazing thighs.' For now, Lianne was naked except for an extra-large Snoopy T-shirt. She swam across the bed and threw Claire a balled-up pair of fishnets. Claire set them to the side, as though intending to return to them, and she looked at herself in Lianne's full-length mirror. Lianne was right – Claire's thighs weren't that bad. They were so pale that she could see thin blue veins, but the shape of them was— You could almost call them toned. She walked to Lianne's tights drawer, wondering the correct etiquette. She had tights at home but would going home seem ungrateful? She searched for something opaque but settled for a pair of ladder-resistant sheer tights from an unopened packet.

'My turn,' said Lianne, dancing to her ransacked wardrobe.

Claire sat on the bed, stretched the tights out, and then rolled each leg down to the toe. She was sitting with her right toe in the air, the tights rolled up to her left thigh, when Lianne turned and asked, 'How about this?' Lianne was holding a roll of black tape. It was the sort of bondage wrap that they sell at Anne Summer's parties. Lianne lifted her T-shirt over her head, pretended to stretch the tape tight across her nipples. Claire laughed, hoping it was a joke. She couldn't help but notice Lianne's depilation. Lianne had no hair at all, but the waxing or shaving had left her red and sore looking. The tops of her thighs were pin-pricked with stubble and bumped with ingrowing hairs. It looked awful. She had been vajazzled on her pubis, but only two crystals remained, looking like sprinkles left on an empty cake plate. She had a tattoo of some-thing – a butterfly, perhaps – on the V just below her panty line, and her navel was pierced with a disco-ball belly bar. Her legs were covered in bruises and her knee was red where a scab had recently healed. When Lianne turned back to the wardrobe, Claire saw the smudged rose tattoo on her left ankle, and, on her lower back, a flowery heart pattern.

An hour later, Claire and Lianne posed hip to hip before the mirror. Claire had persuaded Lianne to wear a bra – albeit a red one under a white blouse – by complimenting her boobs and insisting she had to 'make the most of them' (the alternative had been a pink boob tube decorated with the Playboy bunny). However, she'd been able to do nothing about the plaid skirt and over-the-knee stockings. Lianne looked like a fourteen-year-old boy's realism-tinged fantasy.

Lianne had accepted Claire's comparatively demure black-dress look, on the condition she agreed to 'accessorise it with something, like, dramatic.' And so Claire was wearing an impractically small diamante shoulder bag and silver platform heels in which she couldn't walk. She was wearing glitter mascara with rhinestones stuck to the outside of her eyes. She looked like she was auditioning for the Lady Boys of Bangkok.

Still, it had been fun. It was years since Claire had done something so girly. It was the smell, more than anything else, which transported her back in time. She smelled the struggle between deodorant and cigarette smoke. She inhaled the singe of hair straighteners, the chemical taste of hairspray, the alcohol scent of perfume left bottled too long. She could smell spilled wine, nail polish remover, and body lotion – a smell like a clean baby.

'How do we look?' shrieked Lianne.

'Sexy as hell,' said Claire, attempting the sort of sassy voice she thought appropriate for a party-loving ladette.

Yes, it had been fun, and so Claire was surprised – maybe a little hurt – when Lianne asked for time to do 'some personal stuff.'

'Oh,' said Claire. 'Sure. I'll wait downstairs, shall I?'

'It's kind of private?'

'Okay,' said Claire, unsure what was expected of her. Should she offer to stand in the garden?

'Like, maybe I'd best call in for you when I'm ready?'

'Okay,' said Claire, stumbling down the stairs, bewildered. As soon as Claire was outside, Lianne closed the door, as though her 'personal stuff' was very urgent. What did she have to do? Bulimia? A wall-shaking bout of diarrhoea? Intravenous drug use? She looked up at Lianne's closed curtains, and then she tottered home alone.

Sitting on the couch, waiting, Claire had two thoughts. First, she realised that she didn't want Dan to come home – not now. She had texted him that afternoon on the pretence of checking he was okay, and his silence had hurt her, irritated her, but not really worried her. His refusal to even reveal where he was staying seemed childish, and she had the impression that he was performing their estrangement without really believing in it. It was only a matter of time, she thought, before he came to bed, smelling of beer, and made some clumsy attempt to undress her. At least, that was how his strops had always ended in the past.

That said, before she went out, she had been listening to every engine, hoping it was Dan arriving home. She did miss him. Or she thought she missed him. Or she thought she should miss him. She wanted to talk to him – that was certain – although she didn't know what she would say. She wanted to convince him she wasn't having an affair, but then, surely he *knew* she wasn't having an affair? I mean, apart from anything else, Claire Wilson just wasn't the sort of woman who *had* affairs. And then – this was the truth – she wanted to hear *him* apologise to *her*.

So she did want to talk to him, and she did want to see him; she just hoped he wouldn't come home while she was dressed like this. What would it look like! Would she pretend she had dressed this way for him? She clip-clopped to the downstairs toilet and studied herself in the mirror. She didn't feel sexy. She tried to see herself from different angles, tried to see how her legs looked as she walked. It was no use; she had always felt like a transvestite when she tried to walk in heels.

The second thing she realised, while she was waiting, was that she feared Lianne would not reappear. This was a strange thing to worry about, given how reluctantly she'd subscribed to this night out in the first place, but now that she was slightly drunk and all dressed up, it was horrible to think she'd be left to sit alone. She remembered the night of Kirsty Towner's sixteenth birthday party. Kirsty's crowd had been the coolest in school, and Claire – who at that age engendered ambivalence in everyone – considered it a great privilege to have been invited. At Kirsty's house, she drank too fast, out of nervousness, and somehow didn't register that the plan was for everyone to go clubbing. The other girls had confidence or cleavage or fake IDs, but Claire, who had never been to a nightclub, who queued unsteadily in kitten heels, was curtly refused entry. She remembered looking forlornly at her peers, wishing even one of them would stay with her, but Kirsty only turned with a wry shrug before descending to the shrieking music. Claire meandered homewards, stopping at a wall near her house, where she sat, shivering, until she saw her parents had gone to bed.

So it was a great relief when Claire heard the clatter of Lianne's heels and smelled, through the door, a thick buzz of Britney Spears perfume. Lianne acted as excited as before, and neither of them mentioned her 'personal stuff' again.

Eighteen

THEY STARTED at a bar on Oxford Street called The Temple. 'This place used to be a toilet,' said Lianne.

'Did it change owners?' asked Claire.

'No,' said Lianne, 'I mean it were actually a toilet. Like, an actual public toilet.'

As they got closer, Claire saw she wasn't joking. The entrance, built on a traffic island, was a descending staircase surrounded by original railings. Inside, it was about the size of a tube carriage. Band posters papered every inch of the walls.

'Don't worry,' said Lianne, 'we won't be here long. I just got to meet someone, yeah?' She looked left and right, saw a man in a trilby. She hugged him, kissed his neck. The man did not seem enthused to see her, but after a moment, he stood to go outside, still talking to his mate as he walked away.

'Get me a Bacardi Breezer, yeah?' said Lianne, squeezing past Claire to follow the man outside.

Claire sat with the drinks, conspicuously alone. A man in skinny jeans and dark-rimmed glasses nodded at her quizzically. Claire tapped her foot to the Velvet Underground, sipped her G&T. In her high-school prom get up, she must have looked very out of place.

When Lianne still hadn't returned, Claire went to the toilet – the dirtiest toilet she'd been in since high school. She stood for a while and read the toilet graffiti: 'I used to think that language was all a construct, but now I'm not Saussure'; 'End poverty, eat the rich'; 'Who was the first hipster? You've probably never heard of him,' and below that in black sharpie, 'Heard of him? I've got him on vinyl'; 'Don't hate me cause I'm beautiful – hate me cause I did your dad,' and below that in a different hand, 'Go home, Mum – you're drunk.'

Back in the bar, Lianne was waiting. Everything was cool, apparently, but it was time to bust a groove to somewhere more happening (Lianne talked this way for two or three minutes and then, once they'd left the Temple behind, she seemed to give it up).

Outside – it had *smelled* a bit like a toilet, Claire thought – Lianne held her palm out and offered Claire a choice of small round pills. For a second, Claire thought they were mints. She didn't want to show herself up by asking what they *were*, but she guessed they were ecstasy tablets – did people still take ecstasy tablets? 'No thank you,' she said, as if she'd been offered an olive.

They cut across the street. Drivers in stationary cars watched them, starting at their legs and working upwards. Claire tugged down the hem of her dress. From further down Oxford Street, someone wolf-whistled; Claire didn't know whether they were wolf-whistling at her and Lianne, but she hoped they weren't. It was strange, she thought, how women – women like her, at least – could spend so long curating their appearance, with no ambition other than to pass unnoticed. As she was thinking this, her heel caught on the pavement and she had to grab Lianne's arm. Behind her, women laughed; Claire didn't know whether they were laughing at her, but she hoped they weren't.

Outside the Paramount, a big glass-fronted Wetherspoon's, two gum-chewing bouncers stood, chatting privately, expressionless as they watched Claire and Lianne approach. Claire straightened herself and concentrated on placing one foot in front of the other. Inside, they ordered a bottle of wine and sat on the mezzanine level. The pub wasn't playing music, but noise swelled from below them – a thousand glasses tapped and slammed, shrieks of laughter from big hen-parties in matching pink Stetsons, an argument between a group of men in half-unbuttoned shirts, a drinks order yelled across the room.

'If you ask me,' shouted Lianne, apropos of nothing, 'it's devil worship. I read a book about this sort of thing once.' She was shouting above a group of boys, kids who looked barely old enough to drink, who were banging the table and cheering as they took turns to down weird-coloured shots.

'Really?' said Claire.

'Yeah. The pentagram's a Satanic symbol, right? They're, like, not *that* unusual. Sacrifices, I mean.'

'They're not?'

'It's more often in, like, Scandinavian countries. Norway, Denmark, Iceland, Ukraine. Places like that.'

Claire didn't really buy this, but she was too drunk to argue. When she looked around the bar, the colours bled into each other.

'What normally happens,' Lianne continued, 'is that they start with, like, an animal, so they can get some practice, yeah? Normally it's a family pet or whatever. Then, once they're, like, in the swing of things, they sacrifice a child. Morgana, or Adrian, or the guy with the pram, or maybe all three of them, have killed the pig, right, and so next they'll probably—'

Whether or not Lianne believed this explanation, Claire didn't know; either way, Lianne forgot about it when one of the young guys swayed towards her, glazed-eyed from the recently slammed shots. 'Sorry to bother you,' he said to Lianne. His voice was cracked but not deep and it perfectly matched his body: he had the stretched, thin torso of one whose growth spurt has outrun its supply lines. His face was smooth except for dots of acne. 'I just wanted to say that you have totally amazing tits.' Claire thought he'd probably been bet or dared to make this announcement, because his friends – who'd watched his progress with jittery excitement – now cheered and banged the table.

'Come here,' said Lianne, grabbing the boy's hand. This hadn't been part of the plan – the boy now looked panicked. There was a genuine chance, Claire thought, that he might cry. Lianne pulled the boy's hand into her blouse and placed it inside her bra. 'What's the matter?' she asked.

The boy didn't know what to do. He looked back at his friends for help.

'It's just a pity your balls haven't dropped, innit?' said Lianne, squeezing him between the legs.

The boy jumped backwards as if he'd touched an electric fence.

'Piss off now,' said Lianne. For the benefit of the boy's friends, she indicated the size of his manhood with her pinkie. Then, laughing, she emptied her glass and stood up. 'Come on; let's go out for a fag.'

But outside, on the edge of the smokers' cluster, Lianne went quiet, and then, forgetting about her cigarette, she put her arms around Claire and started to cry. Claire threw down her own cigarette and patted Lianne's back – she had no idea what had triggered this.

'I'm a bitch!' wailed Lianne.

'No, you're not,' said Claire.

'I am! I'm a skanky bitch!'

'You calling my friend a skanky bitch?' said Claire in her best ladette voice.

'You wouldn't be my friend if you knew what I'm really like. If you knew me, you wouldn't be my friend!'

Claire held Lianne by the shoulders, looked her in the eye. Lianne's mouth was open in a silent wail, and trails of drool stretched between her teeth. 'Come on,' said Claire. 'It's okay.' She looked in Lianne's bag for tissues. She was glad she'd worn black because Lianne's eye makeup – of which there was plenty – was now smeared over Claire's shoulders and both their faces.

'I'm *soooo* sorry,' said Lianne. 'You must hate me!'

Not for the last time that night, Claire wondered why she was there. One thing she held on to – every time she worried how she looked or what people thought of her – was that she knew nobody in Manchester, and in a sense was liberated to be whoever she wanted to be. This comforting logic fell apart, sometime after midnight, when she and Lianne had finally been admitted to a nightclub called the Ritz. She was queuing for the bar when she noticed a man looking at her and realised – in this order – that he was uncommonly beautiful, that she'd met him before, and that the place she'd met him had been the old church house. He was Lukasz, the Polish builder.

Later, she would wonder why seeing Lukasz had felt like meeting someone she knew – someone in front of whom she could not stand to embarrass herself. Why was Lukasz any different from the bouncers or the clubbers or the bar staff? After all, she was no more likely to see him again.

'Hey,' he shouted, 'you are . . . Katie?'

'Claire,' said Claire, feeling slightly hurt.

'Yes,' said Lukasz. 'You are here to party?'

'What?' said Claire, trying to push her way to beside him.

'You are here to party?'

'Where do I know you from?' she said. She knew perfectly well, of course. She could, in fact, remember every muscle on his abdomen.

'Party time!' he said.

Claire realised that neither could hear what the other was saying. She smiled at Lukasz but he was now being served. He was leaning over the counter, raising five fingers on his right hand and one on his left.

The club was in an old building, which might have once been a theatre or a cinema or a ballroom. Above Claire there was a balcony level, from which people leant over, extending their hands to their friends or just to salute the beat. From the ceiling there hung a large disco ball. She couldn't see much of the dance floor because of smoke that hissed from under the stage. On the stage she saw girls, dressed like Lianne but prettier and thinner, looking down to admire their own bodies in movement.

She looked back and saw Lukasz shouldering his way through the crowd, holding a circular tray high above his head. 'You are here with your boyfriend?' he asked.

'No, no, my friend, Lianne.'

'You want some tequila?'

'Okay,' said Claire, giggling. She realised that behind her back she was sliding her wedding ring from knuckle to knuckle.

'Oh my God!' said Lianne, when she saw Lukasz. 'Who is *this*, Claire?' She adjusted her breasts, wiggled her shoulders.

'Lukasz, this is Lianne. Lianne, this is Lukasz.'

'Who?'

'Lukasz!'

'You want tequila?' said Lukasz.

'Who are you here with, Lukasz?' asked Claire.

'What?'

'Yeah, I want tequila,' said Lianne, taking the salt and lemon from Lukasz's tray. She lifted her skirt, so there was a clear gap between it and her stockings, and then she sprinkled the salt on her thigh. Next, she put a slice of lemon between her lips, holding the skin of it between her teeth.

As she beckoned him with her hands, Lukasz understood what he was expected to do. Laughing, he bent over her crotch and licked the salt from her thigh. Then he sat up, downed a shot of tequila, slammed the plastic cup on the table, and kissed Lianne's lips, ripping the lemon from her mouth. Claire felt a weird surge of jealousy.

'Wooo hoooh!' said Lianne. 'Now you, Claire – now you!' She started to sprinkle more salt on her thigh, but Lukasz stopped her.

'My turn,' he said. He lay back, so his head was on Lianne's lap, and he lifted his shirt. He sprinkled the salt on the bottom of his stomach, just above his belt, and he held a lemon slice between his teeth just as Lianne had done.

Claire hesitated. This was not okay, she thought. Whatever anyone says, the line of fidelity is a blurred one. There are a thousand ways to suggest physical intimacy – some playful, some openly erotic, some seemingly quite innocent – and each one could, depending on circumstances, be seen rightly or wrongly as a breach of monogamous commitment. For example, on which side of the line should you place a shoulder rub? If Claire gave a shoulder rub to Lianne then that would hardly seem homoerotic, but would she be happy if Lianne gave a shoulder rub to Dan? But then, she wondered, do the rules change if the act takes place within a formally or informally constituted game? Which is to say, if Dan reached his hand between Lianne's legs then Claire would be furious, but if he did so in accordance with the rules of a game of Twister then—

But consciousness is not the most useful tool for making important life decisions. It talks away to itself, often it justifies what's already happening, but the real decision has already been made somewhere else. As Claire's head moved downwards, she told herself she wasn't betraying Dan, because the act was within the context of an informally constituted game, and so, just like in a game of Twister, it was okay for her— In fact, the reason her head was already moving downwards was because she was insatiably titillated. How often had she felt this way in the past? Spin the bottle at Vicky Gallagher's house when she was fifteen? Strip poker during her fresher year at university? Now she was once again pushing her boundaries, risking experiences she normally wouldn't have dared imagine.

She paid more attention to that moment than she sometimes paid to whole days. She noticed how stray grains of salt were suspended in the curls of hair that led under Lukasz's belt. She noticed how her tongue licked through the salt on his stomach, how it formed a wet pathway banked by thin white lines. She noticed how he held eye contact as she glugged the drink, and how he leant forward inviting her kiss. And it wasn't a kiss, of course – not really. She felt the roughness of his stubble for just a millisecond, and then she ripped the lemon clear. They were both laughing. They both had dribbles of lemon juice on their chins.

All that happened in seconds. Then the DJ mixed into 'Paper Planes' by MIA and the club cheered and people ran to the dance floor. Claire cheered too – even she knew 'Paper planes' – but it was Lianne who reacted first. She was on her feet, waving her arms, shrieking in delight. She grabbed Lukasz by the wrist. 'Watch my bag!' she said, throwing it at Claire.

Yes, thought Claire, this was more like it. Claire had always been the bag minder. She watched Lianne and Lukasz run to the dance floor and it occurred to her how many times she had fulfilled this role. Her friends at university had often discussed why Claire didn't like to dance. In fact, Claire had never said she didn't like to dance – she supposed she'd like to dance as much as the next girl, if she ever got the chance; rather, she had become, through habit, the girl with whom the others left their bags. This had become so institutionalised that her friends assumed the role was one she had adopted through choice.

So was it so bad, Claire reasoned, that she wanted to flirt a bit? Was it so bad that just for one night she didn't want to be Mrs Wilson? Was it so bad that she slipped off her wedding ring? Oh, the ways we have to convince ourselves of what we know is wrong.

The lights were strobing, so the dancers appeared one frame at a time, their movements like a jerky animation. Claire looked at her wedding ring, watched the disco lights sparkle on the diamonds. What should she do with it? She briefly imagined explaining to Dan that she'd lost her wedding ring in a nightclub. She put it on her right hand but it was too tight for her ring finger and too loose for her pinkie. She opened her diamante bag and selected an inner pocket, but it closed with a loose buckle and she worried the ring might slip out. In the end, she put it in her purse beside her coins.

She didn't notice that Lukasz was watching her. His smile said that she was ridiculous, and that he was too kind to mention it. He didn't say anything, but Claire knew that he'd seen her hide her wedding ring, and she knew that he knew that she'd done it for him. Had she not felt some loyalty to Lianne, she would have run from the club that minute.

Instead, she looked away from him and asked, 'Where's Lianne?'

Lukasz shrugged and laughed. 'She has left me already. Now I have no one to dance with.'

'What?'

He leant closer, cupping his hand to her ear. 'I am wondering if you would like to dance?'

'I don't dance,' said Claire.

And so they enacted a familiar ritual: he, holding her wrists, tugging her upwards with a force that was only symbolic; she, shaking her head, laughing, repeatedly saying no, terrified he'd abandon his attempts to persuade her. And once they were on the dance floor (and of course, eventually, they *were* on the dance floor), she felt even stupider.

Claire Wilson was a wonderful dancer, when she was alone; but in a busy club, opposite a beautiful man, with two handbags at her feet, she was rooted to the sticky floor, arms swinging left to right, as if she were some malfunctioning children's toy. Lukasz seemed to sense her unease and so he began to dance as ridiculously as he could. He did the robot, then Saturday Night Fever, then churning the butter, then the funky chicken. He did a bit of the Macarena. He dropped to do the worm. When he got up – oblivious to derisory stares – he did the lawnmower, something about shaking cocktails, and finally a weird routine that seemed to involve shining strangers' shoes.

It worked, of course. Soon Claire was laughing and at ease and starting to loosen up. And when they tired, when they stepped together off the dance floor, Claire felt good – as if she'd achieved something. Lukasz was laughing, too. He pulled Claire towards him. His shirt was V-necked and she felt the sweat on his chest. Around them people held their hands up in salute to the chorus of a song Claire didn't know. She didn't flinch or push him away, not even when he kissed her forehead, not even when he slid his hands to her waist.

Nineteen

CLAIRE ROLLED ONTO her shoulder, easing the pain in her lower back. The light was bright and people were talking in a language she couldn't understand. Her head hurt and she had no desire to wake, but this, she realised, was not her house. She was on a sofa bed – it was the sofa bed's frame that had hurt her back – and she—

Lukasz. Oh, God, she had gone home with Lukasz. And now she was in his living room and she— God, she was topless – her bra was thrown over a chair. She pulled the cover to her chin, looked around.

'Good morning,' said a man – a large Polish man – who definitely wasn't Lukasz. 'Would you like some coffee?'

'Where's Lukasz?' asked Claire.

'He has had to go to work.'

'Coffee?' she asked, screwing her eyes against the light. 'May I have a glass of water, please?'

She heard the man's footsteps and a tap running through the wall. While he was away, she surveyed her surroundings. In the bay window there was a big TV surrounded by wires and games consoles; a Legia Warsaw football scarf was draped over the mantelpiece; and on the far wall there was a full-colour A2 poster of a photo-shopped brunette – Megan Fox, perhaps? – leaning against a car bonnet, with one hand on her bosom while the other explored inside her unbuttoned denim shorts. It looked like an all-male student flat. It smelled like one, too. It smelled of cigarettes, unvacuumed carpets, sweaty trainers, sports deodorant. What had she done?

The man returned and passed her a mug of water. 'Lukasz has left you this,' he said. He handed her a note scribbled on the back of a phone bill.

Hi Clare,

Sorry I have had to go for my work. I hope your head
is not too banging. Help yourself to anything we might
have for breakfast please. I had fun so if you would like
to party more then you can phone me.

Lukasz x

Once Claire was alone, she started to piece together what had
happened. She remembered the tequila slammers in the Ritz. She
remembered— God, her chin was sore from Lukasz's stubble. She
remembered the feel of his tongue in her mouth. She remembered
Lianne going— Crap, Lianne had gone home with two older men,
whom Claire had vaguely recognised as two of the unbuttoned
shirt guys from Wetherspoon's. She remembered arguing with her,
pleading with her not to go with them.

She couldn't remember leaving the Ritz, but she remembered
walking with Lukasz and his friend, past shut bars and darkened
windows, at an hour when the only moving vehicles were taxis
and police cars. She remembered Lukasz and his friend climbing on
scaffolding, swinging from it like monkeys. But what then? What
then? She remembered sitting with Lukasz in this room, late-night
TV playing in the background. He had poured her a vodka and
Ribena – a drink she hadn't touched; a drink which remained on
the mantelpiece next to an empty can of Tyskie and a full ashtray.
They hadn't had—

Jesus, her wedding ring – she wasn't wearing her wedding ring.
Where— what— She'd taken it off. She remembered taking it off.
She saw her dress – Lianne's dress – on the floor, but where was
her bag? Had she left it? She searched the floor, scrabbling with her
hand on the carpet, afraid to expose herself in case Lukasz's flatmate
reappeared. The bag was under the sofa-bed. She pulled it out,
ripped it open. Her purse was still inside. She tipped the coins out,
searched among them. There was her ring. She held it to the light
and checked for scratches, and then she slid it back onto her finger.

She remembered Lukasz moving his hand up her thigh, an
inch at a time, and then it had all gone wrong – or right, perhaps.

She had started crying. She had told Lukasz everything – about Dan and Manchester and her disastrous job interview. About the Secret Baby Room and the pig's head and God knows what else. They hadn't done anything but kiss. They hadn't done anything but kiss.

Claire listened for footsteps and when she heard only a radio playing upstairs, she swung her legs from the bed and reached for her bra. Her dress smelled of cigarettes and body odour, but she had nothing else to wear. She'd ripped her tights in half where they'd laddered. She sat on the edge of the sofa-bed and drank the water. However awful she felt – and however awful she looked – she knew she had to get out of that house. She tried to fold away the sofa-bed but couldn't force it back into place. After a minute, she gave up and left it half-folded – neither one thing nor the other.

She found a bathroom and locked the door. Here, too, everything was male. A can of shaving gel – uncapped, the gel dripping and dried hard – sat next to toilet roll centres and a flake of soap that had been worn transparent. She briefly thought of showering but mildew covered every sealant and the bathplug was clogged with male hair. On a soap-marked shelf, used containers of supermarket-brand shampoo lay on top of piles of rusted disposable razors. The bathroom smelled of damp towels. Claire checked herself in the cracked mirror – she looked nightmarish, but what could she do? She ripped up Lukasz's note, flushed it down the toilet, and ran from the house.

Outside, standing in the drizzling rain, Claire felt disorientated by the flow of the world. A woman in a hijab bumped a pushchair over a kerbstone. A man in a high-visibility vest unloaded a box from the back of a van. Two kids on BMXs whizzed past, shouting to each other as they rode no hands. She had no idea where she was.

The shame! The walk of shame! How had this happened? She was a twenty-eight-year-old married woman and she was— Oh God, she thought, catching sight of her reflection in a car window. She looked like a prostitute.

She needed a taxi. She would get a taxi home, shower, go back to bed, wake up and pretend this had never happened. She couldn't stand still and wait for a taxi, because she would look like she was soliciting, but she would walk until one passed and then hail it. She checked her purse and discovered only bar change – shrapnel, as Dan called it. She needed a cashpoint.

When she found a cashpoint, however, she discovered she had no money. She tried the card three times, convinced there was some error, but all the time she was mentally accounting for her savings. She realised it was not improbable that her account might be empty.

So, she thought, it's started. She had known that sooner or later she would exhaust her final pay cheques, and she had known that sooner or later she'd be financially dependent on Dan, but she had imagined that time would come when she was pregnant with his child, not when she was walking home in disgrace having slept at another man's house.

She crossed the road, sheltered in a bus stop. She hoped there would be a map or a timetable, but that bit of the shelter had been smashed into pavement jewels. On the shelter's sloping plastic bench, below a Tippex drawing of male genitalia, an old man drank a can of Super and a pregnant woman ate a Gregg's sausage roll. Claire thought to ask which bus she needed, but both were looking at her – she thought – with unhidden contempt.

So, instead, when the woman hailed a passing bus, Claire followed her inside and, purse in hand, asked the driver whether he went anywhere near St. Michael's. The driver looked at her, screwed his face up. 'St. Michael's?' he said. He looked through the windscreen, shaking his head ruefully, as though her stupidity saddened him. 'This bus is for Piccadilly. You need to get a 43 or 44.'

'From this stop?' asked Claire.

'No, no, no.' The driver's dismay seemed to deepen. 'From Rusholme.'

Claire didn't know where that was either. She sensed the other passengers watching her, irritated by the delay she was causing. 'Where's—'

'Sit down there,' said the driver, pointing to the seats reserved for the elderly and disabled.

'How much do I—'

'Just sit there and be quiet.' The driver was still shaking his head.

They drove through the mid-morning traffic, the city hidden by beads of rain.

After two minutes the driver called, 'Here, love. Across the road, you see?'

Claire thanked him and stepped from the bus, holding the rails for support. The street was lined on both sides with curry restaurants, one or two of whose neon signs glowed dimly through the rain. She walked past a jeweller's, a falafel diner, a dress shop selling gold-embroidered saris. Outside a grocer's, she saw piles of exotic vegetables that she couldn't name. A man drove past, playing Bollywood music from a sports car. As she crossed the road, young men hooted the horn of a beat-up Mercedes. They laughed, shouted things she didn't try to hear. Even at this hour, the road smelled of cumin and garlic and garam masala.

She was at the bus stop when her mobile rang. She thought she wasn't going to retrieve it from Lianne's clutch bag before it went to the answer phone, but she just caught the tail of the final ring.

'Hello?'

'Is that Claire Wilson?'

'. . . Yes.'

'I'm phoning from University Hospital of South Manchester—'

'Oh, yes,' said Claire. 'How are you?'

'Thank you so much for interviewing yesterday.'

'It was my pleasure.' Claire felt her hopes lift.

'I'm afraid you've not been successful on this occasion.'

'. . .'

'The panellists commented on the strength of the applicants and—'

'It's okay. I know, I know. Thank you for calling.' Claire hung up before the woman could continue. She laughed at herself, at the idiocies of optimism, and then she sat at the bus stop and cried.

* * *

When a single-decker 43 arrived, she paid her fare and sat on an empty seat near the back. This, she immediately realised, was a big mistake. Behind her, three teenage girls played hip hop music on a phone, shrieking with the chorus. The girls opened and then slammed shut the bus windows, laughing at the other passengers' startled reactions. They threw chewing gum towards the front of the bus, and they leant over people to write obscenities on the steamed windows: they wrote 'slut' with a dripping arrow pointing at Claire.

Claire, like everyone else on the bus, pretended not to notice them. She was desperate to move to a seat near the front (one of the girls had started to snort phlegm, as though she intended to spit in Claire's hair), but she was afraid of the reaction that would provoke. But it wasn't long before a solution of sorts presented itself. Claire couldn't see where they were or how far they'd travelled – only the red smears of other vehicles' brake lights were visible through the rain and steam – but after five or ten minutes, a man in a bomber jacket boarded the bus with a pram. Claire immediately recognised him as the pram guy from the tower block.

Before she'd thought the plan through, she stood up and hailed the man as if he were an old friend. She walked to the front of the bus, ignoring the shouts of 'slag' from the back seat. 'Hi,' she said, smiling extravagantly.

The man cowered into the pushchair area. He was holding a football sticker album, which he lifted so it obscured his face. The pram, Claire noted, was today filled with an iron, a rusty desk-lamp, and an old Dyson vacuum cleaner.

'I'm Claire,' she said. 'What's your name?'

The man didn't answer. Claire had no way of knowing whether he recognised her as the woman who had chased him. He smelled bad – like clothes that had been left too long in a wet washing machine.

'What have you got there?' she said. From the back of the bus, she heard the girls shouting – slag, slut, whore – insults she knew were directed at her. One girl would shout something obscene, the other girls would laugh, and before the laughter had died, another girl would shout something else.

'Are they football stickers?' Claire asked the man. She was talking to him in the voice she used to talk to children – the voice she had initially used when talking to Jack – and she felt guilty about this, for it seemed to patronise or dehumanise him.

'Yeah, don't talk to her, man. She's got crabs, yeah?'

The bus was full but, besides one old lady who looked at Claire with sympathy, the passengers stared ahead, watched raindrops traverse the windows, or pretended to be busy with their phones.

'You deaf or what?'

Claire glanced to the back of the bus and saw that the shouter was a fifteen-year-old white girl with corn-row hair. She and her friends were all wearing uniform black body-warmers.

'Yeah, you, you slut. I'm talking to you, yeah?'

Claire wondered why nobody helped her. On the bus were half-a-dozen able-bodied men, and all of them were pretending they could hear nothing. A man with a goatee beard was setting the time on his watch. A young body-builder was pretending to read his shopping bags. Were they all really so afraid of these girls?

She had forgotten about the pram man and so she was surprised when he spoke to her. 'Why do those girls hate you?' he asked.

'They— I don't— They just—' Claire feared she might cry again.

'Yo, slag? We're talking to you, yeah?'

'Leave her alone!' shouted the pram man. He had a strong speech impediment and when he shouted, the distortion became even more pronounced. The girls, of course, threw themselves across the back seat, performing exaggerated laughter.

'Spastic!'

'What you saying, mongo?'

The girls laughed for a long time while the pram man looked bewildered. Eventually he said, 'shut up . . . you stupid cows.'

This only provoked more laughter. The girls stood up, wrists bent at odd angles, tongues pressing into their mouths. They were doing the sort of disablist parodies Claire had last seen at primary school.

But then the pram man did something unexpected. He handed Claire his sticker album and lurched to the back of the bus. This movement immediately silenced the girls – indeed, Claire was scared he was going to attack them – but when he stopped in front of them they were once again emboldened.

'What d'you want, you flid?'

'Aw, man, he's stinking!'

'Piss off you paedo spastic, yeah?'

He reached his arms out to full stretch, leant back, and started to sing as loud as possible: 'City till I die! I'm City till I die! I know I am, I'm sure I am, I'm City till I die!'

'Aw, man, he's proper mental,' said one of the girls, but it was obvious they were unsettled.

'Blue Moon! You saw me standing alone! Without a dream in my heart! Without a love of my own!'

The pram man continued to holler, and the girls continued to laugh and goad him, but Claire could see that they had lost some of their bravado. She could also see that to the other passengers she and the pram man were morally equivalent to the girls. There was nothing to suggest that her fellow travellers supported this tattooed man's strange intervention; rather, they saw him – and by association Claire – as just another faction in an underclass dispute from which they'd disassociated.

Soon, the girls shouted that it was their stop. 'Get out the way, spastic!' They didn't press the bell and when the driver failed to stop they yelled that he was a pervert. As they walked down the aisle, they knocked every passenger they could, and, of course, they saved special vitriol for Claire.

'Spazzer shagger!'

'You must be desperate, slag.'

When they'd disembarked, Claire leant over the pram and sobbed.

'It's okay now,' said the pram man. He put his arm around Claire and started to rock her. She appreciated what he'd done, but he did smell very unpleasant, so she wriggled out of his grasp and wiped her tears with her bare wrist. 'Thank you,' she said.

'Me name's Jo-Jo,' said the man, extending his hand with awkward formality.

'Claire,' said Claire, shaking his hand. She noticed again the faded 'MCFC' tattoo across his knuckles. 'Your team is Manchester City?' she asked.

Once again, Jo-Jo leant back to project his voice as loudly as possible. 'We are City! We are City! Super City, from Maine Road. We are City, super City. We are City from Maine Road.' When Jo-Jo sang, his speech impediment faded, and he pronounced with ease words that normally seemed to be a struggle. After finishing his chant, he took back his sticker album and opened it to the Manchester City page. 'Look,' he said, pointing at the club's badge.

When it was time for them to alight, Claire helped Jo-Jo bump the pram onto the pavement. Then they walked together, past the pub, along the pine-needle softened side street. When they reached the cycle path, Claire made her move. 'I saw what's in your pram,' she said.

'Me stuff,' said Jo-Jo.

'Are you taking those things to the tower block?'

Jo-Jo didn't answer.

'Is that where you live?' asked Claire.

Jo-Jo shook his head. 'Just where I store me things.'

'What things?'

'Just things.'

'Like what?'

'Just things I sell. I have a business, me. A proper business. Nothing naughty.'

'That's great,' said Claire. 'What sort of things do you sell? Maybe I'd like to buy something?'

Jo-Jo thought for a moment. Once again, his expression was a measure of concentration. 'I can show you, if you want?'

'That would be excellent. Thanks, Jo-Jo.'

They walked alongside the river. As Claire had expected, Jo-Jo led her across the rough ground to the tower block's loose fencing. He opened the fencing, checking nervously over his shoulders as he did so, and then he pushed the pram over the path of flattened weeds and grass. But when they reached the tarmac, he didn't turn the pram towards the tower's main door; instead, he pushed it to the padlocked utility room. From inside his bomber jacket he pulled a big bunch of keys, and after several attempts he found the right key and unlocked the door. The door screeched on its hinges and slammed against the concrete wall. The room was black.

'Wait,' said Jo-Jo, slapping his hand against the walls. It took him ten seconds to find his battery-powered lamp, but once the room was dimly illuminated, he said 'ta-dah!' and gestured to the contents with pride.

'Wow,' said Claire, strolling among the clutter. It was mostly junk, and some of it was totally unsellable: there was the u-bend from a toilet, a mouldy bean bag, the rails of a rocking chair. But there were also piles of Manchester City flags and scarves, stacks of cigarettes in badly printed boxes, old electric fans. 'This is amazing,' she said.

Jo-Jo was smiling very broadly. 'Is there anything you might be interested in today, madam?'

'Em . . . ' Claire thought it would be politic to buy something, but she didn't want a football scarf or a badly-wired toaster, and given her hangover she could think of nothing more awful than dodgy cigarettes. 'Well,' she said, searching the junk. 'What about that?' she asked, pointing to a baby's high chair. It was old, and the paint had been chipped off its legs, but it had all its wheels and it looked fairly clean. 'How much for that?'

Jo-Jo grinned and ran to retrieve the chair from behind other junk. 'Ace buy,' he said. 'Deffo. For you there's a special price of . . . fiver?'

'Okay,' said Claire, 'thank you.' Jo-Jo's tongue and jaw and mouth all seemed too big for his face, but this gave him an enormous, radiant smile. It was a long time, Claire thought, since she had seen someone looking so happy. That was when she remembered she had no money. 'Oh,' she said, 'hang on.' She searched her purse. 'I—'

'Wait,' said Jo-Jo. 'Four quid.'

'No,' said Claire, 'five pounds is a good price. I'm just not sure I have the money. Hold on.' She started to count her change. She had four fifty-pence pieces and six twenties, but after that she was counting small change. In total she had just £4:34. 'I'm sorry,' she said, 'this is all I have just now.'

But Jo-Jo seemed delighted with the fistful of coins, which he didn't count before stuffing them into his bomber jacket. 'Ace buy,' he said, rubbing dust off the baby chair with his sleeve.

As Claire wheeled the baby chair outside, she looked up at the derelict tower block and saw Jo-Jo follow her gaze. 'Do you ever go into the rest of the building?' she asked.

Jo-Jo shook his head vigorously.

'I went in there,' said Claire.

Jo-Jo pointed at the baby chair. 'Proper ace buy.'

'I saw a pig's head.'

Once again, Jo-Jo vigorously shook his head.

'May I ask you something?' asked Claire. 'Do you know a woman called Morgana?'

'Mor-ga-na? No,' said Jo-Jo.

'Have you ever met a man with red hair called Adrian?'

'No,' said Jo-Jo. 'I don't know nobody like that.'

'You sure? You don't do any business with either of them?'

Jo-Jo thought hard. He looked like he wanted to give Claire the answer she desired, but eventually he shook his head apologetically. 'I don't know them,' he said.

When Claire got home, she wanted only to bathe and sleep; however, it occurred to her that Dan would think her crazy if he came home and found a baby chair in his living room. She had only bought it to be polite and now she didn't know what to do with it. She thought about putting it in a cupboard or out in the garden. Instead, she bumped it up the stairs and shoved it into the spare room – the room she and Dan had once imagined as a nursery. There was no particular reason for Dan to go in there, but just in case he did, she locked the door and removed the key.

It was only then that she went downstairs and found the note on the kitchen table. Strange, she thought, that today men had decided to leave her notes. It was Dan's handwriting, and the unusual absence of kisses made the note look stark and cold. 'Claire,' it said, 'we need to talk.' Had he come home last night after all?

Twenty

CLAIRE SHOWERED, scrubbing herself hard with the loofah. She shampooed her hair three times, trying to rinse away the feeling of seediness. By the time she got out, her fingers were wrinkled and her skin was red from her ablutions. She stuffed her clothes in a bin bag – had they not been borrowed, she might have burned them – and then she went to bed, setting her alarm for three p.m.

She awoke determined to make amends. On her way to the bathroom, she saw the locked door to the spare room and remembered buying the baby chair – the whole incident seemed dreamlike and improbable. In the bathroom, she washed – again – and then moisturised and talced her body. She looked in the mirror and realised she didn't know which was more bizarre: that she had been willing to kiss Lukasz or that Lukasz had been willing to kiss her.

She remembered her mum giving her *the talk* when she was fifteen. Amid stammered mumbles about contraception and STDs, her mum had advised Claire to never be intimate with a man unless she was willing to have his children. It was old-fashioned advice, of course, and it was unrealistically restrictive, but it had stuck with Claire, and she wondered if her mother's voice had played as big a part in stopping her last night as had her love for Dan.

But then again, Lukasz may not have been husband material but he was indisputably gorgeous – easily the most attractive man Claire had ever kissed. And now that she was naked, her face bare, she saw how tired and saggy she looked, and she realised how much his attention had flattered her – how pathetically she'd craved even a temporary boost to her self-esteem. Even now, amid all her regret, she remembered the feel of his hand on her thigh and the bulge in his jeans which she had longed to—

Enough! She didn't ever want to think about Lukasz again. It was time to begin Operation Marriage Rescue. She started on her face: natural foundation, a touch of blusher, minimal eye makeup, and transparent lip gloss. She wore a cardigan and a long summer dress – a look she thought was *wifely*.

She tidied the house, vacuumed the carpets, and then she searched the kitchen cupboards for ingredients. She had no money to buy food, but she was determined to greet Dan with something homely and good. There was little to help her in the fridge. There were some salad ingredients that needed to be used: tomato and lettuce and cucumber that had gone off. The cucumber had turned to mush and its water squelched at the bottom of its wrapper. Grotesquely, it reminded Claire of a used condom.

When she could find nothing else to cook, she decided to bake some bread. She had yet to bake bread in their new house and even if Dan wasn't hungry the smell would make him feel at home. While she was mixing the dough, she wondered what her story would be if Dan asked where she'd been last night? She could tell him the truth, of course. She *could*, but she wouldn't. She was too afraid of losing him. Perhaps he had his eye on someone else. Maybe he had his hands on someone else. She imagined a young counter girl at Dan's work. Perhaps if Claire confessed her infidelity then it would be the excuse Dan needed to propose a divorce.

No, the truth was not an option. She could tell him that she'd stayed overnight at the nursing home again, but she still felt self-righteous that the first time she'd failed to come home she really *had* stayed overnight with a dying man, and she couldn't sully that truth with a lie. In any case, there was a chance that Lianne would mention their night out in Dan's presence and that would blow her story apart. She'd have to say she'd gone out with Lianne, but she couldn't say she'd stayed with Lianne because Lianne lived next door and there would be—

Claire never found an alibi because at that moment the doorbell rang. At first she panicked that it was Dan and he had lost his key, but through the peephole she saw that it was Morgana. She considered staying quiet and ignoring the ring – Morgana was the last person with whom she wanted to speak – but when the bell rang again, she panicked and opened the door. She made a big show of rubbing her hands with a dishtowel, hoping this would explain the delay in her arriving.

'Morgana, hello!' she said as enthusiastically as possible.

'Hello, Claire,' said Morgana. Her hair was tied up in what looked like a dishcloth and her feet were once again bare except for half-a-dozen toe rings. 'I'm sorry if I'm intruding but I've been keeping this for you since last Wednesday.' She passed Claire a crumpled copy of the *Manchester Evening Chronicle*. 'I wanted to give it to you personally, but it's been so long since I've seen you. I thought you'd come to a meeting, or at least send your apologies, but—'

'Oh,' said Claire, 'I'm so sorry. I've just been a bit preoccupied.'

'Well, they printed your letter. Page twenty-six.'

Claire turned the pages, trying to look excited. There it was: 'Dear Sir, I am writing as a concerned resident of St. Michael's who wishes to protest . . . '

'I must say,' said Morgana, when Claire had finished reading, 'that I'm . . . I don't really know what you've been feeling recently. It's as though . . . Well, I thought we were developing a valuable friendship, and it's like you're running away from that.'

'Not at all,' said Claire. 'I've just been—'

'It's like you feel threatened or something.'

Claire shook her head and shrugged. It wasn't a great response, but it was the best she could manage.

'So I don't want to be too . . . recriminatory, because maybe friendship is something you find very difficult, but for my own emotional wellbeing I do need to tell you how *I* feel.'

'Good,' said Claire, 'that's . . . '

'It's like you've been putting up all these barriers and I— I don't know what I've done wrong.'

Claire could identify passive aggression but she was powerless against it.

'You must understand,' said Morgana, sniffing back tears, 'that— is there somewhere else we could talk?'

'Yes,' said Claire, 'of course. Please come in.'

'Are you sure? I need to know that I'm welcome because—'

'You're very welcome.'

'And you're sure this is an okay time?'

No, thought Claire, it's a bloody awful time. 'Yes, of course. Come in, take a seat, let me put the kettle on.'

'I'm so sorry about this,' said Morgana, following Claire into the kitchen. 'Oh, you're baking, are you? I'm not interrupting, am I?'

Duh. 'Not at all. I'm afraid I don't have anything herbal. Is—'

'A cup of hot water would be fine.'

'Right.'

'You must understand,' said Morgana, above the roar of the kettle, 'that since adolescence I've so often been marked as different – as other – and that I'm therefore very affected by exclusion. And you seemed to accept me, and so it's all the more hurtful that now – I just don't understand what I've done wrong.'

'Morgana,' said Claire. 'I'm so sorry if I've— Of course you've done nothing wrong.'

'Oh, I'm probably over-reacting. It's just that when I've seen you on the road you've been so . . . cold. And I've felt so . . . I suffer from feelings of rejection and you've really . . . '

'Morgana,' said Claire, carrying the cups to the living room, 'I'm very sorry I've made you feel that way. The truth is—'

'I just feel I deserve some explanation as to why you've erected these barriers and—'

'Okay,' said Claire, before immediately reconsidering what she'd planned to say. She looked around for Morgana and Adrian's gift – the hand-made Bedouin cushion – and realised, to her embarrassment, that Dan had thrown it behind the TV.

'Yes?'

'Well . . . '

'Come on, Claire. These things are better in the open.'

'I suppose in any neighbourhood people have different philosophies.'

'Strength in diversity,' said Morgana.

'Absolutely,' said Claire. 'I suppose . . . you and Adrian have beliefs . . . '

'Yes?'

'You believe in things that . . . I don't fully understand. And that, I suppose—'

'You're saying you fear what you don't understand?'

'Yes. No. I suppose . . . when you involve the children it's . . . '

'My children? You object to me sharing Wicca knowledge with my children?

'No, that's not—'

'Would you shun a neighbour who raised her children in the Christian faith?'

'No. Maybe. It would depend. If their expression of faith was . . . unhealthy.'

'Ah,' said Morgana, chuckling privately, '"*unhealthy.*" Almost any time someone has told me something is "unhealthy" it's been a male authority figure, who has feared how an "unhealthy" act might empower me. "Don't spend so long reading, Morgie – it's unhealthy." "Don't masturbate, Morgie – it's unhealthy." "Don't discuss menstruation, Morgie – it's unhealthy."'

Claire felt a prick of anger. 'I'm not a man and I'm not an authority figure and I'm not trying to stop you believing whatever you want to believe. What you do in private is—'

Morgana chuckled again. 'Yes, I was wondering when I'd hear the "what you do in private is your own business" line. When I was twenty-two, I fell in love with a woman from my coven, and another male authority figure – my father, this time – finally reconciled himself to my lesbianism because, as he put it, what I did in private was my own business. But the implication's clear, isn't it? My beliefs, like my sexuality, like so much in my life, are not suitable for public exposure. They are something shameful, something to hide, something that should be a dirty secret.'

'No,' said Claire, setting her tea down so forcefully that it spilled into her saucer. 'That's not fair. If Adrian was a woman it wouldn't make the tiniest bit of difference to me. In fact,' she said, voice climbing with emotion, 'I think it's pretty homophobic to equate lesbianism with Satanic rituals and blood sacrifices!'

'Satanic rituals? Blood sacrifices. Claire, what—'

'I'm sorry to bring it up, Morgana. I really am. But I've seen the pig's head and—'

'*A pig's head*? Claire, what are you talking about?'

'In the tower. On the second floor landing. A decapitated pig's head in the middle of a pentagram.'

'And you think *I* put it there?'

'You do wear pentagrams and—'

'The pentagram is an ancient symbol. It's a nurturing, life-enhancing— Stand up, Claire.' Morgana stood up and Claire felt obliged to follow. 'Stretch out,' said Morgana, spreading her legs and reaching her arms out. 'What do you see? A five-pointed star. Each of us has the pentagram inscribed inside us. Every year, Venus, the mother planet, carves a pentagram in the sky. This is not a coincidence. The five points stand for the four elements, plus Spirit. The pentagram represents the unity of the world into one expression of the Divine. Do you understand?'

'That's all well and good, but—'

'The pentagram was worshipped by Pythagorean mystics to whom it meant life and health. In Egypt the five-pointed star represented the underground womb. It's a feminine source of energy that contains the universe.'

'That's great, but—'

'So how come people like you associate it with Satanism and blood sacrifices and evil? Because men have historically used that discourse to repress female knowledge and to disempower women. What do you think was the purpose of the witch hunts? Unknown thousands of women massacred to establish the tyrannical hegemonies of organised Christianity and masculine medicine. Today women have been disconnected from the earth and from their own bodies. I mean, men even control how we give birth. Look,' said Morgana, lifting her top.

Silently, baffled, Claire regarded Morgana's white, stretch-marked belly.

'See that?' said Morgana, pointing to her caesarean scar. 'I had selected a natural birth, but they wouldn't wait. I begged them,

Claire. I wanted to use nothing but herbs. But nature wasn't quick enough for the masculine accountants of time. Look how they cut me!'

This was somewhat baffling to Claire, who had always thought that when she gave birth – *if* she gave birth – she would want to have on tap the strongest drugs known to science.

'Yes, everything you think of when you think of witches – evil warty women turning princes into frogs – is propaganda designed to disconnect you from the earth and from empowering traditions of female knowledge. I am a witch. I am a pagan and a Wiccan. Wicca is a positive movement that has taught me to love everyone and appreciate the gifts provided by the God and Goddess. It has nothing to do with the Devil, who is a bogeyman myth which Christians and Muslims inherited from the Arabic Zoroastrian system. And as for blood sacrifices, what nonsense! There is only one absolute rule of our belief system: "eight words the Wiccan Rede fulfil: An it harm none, do what thou will." Do you understand?'

'Well,' said Claire, 'I apologise if you really had nothing to do with the pig's head. I saw the head and the pentagram and—'

'Claire, people have been trying to repress and discredit the cult of the mother goddess for millennia.'

'But do you concede that you've practised rituals under the tower?'

'Under the tower? No, never.'

'But – and I'm just trying to increase my understanding – you do perform . . . fire rituals?'

'Of course! Pagans have used fire in their celebrations for millennia. Fire is a primary transformative force. It represents the spirit of passion and the light of the Divine.'

'And you do this naked?'

'Some fire rituals are performed skyclad, yes. Unlike the monotheistic religions, we don't demonise or fear the body – we view it as a temple of the Divine.'

'Okay, well, Lianne saw you doing one of these rituals under the tower.'

'*Lianne,*' said Morgana, digging her nails into the leather couch. 'I should have known Lianne was involved in this somehow. What else has she told you?'

Claire shrugged, reluctant to divulge Lianne's private conversation.

'Come on,' said Morgana, 'you were happy enough to gossip about me behind my back. I think I at least deserve to know the charges laid against me.'

And that was when Claire heard Dan's keys in the front door.

Twenty-One

COULD HE have arrived at a worse moment? Maybe Claire could have handled one of these conflicts on its own, but now she felt like a tiny fortress attacked simultaneously from both sides. She stood up, kissed Dan on the cheek. It felt false, but she was unsure whether she was performing for Dan, for Morgana, or for herself. 'How are you, Sweetie?'

Dan received her peck without any gesture of reciprocation. 'Hello, Morgana,' he said.

'Hello,' said Morgana, who was acting almost as coldly towards Dan as he was acting towards Claire.

'How's your day been?' said Claire. She was smiling desperately. Maybe a neighbour's presence would force Dan to act as if things were normal?

'Crap.'

'Oh dear,' said Morgana. 'I'm afraid we're rather in the middle of—'

'I've been looking forward to coming home, opening a beer, sitting on my couch, and watching my TV.'

'Come and sit here,' said Claire, patting the sofa. 'I'll get you a beer.'

'Oh dear,' said Morgana. 'I hope you don't think me rude but what we're discussing is quite intimate, and we were doing so well to be open, and I sort of worry that a male presence might inhibit that communication?'

'No,' said Claire, waving her hands, desperate to disassociate herself from this statement.

'She's right,' said Dan. 'My penis would get in the way. I'll go out.'

'Please don't, Sweetie.'

'Do you mind if I use my toilet before I leave? Will that be okay with the earth Goddess?'

'Dan,' said Morgana, 'I didn't mean—' Morgana stopped: Dan had left the toilet door open and was peeing loudly into the pan. 'You may have some bridges to mend there, Claire.' Morgana laughed and shook her head. 'Why are men so frightened by women's homosocial friendships?'

Claire didn't answer. When Dan exited the toilet, she placed her hands on his shoulders, willing him to show her some affection. 'Please stay,' she said.

'Nah,' said Dan, 'I'm off to drag my scrotum through the undergrowth.'

'Dan—'

'Bye, Morgana.' He stepped outside, tried to slam the door.

Claire blocked it with her foot and ran after him. 'Dan!' she called.

He stopped at the garden gate and waited for her, head drooping.

'I'm *soooo* sorry,' she said. 'I didn't know she was coming round – I promise. I tried to get rid of her but she said all this stuff about how hurt she was and how she—'

'It's okay,' said Dan. He didn't seem as angry as Claire had expected. 'I just can't face her, not tonight.'

'I'll get rid of her. I promise.'

'Nah, I'll go for a pint, observe normality from a distance.'

'She just—'

'It's not just tonight, Babe. Since we moved here . . . It's my fault. I thought you'd started to feel a bit better about— Like, I thought we were going to be able to move on. Start afresh. But you're not over it, are you? You're not over the miscarriage. Nothing seems to matter to you except all this baby stuff. I just— I'm sorry I accused you of cheating – I never really thought that – but . . . '

There it was: the apology Claire had wanted to hear, and how awful it sounded now. How guilty it made her feel!

'But I do feel like I've lost you,' Dan continued. 'It's like you've no time for me anymore. All you care about is some guy whose baby died in the 1930s. And that fucking tower,' he said, pointing.

'It'll soon be gone,' said Claire.

'Good.'

'The day after tomorrow. *Kaboom.*'

'Yeah,' said Dan. They stood staring at the tower. The neighbourhood was quiet except for the distant barking of dogs. 'While I were away I were thinking about how messed up everything's got. I do love you, Babe. I just want things to be back to normal.'

'They will be,' said Claire. 'I promise.' She could see Morgana peering at them from the living room window.

'They better be,' said Dan, 'because I don't want my marriage to be like this.'

'Me neither, Sweetie.'

'Remember when we used to make each other laugh?' He squeezed Claire's shoulder. It wasn't quite a cuddle but it was better than nothing.

Claire nodded. She could still smell his morning routine: his Lynx Africa deodorant, his Polo Sport aftershave, and the tea-tree oil from his shaving gel. His shirt smelled of engines and exhaust fumes. His hair smelled of Brylcreem and her Herbal Essences shampoo.

Dan patted her shoulder. 'You better go back in before Sabrina summons Beelzebub.'

Claire stood at the gate and watched him slump in the direction of the tower. As she returned inside, she realised he hadn't asked anything about where she'd spent the previous night.

Back in the living room, Morgana had retrieved the hand-stitched Bedouin cushion and was ostentatiously plumping it on the sofa. 'Is everything okay?'

Claire shrugged, looked at her watch. She felt viscerally enraged by Morgana's intrusion.

'I'm sorry if I offended your husband. But I think what we were talking about is very important.'

'Then you'll forgive me if I ask you a direct question,' said Claire.

'There will be nothing to forgive – in the spirit of open dialogue, I'll welcome it.'

'On Saturday at twelve, less than forty-eight hours from now, they're going to blow up Sighthill Tower and anything that's inside it.'

'Yes,' said Morgana, awaiting the question.

Claire realised she hadn't yet formulated a question. 'What does Adrian deliver to the tower? Why are you trying to postpone the tower's demolition? And what do you know about the Secret Baby Room?'

'Three questions,' said Morgana. She stood up and paced towards the window. 'Fine. The Secret Baby Room is a game my children played before I forbade them to enter the tower on safety grounds.'

'I've seen their Secret Baby Room. It's . . . macabre.'

'To an adult, perhaps.'

'Unity told me that on the eighth floor of the tower, she sometimes heard a baby crying.'

Morgana shrugged. 'Unity told me she saw a fairy riding a unicorn. Claire, I know what you think you saw, and I know this idea has obsessed you, but I very much doubt there's a baby in the tower. If you're sincerely worried, then, given the impending demolition, I'd be delighted to help you search. Would that put your mind at ease?'

'When?'

'You mean when will we search it? Time's obviously of the essence, but I'd say it's a little dark now. How about first thing tomorrow?'

'Okay,' said Claire, 'thank you.' Even as she agreed to this plan, Claire knew that it wouldn't put her mind at ease, since if Morgana was involved in some sort of . . . God, she had no idea what she suspected Morgana of doing. But if she was storing a baby in the tower for whatever crazy reason, then she would have plenty of time to remove it before tomorrow's search.

'As to your second question,' said Morgana, still pacing like an attorney in a courtroom drama, 'it's harder to explain why I oppose the demolition. Let me try to put it this way. The impending demolition is causing you anxiety, isn't it?'

Claire nodded.

'You think this is because there's a baby trapped inside. Probably your subconscious has chosen that expression of the anxiety because it connects with other anxieties you have about your womb and your role as a life giver.'

'Funny,' said Claire, 'that's almost exactly what my husband says.'

'But that doesn't mean the anxiety isn't real. You may remember me asking whether you've ever been tested for clairsentience? Everything has an energy, doesn't it? Most cultures recognise this, but we all label it according to a different vocabulary: they call it Chi in China, Ki in Japan, and Prana in India. In everyday parlance we call it a vibe – an energy that some laypeople can detect but not define. People, animals, and even inanimate objects give off vibes, and I think you detect those energies, don't you? If you put your arms around a tree, for instance, I bet you can feel it giving off positive energy?'

Claire had never put her arms around a tree, except when she'd intended to climb one. Hugging trees struck her as slightly crazy.

'If you train yourself to feel and interpret this energy, then it's like hearing a silent language of the universe. I had no idea what you thought of me or why, but I could feel your energy trying to repulse me. I knew we had to talk, had to diffuse the negative energy. Similarly, the tower is crying out to me. It's in pain and it needs to be heard. If we blow it up before we've heard it, we'll be heaping a mountain of negative energy into an already suffering earth. I think you know what I'm talking about, don't you?'

No, thought Claire, I haven't the faintest idea.

Morgana took Claire's silence as agreement. 'What was the third question?' she asked.

'What does Adrian deliver to the tower?'

'Oh, yes. That's the strangest of your three questions. I've no idea what you mean.'

'There's this guy,' said Claire, 'called Jo-Jo. He's got learning difficulties, I think, but he's some sort of a market trader. He keeps his wares under the tower block and ports them about in a pram. Lianne told me she'd seen Adrian passing the guy bundles that were about the size and shape of a baby or a small child.'

Morgana massaged her temples with her thumbs. 'Oh dear,' she said. 'We need to have the Lianne conversation.' She sat down, placed her elbows on her thighs, and clasped her hands as if in prayer. 'I maybe should have spoken to you sooner.' She sighed, shook her head. 'It's just that . . . I'd never want to prejudice one neighbour against another, you understand? Lianne Shaw is . . . a very manipulative girl and a very troubled girl. I'm surprised someone as perceptive as you hasn't detected that energy?'

'I knew she had . . . issues,' said Claire, but even to say that made her feel she was betraying a friend.

'Yes, indeed she does. You may have noticed that she's disempowered – she's not at all a free spirit. What I mean by that is that she has a pathological need to appeal to the other – often to a male authority figure. You see, Claire, Lianne suffered – and I have to be careful what I say here – a traumatic episode that meant her spiritual development was arrested at a childish level. I can't say more than that. Let me put this very crudely: how she dresses isn't about what makes her feel good in her body; it's about what she thinks will appeal to men.'

This was hard to disagree with.

'Similarly,' continued Morgana, 'she tries to give you what you want. You asked her about a baby in the tower, and she came to understand that this fantasy is an important channel for your psychic energies. So she feeds your fantasy just as she feeds male sexual fantasies, and this makes her appeal to you more than she otherwise would. What I'm saying, Claire, is that she invents things – and invents herself – in order to complement what the other desires.'

Claire thought about this. She recalled an image from their night out – one she had hitherto forgotten. Not long before Lianne had left with the two older men, Claire had seen her sitting on one man's knee – in her plaid skirt, stockings, and unbuttoned blouse – sucking her thumb. For some reason the image disturbed Claire and she tried to blink it away.

'Lianne has chosen to invent stories about me and Adrian because for some months now she's been angry with me. You see, Claire, I practise spiritual healing. I offer a therapeutic service that uses a range of homeopathic remedies to draw negative energy from my patients. As soon as I met Lianne, I sensed this tragic weight of negative energy, and I wanted to help her. I believe in community, Claire, and I believe in doing one's neighbourly duty. So I waved my charge and treated Lianne for free.'

'What sort of treatment?' asked Claire.

'Obviously I'm bound by patient-healer confidentiality, just like any other medical practitioner. But I can describe my general approach, if you want?'

'Okay,' said Claire.

'I practise auric Reiki healing. I do use hands-on healing but mainly just to massage the patient, to ensure she's relaxed and thus able to receive the auric healing. Every living thing – and, interestingly, this includes buildings – has an aura.' Morgana raised her palms and seemed to be doing a quick Marcel Marceau impression. 'For instance,' she said, 'I can feel your aura even from here.'

'Really?'

'Of course. Anybody can see auras by viewing Kirlian Photography. But I don't want to get bogged down in the physics of it. There are different zones – the etheric double, the inner aura, the outer aura – but that needn't concern us just now. What makes my practice unique is that whereas most healers impart positive energy, I extract negative energy. I take on my patients' negative energy and then replenish myself with positive life force. Another thing that makes my treatment unique is that during therapy I encourage my patients to free talk. I prompt them to give voice to negative emotions, however incoherent or taboo those outpourings might be.

'Now,' continued Morgana, 'depending on the patient's problems, I'll use particular herbs or crystals to help draw out their negative energy. For example, with Lianne, I used an amethyst. As I passed the amethyst over Lianne's chakras – her natural energy centres – I noticed intense resistance, kind of like a blockage, in two places: her third eye and her sexual organs.'

'And what did Lianne make of all this?'

'Well, that was part of the problem. I did warn her that the healing process can be traumatic – that negative energy doesn't always slip quietly from the body, but sometimes it's expelled suddenly and violently. I warned Lianne that spiritual healing can take one into dark places. Of course, at first she treated the whole thing as a joke. She wouldn't listen to me. Session followed session and nothing happened. But then . . . '

'Yes?'

'Then . . . I'm not sure it's ethical for me to say.'

'I understand,' said Claire.

'I can probably share the general themes that emerged without betraying her confidence. As the healing progressed, Lianne started to free talk about a relative she previously seemed to have repressed. His name was Uncle Robert, and all she could recall was that he had disappeared from her life suddenly and without explanation. She thought he must have died, but she couldn't remember attending the funeral. Neither of her parents ever mentioned him.'

'So what had happened to him?'

'She couldn't remember. Session followed session and all this negative energy stayed blocked in those same places. I kept prompting her: "Where is Uncle Robert," I would say. "What happened to Uncle Robert," but she couldn't remember. And then, one day, her chakra opened and everything flooded out. I don't think I've ever taken on so much negative energy at once. It left us both exhausted and hurting. I had to stop treating her while I recovered, and she experienced this as a rejection. You see, Claire, the therapy probably saved Lianne's life, but she was too involved to understand that. She blamed me for the trauma she suffered during the healing process. Since then, she's tried to pass that hurt onto me.'

'How d'you mean?'

'She told Adrian that I'd groped her during treatment. It's a terrible slur to make against a healer – and totally ridiculous of course – but I forgive her because I know what she's gone through. She told you that my husband and I performed Satanic blood sacrifices. Would you believe it, I even had a call from the police to check on the health of my children: apparently a neighbour they wouldn't name had reported they'd been abused in a satanic cult!'

Claire flinched and looked at her feet. Then, in an attempt to disguise her guilty reaction, she laughed raucously, hoping to show she thought such a report to be beyond ridiculous. Morgana was not amused: she looked at Claire with such intensity that Claire feared she was the object of some spell. 'So what happened to Uncle Robert?' Claire asked, in an attempt to change the subject.

'That bit's still uncertain, but Lianne did uncover *why* he disappeared from her life, and why her parents never mention him. I can't tell you that bit, of course.'

'Of course,' said Claire. 'I wouldn't want you to betray her confidence.'

'That said, maybe in these circumstances . . . '

Claire thought she could guess Lianne's secret, and she didn't want to hear it from Morgana. 'I'm sure Lianne would tell me if she wanted me to know.'

'I suppose you do have a right to know, given everything that's happened. Oh, this is a very difficult situation. I fear I've said too much already.' Morgana closed her eyes and massaged her eyebrows with her index fingers. Claire could tell Morgana was going to reveal Lianne's deepest secret, and later she would feel she'd betrayed Lianne by staying in the room to hear it. Strange, she thought, that her desire – this time her desire for information – was once again triumphing over her loyalty.

'You're right,' said Morgana, as though Claire had been begging her to talk. 'I might as well tell you now. He abused Lianne. He abused her for years. Claire, Lianne's Uncle Robert was a paedophile.'

Twenty-Two

IN THE MORNING, walking to the tower, Claire noticed the approach of autumn. Berries had grown plump on her neighbours' bushes, and the pavements were covered with little wounds, where fallen fruits had been crushed underfoot. Overhead, leaves had begun to yellow, their edges curling like old newspaper, and through them the low, damp clouds appeared rust-coloured on the horizon.

In many ways the atmosphere should have been more sinister than when Claire had last entered the tower. But having some company – even if that company was Morgana – made the building seem less ominous. This was true even though Morgana was doing everything imaginable to make their visit as creepy as possible. She was dressed in a long white robe, and she carried a steel tray, which was carved with effigies of a horned god. On the tray, she balanced a blue candle, a bunch of sage leaves, a tub of salt, and a green phial. The phial smelled of rosemary and sandalwood and patchouli oil.

They walked in silence along the path of flattened weeds. Morgana was wearing Huarache sandals and Claire could hear every crunch of plant stalk. When they stood below the tower, Claire pointed to the locked door and said, 'that's where Jo-Jo, the guy with the pram, keeps his stock.' She said it to break the silence as much as for any other reason, but Morgana seemed not to hear. She balanced her tray on the crumbling car park wall and lit the candle with a Zippo lighter. This struck Claire as somewhat bathetic: Morgana should have lit the candle with a ceremonial wax taper, Claire thought. The smell of the smoke was equally unimpressive: the candle had a pleasant lavender scent, but it smelled like something she'd spray after Dan had used the bathroom.

Still, Claire kept these thoughts to herself and led Morgana into the sordid entrance foyer. Except that it was darker, the entrance foyer was exactly as Claire remembered it. The stained mattresses, beer cans, and clumps of tinfoil were all unmoved. Morgana placed her tray on the steps and clumped about in the half-light. She took long bouncing steps as if she were walking on the moon. After a few seconds, she started to whack the walls with her clump of sage leaves. Then, in an affected voice, as if delivering a Shakespearian soliloquy, Morgana chanted, 'With the purifying power of water, with the cleansing breath of air, with the passionate heat of fire, and with the grounding energy of earth, we cleanse this space.' She then threw salt into the room's dark corners, before drizzling the contents of the green phial in what looked to Claire like a pentagram shape.

When Morgana had finished, she said 'Good' and nodded her head at the scene, as though some visible change was evident. It occurred to Claire that if Morgana planned to do this in every room then they could be there for days. She therefore decided to lead them straight to the landing where she'd seen the pig's head. On the way, she studied the gloom for new footprints, but saw only that a pigeon had met its death in the doorway of the burned flat. The floor was covered with feathers and bird droppings, and Claire imagined the poor creature banging against walls in a desperate attempt to escape. Its body lay in the doorway, not yet rotting. Maybe the cat had caught it. Maybe it had starved. Or perhaps its death had a more sinister cause?

One thing that relieved and surprised Claire was that she couldn't smell the pig's head. Though September had brought clouds and drizzle, the weather was still warm, and Claire had imagined that the rotten head would by now have filled the whole tower with its fetid stench. As she and Morgana continued up the stairway, Claire knew there was no way she could have confronted this terror on her own. Even with Morgana at her side, she stopped at the final flight of stairs and braced herself. 'The pig's head is just up there,' she said. 'It's pretty terrifying.'

'I'm sure I'll cope,' said Morgana.

'I'm just saying that the smell and—'

But Morgana was already striding up the stairs.

'Morgana!' called Claire, climbing the steps slowly, dreading when her eye level would reach the landing.

'There's nothing here,' said Morgana.

'What?' Claire caught up, fear turning to confusion. Morgana was right: the landing was spread with black paint but there was no sign the pig's head had ever been there. 'It was here!' said Claire. 'It was right there! Look – this paint, it's— This is where the pentagram was drawn. Somebody's painted over it!'

Morgana nodded and looked at Claire in a way that made her irrationally angry.

'The pig's head was here!' Claire said again.

'What do you think the pig's head is symbolic of in your subconscious?' asked Morgana.

'It wasn't symbolic of anything, and it wasn't in my subconscious. It was a pig's head and it was right there!'

'Would you feel better if I cleansed this space too?' asked Morgana.

She must have moved it, thought Claire. Morgana or Adrian must have crept in here last night and taken the pig's head away and painted over the pentagram. They wanted her to think she was going crazy, imagining things. 'I know what you're doing,' she said.

'*Shhhh*,' said Morgana. 'You try to relax. Breathe mindfully and imagine you're in a safe place.'

'I'm not in a safe place. I'm in a condemned tower block that's been used for black magic!'

'*Shhhh*. With the purifying power of water, with the cleansing breath of air, with the passionate heat of fire, and with the grounding energy of earth, we cleanse this space.' Morgana repeated the whole ritual and then, with a placatory smile, she placed her hand on Claire's forehead.

Claire jerked her head back and pushed Morgana away. She ran up the stairs. Her lungs were bursting but she needed to reach the eighth floor. She needed to see the Secret Baby Room – needed to know she wasn't going mad. As she climbed higher and higher, she thought of movies with big twists – *Shutter Island, Identity, Secret Window* – and she considered for the first time that maybe

Dan and Morgana were right. Maybe she had become so obsessed that she was imagining things. Maybe losing her baby had driven her insane. Maybe everyone was trying to help her and there was no baby in the tower, no pig's head, no Old Man Jack – What had happened to her? What if, maybe, she was the only one who didn't know that she was crazy?

She reached the eighth floor. It had gone. The Secret Baby Room had gone. No, she thought, this must be the wrong floor. She could see the light paint where a number 8 had once been affixed, but nevertheless she ran up another flight of stairs, convinced she must have miscounted. Of course, there was nothing on the ninth floor either.

When Claire returned to the eighth-floor landing, Morgana was still climbing the stairs below. 'It's gone,' called Claire.

'Oh dear,' shouted Morgana, in a tone that betrayed no surprise. Thirty seconds later, she struggled up the stairs, still carrying her tray.

'I promise it was here!'

'Of course it was,' said Morgana, breathing heavily.

'Stop it!' shouted Claire. 'I know what you're trying to do! There was a doll with a melted leg, just there. Its face was cracked and its insides were— I promise, it was pointing this way. And here, right where we're standing, there were blankets and sheets and all sorts of— And all these toys. There were all these old toys: a gollywog and a pregnant Barbie and a teddy with no face and an Action Man that had been set on fire. You know it was here! I know you know it was here!'

Morgana was trying to hush Claire as if she were a baby. The older woman opened her arms, inviting Claire to accept her embrace. She was nodding insincerely, neither contradicting nor believing a word that Claire said. And that was when it occurred to Claire that maybe she really had gone mad.

She dodged Morgana's embrace and slumped onto the floor. She sat there, staring at the concrete, as though the Secret Baby Room might somehow reappear. Poor Dan! she thought. Dan had been putting up with her madness for weeks. She suddenly saw how crazy it all was: a skeleton found on a building site, a decapitated pig's head, a ghostly woman holding a phantom baby in a derelict tower block. *She had imagined everything!*

She didn't feel upset. She felt exhausted but also relieved. She realised that the real Secret Baby Room wasn't in this tower. It wasn't even the locked room in her house. The real Secret Baby Room was in her mind! She had been unable to deal with her miscarriage psychologically, so instead of thinking about what had happened, she was processing her trauma by imagining babies that were dead or in danger. She had become so obsessed that she had lost her job and her marriage was falling apart. Did everybody know? Did everybody just humour her? Dan knew. Morgana knew. Did Lianne know? What about Seth? Was the nursing home really a nursing home or was it a psychiatric institution? Was that where she really lived? And what about Lukasz? Did he know?

And then she heard the baby cry.

She placed her hands over her ears and tried to determine if the wail came from inside or outside her head. When her ears were covered, she couldn't hear anything, and when she removed them and listened, it seemed that the crying noise came from one of the flats. But that proved nothing: if she was going to imagine the sound of a baby crying, Claire thought, then she would imagine a sound that originated outside her head.

Morgana was throwing salt across the landing and chanting. There was nothing to suggest that she could hear the noise. But that also proved nothing: Claire could barely hear the noise, and she was straining to listen. Anyway, even if Morgana swore the noise was in Claire's head, then that wouldn't prove anything either; after all, if Morgana *was* using the tower for some weird ritual, if Claire *had* seen the pig's head, if the Secret Baby Room *did* exist, and if Morgana *was* trying to make Claire think she was crazy, then *of course* Morgana would deny hearing the noise.

However, if Claire was right about the baby, but wrong to think that Morgana was responsible, then Morgana would confirm that the noise existed. In other words, if Morgana said she couldn't hear the noise, then Claire would know no more or less than she did now; but if Morgana said she *could* hear the noise then Claire would know not only that the baby was real but also that Morgana was innocent.

She stood up and filled her lungs. 'Morgana?' Her voice sounded unnervingly quiet.

' . . . with the cleansing breath of air, with the passionate heat of fire, and with the grounding—'

'Morgana!'

'It's okay, Claire; I'm here for you.'

'Morgana, would you just shut up for a moment? Listen!' And so they froze, both affecting the head-tilted posture with which people demonstrate their audial attention. 'Can you hear it?' If I might have one wish, thought Claire, please let Morgana say 'yes'. If Morgana said 'yes', Claire would toss no more coins, catch no more seeds, and blow out no more candles. Please, she thought, let this one wish come true.

Morgana listened hard, face screwed up in bemusement. 'Goodness me,' she said, 'that sounds like—'

'It is!'

'It certainly sounds like—'

'It's a baby crying! Just like Unity said!'

Morgana threw down a cloud of salt and dropped her sage leaves to the floor. 'Well, come on!' she said. 'We need to find it!'

After that, everything happened very quickly. Had Claire had time to dwell on what might have lurked in the flats, then she may not have found the courage to search them. For instance, it occurred to her, as she followed Morgana into the cramped hallway, that there was probably someone with the baby – probably the blonde (or had she been grey-haired?) woman whom Claire had seen at the window all those weeks ago. She imagined that woman as a ghost, or a crone, or a paper-skinned escapee from a lunatic asylum, who survived by eating rats, and who hadn't felt the touch of the sun in months. But there was no time for Claire's fear to grow.

As they searched the flats, she registered only stray details. Behind a broken black door, on which MCFC had been painted in dripping white letters, a radiator had been dragged as far as the hallway and then discarded. A stained toilet sat disconnected in the middle of what had once been the living room. The salmon and brown seventies-style wallpaper peeled off in curls, and there was a fist-sized hole in the window, from which cracks spread out like spider's legs. Every few steps, they stopped, listened.

'In here!' said Morgana, rushing to a bedroom. But it too was empty except for a plastic coat hanger and a broken curtain rail. 'Listen . . . It's coming from through the wall.'

'The bathroom,' said Claire.

Though the toilet had been dragged to the living room, the bathtub remained, and hanging above it – as though expecting to be used at any minute – was a dried-out Mickey Mouse face cloth. But there was no baby in the bathroom, even though the crying was louder. 'We're close,' whispered Morgana, and then she and Claire stood in silence, trying to determine from where the noise originated. There was an unpainted white square where a bathroom mirror had once been affixed – Morgana put her ear to this, but then shook her head.

'The cupboard,' said Claire, remembering from the other flats that there should be a storage area above the water tank. Sure enough, to the left of the sink, she saw there was a loose panel. The handle had gone but Claire used her keys to prise open the door. Inside, however, there was nothing except old newspapers: top of the pile was a yellowed tabloid with a headline about Jade Goody's wedding.

'Listen,' said Morgana.

'It's stopped.'

'It must have been coming from the flat next door.'

'Come on,' said Claire, running back into the hall and jumping over the discarded radiator. But that flat also seemed empty. The floors were scattered with bird feathers and rocks of plaster, and there were holes in the walls where sockets had been ripped out. They searched every room and then stood, disconsolate, in the living room. Here and there Claire saw little reminders that people had lived here until recently: in the hallway there was a poster for the film *Ratatouille*; near the kitchen door there was a calendar with reminders scribbled in red pen: 'mum and dad coming to stay'; 'nurse to take blood pressure'; 'Tony to cubs.' But they could neither see nor hear a baby.

For a minute or so, Claire and Morgana stood like this, both pondering what to do next. Then, from far below, they heard male voices. Instinctively, both flattened themselves against the wall. Morgana put her fingers to her lips, but the only noise was the beating of Claire's heart. They listened as footsteps grew louder on the tower stairs: slow, heavy steps ascending. As the noise approached, Claire heard a man whistling. When he reached their level, he stopped. He must have seen the tray, Claire thought. She heard something rattle. She heard something crack. And then the man walked again. She heard his boots hitting the steps as he climbed higher. He started to whistle again.

'Come on,' whispered Morgana. They slid from the flat, backs to the wall like commandos, and they peeked into the empty landing. They could hear the man whistling on the floor above. Morgana's phial had been knocked over and a dark stain had formed where liquid had leaked through the cracked glass. 'Now,' said Morgana.

Morgana ran to the stairs, her robe extending like a jet trail behind her. Claire saw no choice but to follow her, and so she ran, taking the steps two or three at a time.

'Hello?' she heard the man shout from above. And then, when neither she nor Morgana replied, Claire heard the man give chase. His boots clumped and he shouted, 'hey! Stop!'

They didn't stop, of course – who has ever stopped when a chasing man has shouted 'stop'? Instead, they ran from floor to floor, neither of them looking back. Claire was faster than Morgana, and she overtook her, thinking guiltily that if one of them was caught then it would not be her. But because Claire was now leading their flight, when they reached the first-floor landing, it was she who crashed into the man ascending the stairs.

And she did, literally, crash into him. Had they been of the same height, and had he not been wearing a hard hat, then it's probable that both would have suffered severe concussion. As it was, her head slammed into his shoulder. She bounced backwards and maybe lost consciousness for a moment, because the next thing she knew she was sprawled on her side staring at the graffiti of a red-eyed wailing skull.

The man had also been knocked off his feet. Claire could hear him curse and swear as he lifted himself from the dusty floor. Then she heard the other man arriving from above. He was breathless and wheezing: 'What the hell—' he said. She realised she was completely trapped – both men were looming over her – but she also realised that it didn't matter. In fact, as she lay on the floor, she started to laugh. Both men wore luminous yellow jackets and hard hats – they were demolition workers from Skacel and Black.

The man she had crashed into was rubbing his arm and slapping dust from his trousers, and the other man, enjoying some schadenfreude, pointed and laughed at his colleague. All four of them were laughing, albeit for different reasons.

'Are you okay?' asked Morgana, helping Claire up. 'Honestly,' she said to the men, 'what a fright you gave us.'

'What a fright *we* gave *you*? What the hell are you doing here?'

'Can't you read?' asked the other man. 'This is a demolition area. You're trespassing.'

'You want to get yourselves blown up?'

'You can't blow up this building,' said Claire, struggling for breath, 'until you've—'

'Somebody's hiding a baby up there,' said Morgana.

'We just heard it crying,' said Claire.

'Slow down,' said the man Claire had crashed into. 'You just heard *a baby*? Let's hear this from the start.'

So Morgana, with a little help from Claire, explained the whole story. When she'd finished, the men looked at each other and shrugged. This was obviously not an eventuality for which they'd been trained. 'What we going to do?' asked the man Claire had crashed into.

'I don't know. Take them to the gaffer?'

Twenty-Three

THE SITE MANAGER had an office in a Portakabin a hundred metres from the tower. The cabin was on the undeveloped ground that led to St. Michael's Street, and Claire was sure it hadn't been there a few days ago. In fact, when she and Morgana arrived with the two workmen, a man in an orange jacket was sprawled on the ground, struggling to connect the electricity.

Inside, the cabin was a bit flashier than Claire had imagined. The site manager was arranging his desk – he had just placed a novelty crane-lamp atop a red ring-binder – and in the centre of the cabin four chairs were tucked under a laminated desk. Though he'd evidently just arrived on site, the manager already looked exasperated. His collar was crumpled and the knot on his tie had been wrenched to his chest. His receding grey hair was spiked into a sweat-dampened quiff, and his shirt sleeves were rolled to his elbows. He introduced himself as Paul, but the workmen called him Mr Jeffries. As they explained what had happened, Jeffries' expression became increasingly hangdog, until he was almost sprawled on his desk.

'Sit down, sit down,' he said, gesturing Morgana and Claire towards the larger table, while dismissing the workmen with his other hand. 'Okay. Woah-kay. Let me think.' He typed a rhythm on his desk. 'This is a delicate situati— Wait,' he said, pointing at Morgana. 'Aren't you the woman who complained about the asbestos?'

'Morgana Cox,' said Morgana, extending her hand.

'Great,' said Jeffries, rising to greet her. It was apparent that smiling at Morgana required gargantuan effort. 'We really appreciate having good relations with the community. Of course, there wasn't any asbestos, which I kind of expected, but it's better to be safe rather than sorry, right?'

'Especially when there's a young life involved,' said Morgana.

'Right,' said Jeffries. 'Especially when there's a young life involved.' He typed on the desk again. 'Woah-kay. Let's think about this. On the eighth floor, you say? A baby. What do you suppose a baby would be doing up in my skyscraper? That's what I'm wondering. I don't really see how that would happen, do you? One of the first jobs I ever managed – up in Sunderland this was – involved knocking down these cranes – giant cranes. Morning we were due to start, this guy comes up to me – he's got binoculars and all that kind of thing. And he's a bird watcher, right? "Look," he says, "they're peregrine falcons." "Well," says I, "you better move them cause I'm about to knock these cranes down." "Okay," says the guy, "I'll go phone the RSPB." So what the hell, I think. I tell everybody to stand down, have a cup of Bovril, break for lunch. We'll wait till the bird guys get here, okay? RSPB guy comes along and he says the birds are breeding. "That's nice for them," I say. "Heck, I wish I was breeding too. But you're going to have to move them, cause we're knocking those cranes down." "Oh no," says the guy, "they're an endangered species." And then he hits me with all this legal jargon about the Wildlife and Countryside Act of 1981. Long story short, our equipment idled there for months, while these damned birds laid eggs, hatched, fledged, whatever it is they do. My boss called me up and he said, "Paul, it's your first job and I forgive you. But don't ever let this happen again."' Jeffries was pointing at Morgana and he held the gesture in silence for emphasis.

'Now,' continued Jeffries, 'do you have any idea what's involved in blowing up a building like this one? Do you have any idea how long I've worked to arrange Saturday's blast? Let me give you some idea. There is a fireman who right now is on the phone to his buddy explaining that he can't go to the football because he's got an extra shift this weekend. You know why he's got an extra shift this weekend? He's got an extra shift this weekend because I've had to book two fire engines to park out here in case we set the city on fire. You know who else is coming for this blast? Ambulance men, police officers, three guys from United Utilities who're coming to monitor sewerage damage. From noon today, when we start laying the explosives, we've got a dozen guys with dogs from a private security firm. We've got them building a second security fence *as we speak*. I've surveyed that damned tower so many times I could tell you which room in which flat has which wallpaper. If the blast doesn't go ahead within the permitted window, I've got to reapply to the Health and Safety Executive. Do you know how long that takes? Have you ever filled in an Engineering Survey Report? I supervised the first structural survey in October. I've spent months calculating the collapse mechanism, the fall direction, the pre-weakening requirements, so that now we know exactly where to place our explosives and how we're going to drill them in. Today and tomorrow, we've got to unload and install half a kilometre of blast shielding. We've notified over two-thousand homeowners and, just to be safe, we're going to evacuate twenty houses. We've got a ninety-four-year-old former resident hobbling down to press a symbolic detonator. We've got the local press coming. Come hell or high water, *the blast is happening this weekend.*'

'I understand what you're saying, Mr Jeffries,' said Claire, 'but—'

'We've had to compensate the golf course for fencing off the seventeenth hole. Golfers are going to argue about who would have won had the seventeenth hole not been in the safety exclusion zone of an expertly conducted controlled demolition. And even when the demolition's over, we're going to have to pay for the dust to be vacuumed off their carefully mowed fairways. To try to suppress that dust, we've hired four model-S35 spray cannons, each of which comes with a six kVA generator and a 2000-litre water tank. Guess how long we've got them hired for? That's right, just this weekend.'

'Nevertheless,' said Morgana.

'Right,' said Jeffries, 'nevertheless. I'm prepared to delay by twenty-four hours, to blast on Sunday instead of Saturday, and I'm going to deal with this issue thoroughly but unofficially. Does that sound fair? We've got this infrared camera – we used it when we demolished a chemical plant. I'll get them to send me the camera and we'll hold off laying the explosives until we've scanned the building from top to bottom. If there's a baby or a peregrine falcon or a sheet of asbestos or anything there that shouldn't be there, then my men will remove it. *We* will deal with it, okay? We will place it safely beyond the exclusion area. Then, we're going to lock the area down, we're going to place our explosives, and on Sunday, *no matter what*, we are demolishing this building at twelve noon. Is that fair?'

'That's very fair,' said Claire.

'You see, if there's a baby then there's also going to be a mother. And maybe the mother has some crazy notion of squatting this building. And maybe if the police get involved then some guy from Shelter is going to start quoting section six of the Criminal Law Act at me. And then what? All of a sudden we'll have to apply for a court order. Meanwhile the poor baby dies of dysentery. That wouldn't be in our interests, and it certainly wouldn't be in the baby's interests. You see what I'm saying?'

'Yes,' said Claire, before Morgana could think of some weird objection. 'Believe me, Mr Jeffries, I'm as keen to see this building flattened as you are. I just want you to make double sure it's empty.'

'Good. Then we have a deal. In return I ask only that you leave me your contact details.' He found a pen and slid it across the table on a torn sheet of A4. 'Here.' As soon as Claire and Morgana had written their names, addresses, and phone numbers, Jeffries grabbed the sheet and folded it into his pocket. 'Now,' he said, leaning across the desk. 'I promise to keep my part of the bargain, and I'm sure you'll keep yours. But let me be clear. If this turns out to be some kind of hoax, or if you do anything else – I mean *anything* – to delay my demolition, then I will not rest until you've paid for it. I will pursue you in criminal and civil law, and I will sue you for every penny you have cost us. Do we have an understanding?'

'I don't appreciate your tone,' said Morgana.

Claire put a hand up to silence Morgana. 'Please, Morgana, not now.'

'I'm just saying that—'

'We won't interfere again, Mr Jeffries, and we're grateful for what you're doing.'

'Good,' he said, standing up. He put a mint in his mouth and sucked hard. 'Now, if you'll excuse me, there are thousands of people who need to be informed of this delay.'

And would you believe it, when Claire walked out of that Portakabin, the clouds had cleared and the day was warm and oh God it felt like a happy ending. She held her arms out, felt the warmth of the sun. The ground was still damp from the earlier rain, and on blades of grass and stalks of thistles a million droplets glittered in the sun. She could smell gas and tar and the exhausts of engines, but she could also smell mowed grass and the fructose scent of pineapple weed. She could hear the rattle-slam of fencing dragged off a flatbed, the shouts of workmen, and the arrhythmic strike of an unseen hammer, but she could also hear the contented hum of insects and the whistled rounds of chaffinches. Wow, thought Claire, this is what it means to feel *heroic*.

She trusted Jeffries, for he didn't pretend to be anything he wasn't. The baby was just an inconvenience to him – a time-consuming problem and a potential PR disaster – and because he admitted that, she trusted he would search the building as he'd promised. What would he do with the baby if its parents weren't to be found? Perhaps he'd give it to Claire. Maybe she and Dan would fall in love with it. Perhaps they'd adopt it and name it something quirky like . . . Kaiden or . . . Skyler. Either way, she had been vindicated. She had won. She had saved a baby's life.

That morning, there was just one thing that troubled her. There was one detail that irritated her and conflicted with her sense of satisfaction and wellbeing. One detail that was not quite right.

On her return from the tower, Claire waved goodbye to Morgana and stopped to tell Lianne what had happened. But as she reached the top of Lianne's path, just as she was about to ring the bell, the door opened and Jo-Jo stepped into the sunshine. He was looking backwards, saying goodbye to Lianne, and he almost walked right into Claire. 'Thank you for the breakfast,' he said. 'Take—'

'Sorry,' said Claire, though it was Jo-Jo who was walking into her.

'Watch where you're going, Jo-Jo,' said Lianne. 'What you doing here?' she asked Claire.

'Hey,' said Jo-Jo, 'I know you!'

Claire was bemused. Jo-Jo was dressed, despite the sunshine, in his usual bomber jacket. Lianne was wearing boxer shorts and a Mickey Mouse T-shirt. 'Yeah,' said Claire, 'it seems we all know each other.'

'You're the woman from the bus,' said Jo-Jo.

'Alright,' said Lianne, 'piss off then. Don't stand there with your tongue hanging out.'

'Bye bye, Lianne.'

'He's not right, him,' said Lianne, as Jo-Jo shuffled away.

'I didn't realise you knew each other.'

'Like, *yeah*. He's my cousin, isn't he?' Lianne said this as though Claire was incredibly stupid to need to be reminded. 'What?'

'Nothing. It's just . . . I thought I asked you about him and you said—'

'You said something about a guy with a pram. I didn't know you meant Jo-Jo, did I?'

Claire didn't say anything. She was trying to remember her conversation with Lianne.

'What's up anyway?'

'You won't believe what's happened this morning,' said Claire. She told Lianne about how she and Morgana had searched the tower, how the pig's head and deformed children's toys had disappeared, how they'd heard the baby crying, and how they'd met Mr Jeffries.

When Claire explained how Jeffries had promised to search the tower with an infrared camera, Lianne said 'that's good news then,' but she seemed fidgety, and she didn't invite Claire in. On her walk from the tower, Claire had thought she might invite Lianne out for a drink to celebrate the baby's rescue. It would also be an opportunity, Claire thought, in light of what Morgana had said about Lianne's traumatic childhood and her need to appeal to others, to let Lianne know that her friendship was unconditional. But before Claire could think how to phrase the invitation, Lianne was trying to send her away. 'Sorry,' she said, 'it's just that my dad's coming round soon and I've, like, got to get dressed and stuff.'

So Claire walked home, still delighted with what she'd achieved that morning, but still not quite at ease. Hadn't Jo-Jo appeared as a mysterious stranger in Lianne's tale about Adrian and his kayak trips to the tower? All afternoon this worry lurked beneath her happiness, like an itch she couldn't quite scratch.

Twenty-Four

THAT LUNCH-TIME, just after she'd poured a celebratory glass of pinot, Claire received an unexpected phone call. She'd never expected to hear from Seth again, and the sound of his voice made her weirdly happy. He was phoning to say thanks. 'You know what you said about Amy?'

Claire remembered the nursing home and the polished little blonde receptionist who'd been so obviously desperate for Seth's attention.

'Yeah, well, after you said that she liked me or whatever, I thought fuck it, you know? And I, you know, asked her out and stuff . . . And she's like . . . I mean, she's a total babe, right, but she's also really cool and stuff, you get me?'

'That's awesome, Seth,' said Claire.

'Yeah, right, so basically I wanted to say thanks somehow, you know what I mean? Especially cause I feel kind of bad about, you know, painting on your wall and everything.'

'That's really thoughtful of you, Seth.'

'I was thinking that I could maybe do you a favour in return?'

'Why, you know a doctor you could set me up with?'

'No, man, I was thinking more like maybe I could paint summat for you. Summat nice, you know? No staked babies, I promise.'

'Seth, you really don't need to—'

'I know you think it'll be crap, yeah, that I'm just a tagger, but I promise it'll look proper good. Come on, Claire? Worst that can happen is you don't like it – I'll paint it back the way it was straight away, you get me?'

Claire could tell that Seth really wanted to do this. She was drinking wine; she'd saved a baby's life; why not, she thought. 'Can you do children's designs?'

'I can do anything.'

'We've got this room that we plan to use as a nursery one day. The walls are just plain magnolia, but maybe you could draw some cartoons or something?'

'I can start this afternoon, if you want?'

'Yeah,' said Claire, 'why not? You'll have no problem finding the house – it's the one with all the paint on the garden wall.'

Two hours later, Seth arrived with a rucksack full of paint tins and rollers and brushes and stencils and aerosols. They worked together to empty the room, piling boxes of winter clothes in the hallway. They opened the window as wide as it would go, forcing loose Skacel and Black's anti-dust tarpaulin. Then Seth spread a paint-splattered sheet over the floor and unpacked his equipment. 'You got a ladder?' he asked.

'We've got a kick step.'

He glanced at the height of the ceiling. 'That might do.'

When Claire returned with the kick step, Seth was pouring paint into a roller tray. He seemed to sense that she was nervous. 'Don't worry about a thing, Claire. This is gonna be a serious piece. This is gonna be dope, you get me?'

Claire understood that it was time to leave Seth to work, and so she backed out of the room, stooped in gratitude like a domestic servant. Once she was downstairs, she started to worry. What if she'd misjudged him? What if he went crazy and sprayed obscenities all over the house? She heard a pencil scratching, a noise like a wobble board, scissors cutting through card. She wanted to know what he was doing up there. It occurred to her that she could inspect his progress with the pretext of bringing him a cup of tea, and after half-an-hour she could wait no longer.

By the time she climbed the stairs with the tea, the landing smelled of paint and she saw Seth had slapped a few big blotches of yellow and red and blue. He was drawing fat marker-pen lines here and there, but it looked awful. Still, she thought, it wasn't like he'd painted dead babies all over the landing or anything, and it wasn't like she was paying him. She'd just have to repaint it when he'd finished. When he saw her studying his work, he looked irritated. 'They're just fills, yeah?'

'It looks great,' said Claire.

'This isn't a throwup, you know? I'm just starting.'

'I brought you some tea.'

'Ta,' said Seth. 'Just put it at the door or summat, yeah?' He was clearly annoyed by her intrusion.

For two hours Claire waited downstairs, developing a headache from the paint fumes. She found yesterday's (now risen) bread dough and stuck it in the oven, hoping the smell of baking would combat the paint. She tried to open every window, even if just by an inch or two, to ventilate the house as much as the duct-taped tarpaulins would allow. It was by now apparent to her that accepting Seth's offer had been a very bad idea.

Worse, she realised that Dan would soon be home. Weirdly, she'd felt they'd made some progress last night. Dan seemed to have mellowed during their time apart, and their shared irritation at Morgana had allowed them to bond a little. Claire was determined that tonight they'd be undisturbed, and if Dan came home to find the local vandal painting a nursery in their spare room, there was no telling how he would react. So, intrepidly, Claire climbed the stairs to ask Seth whether he was nearly finished.

The first thing she noticed was that Seth's cup of tea was untouched. He was rollering blue sky, spraying candyfloss clouds, too deep into his work to notice her. But she couldn't believe how much he'd done. The red blob had been transformed into a hurtling roller-coaster train that was crashing through a field of flowers and butterflies. The train's sense of jolting speed was incredible. Cartoon characters leant from its windows, gurning in exhilaration at their helter-skelter journey. She saw Scooby-Doo and Kermit the frog and Sponge Bob and Krusty from the Simpsons. On the ceiling he'd painted a radiant yellow sun, and he'd stencilled Tweetie Pie looking shocked as Icarus's wings melted. The sun's rays faded from the centre and the ceiling darkened to a space-scape. He'd sprayed silver and gold stars and stencilled a tentacled alien. He'd also painted the baby chair Claire had bought from Jo-Jo: it now had metallic buttons and dials like in a cockpit. 'Don't worry,' he said, seeing her looking. 'None of the paint's toxic – I checked.'

'This is amazing!' said Claire.

'You like it?'

'Oh, Seth, it's like . . . *wow!*'

'I'm just starting. On this wall I'm gonna do an underwater scene, I think. You know like with fishes and a submarine and stuff. And here, near the door, I'm gonna do it like a temple, with sand-coloured pillars round the doorframe and then this is gonna be Indiana Jones and here I'm gonna do Xena, if I can get the sketches right.'

'This is *so* amazing!' said Claire – she was genuinely shocked by how good it looked.

'I don't know about this wall yet. Maybe a jungle with lots of different animals? I haven't used much green yet, and the other paints are getting a bit low. Maybe I can do the end of the train coming out the jungle, and reeds growing out the water, and the water flooding the temple, and a shooting star falling from the sky. Kind of merge it all together, you get me? End-to-end it.'

'It's just . . . *wow!*'

'You don't mind if I keep going, do you? It's just once I'm into it, I'm focused, you know?'

'Of course not. Well, there is one problem – my husband's coming home soon.'

'Will he be pissed at me?'

'It isn't that, it's just that . . . I'd like it to be a surprise for him.'

'That's cool. I'm off till Saturday, so I could come back tomorrow, I suppose.' He sounded disappointed.

'No,' said Claire, 'he'd smell the paint anyway. I'll take him out as soon as he comes home.'

'You sure?'

'Of course. Just let yourself out when you're finished. The door locks itself.'

'Props, Claire. That's pretty cool of you.'

Claire hoped her trust wasn't misplaced. 'Could you do me a favour? I don't want Dan wandering in here, so when you're finished could you leave the window open but lock the door?'

'No worries.'

'Maybe leave the key in the bread tin in the kitchen?'

'The bread tin?'

'Yeah, you can't miss it. Thank you so much, Seth.'

'No worries. I owe you big time.'

Claire turned to walk downstairs but then she thought of something else. 'Hey, can I ask you one more favour? I was wondering if I could come to the nursing home and speak to Mrs Shaw?'

'I guess,' said Seth, sounding surprised.

'It's just, maybe you remember me asking about the Secret Baby Room?'

'You were asking about that old tower, right?'

'That's right.'

'You gonna watch it blow up on Saturday?'

'It's going to be on Sunday now.'

'Nah, I'm sure they said Saturday. All the oldies are looking forward to it.'

'They had to postpone it a day – it's a long story. We found the baby—'

'There really was a baby?'

'Yeah. Well, we heard it. But one or two things still don't make sense. You said Mrs Shaw has nightmares, shouts out stuff like "why did I do it?"?'

'That's right, yeah.'

'I think I know what might be wrong with her. You see, the other day I learned what happened to Mrs Shaw's daughter when she was a little girl.'

'Well, Mrs Shaw's always happy to talk – she doesn't get that many visitors, you get me? I doubt you'll get nothing out of her, mind you. You talk to her during the day and it's like everything in the world's wonderful, you know? But you can try. I'm off tomorrow. Would Saturday work?'

'It'll have to.' Saturday was the day before the demolition. Why did that still cause her concern? She left Seth to continue his masterpiece and returned downstairs to ponder what she was going to do with Dan. She had no money to take him to the pub or the cinema. Besides, she wanted to do something special. She looked outside, saw the bright sunshine, realised how desperate she was for fresh air. For some reason it occurred to her that they should go for a picnic.

When Dan arrived home, she met him on the doorstep and pushed him into the garden.

'What you doing?' he said, sounding both amused and irritated.

'We're going for a picnic.'

'*A picnic*? What is this – an Enid Blyton novel?'

'Come on. It'll be fun.'

'Who goes for picnics? Have you packed the raspberry pop and ginger beer?'

'I've packed four Carlsbergs.'

'I work all day and then I have to go *on a picnic*? I'd sooner— What's that smell? What you doing in there, Babe?'

Even from the front drive the smell of paint was strong. 'Come on,' said Claire, pushing Dan further down the path.

'Can't I change at least? Can't I go in for my short pants and field glasses?'

'No,' said Claire, laughing. 'Just carry this and act like you're having fun.'

So she led him, grumbling, along the route she had jogged so often. They walked past Jeffries' cabin, saw men in yellow Castle Security jackets erecting a fence around the new exclusion zone – DANGER: DEMOLITION IN PROGRESS. They passed two newly installed Portaloos, and as they crossed towards the tower, a workman emerged from one of the loos, hat in hand, letting the door bounce shut behind him. They passed rusting girders and jumped a ditch filled with polystyrene cups and Big Mac cartons. They heard and then saw a dog transporter, in which German Shepherds prowled their cages, tongues out like wolves, throwing their heads back to bark and howl.

'You've chosen a beautiful spot,' said Dan.

'Very funny.'

'Should I set the croquet up here or over by the toilets?'

'There's a reason I'm taking you this way.'

'I feel like I've been conscripted.'

'Dan, I don't want to make you mad, but Morgana and I searched the tower this morning. We heard the baby.'

'Babe—'

'It's over, Sweetie. We spoke to the site manager, Mr Jeffries. He's got an infrared camera. He's going to do an extra-thorough search before they blow it up. It's going to be okay.'

Dan stopped walking, looked up at the tower, and then at Claire. His mouth was open and his face was screwed up, as though in his head several questions were jostling for position. Eventually he said, 'You heard a baby?' Claire could tell he didn't believe her. 'Okay,' he said and started to walk again. 'But it's sorted now? You've reached some kind of . . . closure?' Dan pronounced 'closure' as if he'd secretly been consulting a self-help guide.

'That's what I'm telling you. I know this whole thing has put a big strain on us, but it's over now.'

Dan thought about this. 'So whose baby is it?'

'I don't know. But the main thing is that it's safe, right? The baby's going to be okay, and I can relax and start to enjoy our new life here.'

'When they blowing it up?'

'Sunday at twelve.'

'Three days.'

'Less than that.'

Dan looked up at the tower again. Before he could articulate his thoughts, he and Claire were hailed by a workman. 'Hoy,' said the man, 'this is a demolition site. Private property, yeah?'

'We're just looking for a nice picnic spot,' said Dan.

'Ignore my husband!' shouted Claire. She pushed Dan towards the river. They were both laughing. This seemed to irritate the man, who followed them, muttering to himself, until Dan and Claire had left the controlled area.

'Look' said Dan, pointing to where a supermarket trolley was half-submerged in the river. 'Perhaps we can go for a dip before we eat the custard creams?' It had been exhilarating to receive a row from a stranger. They walked on, chuckling with childish abandon. She felt young and naughty and as if anything could happen – she had been crazy to think that Lukasz could offer her anything Dan couldn't. She held Dan's hand – he hesitated for a second, but then his grip tightened on her palm.

As their laughter subsided, Claire felt an explosive urge to confess. It seemed that if she said now what had happened then they could start afresh. She stopped walking, let go of Dan's hand. 'Dan,' she said, 'there's something I need to tell you.'

Dan had tells that Claire had learned to read. When he was nervous or uncomfortable, he compressed his lips and little marionette lines appeared below his mouth. She had first noticed this six years ago when she'd been about to introduce him to her parents. Now, seeing he was nervous, *she* felt nervous.

'Well? What is it?' asked Dan.

She couldn't tell him. 'You know the job I applied for?' she said instead. 'I didn't get it.'

'I'm sorry,' said Dan, his expression thoughtful. 'But I thought you were perfect for it?'

'Well, they didn't.' They strolled downstream towards the bridge. 'I'm bored and broke.'

'Babe, you're not broke – my money's your money! I'm sorry, Babe – I've been so busy at work I— We need to set up a joint account. Or a standing order to your account. I can do it before work—'

'It's not just that. I know you think I've been obsessed with all the weird baby stuff that's been going on round here, but what else would I have been doing? I read this thing the other day that said the best cure for depression is feeling useful. Well, now that we've saved the baby, what am I going to do?'

'Not many jobs are useful these days.' Those little marionette lines had reappeared. 'You're lucky with what you do.'

'What I did.'

He stopped on the bridge and leant on the parapet, peering into the water. Claire stood beside him. In the sunlight, the flat stones on the riverbed looked like coins flicked into a wishing well.

'When I were at Ozzy's—'

'Is that where you stayed?' asked Claire.

'Where did you think I stayed?'

Every now and then Claire saw an image of Lukasz's hand on her thigh, and each time she felt nauseous with guilt.

'I talked to Ozzy about how his life's changed since they've had the kid.'

'How is the baby?'

'Aw, she's amazing. Since you last saw her she's turned into this miniature person. It's unreal. What I'm trying to say is that . . . ' Dan was speaking with the awkward sincerity that he'd assumed when he'd proposed. He was not a man who handled emotion well. His urge whenever he had to say something meaningful was towards irony. 'What I have to say is that I realise I've been a bit traumatised by what happened – I know I wasn't the one to carry it. But I've been . . . It's not been fair on you. But I do still want us to have a kid.'

'Really?'

'Sure. We need someone to mow the grass.'

When they walked on, they found the path fenced off opposite the tower. The diversion took them through the poplar trees and onto the fairway of the golf course. They walked between two sand bunkers and curved around the seventeenth green. The route took them into the nursing home grounds and from there they returned to the riverside track. When they walked past the phone mast, Dan grabbed his neck, spluttered, and pretended to collapse from radiation. From under the flyover, bored-looking skater kids watched Dan's childish cavorting with disapproval. In the shade, where the dank air smelled of marihuana and the water midges swarmed in clouds, they passed the skaters and reached where Claire normally ascended the steps. But from the height of the motorway she had seen open meadowland, and it was there she thought she and Dan might picnic.

They walked on but soon stopped to pick blackberries that grew path-side on tangled canes. A cat slumbered atop the post of a wooden fence, across which children played on a trampoline. Claire could hear the strain of springs and the children's shrieks of laughter, and every two seconds a head appeared, giggling drunkenly at the view from this apex. Soon the path narrowed and passed through banks of gorse. Claire squeezed tight to Dan so that her arms wouldn't be scratched. In the bright evening sunshine, the gorse flowers smelled of coconut. Then the path entered open land and they walked through tall buttercups, whose yellow flowers bobbed with their steps. Ahead of them, where the river curved through the meadowland, two rabbits bounced into clumps of hawthorn. Claire and Dan twice crossed the river on plank bridges, and then Claire saw the perfect place to stop.

'Here?' she said.

'Here's great,' said Dan. So they unpacked the blanket and laid it over the clover. Ahead of them, hogweeds grew in hedgerows, their flowers scattered like lace doilies. Starlings chased each other through the branches of elderberry bushes, and then, in succession, they flew, grew tiny, and disappeared into the blueness of the sky. When Claire lay back, she could feel the sun freckling her face. She listened to the river and the birdsong, and she might have fallen asleep had she not felt a tickle on her arm. She sat up, thinking Dan was pestering her with a sheaf of grass; instead, she saw a ladybird climbing on her elbow. She watched its gutsy ascent, and when it reached her shoulder, she blew it into flight. 'Isn't this perfect?' she said.

Dan rustled one of the carrier bags and pulled out a beer. 'Now it's perfect.'

She stood up, looked back towards St. Michael's. She could just see the top of the tower block.

'Do we get to eat yet?' asked Dan. 'Or do I have to do the sack race first?'

'Wait,' she said. There was something she had to do.

'Where you going?'

'I need to pee.'

'*Here?*'

She followed a small path and stopped when she was out of view. She didn't need to pee, but there was something else she had to do in private. She checked Dan hadn't followed and then pulled out her phone. She scanned through her contacts and hovered over Lukasz's name.

Lukasz, she thought, it's nothing personal. You're a sweet guy, but I love someone else. As she pressed delete, she thought momentarily of the parallel life she was giving up. 'Delete contact YES or NO' said her phone. Yes, she thought. Oh God, yes. Yes.

Twenty-Five

AND WHO would have guessed that all the Wilsons needed were a few days apart and a picnic in the sunshine? The next morning Claire awoke feeling clammy and unwashed and totally, totally, sated. It was after ten and the sun was bright. As she woke up, fragments of sexual dreams faded from her memory, and soon all she could see was her bedroom. The sheets were crumpled on the floor, and their clothes dangled where they'd landed – a weird decoration of belts and underwear. She was naked, her face was greasy with makeup, and her nipples tingled. Wow, she thought, where had *that* come from?

She had once offended Dan by saying that what she enjoyed most about their lovemaking was his enthusiasm. It sounded bad ('you make me sound like the Phil Neville of sex,' Dan had said), but she'd meant it kindly. And in truth Dan probably did lack some finesse in the bedroom – there are probably men out there (though Claire had never been to bed with any of them) who have learned all sorts of smooth moves and kinky tricks to pleasure their partners in ways Claire could barely imagine. But what Dan had that in Claire's mind elevated him above any Don Juan or Casanova was an unaffected zeal *for her.*

And let's face it, she thought, who really wants a suave lothario measuring his performance by counting her orgasms? Who really wants to be forced into positions that require yogic training? In a world of hard core pornography and incessant sex advice, there remained an innocent charm to Dan's sexuality. His sexuality was essentially that of an adolescent boy left alone with a copy of *Nuts* magazine.

They had met at Birmingham bus station where she had worked part-time to fund her degree. He had been her supervisor, and to avoid scandal they had tried to keep their fledgling romance a secret.

She remembered that he would try to arrange for them to have overlapping lunch breaks. They'd rendezvous in a pub a safe distance from the station and usually they would have six or seven minutes of feverish necking before it was time for one or both of them to run back to work. Dan would grope and grind with such urgent excitement that her uniforms were often crumpled and ripped.

Last night, seven years later on, he was still rapturously excited to get his hands on her boobs. That was nice, Claire thought. That was nicer than a man earnestly following cunnilingus advice he's read in *Men's Health*.

She remembered them pulling each other's clothes off. She remembered Dan tripping, trousers caught round his ankles. 'Wait,' she'd said. 'You know I'm not taking the pill just now, right?'

'I know,' said Dan. And so they had made love, both knowing that their lovemaking might create a new life. Upon losing her virginity, Claire had compared *it* to second and third base erotic acts. The difference, she'd decided, was that when you do *it* you give yourself entirely to another person. In any non-penetrative sexual act, she thought, you always still hold something back; you're always still in control of your personal boundaries. And it is both terrifying and thrilling to open yourself to your partner. To consent is to temporarily relinquish your selfhood and to enter into a union you can't entirely control. Well, when having sex without contraception, she was opening her personal boundaries in new and frightening ways. Sex lasts a few minutes, lovers come and go, and even husbands can be divorced. But if she had a child, that bond would last forever.

When she finally left the bedroom, the first thing she noticed was the paint smell that emanated from the spare room. She ran downstairs and found the key in the bread tin. She was so excited that it took her several attempts to open the door.

Seth had finished the train and the meadow and he'd painted the other walls just as expertly. In the jungle scene, Bagheera, Baloo, and a smiling snake peeked out from big green tropical leaves. In the corner of the room, where the walls met, he'd painted a cartoon flamingo. It was stepping from the water mural, its long-lashed eyes winking out from the jungle. What was so impressive about Seth's pictures was how he could generate a likeness with half-a-dozen lines. It was all in precision and proportion. Underwater, a deep-sea diver was wrestling with an octopus, and faces smiled from the portholes of a psychedelic yellow submarine. A shoal of tropical fish swam through the scene like a rainbow and two of them leapt into a waterway that trickled from the temple. The temple was probably Claire's favourite tableau. He'd sponge-painted the bricks and pillars so they had a stony texture, and at the top, overlapping the space-scape on the ceiling, he'd drawn two sphinxes – the left of which had one glinting red eye. Indiana Jones was there – a few simple lines but unmistakeably Harrison Ford – but he'd replaced Xena with Lara Croft (complete with tiny shorts and bulging cleavage). What a difference a day makes, Claire thought: yesterday she'd been terrified that Dan would see the baby room; now she couldn't wait to unveil it.

While Claire was admiring Seth's work, she heard shouting and screaming from Lianne's house. The first scream was so loud that it made Claire jump even though there were two walls between her and Lianne. She heard Lianne shout 'Why! Why! Your moron! What did you do that for, you stupid spastic?' Then a door slammed and the shouting was too quiet to hear.

Claire locked the spare room, pocketed the key, tip-toed to her bedroom, and put her ear to the wall, but all she could make out was the sound of sobbing and 'I trusted you!' wailed over and over again. She wondered whether Lianne was shouting into the phone, for at no point did she hear a second voice.

It doesn't take much to ruin a day, does it? Claire had woken relaxed and filled with optimism. Now, eating breakfast, she felt distracted. She was startled by sudden noises (the postman rattling the mailbox, even a grumble from the immersion tank), and she could feel her pulse throbbing in her temples. She thought about Lianne's paedophilic Uncle Robert and her secret friendship with Jo-Jo. In spite of what Morgana had said, Claire wanted to believe she and Lianne were friends, and she sensed that Lianne needed her help.

And so, when she'd finished breakfast, Claire dressed and left the house. As she walked to Lianne's gate, she waved to Mooncloud and Unity, who were playing a version of hopscotch on the pavement. The dead frog was now just a dark stain – the shape of a stretching amphibian imprinted on stone like a fossil. On Lianne's path, amid cigarette ends, a large black slug lay unmoving, desiccated by the morning's sudden heat.

Claire rang the bell and waited. She listened for any noise from indoors but could hear nothing over the Cox children's playful screams. When there was still no answer, she stepped back and looked at Lianne's upstairs windows. She waited for more than a minute and then she rang the bell again.

While she was waiting, wondering what to do, she heard a car brake by Lianne's house. She spun, fearing it was Neville Shaw, but saw that it was a purple Kia Picanto. The driver reached to the back seat and for a few seconds sat turning pages in a ring-binder. She didn't get out, but when she opened the passenger window and leant over from the driver's seat, Claire recognised her – it was the smartly dressed woman she had assumed to be a salesperson.

Aware that the woman in the car was watching her, Claire rang the doorbell again. 'No answer?' said the woman from the car.

'No,' said Claire, guardedly.

'Same as usual,' said the woman. She settled upright and wrote something in her ring-binder. 'Are you a friend of Lianne's?' asked the woman, leaning back to the window.

Claire considered the most noncommittal response. Eventually she nodded.

'Do you think maybe you could ask her to give me a call? It's been a long time since I saw her and Alyssa.'

Who the hell's Alyssa? Claire wondered.

'I'm Liz Paterson, the health visitor. If you could ask Lianne to call us at the clinic then that would be great.' She started her engine and then leant back towards the window, smiling. 'It's nothing for her to worry about – I'm sure they're both doing very well – it's just that we haven't seen Alyssa since the postnatal check-up.'

Claire watched as the health visitor waved and edged her car forward. She made a three-point turn at the bottom of the street and waved again as she passed. What on earth was all that about? Postnatal check-up? *Alyssa*? Didn't she know that—

And then, of course, it all made sense.

Twenty-Six

CLAIRE HAD only just closed her front door when the phone rang.

'Claire Wilson?'

'Yes?'

'Paul Jeffries here, Skacel and Black Demolition.'

'Oh, hello Mr Jeffries, how are—'

'We've finished the infrared survey. Guess what? The building's empty.'

'No—'

'Yes. I've informed the police about your hoax—'

'It wasn't a hoax! We did hear a baby.'

'Yeah, sure. Listen, the police were already aware of you. Harmless nutter, they reckon.'

'Mr Jeffries—'

'I don't need to remind you, I'm sure, that our demolition site is private property and we won't tolerate trespass, intrusion, or any attempt by you or your friend to interfere with our operation. Is that clear?'

'Mr Jeffries, I promise it wasn't a hoax. Somebody must have removed the baby before you searched.'

'Yeah, yeah, the stork came and took it away. Now, if you'll excuse me, we've got just forty-eight hours to install fifty kilograms of dynamite and RDX.'

After she'd replaced the receiver, Claire paced her home, trying to make sense of everything she'd learned that morning. She'd told Lianne about the search – that had been her big mistake. She'd stopped on her way back from Jeffries' office. Lianne must have sneaked into the tower and removed the baby before— Okay, Claire thought. Calm down. Breathe. Let's think about this. She sat at the kitchen table with a pen and paper. Writing things down made her feel calm and methodical. The universe was unknown billions of solar systems expanding at rates she couldn't comprehend; she was built of billions of atoms, each of them swarming with electrons, all buzzing around at thousands of Kilometres per second. Everything was enormous and complex, chaotic and unpredictable. But there was no problem that couldn't be ordered and contained on a white sheet of A4.

She drew a baby in the middle of the page and wrote the name 'ALYSSA.' Above that, she wrote 'LIANNE SHAW.' Down the side, she drew a timeline from January to the present. Morgana had said that Lianne's pregnancy had ended in tragedy at 'the start of the year.' Claire approximated – she drew an asterisk at the first of February. She wrote '7 months old' beside the picture of Baby Alyssa.

While she thought what to do next, she doodled a skyscraper. She drew an arrow from the skyscraper to Baby Alyssa. She drew in Lianne's house. She remembered that Lianne's garden backed directly onto the demolition site – she would have been able to go in and out of the tower without opening her front door.

Still, she must have had help. Someone else was involved – someone else had to be. Maybe the baby's father? Claire remembered Lianne leaving the club with those two older men, and she realised the father could have been almost anybody. Still, someone had to be helping her. Okay, she could slip in and out of the tower undetected, but what about when she was out? What about when she was *clubbing*? Someone had to be feeding this poor baby. Someone had to be changing it.

She wrote 'JO-JO' in big letters. Below that, she wrote 'Morgana.' She thought about it and then scored out Morgana's name. Then, a few seconds later, she wrote it again – she had to consider every option, no matter how unlikely it seemed. Based on this logic, she wrote 'Dan.' She felt bad immediately and scored his name out. But then again, he had suggested they moved next door to Lianne, he had discouraged Claire from investigating, he had omitted to tell her that he'd been in one of the towers as a child, he had— She considered phoning Ozzy to see whether that was really where he'd stayed. 'Stop it,' she said. Paranoia. Paranoia. Paranoia. Calm down. Breathe.

Underneath the scrawled out 'Dan,' she wrote 'UNCLE ROBERT.' As if constructing a family tree, she drew a branch from Uncle Robert's name and wrote 'Neville Shaw & Mrs Shaw.' She drew a line from their names to Lianne's. She drew a line between 'UNCLE ROBERT' and 'JO-JO.' She drew a line between 'LIANNE SHAW' and 'JO-JO' and along it she wrote 'cousins.'

Perhaps Baby Alyssa was Jo-Jo's child? What happened if first cousins had children together? Did it lead to birth defects? Was it considered incest? Was that why they hid the baby?

Then she wondered whether Uncle Robert was Jo-Jo's father. He had abused his niece, so perhaps he abused his son or nephew? Maybe Lianne and Jo-Jo were mistreating the baby as part of some awful cycle of abuse?

Hours later, when Dan came home, Claire had her ear to the bedroom wall, listening for noise from Lianne's house. She had rationalised her options. She couldn't go to the police – they thought she was crazy – so top of her list was to speak to Lianne. After Lianne, the person she most needed to see was Jo-Jo. In the morning she would speak with Mrs Shaw, Lianne's mother, and she would ask what happened to Uncle Robert – what if he was still alive? What if he had recently been released from prison?

'Babe,' called Dan. 'You home?'

She ran downstairs, sorry she'd not yet hugged him. She was ready to embrace him as if he'd just returned safely from some foreign war. But when she entered the kitchen, Dan was studying her drawings and diagrams.

'What this?' he said.

'Oh,' said Claire. This was going to be tricky.

'Is this what you've been doing all day?'

'Sweetie, I can—'

'"*Baby Alyssa*"? You said this was over. Yesterday, you— Now I come in and find *this*?' He held up the paper and then threw it away in disgust. The paper spread out, caught the air, and then swooped back towards Dan. He batted it in irritation, swatting the air several times as the paper fell at his feet.

'The tower was empty.'

'No shit, Claire.'

'She removed it.'

'Who removed what?'

'Lianne removed the baby.'

'You're crazy,' said Dan. 'That's what's happening here. My wife's gone crazy. Yesterday I thought I had her back, but I were wrong – she's lost the plot.'

'Lianne's baby,' whispered Claire. 'Baby Alyssa. I spoke to her health visitor – Lianne didn't have a stillbirth.'

Dan grabbed Claire by the shoulders – not hard, but not quite playfully either. He shook her gently and pretended to slap her about the face. 'Come on, Babe,' he said, his tone pleading, 'snap out of it now.'

'No, Dan. I'm sick of people telling me I'm crazy or obsessive or so broody I've gone mad. Before we heard the baby crying, I actually started to believe it – I actually thought I'd imagined the whole thing. I need you to trust me, Dan.'

Dan sat down, as if weakened by a sudden realisation. 'Oh God,' he said, putting his head in his hands, 'everything you said yesterday about . . . How did you put it? Closure? You just told me what I wanted to hear, didn't you? You just told me what I wanted to hear so I'd impregnate you.'

'"*Impregnate*"? What am I – a breeding sow?'

'And I fell for it,' said Dan, as if describing his woes to a stranger in a bar. 'My crazy wife told me things were going to be okay and I wanted to believe her.'

'Stop it, Dan.' She sat opposite him and placed her hand on his wrist. 'Listen, Sweetie, I'm going to talk to Lianne's mother tomorrow morn—'

Thump! Dan hit the table with his fist, so hard that his arm jerked away in pain. He was staring at Claire, lips trembling, eyes red. They were both too shocked to speak.

One of Dan's great merits, in Claire's opinion, was that he normally resisted such gestures of rage. Thanks to her mother, Claire's father had mellowed in his old age, but when Claire was a child, she and her mum had learned to fear his temper. It wasn't that he came home drunk or hit them or threatened them or anything like that; rather, he just let his anger build until he had to release it through some physical expression: he'd roar unexpectedly or punch the wall or break a glass. His violence was never directed at any living creature – and certainly not at Claire – but it was terrifying because it was unpredictable. And so Claire had always avoided men who were prone to bursts of temper, and in seven years with Dan this was only the second or third time that he'd lost control of his anger.

They sat in silence for at least a minute. She could hear Dan's breathing – he was aspiring as if he'd just run for a bus. When he finally spoke, his voice was quiet. 'How long's the window for the morning after pill?'

Claire stood up, sending her chair screeching across the tiles. 'Fuck you, Dan. Fuck you.' She ran upstairs, unsure where she was going. At the top of the stairs, conscious that Dan hadn't followed her, she unlocked the door to the spare room. She stepped inside, closed the door, locked it.

Two minutes later, sitting on the floor, knees pulled to her chin, Claire heard Dan climb the stairs. He searched in the bedroom and the bathroom and then his footsteps paused on the landing. He tried the handle, realised the door was locked. 'Babe?' he said. 'Are you in there, Claire?'

She didn't answer.

He rattled the door handle. 'What's that smell? What are you doing in there? Claire, open this door.'

Claire still didn't speak.

'This is my house too, Claire. Open the door. Come on, you're behaving like a bloody child.' He rattled the door handle again. 'This is pathetic, Claire – you need help.' Then he swore, kicked the door, and thumped back down the stairs.

⋆ ⋆ ⋆

Claire hid in the baby room for an hour. Her childhood sulks had normally been brought to an end by boredom, discomfort, and the dispiriting realisation that her parents were quite enjoying the quiet. Aged twenty-eight, not much had changed. When she heard Dan turn on the TV, she realised the futility of her protest. She eased open the door and locked it behind her. Then she stood on the landing and pondered what to do with the key. In the end, she hid it inside her pillow case.

'I'm sorry I were so angry,' said Dan, when she returned downstairs. He turned the TV off and made space for her on the sofa. 'I didn't mean to shout. I'm just frustrated, you know?'

'I know,' said Claire. 'I realise this is hard for you to understand.'

'It's not—' Dan suppressed whatever he'd been about to say. 'I'm not mad.'

'I know you're not, Babe. But you are very stressed. And I think your own feelings about . . . you know—'

'What? Why can't you say it, Dan? You mean my feelings about the baby that we lost? The baby that died inside me?'

'I'm trying to be reasonable.'

'Right. Which is hard when you're dealing with a hysterical barren woman.'

'Claire, ever since we moved here, you've obsessed about that tower block, you've obsessed about that poor girl next door, and you've obsessed about real and imaginary babies. Finally you've put all three together: you think Lianne has a baby that she hides in the tower block.'

'Okay,' said Claire, 'you tell me where Lianne's baby has been for the past month.'

'She doesn't have a baby.'

'Then she's got a very confused health visitor.'

'I don't care! I want us to concentrate on *our* lives. Babe, I want you to go and stay with your parents for—'

'*What?*'

'Just for a few days, Claire. Just until the tower's demolished. Please?'

'I can't.'

'I don't want you mithering Lianne's mum – we have to live with these people, Claire.'

'You're trying to get rid of me.'

'Of course I'm not. I just want you to get away from this environment. Just for a few days. I promise you – you'll come back, the tower will be demolished, everything's going to seem different.'

'I can't rest until I know the truth.'

'And . . . I want you to consider counselling.'

'Listen to me, Sweetie. *You* want counselling, go to counselling. You want to leave Manchester, leave Manchester. I don't make your decisions and you don't make my decisions. Understand? When *I* decide to go to counselling, I'll go to counselling. And when *I* decide to go to my parents, I'll go to my parents. I love you, Dan. But I can't leave Manchester now. I'm not leaving until I've done everything I can to make sure Baby Alyssa is safe.'

Twenty-Seven

ON SATURDAY MORNING, twenty-six hours before the tower was due to be demolished, Claire returned to the nursing home. The bridge at the bottom of their street was now part of the exclusion zone, so to cross the river she had to walk right round the tower, across the far bridge, and over the seventeenth fairway on St. Michael's Golf Course. As she circumnavigated the outer security fence, she could just hear the sound of drills and the shouts of demolition workers. She saw that Jeffries was taking no chances: whereas the inner fence was held together by plastic ties, the wire mesh panels of the exclusion zone fence were locked together with steel clamps. At ten metre intervals, signs announced 'WARNING: GUARD DOGS ON PREMISES. NO TRESSPASSING.' Security guards manned the front gate, their radios crackling in the background. The only gap in the fencing was where it crossed the river: Claire was surprised that Jeffries hadn't installed a decommissioned Second World War dreadnought.

The nursing home grounds had changed since Claire had sat up with Old Man Jack. The rhododendron flowers had wilted and their petals had fallen, forming a pink-brown river at the side of the driveway. Now and then a sycamore seed whirled to ground, landing in the scatter of leaves with a noise like falling paper. Inside, Amy's demeanour had changed even more: she smiled shyly at Claire and hurried to call Seth. When he arrived, he and Amy spent some time tickling and nibbling each other.

'What did your husband think of the mural?' asked Seth, as he led Claire through the peach and lilac corridors. The flowers on the tables had been replaced since last time, but the nursing home still smelled of rose and lavender.

'He— I'm waiting to surprise him. He'll love it as much as I do – it really is beautiful.'

'It was nice to paint something without looking over my shoulder. You okay, Claire? You seem kind of stressed.'

'Just a bit tired.'

'Mrs Shaw might expect you to be her daughter. I've tried to explain who you are but she gets a bit muddled sometimes. Here we go. You going to be alright?'

Claire nodded and Seth knocked the door.

'Who is it?'

'It's me,' said Seth, shoving open the door. 'Mrs Shaw, this is the woman I told you about.'

Mrs Shaw looked at Claire with total blankness. 'You're not Lianne,' she said.

'No she's not, Mrs Shaw. This is your daughter's friend, Claire. Do you remember?'

'Of course I remember,' said Mrs Shaw.

'Then I'll leave you to it.'

Mrs Shaw was holding a Danielle Steel novel called *Matters of the Heart*. 'Good book?' asked Claire.

Mrs Shaw looked confused and didn't answer. Her room was similar to Old Man Jack's except that it was personalised with ornaments: a pink ceramic angel, a plastic cherub, a photograph of a baby kissing a kitten. The room smelled of potpourri mixed with the ethanol scent of antibacterial hand wash. Claire sat in the spare chair and smiled very hard – it was unnerving that her facial expressions were not reciprocated.

Then Mrs Shaw seemed to remember where she was and what she had to do. 'Would you like a cup of tea?' she asked.

'No thank you,' said Claire, unsure what difficulties would result from accepting.

'Do you know how much it costs to stay here?'

Claire shook her head, belatedly realising that the question wasn't rhetorical. 'It's a very nice home.'

'It is, isn't it? The staff are so friendly, even if they do forget my meals. Do you know that they give me the wrong medicine almost every other day? I don't say anything, of course – I don't want to hurt their feelings, do I? But I am very lucky. My first husband was a right miserable sod. That's why my first two girls were such bitches. They always tried to separate me and Neville. Well, good riddance to them, I say. Lianne's dad was no better – pissed off before she was even born.' Mrs Shaw dropped the book – she appeared to have forgotten she was holding it – and Claire picked it up and placed it on the wicker tray atop the side table.

Claire waited, thinking Mrs Shaw would continue, but she was staring contentedly towards the window. 'Are you going to watch the demolition tomorrow?' asked Claire.

'Oh, I wouldn't miss that now, would I? We're having a special tea upstairs so we can have a decent view. It's sad, in many ways, but . . . It was a good home to us. I can remember every family: the Hoggs, the Jenkinsons, the O'Dohertys.'

Claire told Mrs Shaw that she had met the site manager. She talked about the demolition preparations, because she thought this might interest Mrs Shaw, and because she was afraid to ask the questions she'd come to ask. Eventually, apropos of nothing, she said 'Have you seen Alyssa recently?'

'Oh, yes. Alyssa's doing fine. Same old, you know how it is.'

'Has she still got that wooden leg?' asked Claire.

'Yes, yes, she's not changed a bit.'

It was obvious that Mrs Shaw had no idea who Alyssa was. Next question. 'Have you seen much of Lianne's Uncle Robert recently?'

'Who?'

'Robert – Lianne's Uncle.'

'Did she tell you about him?'

Claire decided not to answer.

'I can't believe she's started that nonsense again. After all these years? She'll be getting a slap the next time I see her. She made Neville terribly upset.'

'Because she reported Uncle Robert?'

'Reported? She used to play a game with Neville. Every night he'd go to read her a bedtime story and at some point – she must have been seven or eight – she started to say "Uncle Robert read me a story about a princess." "Uncle Robert did this." "Uncle Robert did that." I don't know where she got the name from – kids say the funniest things, don't they? Neville though it was funny, too. He started to say, "Run to bed, Princess. Uncle Robert's got a story for you." It was their special game.'

'Let me get this straight,' said Claire; 'Lianne doesn't have an uncle named Robert?'

'No, no. That's what she called Neville when he put her to bed. During the day he was Dad or Daddy, but she liked to imagine that she had this uncle who read to her. Who knows why? But Neville liked it. He'd do this funny deep voice and run to her room saying "Uncle Robert's coming – you better be in bed." She used to draw pictures of Uncle Robert and everything. She always drew him with a beard.'

'And then?'

'Well, you know what adolescents are like. Suddenly they don't want to play childhood games anymore. Lianne started to say that she didn't want Uncle Robert to visit her. And then – because kids will be kids – she started to say awful things about Uncle Robert. Suddenly Uncle Robert was a monster who did terrible things to her in the night. Honestly, you wouldn't believe the filth that came out that girl's mouth. And you can imagine how that made poor Neville feel. He'd been playing the Uncle Robert role for years, so it hurt him very much. When I told him what Lianne had said, he was furious. And I'll tell you one thing for free,' said Mrs Shaw; 'my Neville's not a man you want to make angry.'

Claire stood up – she felt sick. 'Excuse me,' she said, with no intention of returning. She had to get out of that room. She had to get away from Mrs Shaw. She ran through the corridors, pushed open the front doors. She didn't look at Amy or hear what she said.

Outside, Claire bent over, afraid she might vomit. When the nausea passed, she stood upright, took deep breaths of fresh air.

It was Neville Shaw. It was all Neville Shaw.

Twenty-Eight

SHE WALKED across the golf course, her head full of hideous images. Across the river, Sighthill Tower looked more sinister than ever. She wondered which floor the Shaw family had lived in. She wondered whether she'd walked in the room where Neville Shaw had abused Lianne. She screwed her face up, trying to force the images from her mind.

When she reached the bridge, she stopped and stared into the water. She could see a hazy reflection of herself, but as she stared she saw a shadow loom over her shoulder. She turned around, startled, imagining the shadow was Neville Shaw. But there was nothing there. When she looked back into the water, her own reflection had been stolen by passing cloud. Instead, she imagined Lianne, dressed up as a schoolgirl, as she had been on their night at the Ritz. Then she imagined Lianne, when a schoolgirl, dressed up as a sexualised adult. The child Lianne reached an arm out from the water. She was silent but her expression pleaded for help. Claire looked up at the clouds, shook the image from her head. She remembered the story about the White Lady, who centuries ago had supposedly drowned her babies in this river. She looked back into the water, but saw only the trickling stream and the trembling green limbs of watermilfoil.

On the other side of the river, as she strolled homewards, she heard a commotion coming from near the tower. In the distance, she could see two police vans and a patrol car, their siren lights wheeling dim-blue circles against the cloudy sky. At the fence, two security guards were smoking, watching the scene from a distance.

'What's going on?' Claire asked the Guards.

'Police nicked some boy for dealing counterfeit fags.'

'They've got him up there, right, and then all of a sudden he goes mental.'

'Jo-Jo,' said Claire, and she started to run. She ran past the church house and over the rough ground at the side of the exclusion zone. She jumped ditches and hurdled piles of rubble. As she got closer, she saw four policemen pinning a man to the ground. She could see only the man's jeans and the black of his bomber jacket, but she knew it was Jo-Jo.

Closer still, she saw that one of his shoes had come off. His hands were twisted behind his back, his wrists red and scraped, and where his jacket was pulled up she saw that his side was grazed and bloody. PC Young – or was that PC White? – had his knee pressing into Jo-Jo's back, but he was still writhing and struggling. He was twisting his neck round and he looked like he was trying to bite the police. Another policeman, whose hat had been dislodged, punched Jo-Jo hard in the side. They were shouting at him to calm down, but his rage was animalistic.

Eventually, a big bald policeman sprayed a canister of CS gas into Jo-Jo's face. Jo-Jo screamed in pain and instinctively Claire ran forward to aid him.

'Get back!' said the fourth policeman. 'Get back!'

Even from this distance, Claire could feel the sting of the gas; from where she stood, the sensation was like smelling freshly-chopped onions and chillies. The policeman who'd sprayed the gas now grabbed Jo-Jo by his hair and forced his face into the ground – Jo-Jo was trying to shout something. Then the police lifted him – each holding a leg or one of his handcuffed arms – and carried him to the nearer of the two police vans. Jo-Jo looked like a carcass being hung up to roast.

But as they neared the van, Claire finally understood what he was trying to shout. 'Baby!' he was saying. 'Baby Alyssa! Got to get her out! She's in there – Baby Alyssa!' Just before the police threw Jo-Jo into the van, he seemed to catch Claire's eye. His face was red and wet with tears, but it was as if he'd recognised Claire among the onlookers. The last word he shouted was 'Help!'

And even once the police had slammed the van doors, she could still hear his muffled shouts. He was thudding against the van walls, throwing himself around his temporary cell, slamming the sides so hard he rocked the van. Meanwhile, the policemen dusted themselves down, caught their breath, laughed and shook their heads.

'Excuse me,' said Claire. 'I think maybe you should investigate what that man said because—'

'Ignore her,' said PC Young. 'She's one of the local crazies.'

A minute later, the van departed. Its siren emitted three short yelps, and then its undulating wail faded into the distance.

Okay, thought Claire, the baby's still in there. Calm down. Breathe. Jo-Jo must have been trying to get Alyssa out of the tower when he was arrested. Directly overhead, the sun broke through the clouds; Claire looked at her watch and saw it was almost noon. Twenty-four hours to demolition.

She had to find Lianne – if Lianne had trusted Jo-Jo to take the baby to safety and Jo-Jo was now in prison then – Looking back over her shoulder, she saw a policeman taking a statement from one of the security guards. She started to run. She was convinced she could persuade Lianne to go to the police.

What happened next was one of the most terrifying incidents of Claire's life. When she reached her street, she saw Neville Shaw dragging Lianne to his car. He was shouting, 'Shut your mouth, you drunken wee tramp! You stink and you're pissed! You disgust me.' Lianne was struggling and crying and Neville was tugging her by the hair.

By the time she reached Neville's car, he had forced Lianne onto the back seat and he was pacifying her with a fierce grip on her wrists. 'I'm gonnae sober you up, even if I need tae tie you down.'

Lianne was crying, speaking softly. 'Tomorrow, Daddy. I'll come tomorrow, Daddy. Please, I promise.'

'Look at yourself – look at yourself!' He wrenched her head up and forced her to look in the rear view mirror.

Claire could see that Lianne *was* very drunk. Her head lolled and she looked to have sick in her hair. Both Neville and Lianne were oblivious to Claire's presence until Neville slammed the door and turned towards the front of the car. Then he saw Claire. 'What you looking at? Eh? What you looking at?'

'I need to speak to—'

'Not now,' said Neville, opening the driver's door.

Lianne had her hands over her face and Claire knocked the window to get her attention.

Neville stood up, one foot in the car, shouting over the roof. 'Listen, you fucking bitch. Get in my way and I'll kick your fucking teeth in. You understand?'

Claire stepped back. She was trembling – too scared to cry. Before the car sped away, she caught Lianne's eye and whispered two words: 'I know.'

Twenty-Nine

THAT AFTERNOON, Claire watched internet footage of controlled demolitions. She read that most demolition companies sounded a five-minute warning siren. She heard, on the videos, that fifteen or twenty seconds before the blast, the demolishers set off a banger to scare away roosting birds. The watching crowds were invariably startled; they would gasp, then laugh at this false alarm, and then seconds later they would begin to chant 'ten, nine, eight . . . ' And at zero, every time, the buildings would crumple, chopped at their bases, and the crowds' whoops would give way to fearful exclamations of awe. Claire watched with horror how the buildings seemed to disappear into themselves, and how, a second later, a cloud of dust spread out and grew and grew and grew.

By evening, she had formulated a plan – of sorts. Jo-Jo was in prison, and, in a way, so was Lianne. The construction site manager already thought Claire was a malevolent hoaxer. The police thought she was crazy – even her own husband thought she was crazy – and Morgana, while maybe not the leader of a satanic cult, was a deluded busybody. This was now up to Claire alone.

It was Claire's guess that Lianne hadn't abandoned Alyssa to die in the demolition. More likely, after removing her from the tower before Skacel and Black's infrared search, she'd entrusted Jo-Jo to look after her, and Jo-Jo, being Jo-Jo, had for some reason put her back in the tower. On Friday, Claire guessed, it was Jo-Jo that Lianne had been shouting at on the phone. If she was right then Baby Alyssa had been alone in the tower for more than twenty-four hours. How long can a seven-month-old baby last without being fed? She remembered something about an earthquake in Mexico City, which had buried a maternity ward under rubble – it took rescue workers seven days to dig out the new born babies and almost all of them survived. This thought comforted Claire, but when she tried to remember more details, she couldn't be sure whether she'd seen this on the news or in a film.

Jo-Jo must have been trying to rescue the baby when he was arrested. If Jo-Jo, who knew more about that tower than anyone else, had been unable to sneak in, what chance did Claire have? She had no chance, but she also had no alternative. The demolition workers would not stumble upon Baby Alyssa – Claire and Morgana had been unable to find her even when they'd been purposefully looking – and so long as they were drilling and hammering and shouting, there was no chance of them *hearing* her either. No, whichever way Claire looked at it, this was something she had to do on her own.

That night, she waited until Dan had gone to bed, and then she removed two chicken drumsticks from the fridge. She stuffed the drumsticks into her gardening jacket and then she slipped outside, wincing at the click of the Yale. The air was cooler than any she had felt in weeks, but the night was dry and still and lit by a full moon. She realised that none of these facts were in her favour. Had the sky been overcast, the night lashing with rain and gusting with wind, her chances of sneaking into the tower undetected would have been greatly increased. As it was, her mission seemed fairly hopeless.

The best plan she'd come up with – and it wasn't much of a plan – was to fill her pockets with stones, creep up to the fence, and throw the stones and the drumsticks into the exclusion zone. While the dogs and the guards were distracted, she would creep to a by-then-unguarded part of the fence and climb over as quietly as she could. Once she was in the exclusion zone, she'd have to hope that the inner fence was unguarded, and that the gap opposite the church house hadn't been repaired. Then she would enter the tower, climb to the eighth floor, and find the baby.

★   ★   ★

What Claire needed, obviously, was a flashlight. Remembering Dan's torch, she doubled back towards the garage, hoping that the torch's battery wouldn't be flat. She hit the fob on her keys, forgetting to direct it at their garage exclusively, and the Cox's door began to rise. In the midnight quiet, the two garage doors seemed to make an awful rattling, screeching, engine noise. She hid against the wall, listening to the occasional hoot of an unseen owl. Now and then the neighbourhood dogs barked, perhaps perturbed by Skacel and Black's German Shepherds, and she could hear the faraway murmur of lorries on the flyover. When she thought it was safe, she tiptoed into her garage and searched Dan's tool truck for the flashlight. She had become accustomed to the dark and the garage light stung her eyes. When she found the torch, she couldn't at first tell whether it was working, but when she turned off the garage light she saw that the torch did produce a weak beam. It would have to do; she stuffed the torch into her jacket pocket. And then, as she ran to close Morgana's door, Claire saw something that inspired in her a new and daring plan.

There was no space for the Cox car in their garage because, in addition to the Wiccan altar (which Dan *hadn't* been joking about), their garage held camping equipment, folding canvas chairs, several bicycles, and – the object that grabbed Claire's attention – Adrian's kayak. The kayak was on its end, leant against a wall, surrounded by paddles and helmets and lifejackets. This, thought Claire, was the answer.

She inspected the kayak, wondered whether she was strong enough to transport it, and saw that near the kayak there lay a pair of wheels – a small cart on which she could rest one end of the boat. She saw that there was a paddle, too – a heavy-looking double-ended thing, like a giant plastic cotton bud. She had seen people kayaking and vaguely knew the technique. The new plan was growing on her with every second.

Returning to the garage doorway, she checked that everything was still quiet, and then she stood for a moment, asking herself whether she was really going to do this. Strangely, the hardest part of the whole plan seemed to be getting the kayak out of the garage without waking Morgana or Adrian. It took Claire a while to realise that the boat was strapped to the wall, but once she unbuckled it, the kayak fell into her arms. It was made of fibreglass and it sounded hollow, so the weight of it surprised her. She slumped underneath it, bent onto her knees, and dropped it five inches to the floor. The noise it made was a sharp crack and again she returned to the doorway and listened for any sign that she'd disturbed her neighbours. When she felt calm again, she walked back to the boat and tried to lift its end onto the wheels. The first two times, the wheels scooted away from the boat and clattered onto the concrete floor, but the third time she clicked the rear of the kayak into the cart and realised, testing the weight, that she'd be able to drag it easily. She pulled down the paddle and slid it into the boat's cockpit. Before leaving, she spent a minute deciding whether or not she should take a lifejacket and helmet. She decided against the lifejacket – its fluorescent-orange colour was too conspicuous, and in any case the river, still low from the summer drought, was never much deeper than waist height – but she donned the helmet and clipped it under her chin. As she crept from the garage, tugging the boat behind her, it occurred to her that now would be a very bad time to see Dan.

The bottom of the street was fenced off – the street itself was to be evacuated from eleven a.m. – and this meant Claire had to drag the boat a long way to meet the river. She pulled it to the top of her road, aware of the soft trundle and clicks of the wheels, and the gentle rattle of the paddle. As she passed the church on St Michael's Street, a car drove from behind the shops. Its full-beam headlights momentarily illuminated Claire, and she felt as if she'd been caught by a searchlight. The car slowed as it passed her. It was a taxi, and both driver and passengers turned to watch this bizarre sight: at half-past midnight, a woman in a helmet was dragging a kayak through suburban Manchester.

She hurried down Riverside Grange, sure now that she'd made good her escape. She passed Mrs Brompton's house and bumped the kayak onto the riverside path. Opposite her, on the far bank of the river, the red light at the top of the phone mast blinked warnings in rhythm with her pulse. She pulled the paddle from the cockpit and waved it about, swishing through the air in some attempt at a practice stroke. While she was doing this, she noticed that at the side of the path a small creature was snuffling around in the dirt. It was a hedgehog, clearly visible in the moonlight, meandering with no apparent sense of direction, its nose pressed into the ground. The hedgehog didn't seem disturbed by her presence, and she felt it was some sort of an omen – by some inscrutable logic, she decided the hedgehog was a sign that what she was doing was right.

And so she found the courage to push the boat towards the water edge and lift it from its wheels. Immediately a problem became clear. As soon as she put the boat in the river, it was going to float away without her. Clearly, there had to be some trick that kayakers used to launch themselves, but to Claire such a manoeuvre seemed unimaginable. She hoisted the boat on her shoulder, stumbled over the rocks, and when her feet were getting wet she splashed it into the black water. After a few attempts at getting in – holding the coaming with one hand and stretching a foot into the cockpit, as if playing some aquatic version of Twister – she gave up and pulled the kayak back onto dry land. The only option, she decided, was to get into the boat on land and then somehow propel it to the water. So she stuffed herself into the cockpit and sat there wondering what to do next.

At first she tried to lever herself into the water with her paddle. Then she pushed at the ground with her bare hands. Finally she wriggled and gyrated, rather how one shuffles across the floor in a sleeping bag. This had some effect and after a moment the boat slid over the grassy bank and crashed hard onto rocks. Nearby, lost in the dark, birds squawked awake, shrieking as they beat the air. Pain surged through Claire's coccyx, and she worried she had cracked the bottom of the boat. She imagined herself sinking into the river and hitting the bottom so that just her head stuck out, like a buoy. Before that happened, however, she'd have to reach the water. She continued to wriggle inside the boat, bumping it on the rocks, producing an awful noise of chipping and scratching and carving.

She felt sorry for damaging Adrian's boat and stopped to catch her breath. Some unseen creature plopped into the river and then a giant HGV crashed across the flyover in a blaze of noise and light.

When Claire realised that she'd reached some water – albeit water too shallow for the kayak – she felt encouraged and with a final effort pushed herself diagonally into the stream. To her surprise, the boat glided into the water, aligned itself with the river, and for a few feet carried her contentedly downstream. Then she remembered Adrian's kayak cart, looked back to see the wheels stranded on the riverbank, and almost capsized the boat. She tipped the thing over and only her proximity to the river's rocky sides prevented her from splashing into the water. She was able to push herself upright and wobble onwards, but in doing so she grazed her knuckles. She held the paddle aloft, too afraid to dip it in the water.

Soon she passed into a stretch of river where the water spread flat and black and the boat slid forward with a melodic trickling noise. The full moon cast a white stripe down the centre of the river and Claire used this to navigate her course; she dipped the blades of her paddle to steady her line and felt reasonably in control. Unfortunately, as she approached the bridge at the bottom of her street, the pace of the river quickened, and she was once again at its mercy. But as she splashed under the bridge, she noted that she was now within the exclusion zone. All she had to do was dock the boat riverside.

That, of course, was far beyond her boating skills. She thought that if she paddled on the boat's left side, then she would steer towards the right, but when she submerged the blade, she veered the craft dangerously across the stream. The current wasn't fast – a little slower than walking pace – but Claire felt completely help-less as the river carried her side on. Worse, she realised that she was now passing the tower – she had to stop, even if it meant rolling into the river. And so she reached out and grabbed the site's inner fence.

The crash of the metal seemed to echo across the city. Birds screeched and dogs barked, and Claire hung on as the water splashed into her boat. She dropped her paddle and watched, helpless, as it bobbed downstream. Her fingers were red and white from gripping the wire and she could feel water filling the cockpit.

Such was her position when the security guards arrived.

Whether they had been alerted by the noise, had been positioned there all night, or had happened to be doing a patrol, Claire would never know. Although she was dismayed to see them, their first thought – after a beat of incredulity – was to help her. They ran to the riverside and one of them grabbed the boat's stern, while the other pulled Claire to shore by her hand. They dragged her from the kayak and pulled her onto the riverbank, and then they pulled the kayak beside her.

'You okay?' one of them asked.

'What were you doing?' asked the other one, more perplexed than angry.

Claire was shaking and cold and her legs were wet, but what made her cry was the thought that she'd failed Baby Alyssa. 'I need to—' She stopped herself. To admit she was there on purpose would surely see her detained. 'I often kayak at night,' she said.

'Do you need an ambulance?'

'Oh no, I'm fine. I'll just catch my breath and then paddle on.'

The security guards looked at each other – this was beyond eccentric. 'Why would you kayak at night?'

'For the nocturnal wildlife,' said Claire, trying to nod sagely despite her tears.

The security guards thought about this. Her story was incredible but there was no reason for them to think her suspicious: after all, they were used to deterring drunks and vandals and copper thieves. The taller guard shrugged. 'Takes all sorts, I suppose.'

'We'll need to escort you off the site,' said the shorter guard, who seemed the more officious of the two. 'Now that you're on it, I mean.'

'No need,' said Claire. 'You've been very kind, but I don't want to keep you guys from your duties. You get on and I'll set sail when

I've got my breath back.' She tried to sound light-hearted and calm but the pitch of her voice was unsteady with emotion.

'Do you want us to call someone for you?' asked the taller guard.

'No thanks,' said Claire. 'I'll be sailing home in a minute.'

'We can't leave you here alone.'

'Okay,' said Claire, thinking fast. 'Let me just stretch my legs before I continue my journey.' She kicked her legs out and shook her ankles; then she held her feet to her bum, stretching out her quads. The guards watched, bemused, as she wandered further and further from the river. When one of the guards shouted something about staying away from the building, she decided she'd put as much distance between her and them as she could. She seized her moment and ran.

It took them a beat to react, but then she heard them roar 'Hoy! Stop!' and their feet thudded in pursuit. Their strides were longer than hers, and she knew they'd soon catch up, but if she could make it into the tower then she could lose them in its labyrinth of flats. Perhaps they'd be too afraid to even enter now that the building was wired with explosives? For the first seconds of her run, Claire was lucid and composed. She saw the ground beneath her rush past like something seen from a train. But when she saw that she might actually make it, when she saw the door was only fifty metres away, she was seized by panic and her muscles started to tighten. She could hear them behind her, getting louder all the time. Her movements felt slow, like the running-through-treacle feeling she sometimes experienced in nightmares.

And then she had lost her balance and was flying, hands out – She hit the ground and then – there was a tiny separation between the two impacts – she felt a guard land on top of her. She realised she'd been rugby tackled. She was winded and felt like she couldn't breathe. She was flapping her arm, trying to explain that she was suffocating, but no sound was coming from her mouth. She heard a radio blast half a second of static. 'I can't breathe,' she was trying to say. 'Help,' she was trying to say. But all she could hear was the security guard's breathless request for police assistance.

Thirty

AS A TEENAGER, Claire Wilson could have imagined hypothetical scenarios in which, conceivably, she might have ended up in a police cell (a drunken night out, a case of mistaken identity, an over-zealous police officer). But as a twenty-eight-year-old married woman, it was hard to believe this was really happening. She felt detached from the whole experience, as if she were watching her part being played by an actress, and though she was afraid – being arrested was terrifying – she disassociated from what was happening to such an extent that outwardly she appeared calm.

Everything was either like a scene on TV, in which case it seemed unreal, or it was unlike a scene on TV, in which case it seemed even more unreal. For example, when the policeman cautioned her, he said exactly what policemen say on TV: 'I'm arresting you on suspicion of aggravated trespass. You do not have to say anything but it may harm your defence if you fail to mention when questioned something which you intend to rely on in court.' Similarly, when she met the duty sergeant, when she was patted down by a WPC (a bit like going through airport security), when she turned her pockets out and signed the record of her possessions on her custody report (embarrassingly, her possessions included a helmet, a kayak, and two chicken drumsticks), she felt as if she'd stumbled into an episode of *The Bill.* When she was led to her cell, the jailer really did have a clanking key chain, and the cell door was, as Claire would have expected, a heavy metal thing that slammed shut and locked with an intimidating *ker-thunk.*

On the other hand, when the duty sergeant asked whether she wanted him to contact anyone on her behalf – which is to say, when she realised she *wasn't* entitled to make one teary phone call from a graffiti-covered payphone (while being heckled by a long queue of impatient criminals) – the scene didn't correspond with what she'd seen on films and television, and therefore the experience seemed flagrantly unreal. (As to the question itself, she couldn't decide whether she wanted Dan to know or not, and when she didn't reply the duty sergeant shrugged and said, 'Let us know if you change your mind.') Similarly, her cell should have been covered in graffiti, she felt. In fact, the walls were whitewashed and the only evidence of graffiti was a few painted-over initials carved into the plaster. There was, however, a line of grime – like the tide mark left on a bathtub – where the wall met the bed. The bed was a shin-height wooden platform, on which there was a thin blue mattress and cushion. The cell didn't smell of urine and sweat – it smelled of bleach. Behind a waist-high partition, there was a metal toilet (sans toilet paper, Claire noticed), and this was something else Claire wouldn't have expected based on television.

Until it happened to her, Claire had never known how terrifying it is to be arrested. It wasn't that the police threatened her or were even particularly unpleasant; the frightening thing was that she had lost any right or power to determine her own safety and was completely at the mercy of uniformed strangers. For instance, they made her surrender her shoelaces and belt (which left her wet trousers falling down), and they took her watch and mobile phone, so she had no sense of the time, and no means of communicating with the outside world. The sense of isolation and vulnerability – the sense that here anything could happen to her – was petrifying.

And there were other things to be afraid of, such as the shouts and chants and banging on doors. One man kept shouting, over and over again, 'Mark Duggan, Smiley Culture, Sean Rigg, Ian Tomlinson, Kingsley Burrell, Jimmy Mubenga, Jean Charles de Menezes – murdered by the police!' The police ignored him for a long time, but soon after he started chanting 'Simon Harwood – killer! Simon Harwood – killer!' Claire heard thudding boots, the slam of a door, yelps and thuds. She heard a policeman shouting 'Shut it! Shut your face or we will fuck you up! D'you understand?' The cell door slammed and there was a moment of silence, but seconds later the man resumed shouting, this time about unpunished deaths in police custody. At this point, a female prisoner shouted back that if he didn't shut up, she'd kill him herself.

It was probably this fear that made Claire such a placid prisoner. She should have been banging on the doors, screaming for justice. She should have been yelling about the baby, demanding they act to save a child's life. How many hours until demolition now? Ten? Nine? She should have been throwing herself against the walls, screaming and beating down the doors. Instead, she kept thanking the police as if they'd just carried her luggage in a hotel. Once an hour, a WPC opened the latch in Claire's cell door. The latch made a noise like a shotgun being cocked, and every time it opened, Claire jerked in fear and felt her heart. 'You alright in there?' the WPC would say.

'Yes, thank you,' Claire would reply.

In fact, her trousers were wet and she was very cold. She badly wanted to ask for a blanket, but she was too afraid. And what she most wanted was some information – some idea of what was happening to her. There were so many questions in her head. For how long would she be held there? Why hadn't she been interviewed? When would she eat? What would happen if she started her period? Was she going to court?

Though she was exhausted, at no point did she sleep, and as the night dragged on, frustration began to compete with fear. Why was she there! Every minute brought the demolition closer. She had no idea how long she'd been detained for, and there was no natural light in the cell. Was it morning? They needed to let her out!

On Sunday morning at 9:15 a.m., Claire was escorted to Interview Room 3. She was relieved to be out of the cell but self-conscious about her stale breath and unwashed body. Her jeans smelled of damp, and dried blood covered her right hand where she had grazed her knuckles kayaking.

And then it occurred to her, as she was waiting alone in the interview room, how ridiculous these thoughts were. What did it matter? So much of her life she had spent caring about the wrong things: what did it matter whether she had stale breath? What difference did it really make if her bra was visible through her shirt? Why did she care about her BMI or her . . . underarm fat. *Underarm fat!* Who even decided such a thing should be added to the catalogue of female worries? It was all absurd. She remembered that as she was being driven to the police station, her hands cuffed behind her back, among her many terrors was the thought that she might be strip-searched. As much as she feared the violence of the act, she had also worried because her legs were unshaved and it had been ages since she'd attended to her bikini line. What a moment at which to worry about depilation! 'Who cares?' she said aloud. 'Who really fucking cares?'

When the door opened seconds later, Claire worried that the police woman had heard her shout 'who cares?', and had interpreted it as the recalcitrant outburst of a defiant criminal; so she readjusted her countenance into one of extreme contrition. To Claire's surprise, however, the woman conducting the interview was more interested in the suspected theft of the kayak than in the alleged aggravated trespass. She never mentioned that Claire had been arrested on a demolition site (or asked why she'd gone boating in the middle of the night), but she was keen to know where Claire had acquired the kayak.

Claire's first thought was to claim that the kayak was her own, but she was too tired to defend this story convincingly. 'It's my neighbour's boat,' said Claire. 'I borrowed it.'

'You're saying your neighbour leant you the boat?'

Claire nodded.

'Can you confirm that for the video camera, Claire?'

Claire nodded more vigorously and said, 'Yes.'

'And this neighbour will be able to confirm your story?'

Claire didn't say anything.

'You're not doing yourself any favours by lying. The boat you had in your possession at the time of your arrest was reported stolen this morning.'

Claire imagined Adrian emerging from number thirteen, ready to lash his kayak to the roof rack. She saw him opening the garage door, thermos and camera in hand, only to find his beloved boat was missing. 'Adrian Cox,' she said.

The policewoman stared back, pokerfaced.

'Adrian Cox is my neighbour.'

'The man who leant you the boat?'

'Yes.'

'So why did he report it missing?'

Claire looked at the clock and watched the second-hand hop. 'It was his wife, Morgana, who gave me the boat. She must have forgotten to tell her husband. It's just a misunderstanding.'

The policewoman stared across the table and tapped a pen against her teeth. 'Wait here,' she said. She locked the door. The video camera continued to run.

Claire guessed the WPC had gone to phone Adrian. He would ask Morgana whether she had leant the boat to anyone, and she, of course, would say 'no.' For the first time it occurred to Claire that she might be in serious trouble. Was stealing a kayak similar to stealing a car? She now thought she'd been an idiot to begin this interview without a solicitor present. She resolved to answer every subsequent question 'no comment,' but worried that doing so would make the woman angry. If the police shouted at her, she would do whatever they said.

She looked at the clock again. Hop, hop, hop, hop. Every second brought the demolition closer. In a way Claire was glad to be in prison – at least she wouldn't have to hear the explosion. On the videos, the noise of a building collapsing sounded no louder than the snap of a chocolate bar, and as the clouds of dust spread towards the cameras, the noise was like a wave washing over shingle.

The policewoman returned. 'You're in luck, Claire. It turns out that when Mr Cox had a think he *did* remember lending you his boat.' The policewoman seemed to find this intensely frustrating. 'Interview suspended,' she said. 'Nine-twenty-two a.m.'

Claire was released two hours later. For the aggravated trespass, they issued her with what they called a 'simple caution.' The simple caution did not seem simple at all. Back in Interview Room 3, a policeman asked her to confirm that she had unlawfully entered private property in the early hours of Sunday ninth September, and had there behaved in a way likely to cause an obstruction to lawful business on said property. He talked fast and at length. Claire was tired and desperate to be home – she nodded to everything he said. Now and again a phrase registered – criminal record, enhanced disclosure, Criminal Records Bureau, prospective employer, admission of guilt. Just before she signed in confession, she hesitated – the document was pages long. 'Do I need to sign this now?'

The policeman shrugged. 'It will help speed things up,' he said. 'You'll be on your way home in a few minutes.'

Claire signed.

A few minutes later, waiting in the lobby of the custody suite, she heard the duty sergeant bemoaning the standard of the previous night's arrests. 'They nick someone,' he said, 'come back to the station for a cup of tea, piss off out again, and forget that we have to look after these mugs.'

She signed for receipt of her possessions, less the chicken drumsticks, which had been disposed of as perishable goods, and the kayak, which was in secure storage. The duty sergeant explained the process by which she could apply to recover the kayak, but of course Claire wasn't listening.

Leaving the police station – not daring to look back – she felt a pang of relief and elation. It didn't last. Five seconds later, Claire saw her husband. Straight away, she knew that Dan had been crying.

Thirty-One

THEY DROVE in silence for five minutes and then Dan pulled over at the entrance to a school. He stared out of the side window and didn't say anything. Claire looked at the clock on the dashboard: 11:24. She wanted him to drive. She didn't have a plan, but if she could get to the tower in time then maybe one would occur to her.

'Last night,' said Dan, 'I woke up and you weren't there. I looked for you downstairs, expecting that you'd fallen asleep on the couch or summat. I didn't know you'd been arrested for stealing our next door neighbour's canoe. I'd never have seen that coming, cause I still imagine you as . . . my Claire. My Babe. You know? When I realised you were out, I wanted to phone the hospital or the police. But I feared how the conversation would go, you know? At some point they'd have asked me, "Has your wife stayed out all night before?"'

Claire started to say that she was sorry but then she stopped. That was another thing – why had she spent her whole life saying sorry? She said 'sorry' when she edged through a crowd, 'sorry' when she walked in front of the TV, 'sorry' when she and Dan started sentences simultaneously, 'sorry' when she took her seat on a train. She *wasn't* sorry. The only thing she was sorry about was that her attempt to break into the tower had failed. The only person to whom she owed an apology was Baby Alyssa.

'When I went to bed,' continued Dan, 'I found the key to the spare room. For fifteen minutes I didn't dare use it. I were terrified of what I might find in there. And then when I . . . The paintings were— I opened the door and it were so beautiful. And I— Oh God,' said Dan, tears running down his cheeks, 'God, I just want my wife back. Oh God, please, I had a wife – I just want her back.'

In all the time she'd known him, Claire had only seen Dan weep like this once before. It had been at his parents' house, the night before his father's funeral. Dan had dealt with his dad's illness so stoically that a stranger might have thought him dispassionate. But Claire knew that Dan channelled his fear and worry into helping his parents – he was at their house every other day, clearing drainpipes that didn't need to be cleared, moving furniture that didn't need to be moved, buying food that was never eaten. Even when his father died, Dan restrained his grief. His brother was on honeymoon (having married in haste so his father wouldn't miss the ceremony), and so Dan carried his father's possessions home from the hospital in a grey plastic bag. He took responsibility for the funeral arrangements. He placed a notice in the local paper. He obtained a death certificate. He notified the Department of Work and Pensions. He did things Claire would never have known to do, and he did it all with a stoicism and maturity that awed her. And then, the night before the funeral, while smoking a cigarette in his parents' garden (this was before Dan quit), he showed Claire the stump of a tree – the only one there had ever been in his parents' small council garden – from which, two decades earlier, his father had hung a rope swing. At that point, he covered his face and sobbed.

He was crying the same way now and Claire could imagine no sight or sound more awful. She unclicked their belts, held him close, let his tears soak her neck and shoulder. Then she pulled away and looked him in the eye. 'Yes, you had *a wife*,' she said, 'and I'm not sure you'll ever get her back. You'll get something much better: you'll get *me* back.'

Dan looked baffled.

She held him again. 'I love you,' she said, over and over. She meant it every time she said it. And yet, as she held him, she couldn't stop looking at the clock.

11:26.

11:27.

11:28.

They were still parked at 11:32. 'Come on,' said Claire, 'let's go home.'

'We can't go home – the street's evacuated until after the blast.' Dan had wiped away his tears. He now seemed embarrassed by his crying and irritated by Claire's touch.

'We can't just sit here.'

'Why not?' said Dan. He stared at her – the question was a challenge.

'If you're not going to drive, get out of the way and let me do it.'

'Where's Adrian's canoe?'

'The police have got it. I need to apply to . . . ' Claire trailed off. She hadn't heard what the policeman had said about reclaiming the kayak. 'That's not the most important thing right now, is it?' A police motorcycle roared past, its siren light whirling purple.

'You need to phone him,' said Dan. 'You owe him big time.'

11:33.

'They'll have been evacuated.'

'Phone Morgana's mobile.'

'Stop ordering me ab— Tell you what, I'll phone if you drive,' said Claire.

'Tell them we're getting you help,' said Dan, turning the ignition.

Morgana's phone rang for a long time and Claire hoped there would be no answer. Eventually the ringing stopped but the only noise was a haze of background commotion.

'Hello?' said Claire.

'Hello?'

'Can you hear me?'

'Claire, you need to—' The end of the sentence was obscured by a siren.

'I'm phoning to apologise about the kay—'

'Never mind that – Lianne's . . . ' Morgana sounded out of breath and the end of the sentence was spoken incomprehensibly far from the phone.

'What?'

'—on the flyover. Police everywhere but . . . talk to you. I don't know what's got into her but . . . might actually do it. Hold on, there's a . . . It looks like she's . . . The whole flyover is closed off.

She might be— No . . . threatening to jump. Get off the phone. Just get . . . soon as you can.'

'What was that all about?' asked Dan.

'It sounds like Lianne's on the flyover – she's going to jump!'

'Lianne?'

'Come on, drive!' How strange it was that, in spite of every-thing, Claire should feel such a surge of love and empathy for her friend Lianne.

Dan drove like he was in a car chase. When she looked back on this day, as she would so many times, Claire thought that Dan had waited all his life for a legitimate excuse to drive like a nutter. She imagined he'd always wanted to meet a pregnant woman who was having contractions or an expectant father who didn't want to miss the birth. He jumped red lights, swerved in and out of traffic, over-took on the inside, bumped onto the pavement to avoid a queue, and escaped a cul-de-sac with a handbrake turn. It was simultane-ously the best and worst piece of driving that Claire had ever seen.

Near the flyover, bewildered drivers were performing three-point turns, bumping across the dual carriageway, hooting their horns – the noise like some discordant orchestra tuning up. Motorcycle cops revved their engines and moved from junction to junction, looking as confused as everyone else. Not only was the flyover shut but some of the most obvious diversions had been closed to traffic in advance of the demolition. Claire looked at her watch: 11:42.

They left the car on the hard shoulder and ran through the queuing vehicles. Where the road climbed towards the flyover, pedestrians scaled the embankment on the east side. Some carried flasks and camping chairs. A man with a camera on a tripod stood on crash barriers, straining to see over the police vans. None of them knew which way to look: should they focus on the building they'd come to see destroyed, or should they follow the suicide happening to their left? A helicopter hovered overhead, chopping up the sky.

Police had stretched incident tape over the flyover and were guarding the line, arms folded. Morgana was sitting on the road, cross-legged, eyes closed, fingers on temples. Beyond all that, Claire could just see Lianne's head. She was midway across the flyover – balancing at the highest point. She must have been standing on the railings to be visible above the throng of police.

Claire felt someone tugging her sleeve and heard a voice saying, 'This is her! This is her!' It was Adrian.

At first she thought that Adrian was pointing her out to the police so that they could re-arrest her for thieving his kayak.

A helmeted policeman put a hand on Claire's chest and said, 'Wait there!' He spoke loud and slow, as if English wasn't Claire's first language.

'Inspector Page!' shouted Adrian. 'Inspector Page! She's here!'

A grey-haired man jogged towards them, holding the butt of a cigarette. His sweat-stained police shirt was untucked and his trousers were too big for him. A younger man in a peaked cap ran behind him.

'You Claire Somebody?' said the grey-haired man. 'I'm Inspector Page.'

'Hi,' said Claire, still unsure whether she was in trouble.

'You're Lianne Shaw's neighbour, is that right?'

'That's right.'

'She says you know.'

'I know what?'

'I don't know. She says *you* know, not me.' Inspector Page remembered about his cigarette and threw it to the floor. 'She says there's something she needs to explain to you. Does that make any kind of sense?'

'Yeah, it does.'

'You up to talking with her?'

'Inspector, don't you think—' said the man in the suit.

'Are you up to this?

'Let us through,' said Claire. 'My husband needs to hear this too.'

'I don't think we should involve civilians, Inspector. The guidelines say—'

'The guidelines won't be awake all night if this goes tits up. Let's go,' said Inspector Page.

The four of them jogged out across the empty highway. As they neared the roadside, Claire looked down at the drop. Far below, she could see a fire engine and an ambulance parked on Riverside Grange. Beyond her own house she could see Sighthill Tower. From the flyover, the only signs of the impending demolition were the emergency vehicles and spectators gathered near St Michael's Church.

'Lianne?' shouted Inspector Page. 'We've got Claire here, the woman you asked to speak with? Her husband – what's your name, son?'

'Dan.'

'Her husband, Dan, he's here too. What d'you want to tell them?'

'Let them through!' shouted Lianne.

Page nodded. 'Keep your distance. Don't be confrontational. Don't make any sudden movements.'

Claire held Dan's hand and they walked towards Lianne. They could hear the policemen shouting advice, but the words were lost in the noise of the helicopter. Lianne was barefoot, wearing only a T-shirt over her underwear. She had a black eye.

When they were two metres from her, Lianne held up her hand. 'Don't come any closer, okay?'

Claire stopped, held her hands up in a gesture of non-aggression. They were high enough to feel new strength in the breeze.

'Listen, Claire,' said Lianne, 'there's stuff I got to explain to you before I jump.'

Thirty-Two

'FIRST THINGS FIRST,' said Lianne. 'I'm not mad, right? I'm jumping cause it's what I have to do – it's what I want to do. This isn't some freak out, so don't tell me how you knew some guy who, like, tried to kill himself and now he's so glad he didn't. This is what I want to do, right?'

'What about Alyssa? I know about your baby,' said Claire. She looked back over her shoulder at the police. They seemed very far away. They were watching the conversation blankly, with no chance of hearing anything said.

'Yeah, I know you know,' said Lianne.

'Oh, Jesus,' said Dan.

'She's gonna die too. Any minute now they're gonna blast that building to pieces, and there's nothing I can do to stop it. I'm gonna stand here, as close to me baby as I can be, yeah, and we're gonna go together. I'm gonna jump the moment they blow the building, so we die at the exact same moment, yeah? Whether we're going to heaven or hell, we're gonna walk in there holding hands. Cause that's the only thing I can do for my baby now.' Lianne started to sob in great heaving wails. She had run out of tears, as if her grief was beyond anything her body was designed for.

'That's not true,' said Claire. 'There's still time to save her. We can sort all this out, I promise.'

'Yeah,' said Dan, who looked shocked and confused.

'All you have to do is come down and explain to the police what—'

'SHUT UP! Don't you think I've tried?' said Lianne. 'This morning I escaped from my Dad's. I climbed out the skylight, and—'

'Did he do that to you?' Claire pointed towards Lianne's swollen eye.

'Yeah,' said Lianne, 'he did. Like, you think you've got it all figured out, but you don't know anything. I climbed out and I, like, walked barefoot and I begged them to stop. *I begged them.*'

'Who?'

'The demolition bastards. But they saw me and they saw some, like, proper crazy woman. And what d'you think they told me? Yeah, that's right: they said some crazy bitch had already tried that crap on them. And who were that, Claire? You just couldn't mind your own business, could you?'

'I'm sorry.'

'No, you're not. You're just pissed off cause you haven't been able to save the day. You think you're, like, some big hero, and I'm some monster who's killed her baby. But you don't know anything about me. You don't know why—'

'I know about your father. I spoke to your mother yesterday.'

'See what I mean, yeah? You're a proper nosy bitch, aren't you?'

'I know that Uncle Robert was really your dad. I know he – I don't think you're a bad person, Lianne. I don't blame you for any of this.'

'Then since you know it all you probably know that he also raped my step sisters, yeah? That the only reason he ever shacked up with me mam in the first place was cause she had two little girls and a baby daughter. But you knew that, right? You know that it took me till I was in high school before I realised what he were doing were weird, right? When I— STAY BACK YOU PIG BITCH!' Lianne was pointing at a policewoman who had edged a step or two closer, trying to get within earshot. 'When I were a child,' she continued, 'I had this secret den. I found out that there were this, like, space behind the water heater. There were a sort of plywood board, but if you unscrewed that then you could crawl through and drop into the space. I put all me special things in there, like me teddies and stuff. I put them there cause I didn't want them to see what happened to me in the night.'

'Shit,' said Dan. 'That's like where Abukar and me had our fort. I know where you mean. Behind the water heater, right? Shit,' he said again.

'Who's Alyssa's father?' asked Claire.

Lianne shrugged.

'Is Neville Alyssa's father?'

Lianne started to cry again. She didn't answer.

'That sick bastard,' said Dan. 'I can't believe the same time we were playing in one tower block you were . . . '

Claire looked over her shoulder. The police were nodding encouragement. Some were half-crouched, as if about to start a long-distance race. She saw Inspector Page glance over the drop.

'When Neville found out he said that I weren't fit to raise a child. He said I were a tramp and a slut and an alcoholic and a junkie. And he said . . . ' This last sentence became a wail. 'He said he were gonna look after it for me, cause I weren't fit to be a mother. And then I had a scan, and I saw it on the screen, and I saw that it were a baby girl. Once I knew it were a girl, I just couldn't let it happen again. I couldn't let him take her.'

'So you told him the baby was stillborn?'

'What would you have done?'

Claire didn't know.

'I were lucky,' continued Lianne. 'I went into labour a week early. He didn't know. I were in labour for eight hours and he must have phoned me twenty times. The nurses were, like, can we call the father? Can we call your parents? Can we call a friend? Cause I were so scared to be doing it all alone. But in the end, Alyssa were perfect. I remember hearing her crying and then it were like the next thing I saw she were just this little face peeking out of a blanket. And after that I've phoned my dad, yeah, told him I'd had a stillbirth. And he were like, "well that mustae been God's way." And he said it proved I weren't fit to be a mother. So when the hospital said I could go, I took Alyssa and I went to stay at Lynn's house in Salford – Lynn's me cousin. I stayed there nearly three months—'

'Did your dad try to find you?'

'I told him I'd gone away to get me head together. Said I were, like, too upset to be at home. And it were okay at first. Like, even Pigeon – that's what folk call Lynn's fella – were alright with me.

But they've only got one room – Lynn and Pigeon – and soon they needed me out, yeah? So Lynn said I should go stay with Jo-Jo, who's her brother, but he lived in some sheltered accommodation bollocks, so I'd nowhere to go. And that were when I phoned Neville and told him I were coming home.'

Claire nodded.

'Neville has keys to the house – he comes in when he pleases, does what he wants. I couldn't let him find Alyssa – he'd have taken her from me. So I put her in the only safe place I knew. I put her behind the water tank in the old flat. I put her where I used to hide.'

'On the eighth floor?'

'Yeah. I meant it only to be for a few days, but it were like she were happy there, you know? I made it all soft and padded and put in glow lamps. And she had her blankie and her toys.' Lianne started to sob again. She ripped at her hair – the exact gesture Claire had seen Lianne's mother make – and then she leant forward. Was she going to throw herself now? Claire saw Dan readying himself, contemplating some sort of diving intervention.

'And Jo-Jo helped, right?' said Claire. She had to try to keep Lianne talking. 'He fed Alyssa when you couldn't?' She remembered the night when she and Lianne had gone clubbing, when Lianne had asked Claire to leave her house while she attended to some 'personal stuff.' She must have crept into the tower to put her baby to sleep. She'd left her baby asleep in a derelict building while they went *clubbing*?

'Yeah, Jo-Jo helped me. I gave him the pram I'd been using for Alyssa and I suggested he stash his gear in the utility room. Jo-Jo would do anything for me. He's simple, you know? I had to write 'MCFC' on the door so he'd remember what flat it were.'

'Shit,' said Claire. 'We were in that flat. We looked in the bathroom cupboard.' They'd been so close!

'It were all going okay, till you moved here. After you came to my door, I were scared to take Alyssa to the window. Then that stupid hippy's kids started playing in the tower. Like, one day I've gone up to the eighth floor and found all these old kids' toys. I thought someone knew my secret and were trying to mess with me head, you know? Then one day, when I were with Alyssa in the flat, I heard those stupid kids going on about their Secret Baby Room and I knew I had to scare them off.'

'So *you* put the pig's head there and tried to frame Morgana?'

Lianne nodded. 'You wouldn't stop snooping around, Claire. Eventually you got them to do that big search, but you stopped to tell me about it. As soon as you'd gone home, Jo-Jo and I went in – there's loose planks on me garden fence – and got Alyssa out. Jo-Jo was supposed to keep her till I could come and get her. Like, I'd been saving money out of what me dad gave me and I were gonna run away – with Alyssa, yeah? But after the search, Jo-Jo put Alyssa back in the tower. It's not his fault – he's just a moron. He had to sign on and he thought it'd be okay to leave her for a couple of hours. But when he got back, the security were too tight and they'd put up blast shielding against my fence. We couldn't—'

All three were startled by a sudden squeal of megaphone feedback. 'Hello, Lianne,' said Inspector Page. 'Can you hear me okay? We've got your father here.'

'No!' shouted Claire.

Dan was shaking his head and waving his arms in big X-shapes, but Page had already passed Neville the megaphone.

'Lianne,' he said, 'I want you tae ken that I love you.'

Lianne looked over the drop, shuffled her feet forward.

Neville started to walk towards them, unhindered by the police. 'I'm sorry if I've been over harsh – I didnae mean tae upset you.' He walked on, holding the megaphone at his hip. With each deliberate step, he looked to Claire like a gunfighter pacing strides before a duel. Lianne had covered her face – it was impossible to tell her expression or guess what she would do next.

'I think that's close enough,' said Dan.

Neville ignored him. 'Princess?' he said. 'I need you tae come doon off the railings.'

Lianne's toes were now sticking over the edge – only her heels were still on the railing. Even if she didn't decide to jump, one gust of wind could kill her.

Neville set the megaphone on the tarmac. He walked between Dan and Claire. A silence of concentration spread from the police, the demolition spectators, the emergency crews far below.

'Princess, come doon. I promise everything's gonnae be okay. Whatever's wrong, your daddy's gonnae make things better, okay?' He was now close enough to grab her. One way or another, this was about to end.

And when it did, there was no dramatic lunge; Lianne didn't slip; Neville didn't grab her ankle. Instead, Lianne seemed to fall back into Neville's arms. Claire heard distant applause and cheers, the police running to meet them. Only she seemed to notice that Lianne was eerily white, her face frozen in an expression of absence. Her eyes were open but unfocused, and her mouth suggested neither speech nor thought. Her head and arms swung loose, jolted by Neville's embrace. Neville was whispering something in her ear, but she showed no response.

Meanwhile, Inspector Page was wiping his brow with one hand and slapping Neville's shoulder with the other. 'Well done,' he said. 'Daddy saves the day.'

Two policewomen had placed an aluminium emergency blanket over Lianne's shoulders. The cop in the peaked cap was saying something about powers under section 136 of the Mental Health Act. A small tug of war had developed between the two WPCs, the sergeant in the peaked cap, and Neville Shaw. None of them spoke to Lianne.

Claire held Dan's hand. She felt relieved and horrified and angry all at once. Then a siren sounded from the demolition site below. The noise echoed up to merge with the clatter of the helicopter and the expectant cheers of the implosion enthusiasts. 'Five minutes,' said Claire.

'Come on!' said Dan. He started to run.

Thirty-Three

THEY RAN PAST Inspector Page, the WPCs, Lianne draped in her tinfoil blanket. They ran under the police tape, through the patrol cars and motorcycles. They jogged down the central reservation, past irritated drivers who beeped and hooted, oblivious to the day's drama. 'This way!' shouted Claire, leading Dan towards the St. Michael's Street steps. They ran between the photographers and day trippers – a child on his father's shoulders, a man filming the helicopter on a video camera.

Claire had jogged these steps dozens of times. She always took them three at a time, feeling good because she knew her run was nearly over. This time, however, she and Dan struggled against pedestrians moving in the other direction. There were families climbing for a better view. A man with a camping stool. A child crying. An older couple who'd stopped on the mid-section, content with the view from halfway. 'Hey!' shouted a man in a raincoat. 'Watch where you're going!'

They ran down the middle of St. Michael's Street. The road, closed to traffic, was full of spectators strolling back and forth. They passed a food kiosk, ran between two pushchairs. Lungs bursting, they reached the church, merged with the crowd: a father pointing at the helicopter; a mother putting sun cream on a child's arms; kids scrabbling under trees in the churchyard, fighting over the early-season conkers. The air smelled of coconut and hot dogs. A man in a football shirt, sweating under polyester, bent to speak to his son. 'Any second now,' he said.

She saw Dan, hands on knees. 'What now?' he asked.

'Excuse me. Move. Come on, get out the way!' Claire shouldered through the crowd, oblivious to tuts and insults. She saw Seth and Amy, perched on a wall, beneath the billboard he had defaced. She saw a fire engine and two ambulances, idling, doors open, parked on the dirt. The paramedics and firemen mingled in the sunshine, trading jokes, looking at the tower, as expectant as everyone else. She reached the front – a line of trainspotter types, the full-time implosion enthusiasts, pointing, explaining, debating tactics. Beyond them, two cops – Young and White – leaning against the perimeter fence. Security guards. Demolition workers in hard hats. Someone said, 'Here we go.'

She heard the jingle of an ice cream van, the helicopter circling lower overhead. Then she heard a staccato of explosions. *Bang. Bang. Bang – Bang – Bang.* She was too late.

She heard the gasps of onlookers, the click and flash of cameras. She looked up, expecting to see the tower crumble. Then she heard the flap and squawk of birds, saw their silhouettes fly from the tower, remembered about the warning blasts. A pause in the crowd hum – a worry the demolition had failed. Then laughter spreading. Wives teasing their husbands.

No time to waste – one last desperate attempt. She ran and jumped on the fence, started to scramble, hand sore and grazed. She could hear people screaming alarm, a police radio. She felt hands on her ankles, tried to climb anyway. She heard the crowd booing, then cheering as she was pulled down. She felt her arms crack, her hands pulled to her shoulders. People were clapping. She heard the handcuffs locking. The metal cutting into her wrists. Children chanting 'Blow it up! Blow it up! Blow it up!' Her face was pressed into the fence and through the mesh she saw Jeffries nodding, giving thumbs up to his demolition team.

'I'm arresting you for public disorder. You do not have to say anything but it may harm your defence . . . ' Halfway through the caution, the countdown started: 'Ten, Nine, Eight . . . ' The crowd shouted louder with each number. ' . . . you say may be taken down and used in evidence.'

'Seven! Six!'

She could hear Seth shouting at the police, telling them to let her go.

'Five!'

'You're hurting her, you pigs!'

'Four!'

'Get back!' PC White had drawn his truncheon.

'Three!'

In the exclusion zone, she could see an ancient man in a hard hat, hunched over an old wooden rack-bar detonator, and further forward, wearing a headset, a demolition worker held an electronic control box – at this distance, it looked like the controller from a Playstation.

'Two!'

'Stop!' screamed Claire, her voice lost in the chanting. 'I'm sorry, Alyssa', she said. And then she waited, knowing that in a second all this would be covered in dust.

'One!'

She scrunched closed her eyes, braced herself for the rat-a-tat-tat of explosions. When the building fell, the noise would sound no louder than someone snapping a biscuit. The dust cloud would grow and spread. It would look like something from the apocalypse, but Claire would hear only waves on shingle.

'Zero!'

Screams and cheers. Camera flashes. A millisecond of pause. A millisecond more. Still nothing. 'Zero!' someone said again. Laughter. A murmur of consternation.

Claire opened her eyes and peered through the fence. She could see Jeffries, cursing, a hand held aloft to signal delay. He was looking over to his right, his eyes tracking something that moved.

'You stay with her!' said PC White, scrabbling on the fence. He reached the top, leapt, landed, cried out in pain.

Only then did Claire see what White had intended to chase. Dan was running towards the tower, pursued by police and security guards. Midway towards the inner fence, a demolition worker waited for him, crouched like a rugby player intent on a try-saving tackle. 'Go on, Dan,' said Claire.

The crowd had seen him, too – they were booing and jeering. PC White limped for three metres, gave up, and lay in the dirt holding his leg.

'Go on, Dan,' said Claire.

As he neared the demolition worker, Dan dropped his hip, side-stepped, accelerated. The workman dived, grabbed for Dan's legs, missed. The crowd groaned and booed. Just for today, Claire thought, let there be glory and praise for all the world's football practices. 'Go on, Dan,' she said again.

He leapt onto the inner fence. He looked like a man on an obstacle course. His pursuers ran, jumped, grabbed at his legs. A guard had a grip on his shoe. It seemed Dan was caught, seemed he'd be dragged to ground, pinned, handcuffed. Then he kicked off the hand, tumbled over the fence, crashed onto his side. Momentarily, it seemed he might not get up. The spectators held their breath, their loyalties divided by Dan's gallant run.

Then he crawled onto his knees. He stood up groggily, looked back through the fence, and then he limped, stooped in pain, towards the tower. Nobody followed him. The demolition workers restrained the guards and the police, pointing at the tower, gesturing explosions. They slashed the air with their hands, frantically signalling Jeffries to stop the demolition. Jeffries had already stopped the demolition. He was shouting into his radio, pointing at the tower, pointing at the ninety-four-year-old former resident (who had long ago pressed the plunger on his symbolic detonator, and who was now looking at said plunger as if he suspected it was faulty).

'What's going on?' someone said.

'Looks like another suicide.'

'They're all doing it today.'

She heard a police siren, saw the helicopter circle lower. She closed her eyes and imagined the inside of the tower. She pictured Dan in the entrance foyer, squinting in the gloom. She imagined him climbing the stairs; would he remember where to find Baby Alyssa? She concentrated on her thoughts, as though she could direct him telepathically. Remember, Dan: eighth floor, the flat with MCFC on the door, in the hidden space behind the water tank, same as where you used to play with the Somali kid. She was on her knees, face pressed into the fence, as if in prayer.

When PC White returned, he was hobbling on a twisted ankle, muttering obscenities under his breath. The children started to chant 'Blow it up! Blow it up! Blow it up!' and then, to the tune of 'O Come all Ye Faithful,' they sang 'Oh why are we waiting . . . '

'Let's get her in a van then, shall we?'

When they lifted Claire by her handcuffed arms, she screamed in pain.

She heard Seth shouting at the police, calling them pigs, accusing them of brutality.

'November Foxtrot nineteen to Zulu five, request PNC check.'

'Go ahead, nineteen.'

'Claire Wilson, twenty-eight, IC1.'

She heard a child say, 'Why's that woman tied up?' and the mother answer that the police had to stop baddies like Burglar Bill. As they pushed her towards the van, Claire saw the nursing home in the distance and wondered what Mrs Shaw and her friends thought of this delay.

Beside the van, Inspector Page was stepping from a patrol car, and he registered Claire with a double take. He glanced between Claire, the bridge, and the arresting officer. 'What's going on?' he said, unashamedly confused.

'Section five Public Order offence, Sir. We caught her trying to climb over the fence.'

'You're the woman from the bridge, is that right?'

'Yes. I'm Claire Wilson. While we were talking to Lianne, she told me that her baby is hidden in this tower.'

'Sir, Mrs Wilson is a known fantasist.'

'That tower? The one they're supposed to be blowing up?'

'Yes, my husband's in there too.'

'Sir, we've dealt with this one in the past – she's a known nuisance caller.'

'Lianne's dad, Neville Shaw, the guy you've probably left her alone with, is a violent paedophile – a serial child abuser.'

'Alright,' said PC Young, pushing her towards the van, 'that's enough.'

'Let her go!' shouted Seth.

'Shut it!' said PC White.

Then Claire heard a murmur spreading from the front of the crowd. She heard gasps then a mass whispering. 'What is it?' 'What's going on?' 'I can't see!'

'What's going on up there?' said Inspector Page.

Claire tried to turn, straining against her handcuffs. At first PC Young forced her arms further up her back, but then he unexpectedly released her. People started to clap. Someone cried 'Halleluiah!'

'What's going on?'

'People are clapping.'

'He's got a baby!'

'I'll be damned,' said Inspector Page.

As Claire turned to see her husband cradling Baby Alyssa, the applause spread around the fence and back towards the church. All she could see were hands raised above heads. Even on the flyover, people started clapping. And then, through a gap in the crowd, she saw Dan, holding the baby as if he'd been holding babies all his life.

He was flanked by policemen, demolition workers, and security guards, but Claire saw only him. As the cheers grew, the breeze lifted, and it carried seeds from the purple-white clumps of rosebay willowherb. It was as if Claire were dreaming – as if Dan were walking through a thousand floating feathers.

Such was everyone's shock that for a long time nobody – including Claire – remembered that her handcuffs should be removed. Eventually Inspector Page shouted at PC Young, 'Well, come on, damnit – unlock the woman.'

'Sir—'

'Now! You too, White – stop pissing around. I want all units alerted – get that bastard in for questioning.'

Claire flexed her wrists, getting the blood flow back into her arms, and then she pushed towards the front of the crowd. 'Let me through,' she said. 'That's my husband!' When Dan reached her, Jeffries was slapping his back, saying over and over again, 'I've seen it all now. I've really seen it all now.' Men were trying to shake

Dan's hand, or reaching to pat his shoulder. A woman kissed his cheek. He shrugged diffidently, passed the baby to Claire.

As Dan directed the applause to Claire, she concentrated on the tiny creature in her arms. Baby Alyssa was wrapped in a blanket, totally unfazed, blowing spittle into the creases of her dimples. 'I've waited a long time to meet you,' said Claire. She kissed her on the nose. Okay, Claire thought, that's why Dan passed you to me: Alyssa did badly need to be changed.

As the applause faded, a queue of men waited to apologise to Claire. She had never heard so many men say so many apologies so fast. Of course, only one apology really mattered. 'Babe,' said Dan, 'I'm sorry I didn't believe you.'

'I think you made up for it.' Claire kissed her husband and promised herself that when the time was right she'd admit what had happened with Lukasz. She looked at the nursing home and imagined she could see Mrs Shaw pressed against a top-floor window. However awful and destructive a secret might appear, Claire thought, a secret shared is a secret disarmed.

She took one last look at Sighthill Tower and then she turned her back on it forever. 'Mr Jeffries?'

'Yes?'

'Blow it up,' said Claire. 'Blow it up.'

Acknowledgements

Thanks are due to Dr Duncan Dicks, who kindly permitted me to use 'Uncle Robert,' a character inspired by his short fiction; to James Thornton, for his comments and encouragement; to my editor, Martin Goodman, whose faith in me I hope to repay; and to Lucy Tyler, whose creative insights repeatedly rescued and revived this book.